GENTLE
ANNIE SOAMES

Sara Powter

Bible Quotes from the King James Version

ISBN: 9780645441574
Paperback edition

ABN 99 768 734 831
Pacific Wanderland Publications
Kincumber, Australia, NSW, 2251

saragpowter@gmail.com
www.sarapowter.com.au

1st edition 2024 printed by Kindle
an Amazon Company; available on Kindle Unlimited & KDP
2nd edition, Large Print 2024 Pacific Wanderland Publications

Dedication
This book was released on the 200th anniversary
of Lachlan Macquarie's death on the 1st of July 1824.

Lachlan Macquarie, also known as the
'Father of Australia,'
became the fifth governor of the penal colony of New South Wales by
default. He arrived in 1809, after the Rum Rebellion, and found a
primitive and squalid colony. However, he and his wife, Elizabeth, were
determined to improve the lives of the convicts and those willing to
work.
They dedicated themselves to this task for twelve years and turned the
penal settlement into a thriving community of emancipated convicts.
Their hard work and dedication transformed Australia into the place we
love today.

Thank you!

Australian Historical Novels

(All stand-alone books)

A First Fleet Stories (1788+)

Gentle Annie Soames
The Emancipated Potter
Paternity Unknown

The Hunter to Macquarie Collection (1795-1822)

When Upon Life's Billows (2025)
The Saddler's Song (2025)
Tuppence to Pass (2025)
His Majesty's Pageboy (2026)
A Fist Full of Holey Dollars (2026)
Far From the Whispering Sheoaks (2026)
Bound Down in Iron Chains (2026)

Unlikely Convict Ladies Trilogy (1792-1840s)

Dancing to Her Own Tune
(co-authored by Sheila Hunter & Sara Powter)
Amelia's Tears
A Lady in Irons

The Lockleys of Parramatta (1800-1901)

Unshackled Lives - *Prequel novella - free with newsletter signup*
Hands Upon the Anvil
Out Where the Brolgas Dance
Diamonds in the Dirt
The Earl's Shadow
Once a Jolly Swagman
Jonty's Journey

The Convict Birthstain Collection (1820-1840s)

No More, My Love
The Vine Weaver
Scotch at The Rocks
Waiting at the Sliprails
Convict Shadows of the Past
In Defence of Her Honour
I Can't Stop Tomorrow
Madeline's Boy
Jam or Marmalade for Tea

Shelia Hunter's
Australian Colonial Trilogy (1840-1850s)

Mattie
Ricky
The Heather to the Hawkesbury

MY SPECIAL THANKS:-

I say thanks to all those who came before us,
Our convict ancestors were torn from the loving arms of their families
and sent across the seas; more often than not, they never returned home.
And to the unsung heroes of the convict journeys,
and that was the many naval doctors and surgeons
who endeavoured to make the latter voyages safer.
To them, I bow in homage, for they cared!

I have used Doctor Arthur Bowes-Smyth Journal
as a primary source of the first Fleet Trip.
(*Transcript*) http://acms.sl.nsw.gov.au/_transcript/2015/D02131/a138.html

1787-1788 First Fleet Route

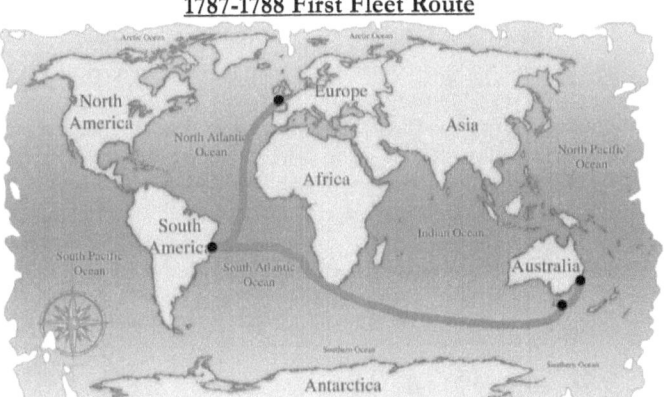

My husband and I can claim seven tortured souls from later fleets.

Thanks also to my husband, Stephen
who faithfully reads all my stories and gives me feedback.

Thanks also to Roby Aiken, who is my punctuation angel.
And my Beta readers, Noreen Robertson, Linda Upcroft and Lee Boehm.

Cultural Advice

Aboriginal and Torres Strait Islander people should be aware that this book contains names and stories of deceased persons.

Acknowledgement of Country:

In the spirit of reconciliation, I acknowledge the Traditional Custodians of country throughout Australia and their connections to land, sea and community. We pay our respect to their Elders, past and present, and extend that respect to all Aboriginal and Torres Strait Islander peoples today.

Author's Note:-

A few First Fleet facts

In 1787, the First Fleet of Convicts was sent to Australia.

The **Lady Penrhyn** was one of the eleven convict ships of the First Fleet that sailed from England to what was to become Sydney.

My character, Annie Soames, sailed on the *Lady Penrhyn* from Portsmouth laden with a cargo of women.

Many were accused of theft, and **two women were charged with highway robbery**. None were charged with prostitution, as in England, it was not a crime. However, by being poor, you could be forced from your home and made to return to where you were born. Some already had syphilis or gonorrhoea.

The **Lady Penrhyn** was one of six transport ships,
Alexander, Friendship, Scarborough, Charlotte, Lady Penrhyn,
and the **Prince of Wales.**
The **HMS Sirius, HMS Supply, Borrowdale, Fishburn,** and the **Golden Grove**
escorted them, bringing supplies and more marines.
The trip out to New Holland, as Australia was then named,
meant that many women were on board for over a year.
They first called in at Tenerife, where their official doctor was replaced.
From there, they went to Rio de Janeiro, where they holed up for a month,
resupplying and preparing for the next leg of the trip.
The arrival in Cape Town marked the halfway point of their journey;
again, the Dutch resupplied them. However, the worst was yet to come.
The fleet took a shorter southern route and hit the colossal seas
of the Great Southern Ocean.
They were caught in such horrific storms; all wondered if they would survive.
All were on their knees, praying for God's protection.
Yet, according to the doctor's journal, only days later,
'The foul diatribes heard emanating from below
were enough to make a hardened sailor blush.'

The stories about the arrival of the *Lady Penrhyn* in the new colony
of Sydney Cove were enough to turn the hardest woman hater to pity them.
Doctor Bowes-Smith, the surgeon on the *Lady Penrhyn,* wrote in his journal:-
"At…about 6 O'Clock p.m., we had the long wish'd for pleasure of seeing the last of them leave the
Ship - They were dress'd in general very clean…The Men convicts got to them very soon after they
landed, & it is beyond my abilities to give a just description of the Scene of Debauchery and riot that
ensued during the night."

This official report has since been debated as embellished; however, it makes you
wonder as laws were changed to ensure it was never to be repeated.
The morning after the orgy,
Governor Phillip assembled the masses and banned such acts from being repeated.
Up to three hundred lashes were used as punishment for such infringements.
This proclamation would not have been issued if nothing had occurred.
I have used Doctor Bowes-Smith's report as inspiration for my story.

The Lady Penrhyn was in easy view of the foreshore so that he would have had a clear view. *(See map)*

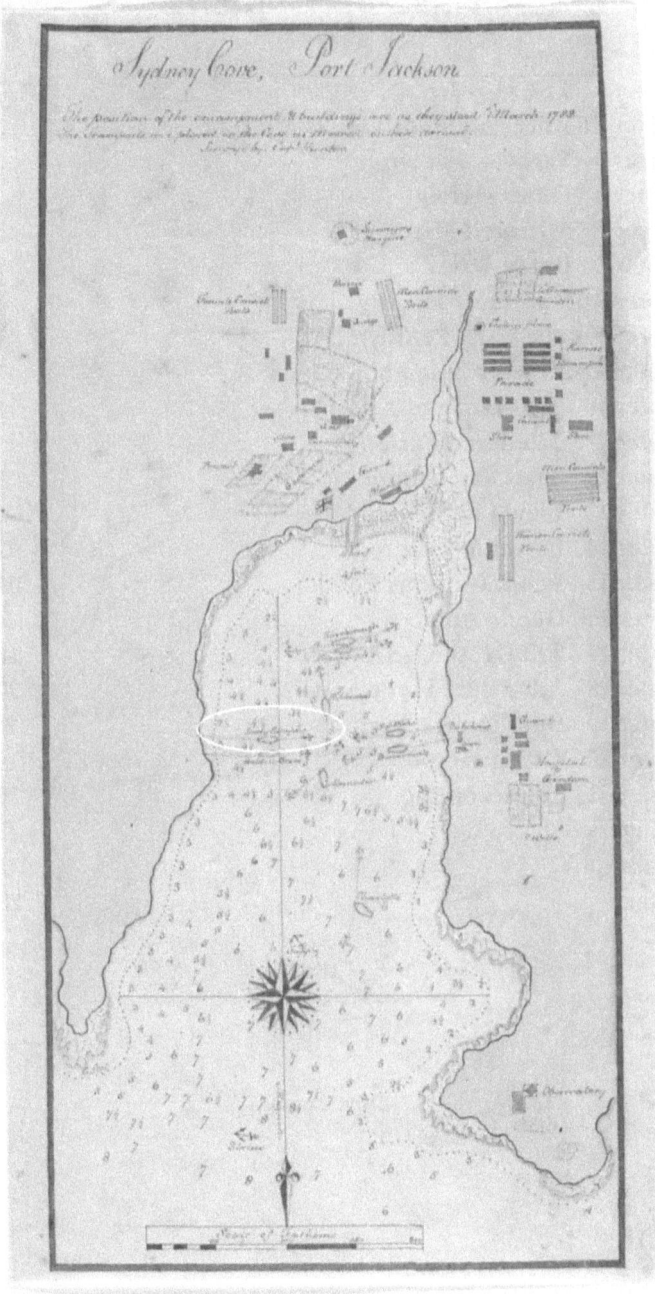

Table of Contents

The grammar and language in this book are
Australian English spelling

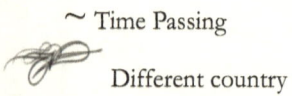

~ Time Passing

Different country

Chapter 1   The Hoyden

A whistle was heard from outside the rectory study. The rector stood and watched his sixteen-year-old daughter call her uncle's unbroken colt to the fence. The beautiful golden chestnut horse was there to keep the grass down in the rectory paddock. The old nag the rector used for his gig could not eat all the lush grass by itself, so his brother-in-law asked if he could use this field to hold a young cantankerous colt that needed a few months under his halter before being broken in. The Reverend Godfrey Soames was in awe at his daughter's skill. Over the past weeks, he watched as she befriended the magnificent young stallion. He knew he should stop her, but with no siblings, she was lonely, and the colt had filled a vast hole in her life. Her work assisting her mother in the parish was time-consuming and vital, and the horse's arrival from Annie's uncle had been a blessing. Annie was bored, so the colt's presence some three months ago had given her an excellent diversion.

Godfrey watched her progress as she gained the trust of the frisky animal. She sat on the fence daily for a month, just watching him, doing nothing more than being there. Each day, she would bring an apple in the hope that he would come close to her one day. On her arrival at the fence, the skittish colt would buck and frolic in the paddock but never come close enough for her to touch. Her daily routine never changed. She would sit quietly, allowing the colt to get used to her. After some time, she would throw the apple quite a distance away, and daily, it was thrown closer and closer. Soon, the colt would walk to it and eat it while she watched.

After another month, the colt drew close. Godfrey watched with his heart in his mouth. A magnificent beast he may be, but one ill-aimed kick, and he could kill her instantly. This morning, Annie again sat on the fence as still as a statue, and Godfrey watched as the colt gingerly drew close. He saw the beast's skin shivering with nerves. The colt threw his head frequently to discharge his stresses, but step by step, he drew closer. The young horse realised that Annie would not throw the apple this morning. Her arm was outstretched, and the juicy red apple sat enticingly on her hand.

The colt wanted it, and Annie wanted the colt's friendship. The colt soon lost the battle of wills. He had learned to trust the body on the fence. All it did was feed him apples. Step by step, the golden animal approached.

Godfrey watched the age-old battle of wills between man and beast. That morning, Annie broke through. Godfrey didn't even realise he had been holding his breath. Finally, the colt came and took the fruit from her outstretched hand. With it held firmly in his teeth, Godfrey expected it to scarper once it had its treat; however, it didn't. It took a bite and let it drop to the grass at Annie's feet. He remained close enough for Annie to reach out and pat its neck. Godfrey wished to call to her not to risk it, but he held his words. He knew a sudden sound could break the spell of the moment. Instead, he called his wife, Anne-Marie, to his side, and they watched the magical moment together.

Within a week, the colt, now named Midas after his reddish-gold coat, would come for his apple each morning when she called with her distinctive whistle. Soon, Midas was waiting for her arrival at the fence. His skin shivered with anticipation, and he now greeted her with a whinny and a toss of his head. Godfrey watched as each new day brought the two a step closer.

Annie was a child of slight build. She had developed into a beauty, but as her mother claimed, she was somewhat of a hoyden. She went about the village without a hat as the village children did. In summer, she was as often as not barefoot as her friends had no shoes. Annie seemed fearless in the face of this magnificent horse. Now, at his full height, he just needed to fill it out before returning to Basil Armstrong's estate next door.

The village of Bowbelle sat between two estates. One was *Bowbelle Hall,* belonging to the marquess of the same name, and the other was Anne-Marie Soames' brother, Sir Basil Armstrong, at *Armstrong's Keep.* Godfrey had started as the curate in the village church and inherited the parish when the incumbent had been killed in a carriage accident with the current marquess's grandfather. The marquess asked him to stay on as Godfrey was about to be fully ordained. That had been nearly twenty years ago. Godfrey already had eyes for the daughter of the Armstrong estate, but as an eighteen-year-old girl from a different class to himself, he held little hope that her feelings would be returned. How wrong he had been.

Anne-Marie Armstrong was as headstrong as her daughter. She had put her foot down to her brother and refused to be presented at court in London, but also said that she was going to marry Godfrey. At that stage, the curate had barely even spoken to her. Her brother, Sir Basil, was not impressed. Basil was a few years older than his sister and was well out of his depth trying to deal with the head-strong teenage sibling.

Reverend Godfrey Soames married Anne-Marie on her nineteenth birthday. He never regretted a single day of their union. His joy was fulfilled when she presented him with a perfect daughter, Annabella-Marie. Sadly, his wife never fell with child again, but Annie delighted his soul.

Annie was an adorable child with honey-coloured eyes and golden ringlets that darkened slightly as she aged. She was drawing close to a time when she would have to be presented in court. Her Aunt Violet, Basil's elegant wife, had drilled her for such an occasion. They were now waiting for her to turn seventeen. Basil and Violet would then take her to London for a season.

After three months of the daily excitement of watching Annie befriend the horse, Godfrey knew she could now pat him and place a rug on his back. The colt trusted her so much that Godfrey expected her to hoist herself onto him. Would it be today? No matter what his occupation, as soon as he heard her whistle, he stopped what he was doing to watch the saga unfold. Annie had already managed to get a halter on him and added a loose strap for a rein. Midas was now also used to being rubbed down with the bag.

This morning, Godfrey dared not call his wife in to watch, but he knew this would be the day Annie finally rode Midas. He was not wrong. Godfrey moved to the office door and watched from there. He stood ready to run if she should need him, but he watched as she moved Midas into position beside the fence. With no saddle to assist her, she sprung lightly onto the colt, bareback and sidesaddle. Midas stayed standing passively. Annie kicked her heels, and Midas moved off in a gentle walk. Godfrey was astounded that the wild nature of the unbroken colt had been won over with apples and love. He knew now Annie would be safe. They rode gently around the paddock and out of sight of his office. Godfrey returned to his desk and prepared to pen his sermon for the week. How could he not liken what he had just witnessed to God's love and acceptance of mankind? For thousands of years, God had held out the apple of grace to us; for thousands of years, mankind had taken it and skittishly ran away from Him. Godfrey knew that, like Annie and Midas, God's love finally broke through with each and every one. Godfrey picked up his new quill and started writing. Soon, only the scratch of the nib on paper was heard.

~

For months, Annie rode Midas every morning. The two were seen tearing hell-for-leather over the hills and dales of the village. Annie had found a pair of trousers belonging to one of her older cousins and sewed the hem up so she could wear them under her skirts. Once out of town, she would flick her leg across the young stallion's back and ride astride. She could ride low on his back and be one with the horse. Annie still didn't wear her hat; if she did, it invariably came off and was hanging down her back, held on by the ribbons.

Then, eight weeks shy of her seventeenth birthday, tragedy struck.

Annie had been for her regular ride when the rectory was empty on her return. The doors were open, and no one was at home. The gig and her parents were both gone. Eventually, she found their cook sitting in the pantry weeping. Mrs Bailey had been at the rectory since before her father had come as curate. She said, "Lovey, there's been a horrible accident, and your auntie has been hurt real bad. Your folks have gone to be with your uncle and see if anything can be done for her." With that minimal explanation, she set to weeping again. She didn't even notice that Annie had gone.

Annie again whistled up Midas, who came at her call. She was on his back and off to her uncle's house two miles away without even bothering to harness Midas up. The exhilarating ride had left her hair in disarray, and of course, she was hatless; she presented herself at the front door in a state of untidy breathlessness.

The debonaire butler knew her wild ways and suggested that she tidy up before presenting herself to the waiting family. The hall stand had a hairbrush and various ribbons in the drawer as she frequently arrived in such a state. The butler had adored the girl since she entered the world. He knew she was about to take London by storm. Her freshness and unspoiled ways would be attractive to some lucky country gentleman; however, she would never settle into town life. Nigel Hawthorne had learned to plait her hair when she was a child. She was too old for those now, as her hair was up. With a few brush strokes, she had her hair secured into a loose bun and tied with a ribbon. She turned to her friend with a look and raised eyebrows.

Nigel nodded approval and said, "You'll do, miss." Then led her to the sitting room on the first floor, where the family awaited them. "Miss Annie, My Lord."

Annie tripped in, aware of the concern on everyone's faces. "What has occurred, and where is Aunt Violet?"

All spoke at once.

Her uncle started, "She had a fall…" he could say no more.

Annie was beckoned to her mother's side with her hand held out to her. "Darling, Violet was out for her normal morning ride with Basil. A fox ran out of a hide and startled her horse; it propped and then reared. Violet must not have had a good hold of her reins, and she fell awkwardly. Darling Annie, we think she has broken her back." Anne-Marie now could not continue. She adored her fun-loving sister-in-law.

Her father took over. "Sweetheart, we are hoping for the best, but if she lives, she may not be able to walk again. We are waiting for the doctor to give us the prognosis."

The news was horrible; Annie now saw why the family was distraught.

"Oh, Uncle Basil, that is so sad. May I wait with you all?"

Basil just nodded silently. He had been unable to do anything to stop the accident from occurring. He had sent the groom who rode with them back for help. Violet remained conscious but said she could not feel her legs. She was lying at an odd angle, so Basil immediately knew something was terribly wrong.

Annie settled beside her mother and leaned into her for a hug. She adored her Aunty Violet. "Can we pray, Mama, or have you already done that?" she whispered to her mother.

Anne-Marie's gaze flew to her husband. "Godfrey, we have not taken this to the Lord. Please, can you pray for us all now?"

He did. With their heads bowed in reverence, they committed Violet's health to God.

An hour later, the nerves of the four in the sitting room were decidedly frazzled. The doctor had yet to appear, and although the tea tray had been brought in, no one had touched it.

After three hours of examination and treating her ladyship's other wounds, the young doctor finally emerged from the bedroom where Violet lay. He had given her a sleeping draught, and she was now tied into a makeshift frame so she could not move more than her arms, shoulders and head.

Doctor David Clarke had just graduated from college, and his skills and techniques were still new. Few locals trusted him, and many wished that the previous doctor, Keith Waddy, had not died.

Basil had no choice but to use his services. The young doctor still knew far more than any of the waiting family.

Doctor Clarke was exhausted. It had taken all his skill as a doctor to treat the wounds, let alone the broken back. He was sure she would never walk again… if she lived. Her skirts had protected her lower limbs from injury, but her face and arms were almost shredded from the deep briar into which she had fallen head first. Extracting her had been horrific, and only by cutting the mound of thorn bush down could they get her Ladyship out. Realising that she could already feel no pain in her legs, she was placed on a door and carried home carefully. The walk itself took an hour.

As Doctor Clarke left the room, he knew he had yet to tell her family about his patient's prognosis. Lady Armstrong would need to be kept absolutely still for months, and only if her back stabilised would she be permitted to sit up. Life would change for them all. David had worked with a similar case in Edinburgh, where he had recently graduated. He had seen the frame that they had strapped the patient into. He had no such structure here, so he had to invent something by cobbling together a container of walking sticks and leather thonging. He would try to source a proper frame later, but for the moment, she was immobilised.

The family all jumped up when he entered the room. The harrowed look on his brow told them the news was indeed bad. He said, "Her Ladyship is sleeping; that is the good news. Sadly, as I suspected, she has broken her back, and if she makes it through the first few days, that will be a miracle. Unfortunately, she will be unable to walk again." David sank into a chair offered to him, and Annie brought him a cup of tepid tea. He threw back the liquid and held it out for a refill. Turning to Basil, he said, "Sir, I wish I could have brought you better news, but at least she is alive. For her to have survived this long is a good sign. She will feel no pain from the break. However, her face and arms are badly scratched and could become infected. I will call in daily to treat those, probably both morning and evening and to see how she is. Sir, she is not to be left alone at all in case she tries to move." He gave more detailed instructions about changing bedding and said he would try to arrange a frame for her. Then he took his leave. He had already instructed some upstairs staff how to change her soiled towels and turn her over. He had more patients to see, and until he sourced a frame, he could do little else for her.

Basil barely noticed the doctor stand to go. He was in shock, and Godfrey escorted the medical gentleman to the door.

As Doctor Clarke stood in the open doorway, he turned and said to the reverend, "Sir, if you know of someone who could become a companion for her Ladyship, I would install her as soon as you can." David turned to look at Annie. "Mayhap your daughter can fill that role for the time being, as I know they are close."

Godfrey nodded, knowing that Annie adored her aunt. He would move her in that very day. He would also call the boys from the university to see their mother.

~

With Annie now living at *Armstrong Keep*, her life was vastly different. Gone was her freedom, the ability to sneak away when she wished and ride Midas wildly across the fields. She also missed her parents, but they knew they would have to cut her free soon anyway.

Violet had already been teaching Annie how to behave and be a lady. But now she was at the beck and call of a frustrated and grumpy patient. As much as she adored her aunt, Violet was understandably terse and tetchy.

Annie tried hard to put herself in place of her previously very active aunt. She understood her inaction.

Soon after her boys returned to college, Violet awoke one day to find Annie staring out the window. Midas had never returned to the paddock at the rectory but stayed in the field close to the big house. Annie watched him lustfully, wishing she could be out riding over the verdant pastures. Today was her seventeenth birthday, and there would be no party and no London visit. She released a deep sigh, not intentionally loud, but still heard by her aunt.

A soft voice from the bed brought Annie back from her daydreams. "Annie, I'm a morose and cantankerous old lady with a prickly attitude. I'm sorry you're stuck here with me for a while."

Annie returned to the bedside, horrified that her aunt had heard her. "Oh, Aunt Vi, I'm not worried about that. I'm watching Midas frolicking in the field, and admittedly, I wish I could be out there with him occasionally." She sighed. "I'm just being selfish."

Violet took her hand and squeezed it. "Darling girl, I do not know what I would have done without you being here with me these last weeks. I'm just sorry that your presentation must be cancelled. I was looking forward to you as the belle of every ball. You would have taken London by storm. You are a breath of fresh air in a turbulent and immoral world." Violet adored her husband's niece. They had two grown sons but no daughter, and Annie was spoiled by her relatives, especially by her aunt.

Annie sat down to read her aunt more of the book she had chosen. It was *Evalina* by Frances Burney. She had already finished the *Barber of Saville*, which was certainly an unusual choice for the unfledged young lady.

Violet was sick of being tied to the cage the doctor had provided. The indignity of her situation was abhorrent to her. Unable to even use a chamber pot, the humiliation of having her bedding and flannels changed like a baby was embarrassing. She sent Annie out of the room when this had to be done. At night, Violet would dream that in the morning, when she awoke, the feeling had returned to her legs; every dawn brought disappointment.

The dismay that Basil could no longer share her bed was something they also had to address. Once, when the doctor was alone with her, she asked him directly about resuming that side of marriage. With perfect bluntness, he answered her. "Madam, once the frame is removed, you will be free to resume marital relations; however, you will no longer feel anything at all. Paralysed women have even been known to carry children to term and deliver them without pain. If it were a male, for some reason, if the man was active in that way prior to the accident, he might be able to perform his husbandly duties but once again unable to feel anything. There have been far too few cases investigated to have a definite answer. I do not imagine there will be any ongoing problems that way, but it will take some months before that is possible." This was a topic that he had heard discussed by some of his lecturers at university. He was embarrassed, as he was sure she would be; David had not been looking at Violet as he spoke as he was cleansing the infected cuts on her arms. The ones on her face had thankfully healed well, but there were a few deep ones on the underside of her arms that had borne the brunt of her fall.

Violet wished Basil to share her bed even if they could not be together that way. "Doctor, could he share my bed without… well, you know what."

David considered that before answering: "I would give it a few weeks, but with the frame in place, I don't see why not."

That brought great relief to her. Basil joined her three weeks later.

~

For six months, Violet suffered in the cage until finally, the doctor said that she would soon be able to be slowly raised to a sitting position.

For over a month, the doctor arranged her pillows until she could finally sit upright. With this momentous achievement, although Violet was extremely dizzy, the household cheered.

Doctor David had a reward for her but would not tell her what it was. Annie had already been sworn to secrecy and knew what modifications were taking place in the house; ramps were built, and rooms rearranged. Soon, Violet could move from room to room with relative ease. Annie's job had been to keep her aunt occupied, and she had done this admirably. In the months before her accident, they shared and discussed many of the things she would have experienced in London.

Annie's innocent heart pattered quickly with the delights they would have been doing had Violet not had her accident. That, too, was washed away, but Annie was not as shattered as she thought she might be. She realised that with a presentation, a marriage would usually follow, and she didn't wish to leave home or her uncle's place just yet.

With Violet now able to sit, Doctor David suggested that once she felt up to it, Sir Basil might take her to London to have a custom-made brace created for her. If she took the trip laying down for most of the journey and they took it slowly, then a sojourn there would have the benefit of being an excellent change of scenery for the family.

This plan was set in motion, and Basil modified one of his travelling carriages so a bed was constructed to stretch from seat to seat. Out of necessity, the journey would be taken most of the way at a walking pace due to the appalling state of the roads.

London was everything Annie dreamed it would be. She didn't care about the parties and the presentation to society. She just wished to see everything. There was so much activity and so much to view that Annie's eyes darted from side to side of the carriage. Yet, the stay in London was both a success and a disappointment to Violet and Basil. The doctors and specialists there agreed that Violet's case was permanent. There was little more they could do for her other than build her a sitting brace and stabilise her back.

Before they had left home, Basil had added some wheels to a chair, but now, in London, they purchased a special cane chair with a steering handle and wheels. Once Violet was in this, she could steer where she wished as long as someone pushed her. This gave her some measure of control over her life. However, there was another one ordered where Violet could push herself where she wished. The chair had two large wheels she could use to move should no one be around. Now she was finally mobile again; Violet's laugh was once again heard in the house. She could not dance or ride but quickly realised that her attitude to her condition reflected throughout the household. Thanks to Annie, she learned to laugh again.

After three months of watching the high life in London, Annie reluctantly left the city with her family. She had not been to any balls, but her uncle had taken her driving most evenings, and she could watch the lovely gowned ladies heading in and out of the various palatial homes in London. The houses themselves were eye-opening. Her uncle pointed out the Marquess of Bowbelle's palatial London home in St James Place. He was her Uncle Basil's nearest titled neighbour.

As the carriage bounced along the cobbled streets leaving London, Annie knew Midas was waiting for her. Her parents' weekly letters had kept her informed, and she knew no one could get near him again. Unbeknownst to her, Basil sold her beloved horse as he had injured a groom.

Annie was resigned to the sedentary life that now lay ahead of her. She wondered if it would ever change.

Chapter 2   Roses are Red; Violets are Blue

Sir Basil saw to everything possible for his beloved wife. Soon after their return from London, a new wheelchair arrived that was far more comfortable for Violet. It had a single small wheel at the back and two large wheels on the sides. Violet found that by wearing kid leather gloves, she could quickly move herself around the rooms that had been converted for her use. The chair with the steering handle was kept downstairs as it was wonderful for an outdoor wander in the gardens, but it needed to have someone pushing her. Still, the occasional bout of melancholy settled on her.Basil also had a special gig made for her, and it was always at her disposal so she could get out and about should she wish for an outing. Her chair could be hooked on the back.

~

Nearly a year after the accident, Violet had mastered all the various techniques of manoeuvring herself from place to place. She was regularly able to get downstairs with the assistance of two strong footmen carrying her chair while she was strapped in. She would push herself to the top of the stairs and wait for her burly footmen to carry her chariot, as she called it, down or up to whatever floor of the house she wished to go. From there, she could get from room to room with ease. Violet's attitude underwent a change when Annie was nearing eighteen. She regained her zest for life. The upcoming celebration of her niece's eighteenth birthday gave Violet something exciting to do. She adored parties, and *Armstrong Keep* was known for the best garden parties and balls. Violet would usually have everyone laughing, and the household's mood once again returned to the enjoyable place it had once been. As a special surprise for Annie, Violet had her dressmaker fit her into a proper ball gown. Until now, Annie had worn the old-fashioned skirt and top like a peasant girl. She had good dresses for family dinners, but she had never had a ball gown before. She was always neat and tidy, well, usually, but the dress Violet had her dressmaker create for her was a pannier-style ball gown. Being un-presented, the gown was predominantly white, with ruches of pastel colours and rosettes on the flounces around the hemline. The inset of the divine dress was embroidered with tiny grub roses on the front horizontally pleated gauze panel. The gown was far more beautiful than Annie had seen in any London shop. While in London, her Aunt Violet's maid had needed to order special outfits for her aunt, and Annie had been able to gaze adoringly at the partially finished creations in the shops they attended.

Basil had decided to give Annie a ball at the house now that Violet could play hostess from her new wheelchair.

Annie's season in London had been curtailed, but at eighteen, she was going to have a private come-out ball like the area had never seen before.

Every local dignitary had an invitation awaiting delivery. Rumour of the magnificence had already preceded the distribution of the invitations.

The magnificent gown hung in pride of place in Annie's bedroom. Her parents were coming to stay, and they would sleep in her mother's old room. For three weeks, Annie had helped her aunt write the invitations. They had been sent out the afternoon before. Annie rose and dressed with the excitement of a child.

Two days before the function, Violet was impatient to head downstairs to continue with the various tasks that needed to be completed. She had long ago refused to be strapped into her chariot. She pushed herself from her bedroom and out onto the landing to await her carriers. She spun her three-wheeled chair around and laughed with one of the maids heading to clean her room. Neither noticed her chair had rolled close to the top step. As Violet was chatting and laughing, the action of her laugh made her chair roll back a little. Violet hardly noticed the slight movement. It only took moments, but the back wheel of the chair rolled over the top step.

Before anyone could reach her, the chair and Violet plunged down the sweeping staircase. She took the steps backwards, screaming as she fell. Halfway down, the chair finally tipped her over and slid upside down the rest of the way. Silence ensued. Violet lay in a tumbled heap at the bottom of the stairs, and the chair came to a stop at the front door as it righted itself. It rolled on undamaged as though pleased to have evicted its cargo. The life-loving Violet, Basil's adored wife, lay dead. Her neck broke in an instant on the first flip of the chair.

Life stopped at 'Armstrong Keep' that day.

What followed was an inquest that found that no one was at fault. Violet's untimely death was a catastrophe for everyone.

Annie's world was in turmoil; her life and future were now in limbo. The family would go into a year of mourning, and Annie would have no birthday party or come-out ball. Not that she was really worried about that, but most of the preparations had been made, and the invitations had been sent. Now, everyone would be coming for a funeral instead of what should have been a celebration.

Violet was laid in state on the dining table, and Basil or one of the staff remained with her until she was buried.

Annie packed her things, planning to return home with her parents after the funeral. With Midas no longer at her disposal, life would become dull and uninteresting again. She would resume her parish work with her mother.

Aunt Violet was from Scotland, and in honour of that, Uncle Basil had planned a modified post-funeral gathering. The attendees returned to the house, were fed, and shared about the deceased. This was called a *coronach* or *keening* in Scotland. While awaiting the post-funeral *keening* where the family would traditionally sing laments, Annie wandered outdoors, not wanting to be part of that. She was sitting in a hedged arbour in the garden, trying to keep out of the way, when a conversation floated across the hedges.

The smooth voice said, "We've been married three months now, and Verity is becoming crotchety, demanding my attention every moment of the day. I am thinking about hiring a companion for her, someone who can be at her beck and call as she wishes. She is only three months gone with child; goodness knows what she will be like when she is ready for her confinement."

The well-modulated voice spoke to Annie's Aunt Violet's second cousin, the toffy-nosed Scotsman, Rupert. Rupert had already made unwelcome advances on Annie, but his reply made her heart sing.

"Oliver, Violet had the most wonderful lass to run her chores and get her things. I think she may be some poor relation of Basil's, but I'm not quite sure where she fits in. With Violet now gone, I presume the lass will be at a loose end and may need to find another position. Basil said he might travel for a while. It's been a tough year for him. In any event, she can't stay here. Ask him about her."

"I shall, thank you, Rupert," the suave voice said.

"How is the Lady Verity otherwise?" Rupert enquired.

The cultured voice replied, "Other than making everyone's life sheer hell, she is well. Rupert, have you seen Sir Basil? I will speak to him."

Rupert replied, "Leave it with me, Oliver; I shall see him over dinner tonight. Now is not the most appropriate time. He's not quite himself anyway."

The voices drifted away from the garden, but Annie had heard enough. She made a beeline for her mother and sought her consent to accept the position at the man's establishment should it be offered. It would be better than sitting around all day doing nothing.

She found her mother and begged for her to acquiesce. "Mama, please say yes, oh please, please," Annie pleaded with her mother.

Anne-Marie Soames stood holding her daughter at arm's length. Annie had flown into the room and catapulted into her arms. "Annie darling, I have no idea what you wish me to say *yes* to, so until you explain, I will not commit myself."

Annie set about filling her in on the overheard conversation. "Mama, with Aunt Violet gone, I'm not likely to enter society without her patronage.

She was a Scottish earl's daughter, and I am but the poor niece of a baron. I have no dowry and nothing but an ability to ride a wild horse and a pretty face to endear me to anyone. I don't even have Midas anymore. I care about nothing in society, so a paid companion's position is far better than being left on the shelf. Please, Mama, talk to Papa and let me go." Annie stood beseechingly in front of her mother, her eyes meeting her mother's and flicking from one to the other. "Please, Mama!"

Anne-Marie looked at her pretty daughter and realised that now eighteen, she was far more than just beautiful. She was still a hoyden in many ways but enchantingly lovely. "I suppose there is very little option now than for you to earn your keep. Your uncle always said there would be a £1000 dowry for you, but I would not hold your breath about that. At forty-four, he is still young enough to remarry and have more children, and then there are their boys. If something were to happen to Basil, I'm not so sure his boys would honour the promise of a dowry. Basil adored Violet, but their past year has been harrowing. The boys are both old enough to cope with whatever he does; I hardly recognised either Douglas or Roderick when I saw them today. It's hard to believe they are nineteen and twenty-one. Both have become men of fashion, even though they are still at university." She paused for a while, obviously deep in thought. "So, yes, my dear, I will talk to your father. I wonder who the gentleman can be. It may be the marquess, as I heard his wife is in an interesting way." She saw interest flick across Annie's face.

Anne-Marie set about pondering the possible candidates. It has to be someone Rupert Sidley-Smyth knew well, or he would not make a recommendation. "I don't suppose Rupert said the man's name?"

Annie nodded. She thought pensively for a moment. "Yes, Allan, no, Olwyn, no, it was Oliver. Yes, definitely Oliver," Annie stood with the curls surrounding her face; her ringlets were wobbling vigorously as she nodded.

Her mother said, "Ahh then, that is the marquess. You should be safe enough there." Her mother had a beautiful smile settle on her lips. "He's newly married and so pompous and aloof that he'll be unlikely to notice anyone but himself. I've known him since he was a boy."

Annie was beside herself with excitement. "I've heard the marchioness is very beautiful, Mama."

Her mother gave her a funny look. "Beauty is not everything, my dear. It's only skin deep; sometimes, the person underneath is not nice or good. I have told you that before. My mama used to say that a pretty face can often hinder a nice personality development. Remember that sage advice, sweetie. If you go there, you will work harder than at Aunt Violet's, and unlike at your uncle's house, you can't go to him and complain you are tired or wish for a ride. I believe that it was an arranged union, and they had barely met before the service."

Anne Marie fell silent, wondering how much she should reveal to her daughter. She was aware they disliked each other intensely. They appeared at church each month and barely spoke to each other. She had known the family all her life. Oliver had been all but brought up by servants when his mother died after a traumatic birth. She remembered when the old marquess had called her mother over to come for a visit after their daughter had been stillborn. His wife had all but withdrawn from life. Even Oliver was not permitted near her. The old marquess had managed until she started sleepwalking and having nightmares. These had started after they were returning from a trip, and a highwayman held them up. Oliver, too, had been subject to this incident; the big house was unsettled. The old marchioness became so badly affected that she needed to be locked in her rooms, and they eventually sedated her. They did not know if laudanum helped or hindered her as she withdrew even more. The nightmares grew more and more violent; then, she started seeing apparitions.

Anne-Marie was ten years older than Oliver, so she would come over and occupy the little boy while her mama spent time with his mother.

Anne-Marie knew that the hold-up had affected him greatly, and on top of the eerie screams coming from his mother's room, the poor boy kept dreaming about being chased by the highwayman. He seemed standoffish even as a small lad, but he wondered if it was because he had never known a mother's affection. He had been palmed off to wet nurses as soon as he was born and had never had any nurturing. She decided then and there that she would give her children as much love as she could. Anne-Marie realised that he barely knew what was occurring around him. He lived in his own little world of lead soldiers and a rocking horse. She wondered if he'd been informed that his mother was not coping with losing her baby. Anne-Marie was even more concerned after she had chatted with the grieving mother. It seemed that she had not just lost the baby but her mind. Anne-Marie had heard of other mothers whose childbirth had robbed them of all reality. All she could do was pray for her.

It had not worked, and the marchioness died while sleepwalking. She had fallen off the top parapet. Their visits had ceased, and the marquess wrapped the knocker on the front door and withdrew from society.

Anne-Marie had not thought much about the boy until she heard his father had died last year. When the news arrived that Lord Oliver agreed to the arranged marriage with his father's Scottish friend's daughter, Anne-Marie wondered if it would work.

Oliver knew little about what went on in his villages as although he owned the parish endowment and village; he spent most of his time in London.

Annie knew much of the history, especially about the nightmares, as some of her friends had them occasionally.

Anne-Marie's gaze rested on her daughter; Annie did not need to know any of this. With a smile on her lips, she said, "Annie darling, you will have to work when told and do things you have no wish to do. But that is the price your Papa and I must pay because we fell in love and have little money."

Annie grinned.

Her mother cupped her face. "My darling girl, if you must go out to work, this is probably the best job I could imagine for you. I met the current marquess when his mother was ill. She became quite unbalanced before she died." Her mother kissed her brow and enfolded her in a loving embrace. "Yes, sweetheart, I will speak to your father."

~

Annie started work at 'Bowbelle Hall' the week after she turned eighteen. Just before Basil left to spend some time away overseas, her uncle had written her a glowing reference in which he had not mentioned his relationship with her. Her cousins had returned to university and acted as though nothing had happened.

The past year had tested Basil's sanity, and he needed an escape. A friend had a house on the coast of Italy, and he had decided to restore his health in peace. He loved ancient ruins, and Italy was full of them. He said farewell to his sister and the family and left in a daze.

Annie was delivered to the Hall in the Armstrong carriage. Her mother had been given use of the old family home's facilities while everyone was away. She was to oversee the family estate for her nephews.

Verity, Marchioness of Bowbelle, took Annie's breath away with her beauty. She was everything that Annie was not. She was dark, and Annie was fair. Verity had ice-blue eyes that looked straight through a person; Annie's eyes were such pale golden brown that they looked like the colour of sweet honey. Verity was extremely tall, and Annie was average. Annie thought everything about herself was just average. She could not see the fresh beauty in her young face or the loveliness reflected back at her each morning. But Annie was lovely in looks and nature, and the staff and village knew it.

When word spread that the minister's daughter would be her ladyship's companion, a sigh of relief flooded below stairs.

Verity's condition was not yet showing, yet she wanted everyone to dance to her every whim. She demanded rather than requested, and she ordered rather than asked.

In the first days, Annie learned that her mother was right; a pretty face did not mean an appealing nature. Annie even saw animosity on her face when the very handsome marquess was in the room.

Her mother was right; Annie soon became run off her feet. 'Go get this,' 'Do that,' 'Run here,' or 'Deliver this or that.' Annie was in no position to criticise, but she did so to herself.

Once alone in her bedroom each night, she would let off steam. She would say to herself in rants to her mirror or while lying on her back, exhausted and gazing at the ceiling. "What makes her think that just because she's pretty and has a title, she can laud it over everyone?" She let her frustrations vent.

Annie was regularly exhausted before luncheon each day, but on the whole, the household was a pleasant place to work. The staff were wonderful.

Being a paid companion meant that Annie was neither upstairs important nor a downstairs servant nor in-between like a governess. She was welcome to eat with the housekeeper, Mrs Durham, or sit on that lady's right at the staff table. The butler, Mr Greening, always sat at the head of the table.

In this house, Annie was one position up from her ladyship's maid and his lordship's valet. Her pleasant nature, happy disposition, and willingness to sit and chat over a cup of tea or chocolate soon made her popular with all the staff who had not previously known her. They came from all walks of the below-stairs social scale.

Upstairs, though, life was vastly different. It was as silent as a mausoleum.

There was no conversation between the married couple other than essential discussion.

Preparations were made for the child's birth, and Verity often said that she hoped this child would be a boy to inherit the title.

Within weeks, Annie knew the names of all the staff, from the eleven-year-old stable boy to the butler's grandchildren. Annie already knew some of the junior staff from her years in the village. She quickly befriended the outdoor staff from the stables and volunteered to exercise his Lordship's horses with the grooms. Bob Brown, the head groom, knew her riding skills of old as he had grown up in the village. His mother was the village midwife.

Bob needed no second offer; Annie received his blessing to ride whichever horse she wished except his lordship's black Godolphin Arabian stallion, King's Majesty.

She may not be permitted to ride him, but she befriended him in the stables. Each morning in the early gloom, he would be greeted with half an apple and would get a nose rub.

Annie rose at dawn and, with a few grooms, took whatever horse needed to let off some steam. They would walk them from the stable yard and then give them their head at full gallop. She was again unaware that even doing this, she was watched from the master suite. Although she rode sidesaddle, she was always seated on a regular saddle. This was a difficult feat at best, as at full gallop, only a superb rider could hold her seat without the knee pommel.

After witnessing one of her first gallops himself, Marquess Oliver rose early and now looked out for her exit to the vast green fields. His gaze would follow her to the stables, but later, he always rode in the opposite direction.

His valet would invariably arrive to assist him in dressing and would catch him watching her.

Both stood admiring the fabulous horsewoman's seat; the valet would typically say something like, "Oh my, she can ride like the wind, sir."

"She can, Giles. Dare I say she is magnificent." Oliver's emotions were in turmoil. Miss Soames was his wife's companion and, as such, was out of his reach. He had made his marriage vows and meant them. His wife was expecting their child, and he should be content. He knew he should actually be thrilled, but since his marriage, the household was no longer happy. In fact, he was decidedly unhappy. Verity was not his choice of wife. This wild girl was far more his style, but he had married whom his father had chosen. The engagement had been long-standing; soon after the engagement was announced, his father died. They married as soon as the year of mourning finished. He had no desire for an arranged marriage, but it was *fait accompli* before he knew what had happened. He needed an heir, preferably one with good breeding as society demanded. Oliver could admire the girl from afar, so he did that as often as possible.

Annie had much to think about on her rides. Once the bay stallion she was riding had galloped off the morning jitters, he settled down to an easy canter and took the green fields in his stride. She then let her mind wander to her very handsome employer.

Following a conversation with the butler over a pre-breakfast cup of tea, Annie didn't know the senior staff were permitted to marry, but apparently, Henry Greening had served as a batman for the previous marquess's grandfather in some war. On his return, he was permitted to marry his sweetheart as a reward. Annie thought it was pretty grim that most household staff were never allowed to marry. If they did, they had to leave. Having grown up with access to the house where her uncle would rather everyone be happy than merely conform to society's archaic rules, Annie knew that she could always go home whatever happened. From where she now worked, it was only a few hours' walk to the parish church and even closer to some of the parishioners' homes that she knew so well.

Annie had delivered calves-foot jelly and homemade broth to many of them. Bob Brown's mother had been a frequent recipient. The cook's ailing sister was another, as was her sister-in-law. Annie had celebrated their births and anniversaries and mourned their deaths.

Annie knew the stories behind each person. She and her mother had visited most of the people in the next village on the estate, as the minister there had been taken ill soon after his wife had died. They had heard of some who were ill and poverty-stricken, so the rectory ladies had set off on their gig with baskets full of homemade goodies to deliver where needed.

Below the stairs, Annie was loved by all. Nothing was too small a request for her to jump up and assist them. Likewise, she found they, too, would find out her likes and dislikes, and she discovered that the cook would make her favourite desserts or cakes. A small flower was often in her place at meal times as a thank-you from some garden staff member.

Chapter 3   Verity's Disdain

$\mathcal{T}$he first Christmas at the house came and went. All the female staff were given a five-yard length of red flannel.

Annie wondered what she would do with her gift and ended up giving it to Bob Brown for his mother. Annie was puzzled as to why they would want red flannel.

Everyone but the aristocracy understood that when they washed clothes in a copper, all knew that any red ran like a blaze up a hillside. Red could only be washed with red and always needed to be done last. She wondered how long the ridiculous gift list had continued.

This thoughtless gift was just another thing to add to her long list of gripes. It had not taken her long to discover that the staff were underpaid compared to her Uncle Basil's household. In a house this size, the staff had to share tiny rooms or dormitories, while in other houses, each had their own private room. They may have been small, but they had privacy. There was plenty of room here, but they had to share a dormitory to save coal for the fire and candles.

Winter was now a distant memory; the days grew warm again, but the dawns were earlier and earlier. Annie was itching to get outside and ride again. She missed Midas; she missed home.

As Verity's condition progressed, so did her temper. Her petite figure was now gone as she sat eating sweetmeats and treats rather than staying active. Consequently, she piled on the weight and bloated quickly, thus exacerbating the situation.

Annie did everything she could to encourage Verity to walk and get some gentle exercise. Her efforts were rudely rebuffed.

Verity's temper flared, and she shot a comment to Annie. "You, girl, were employed to be my legs; why should I have to do anything that I have no wish to do? I am carrying the marquess's heir. I shall do what I wish, so silence your silly orders, girl." Verity always called Annie just 'girl' and never by her name. This riled her, and she wished to spit back words in anger, but she bit her tongue. Her mother's words came back in a flash.

Annie gave up and nodded, acknowledging the statement. Here, she was nothing but a paid employee. She almost wished to return home now, but she bided her time. Her parents had little money, and she must learn to be independent. However, she had already decided she would leave after the child was born.

The marquess had heard the vitriol in his wife's voice and caught Annie's hand as she exited the room. Annie didn't pull away but somehow ended up in his arms, weeping. He did no more than comfort her, but his look of pure adoration shocked her. He kissed her brow and reluctantly released her. With a hooked finger, he stroked her cheek and said, "Bear up, my gentle Annie. The child will hopefully ease her anger." He touched his finger to the tip of her nose in a fun gesture and said, "I can never thank you enough for being here for us."

His smile did silly things to her insides. She finally admitted to herself that she loved him, which scared her. He was married and well out of reach.

~

Days slid into weeks.

Annie often caught the staff pulling faces behind their mistress's back. They would bring a tea tray, and when they turned their back, they would pull faces at the beautiful shrewish lady of the nobility who demanded that everyone jump to her every wish. She tried not to smile, but she normally had to look away to hide her grin. She knew exactly what they meant but remained silent. Verity was nasty, and Annie would not like working for her for long.

The very handsome marquess's penetrating gaze was off-putting. Since their hug, he never made a move towards her, but she felt his eyes following her around whatever room they were in together. She blushed but returned his smile.

For some reason, his frown eased if she dared acknowledge him. She liked him, and she felt that he understood her predicament. The marquess never spoke unkindly to her and always called her Miss Soames very politely. Annie noticed his eyes were fixed on her lips, particularly if she sat near his wife reading to her. He seemed to relax as he listened to whatever she was reading, be it the society columns or a romantic novel. Occasionally, he would request her to attend to some trivial matter on his behalf, but never when he was alone.

However, after the first few months, he would excuse himself as soon as she entered a room. She now saw the marquess little. When she did, he often held himself aloof, watching her with his hands clenching and unclenching behind his back. When he did notice her, his gaze bore into her.

She saw something in his eyes that almost scared her: lust. Her own heart fluttered, knowing it was not unmoved by his desire.

~

As months passed, Annie lived in a near-silent world above stairs, speaking only when spoken to or reading to the marchioness. Of the marquess, she saw very little, but when they did meet, her heart beat somewhat faster when his eyes met hers. She found that it was hard to break their gaze if their eyes locked. He still made no move to touch her. She, along with all the maids, was half in love with the incredibly handsome man. Her breathing rate certainly increased when he was near her.

Verity barked out orders when her mistress spoke and rarely addressed her politely. Annie had to bite back comments regularly. Her greatest pleasure was being relieved for a few hours when her mistress rested. Annie would then take herself into the gardens or back into the stables.

One morning, she took a long walk as the head groom, Bob, now a good friend of hers, had mentioned the delivery of some new stock and pointed her in the direction of the new horses. One horse was a particularly obstreperous near fully grown colt. Bob had mentioned that this beast was brother to the marquess's stallion and had a temper to match.

Annie's face lit up with delight. "Bob, where is he? I'd love to see him and the other new horses."

With the possibility of befriending another horse like Midas, Annie made the cross-country trek to the far field.

There stood an inky black Godolphin Arabian colt. He was a younger version of the Marquess's steed, King's Majesty, and such a magnificent animal that Annie decided he would be her next conquest. It would give her something interesting to do to while away her time. The flighty colt stood eyeing her with trepidation. His withers were shivering with nerves, but he stood his ground with his ears back on his head.

Annie had three months until the marchioness's child was due, which gave her time to charm this new horse. As she had done with Midas, she whistled her arrival and slowly gained the trust of the unbroken young colt. He had been handled a little more than Midas, so in a few days, Annie had him taking the apples from her hand.

By the end of the week, as she whistled, he would whinny and throw his head in the knowledge of the forthcoming apple. Then, he would pace to the fence and await her arrival. His head-tossing and neighing antics would make Annie laugh.

Only two weeks after her first sight of the young stallion, she climbed the fence and found that he almost slid alongside her, wishing her to ride him. She accepted his invitation, slipped on his bareback sideways, and waited for the bucking to start.

It didn't come. He accepted her weight without a murmur and without reins; just holding his mane, she eased him away from the fence for a walk around the field. With no bit, bridle, halter, or saddle, it was just woman and beast alone in the world.

The house was well out of sight, so Annie decided to see what he was like to ride. She lowered herself so she was almost in line with his neck and gently urged him to pick up his pace.

That morning ride gave the colt his new name. Aladdin was like riding on a magic carpet; his gait was so smooth, and his nature was so calm that Annie felt like one with this beast, even more than her beloved Midas.

Although she still did her dawn exercise rides on the other horses, she always made time for Aladdin. Often, it was just after she was released from her daily chores.

Madam insisted on still dressing for a meal, even though she refused to leave her room. This gave Annie an hour before she had to appear in the staff dining room. With no one to answer to, she fled as soon as she was free.

Aladdin was usually waiting for her or would come when she called for him.

"Oh, my beautiful boy, I hope they don't try to break your spirit. You are so adorable, just as you are."

She would chat away merrily to the giant beast as she rode. Her only means of holding on was to his mane. His ears were back listening to her gentle words.

Occasionally, he would give a buck of happiness at her arrival, but rarely did he do so once she was mounted; even so, she stuck to him like glue, being one with the incredible animal.

Bob had taken a late ride on a mare to test if her fetlock had healed fully. Whilst out on the horse, he was shocked at what he saw. He drew an intake of breath when he realised the rider before him was Annie, and she was on the unbroken beast. They were as one, blended and in harmony with each other. She barely moved as she rode and had nothing to hold but his mane. It was as though she was glued onto the animal.

Bob caught sight of her tearing across the backfield and stood watching in awe of her skill. Few could have ridden the animal with a saddle, let alone bareback and sidesaddle.

Annie knew no fear and took hedges as though they were mere inconveniences. He had been very hesitant when he first mentioned the colt's arrival. He was aware of her wild rides on Midas and knew she would soon have this Arabian stallion eating out of her hand, but he thought it would be months before she dared to mount him. Not so!

Bob waited to escort her back to the house as it was now getting dark. With the discovery that the fetlock on the mare was still causing some discomfort, he had dismounted and stood waiting for Annie to reappear.

Annie took the hedge on the return to the field and hardly moved as Aladdin landed. She saw someone waiting for her and made her way towards them. She knew she should brush Aladdin down, but she had nothing to do this with. She slid from his back and saw that he was not lathered. She rubbed his nose and kissed him. "You are my magic carpet ride, boy, and I shall ride you as often as I can."

Bob listened to her endearments. He had not even been able to get close to him to put on a halter, and here was Annie kissing him and hugging the magnificent creature.

Bob spoke as she approached, "I thought I would walk back with you, Miss Annie." He paused, waiting for any words from her; she said nothing. "You are amazing, you know, miss. That colt was so cantankerous when he arrived that he bucked and propped until it took all of my skills to get him into this field. Here you are a month later, riding Aladdin as though part of him."

She was still on a high from her ride. "Oh, Bob, he's magnificent. He is like riding the wind. I've called him Aladdin, as he is my magic carpet ride."

She merrily chatted with the head groom all the way back to the house, gushing about the exhilarating ride.

Bob knew her skills and wasn't worried, but to ensure her safety, he said, "Well, Miss Annie, you may ride him all you wish, but will you tell me when you go and come back, just so I know where you are? I've known you all of your life, miss, and I feel responsible for you. If something happened to you, your mama would have my head."

"All right, Bob, but you know I'm safe. You saw today how magnificent he is. He won't throw me. He almost asked me to ride him by shinnying up to me, and he didn't even buck when I hopped on." Her bubbly enthusiasm was infectious. "I'd love a brush and bags to rub him down, though."

"I'll sort it, Miss Annie; I'm just being careful, that's all. There's a shepherd's slab in the far corner; you can stow things under there." Bob looked at the reddened cheeks of the lovely lass beside him. She was not even wearing a riding habit and could still ride easily. He knew she refused ever to wear spurs or carry a whip. She needed nothing more than herself. Herself and her steed, that's how she liked it. He had been at hand when her father had first sat her up on their old nag. Her joyous giggle at being so high had delighted him.

~

The day of the birth finally arrived. If Verity had been crotchety before, she was downright horrible for the week leading up to the delivery of her child.

Everyone knew she was travailing in childbirth; the windows of the house almost shook with her screams. Hour after hour of appalling language echoed down the halls. Thankfully, some were in Gaelic, and she didn't know what they meant.

Maids came and went carrying towels, hot water, and whatever else was called for.

Annie had been banished from the birthing room as she was a maiden.

The housekeeper's attendance was demanded. The sounds were enough to make her wish to clear out completely. She took the opportunity to visit Aladdin. After telling Bob, she headed to the backfield. He had a bag and a brush ready for her, as well as some apples and a half cob of corn.

Knowing she would be free for some hours, Annie donned her habit and took her steed for a long ride. There was a hilltop path that Bob had recommended, and the five-mile ride was one she had wished to do for some time. With a whistle, Aladdin came at her call, and she let him munch on the cob of corn. She was soon mounted and in hot pursuit of freedom. The melded form of horse and rider took off up the hillocks and headed for the lookout. With the palaver of what was happening at the house, no one would miss Annie for hours. She was not going to miss this time of freedom.

Aladdin was also enjoying the flight. He barely was huffing, let alone any heavy roaring as he galloped. Annie was feather-light on his back, and he barely noticed her weight. Again, she had no saddle, although this time, she had added a halter and reins, but no bit. She had only added the halter and reins as she had no wish to walk the five miles home should Aladdin take off from her. Once there, Annie dismounted and walked over to the top of the hillside, Aladdin matching her every step.

He nuzzled at her neck and occasionally whinnied with delight at the unexpected outing.

Tiredness overwhelmed her. She left him cropping at the grass as she lay in the sunshine on the hillside. The birds chirped overhead, and the bees buzzing around her lulled her to sleep. The week's stresses had left her tired and at the end of her tether. She rested in the cool green grasses and dozed.

The shadow of Aladdin woke her sometime later as he had come to nudge her awake. Realising she must have been asleep for some time, she knew she must return to the house. Leading Aladdin to an outcrop of rocks, she soon mounted with her skirts hitched up and sat astride as she had done as a child.

Aladdin was unfamiliar with her sitting this way but soon fell into an easy pace as they walked down the steepest part of the hill. She reached the rolling fields, and as she was now astride, she kicked him to a canter and then to a full gallop. Aladdin had not stretched out his full pace before, and she let him have his head for over half a mile. After he blew his cobwebs away, he settled down to a canter. Finally blown, he slowed to a walk.

Annie felt exhilarated. She had not had a ride like that ever. She was sitting so low on his neck and holding on as tight as she could with her knees; she was not sure that, had the need arisen, she could have either pulled him up or turned him. Thankfully, his stride and pace eased.

After a while, they saw the flags on the tops of the hall's turrets; Annie kicked him to a canter again. She wondered if she should take the hedge or go through the gate. Aladdin decided to fly home and easily took the stone fence. He landed easily and walked to the corner where she had left the bag.

Annie fed him an apple and brushed him down. By the time she arrived at the stables, the sun was reaching the tops of the trees.

Bob greeted her with the news that the child had only just been born, and it was a boy.

The joyous celebrations in the staff quarters were still quite audible. The marquess had an heir. Bob relieved her of the bag and sent her indoors to clean up. She would tell him of her day on the morrow.

Annie entered the kitchen and asked if any hot water was left over from the birth. She crept up the back stairs and removed her habit. She waited for the bath water to arrive.

The luxury of a bath in her room did not occur often, but today, she was hot and sweaty and relished the warmth of the hot water.

Annie was greeted by two giggling young girls who had somehow beaten her to her room. They already had the hip bath there and had prepared her bath. Annie chuckled. "Am I that obvious, girls?"

Alice, the younger of the two girls, giggled, "Yes, miss, when you were gone for so long, we knew you would wish for a long hot soak on your return. You've had to bear the brunt of Madam Toffee-nose for long enough, and the cook told us to keep the pots hot for a bath for you. Mrs Durham told us to help you."

Annie wondered how many of the staff knew about her riding. She guessed that quite a few did.

The other young maid, Milly, said, "Miss, you are not quite downstairs staff, nor upstairs either, yet you jump to our defence when someone wrongs us. We all see how lady muck treats you, and we don't like it no more than you." She had emptied the can of hot water into the bath, and it was joined by three more. The girls left to get refills.

Annie tested the temperature before sliding into the perfectly warm water. She ached because she had not spent so long on a horse for months. The heat seeped into her bones, and she relaxed, relishing the magnificence of a long, hot soak. Annie also decided to wash her hair while the water was hot. She had just soaped it up when the girls returned with the next four pitchers of water. She had rinsed the bulk of the soap out but said, "Milly, please add a few drops of that oil from that tiny vial into the final pitcher. It's violet oil, a gift from my aunt. It makes my curly hair soft and not frizzy."

Milly was somewhat heavy-handed with the scent, and a slosh went into the jug instead of a drop or two. The three girls looked at each other and giggled, the room filled with the heady aroma.

Annie shrugged. She loved the smell and wasn't going to throw it out just because the water was overly scented. She had her bath and stood for the final pitcher of scented water to be poured over her head, rinsing out the soap.

The three girls were chuckling at the violet perfume now filling the room.

Milly said, "Oh, Miss Annie, that is a beautiful smell. Would you mind if I used some water and washed my hair while you dressed?"

Annie knew the staff didn't have access to hot water but had to wash in cold water once a week. "Girls, feel free to have a full bath. The water is warm and soapy, and there are enough towels for us all, and I won't be telling anyone."

The maids, Milly and Alice, were only a year or so younger than Annie and were some of the staff Annie had known all her life. They had only started working at the big house when the marquess married nine months ago.

One after the other, they stripped off and bathed.

Soon, all three clean girls sat in front of the fire, and the two younger ones brushed their straight hair with brushes borrowed from other guest rooms. The marquess provided everything in every room, and the girls grabbed what they needed from the vacant rooms on either side of Annie's room. As a companion, Annie was not in the staff quarters but in the second-grade rooms. The main suites were reserved for special guests and family, but Annie would not have wished to be that close to the family anyway.

With the birth occurring in the master suite, all the rooms downstairs had been thoroughly cleaned early in the morning. The girls normally had to dodge the family while trying to finish all their work, but this evening, they were free to be with Annie.

For an hour, the three girls dried their hair, and then the two younger ones experimented with dressing Annie's hair into a new style, trimming the side lengths to let her natural curls cluster in spirals framing her face. The effect was both charming and alluring. Annie's fair curls also smelled heavenly. The scent of violets wafted every time she moved.

The two younger girls had straight hair, which they had to wear tied up into a tight bun under their linen mob caps. Both were delighted to have clean hair.

If the housekeeper noticed that the maids were cleaner than when they had left, she said nothing. Annie was sure she knew they had all bathed as she caught her eye over dinner and winked at her.

A few noted the heavenly violet scent that Annie exuded. However, her perfume covered the same smell on the girls.

The news of the protracted delivery of the child was discussed at length.

The baby boy was strong and healthy, but he was surprisingly dark. As the marchioness had brunette tresses, this was not so unusual. However, the housekeeper saw the cleft in the baby's chin when she handed him to the marquess. Mrs Durham knew that his chin was square. Her eyes turned to the marchioness, and Annie realised her chin was pointed. Neither had a cleft, which the baby had, though. She knew someone who did, though. A frown settled on her brow. She remained mute and watched as the marquess cuddled the squawking infant. She saw him frown and then look at his wife.

A seed of doubt was sown.

Chapter 4   Oliver's Heir

$\mathcal{M}$arcus Neville Quilpie, Earl of Martindel, was born on the seventeenth day of August 1786. He was a bonny baby; even Annie had snuck into the nursery to view the sleeping child. She had overheard the housekeeper and butler discussing the babe and his cleft chin.

The household had been given extra rations to celebrate the joyous event. When Annie entered the room, the conversation was abandoned, but she had heard their words and heard the questions in their voices. She wished to see the babe for herself. She had cuddled many a parishioners child. She adored the little ones especially. This baby was adorable. However, Annie also noticed a deep cleft on the child's chin.Annie had not been called back to Verity's room, as the lady had been sleeping for most of the daylight hours. She had snuck out and had a quick ride the afternoon before, but as she had not brought anything to rub Aladdin down, she did not wish to bring him to a lather.

For two days, she had not been needed. She felt like she was having a holiday. The next morning, she was told to stay within call, so she was unable to ride Aladdin for long. However, the following day, heated words echoed from the master bedroom; the staff were told to make themselves scarce, and Annie took this opportunity to go for a long ride.

On returning, she noticed the door to the marquess's office open. It usually was closed, so she quickly looked inside from the doorway. She could see all the chairs were empty, and no one was at the desk. Sitting on the desk was a grog tray with a dirty glass and an empty crystal carafe. As she would pass the butler's room, she thought she might as well take the dirty vessels to be washed.

Annie walked directly to the desk. As she approached the tray, the door clicked shut behind her, and worse still, she heard the snib of the lock. Spinning around, she saw the Marquess, obviously inebriated and in a partial state of undress. He had recently used the chamberpot in the cupboard in his office and had not covered himself properly.

Aghast at what she saw, the man she had come to adore moved towards her with inappropriate intent. The look on his face showed his lust for her. His eyes were hooded with desire.

Annie was petrified.

"Oh, my gentle Annie, how I have waited for a time like this. Oh, my darling gentle Annie, do you know how I want you? I have watched you ride and watched you laugh; you are a balm to my hurting soul." With each slurred word, he moved a step closer.

Annie quickly moved to put the desk between them. As he crossed the room, she made a quick movement and made it to the door. The tray was now well forgotten, and she sought a way to escape. On reaching the door, she realised that he had locked it but removed the key. Panicking, she had nowhere to run to. Now completely cornered, Annie feared what he would do to her. Her eyes searched the room for another way of escape but found none.

Too late, she realised he was now within reach and soon caught her and took her in his arms. He reeked of alcohol. His words were slightly slurred. "Gentle Annie, you are mine and mine only; I want you, I need you." One hand cupped her cheek while the other encircled her and held her captive. He silenced her protests with a deep, wet kiss. His tongue invaded the depths of her mouth.

Having never been kissed before, the emotions raging through her were anger and fear, yet there was a hint of awe. She had dreamed of being held so, but she was frozen, trapped in his arms, and not knowing how to extricate herself.

The man himself, the marquess, was so handsome that all the maids were half in love with him. She often saw the girls blush if he merely looked in their direction. Since his hug, he never made any inappropriate moves towards her. Admittedly, his eyes bore into hers if they happened to meet across a room. Annie had tried not to respond to his subtle smiles but often caught herself grinning like a schoolgirl. He made her uncomfortable as she adored him, so she avoided him as often as possible, yet she now found herself in this position. She struggled in his arms and said, "Sir, you must release me. Please, sir, I am but a maiden. I have not known a man, and you must not do this."

Oliver's brain was more than just fogged with brandy; he had been drinking steadily since the night before. Annie, his ideal girl, had just walked willingly into his office. This was his dream come true. She must want him as much as he lusted after her. His own gentle Annie. He took a deep sniff of her fair hair. What was that scent? It was heady and had haunted him for the last few days. She was unaware that he had unbuttoned the remaining part of his trouser fall.

Annie felt him lifting her skirts, and she tried as hard as she could to push him away and brush her gown down. Before she realised where he was pushing her, she had fallen back onto the chaise lounge that sat in the centre of his office. As she fell, her legs flailed in the air and over the side of the furniture. Her skirts were soon pushed up. Access for him was now unimpeded. Like most ladies of the day, she only wore her split drawers as undergarments; her chemise and petticoats were flimsy and easily lifted for him to access. She was now desperately fighting him off as he lowered himself on top of her. Unaware of the danger about to befall her, Annie was still more worried about him lying on top of her and being able to breathe rather than what he could do to her once there.

With one of his hands, he held her arms aloft and with the other, he pushed her legs apart. Searing pain hit momentarily, but he didn't stop his attention. She was horrified to realise something was now moving inside her, and it was hard. She had no idea what he was using, but it hurt dreadfully. He still had her arms pinned above her head with one of his own, and he held her tightly to him with the other. The smell of brandy invaded her nostrils as the thing kept moving in and out within her. She was still fighting as hard as she could, twisting one way and the other. His mouth held hers captive, so she was unable to scream.

He continued moving. He repeatedly pumped into her. After a few moments, he arched and released a long, contented sigh; she felt him relax on top of her. He murmured, "Oh, my gentle Annie, dearest girl, you feel so real that I can smell your heavenly-scented hair." He breathed in her aroma. "Your scent has nearly driven me crazy these past two days. You are so adorable, my dearest gentle Annie. So very, very lovely." With those words, he collapsed on top of her, asleep.

With him now passed out, he had released his tight grip on her arms. She was now able to push him onto the floor. She felt him pull from between her legs and saw his elongated manhood fully exposed and somewhat bloodied; the horror at what had just befallen her sunk in. The marquess had just deflowered her and stolen her innocence. She now realised what the hard thing was that he had used. She had no idea that a man's thing could grow so big or that it would go hard. She had changed napkins of little boy babies for village mothers, so she knew there was a difference between girls and boys, but his size was far more significant than a baby boy.

Pushing down her skirts, she realised that she, too, had some blood on her legs and drawers. What he had done to her had hurt. She remembered the searing pain that shot through her as he plunged into her. With him lying unresponsive on the floor, she watched as his manhood deflated and noted that it shrank quite quickly. Soon, it was flaccid and quite small. After watching him for some time, Annie found herself still gazing at his intimate parts and realised that they must not be found like this. She was in shock but knew if anyone found out what he had done to her, she would be totally shunned. She was already ruined; she knew that, but so far, only she was aware of it. Sometime during the struggle, she must have clawed at his face, for he had four long fingernail scratches on his cheek. These were now bleeding freely. She checked her nails, and they were filled with his skin. As she settled her skirt, she shoved him with her foot, and he roused a little. Annie shook his shoulder, "Sir, cover yourself, lest someone finds you in such disarray."

He grunted at her words so she was more direct: "Sir, your fall is undone." Her words must have sunk in, as in his stupor, the marquess re-buttoned the flap on his trousers, rolled over, and started snoring.

Annie stood to leave and realised the door was still locked. She could not escape. Knowing the key was somewhere on his person, Annie waited until his snoring was deep and regular, then carefully checked his coat pockets. Even feeling around a sleeping man's unresponsive body was something she had never done before. She saw no pockets in his breeches, and for that, she was thankful, as she had no intention of fingering his person more than was necessary. His arm was covering a coat pocket, and she just hoped she didn't have to roll him over to access the other side.

The exposed coat pocket also drew a blank. She sighed in frustration. Knowing that she now had to roll the insensible marquess onto his back. She carefully moved around him and pushed him over. This action roused him again. "Oh, my gentle Annie, I can even smell you in my dreams; we are lying in a field of violets and…" what he would have said; Annie never found out as she was once again grabbed, and he drew her into his arms. As he had done before, he kissed her, but this time, it was more of a gentle and loving caress. His lips were soft, and his tongue teased her lips apart. He kissed her in such a way that Annie found herself responding to his embrace. Realising what she was doing, she didn't draw away but took the opportunity and started checking the various hidden pockets in his shirt and vest. Finally, she felt it; the key was in his shirt pocket above his heart, and she carefully slid her hand under his vest and grabbed the elusive item. Only then did she remove her lips from his. She found that she enjoyed the more gentle and loving caress than being forced. It had been the kiss of her own dreams. Annie felt somewhat guilty as she had used the kiss to divert his attention from her ulterior purpose. She stayed unmoving until his arms dropped from around her, and his snoring was once again heard. She noticed that his flap was not properly secured on one side, but there was no way she would fiddle around with that part of the marquess's attire, even though he had been intimate with her.

With the key now in her hand, she felt like giving him a swift kick but held back lest she did him some damage. Her nether regions still hurt, and her anger was now growing. He would not hear the last of this; she was determined to confront him on the morrow when he had sobered somewhat. Knowing there was little point in hanging around and accosting him now, she unlocked the door and checked to see the hallway was clear before fleeing to her room.

She rang for a pitcher of hot water and pleaded a headache, asking for a meal to be sent to her room. Once the water arrived, she locked her door and scrubbed her *derriere* and private parts until it felt like she had washed off his odour. However, she could still smell him on her and decided to wash all over. His odour and brandy still permeated her clothing, and she wondered if the cleaning maids would notice the aroma if she put her gown out to wash. She looked around the room and saw the obligatory drink tray on the side table. She knew each room in the enormous house had a grog tray with clean glasses and two decanters of spirits. Her room was no different, and it normally sat untouched. She decided to slosh a quantity of the brandy on her gown and then send it for immediate cleaning. One smell would cover the other. She hand-washed the blood off her drawers and hung them up to dry. With her first dilemma sorted, she unlocked her door and got into bed to await her meal tray. She would spend the evening thinking up a way to give the egotistical and selfish man his comeuppance. How dare he do that to her!

~

After a restless night, Annie slept in. She decided to confront the man as early as possible. She knew his routine well and knew that he would be in his study as he would not have been for his morning ride after such an evening of drinking.

Dressing in haste, she slipped unseen down the main staircase and towards his study. She was one of the few staff members permitted to use these stairs. The butler, Henry, had yet to take up his position at the door, so he must still be at breakfast. She didn't knock when she arrived at his door but marched in unannounced. The marquess was sitting slumped in his chair. His hair was unpowdered as usual when at home, but he was dressed in a coat rather than his typical smoking jacket or riding clothes. She knew that from the few times he had previously imbibed, his head would be pounding.

He lifted his head slowly to see who dared enter his sanctuary without knocking. A slow smile spread across his face as he saw who it was. He waited for her to speak as he knew from her stance that she had something to say. His dream last night was so vivid; at least, he had thought it had been a dream until he looked in the mirror. He realised it may have occurred if his cheek and her temper were anything to go by. "Annie… Miss Soames…" More he could not say. Her anger was tangible. She looked amazing when angry, and he could not help but smile. He gasped as he realised he loved her.

Annie was standing with her hands on her hips. "Sir, do you remember much of yesterday?" Her ire was apparent.

He could hardly focus on her beautiful face. He wished she would lower her voice. His head hurt. He softly replied, "No, but I know something occurred because of this." He turned his cheek, and she saw the red and inflamed channels her nails had dug into his face.

Annie didn't realise the wounds she had inflicted upon him were quite so deep. Her hands remained on her hips. She was livid at her employer. "You attacked me, sir, and had your way with me. I had not known a man before and… and… well, you deflowered me."

The marquess looked at the enraged beauty standing before him. She was truly magnificent. Her words hardly sank in, but he smiled at her again. He wished he could recall what he had done to her and was angry at himself that he had been so inebriated that he could not remember. He gave a half-laugh, "What is done is done, ma'am; I cannot undo the deed. Also, I cannot recall my actions." He gave a nervous laugh. He had no excuse for what he had done to her, but he did not know what to either do or say. He was right; he could not undo his actions but dearly wished he could remember. He could not even marry the woman he wished to spend his life with.

Annie's anger nearly exploded, "You… you… you are a spoilt, shallow, self-centred, egotistical, poor-little-rich-boy who has never been crossed. You are conceited and stubborn, and… and… a cheese-paring toff who underpays your staff, and now you have violated and molested me too. At least because of the scratches; you can't deny something happened."

The marquess remained seated, knowing he would still be unsteady if he stood. He knew that he still had to explain the wounds to his valet. He had no idea what excuse he would use. He cared not for what his wife thought. However, Annie's words had sunk into his brandy-soaked brain. He admitted to some of those faults, but cheese-paring? He finally said, "How am I cheese-paring? You are paid well enough."

Annie stared at him, stunned that he swallowed her insults as if they were water off a duck's back. She knew she deserved to be sacked for her rudeness, yet the words he objected to were being called cheap. Really? The anger in Annie bubbled over. "Sir, if you wish for me to explain, then I will. Your lowest maid is paid less than one pound per year. How much did that one lace kerchief you are dabbing your cheek with cost you? Two pounds? And you expect them to serve you without fuss? Many of the girls are ready to leave and find more profitable work with less harassment or abuse by the footmen whose behaviour is condoned by you. I am reasonably well paid, as the amount I asked was exorbitant. However, as I will leave soon, that is neither here nor there."

His head jerked up. "Leave? You can't leave; Verity needs you." He paused and dropped his voice. "I need you, Annie; you have been my sanity. Don't go, please don't go." His begging cut Annie deeply. In a very soft, apologetic voice she almost missed, he added, "Don't leave me."

Annie presumed that she would be dismissed when his child arrived. Not so! She said, "After your abuse of me last night, I have little reason to stay, sir. I have no idea if anything should come of your actions, but if it does and I fall with child, then be that on your head."

He merely gave a nod of acknowledgement of the possibility but said no more. She stood, continuing to rail at him for some minutes. Her words flew over the top of him, his eyes not leaving her beautiful face. Oliver thought she had no idea how desirable she was when she spoke. He sat passively, letting her berate and chastise him as he would not have permitted any other person on the earth ever to do. He didn't care what she said as long as her words were directed at him. She spoke of red flannel and dormitories, but he could not remember in what context. Her diatribe, exhausted, she was waiting for an answer from him. As he had not listened to most of what she said, he replied softly, "Don't leave me, gentle Annie; I need you here, especially now. Please don't go." His voice broke, and his eyes were watering. "I don't want you to go, my Annie." Her eyes were flashing like flickers of golden fire. He heard her harrumph. His fear of her departure made him rashly promise, "I swear I will not touch you again." He held out his hand to her but then let it drop. "Gentle Annie, please stay." His words were full of raw emotion. He was so close to tears.

Annie was shocked rather than angry; all he wished was to keep her near him. To say she was stunned was an understatement. She had verbally abused the Marquess of Bowbelle to his face, yet he still wished her to remain. Flabbergasted, she asked, "Why?"

Staying was one of the last things she wished to do, but if she did, by any chance, fall with his child, she would need his support. As it was, she was ruined; she could no longer go home; her mother would know in an instant that something had occurred, and Uncle Basil was still away. At least here, she would have a roof over her head.

The silence stretched on.

The marquess looked directly at her as though seeing her clearly for the first time. He held his hand to her again for a moment, then dropped it to his lap again. "Why, my Annie? Because I want you near me. I need to know that at least one person can see through my false bravado and challenge me without fear. I need you to call me out when I do things wrong. I need you, gentle Annie, far more than you will ever know." His eyes drank in her face, and his nose delighted in her scent. It was that smell that he now remembered. "Violets, I remember your violets, Annie. I thought I was seeing things again as I used to when I was young. I used to have dreams of being haunted when I was a child, of being shadowed by the highwayman who once held us up."

Annie knew that. She remembered the stories of his family being held up by a highwayman. Her mother had said that he'd had nightmares about it for years. She was not persuaded. How could she stay in the house of her abuser? "Sir, what if I conceive a child? What then?" She asked these questions and expected an evasive answer.

He was still seated, but the look he gave her made her feel like her legs had melted. Annie understood that he felt something for her; she had not realised that before. "My gentle Annie, I need you, but I swear I will not lay a hand on you again without your permission; that is my first promise. If you find you are carrying my child, I will do everything I can to aid you. But let's not cross that bridge until you know. I will ask that if you find that you are carrying my baby, you must swear to me that it's mine." He reached out his hand to her for a third time.

She left it hanging in mid-air again. Her mouth fell open. Annie was indignant. "Considering that your, um, man-member was covered with my blood last night, that is evidence enough that I was a virgin. I have no beau and do not wish for one. So, sir, I consider that an insult. As to your feelings, you are a married man, and I am no whore."

Oliver nodded; he knew her statement was true. He had noted the staining when he washed it this morning. "Tell me as soon as you know." He was slowly sobering; he felt gutted but had no idea what to say to her. In a way, he wished the act undone, but wishing would not change anything.

Annie still had not received an apology from him. "I will stay for a while, at least until I know. More, I cannot promise. I have nowhere else to go as I can no longer go home." She turned to leave the room, but at the door, she turned and said, "Sir, congratulations on the birth of your heir." As she left, the perfect revenge occurred to her. It would be something that would disturb him, more than just his dreams.

Before he could reply, she was gone.

The door shut quietly behind her.

His grey-green eyes stayed fixed on the closed door. His head sank onto his hands. His heir, his damned heir! If only she knew! The child was born nine months after their marriage, but it was not his child.

He had suspected on their wedding night that Verity had been with a man before him. That had been the first time he doubted her, but she told him she rode astride, and that had been the cause of the lack of blood on the sheets. Now Verity's lie was doubly confirmed, as he knew Annie rode astride and had seen how much blood there had been from their union.

Verity had just laughed at him when he asked if the child was his. He groaned to think of being cuckolded by his shrew wife. Neither of them had a cleft chin like that.

Knowing he shouldn't, he took another drink.

~

Annie settled on the exact punishment for the marquess. He had so many clothes that he would not miss some.

Early one morning, soon after the attack, Annie stole into his dressing room and placed a stolen cloak, tricorn hat, dark riding breeches, scratched top boots and a coat into a carpet bag, then carefully carried them downstairs while the staff were eating their breakfast. She had intentionally chosen old garments the same style as he wore riding but similar to what a highwayman wore. The ego of the man still riled her. She may love him, but liking his behaviour was another matter. She would make him think twice about mistreating a lady. She was no maid to tumble, and his behaviour was abominable.

On one of her many rides, she had found a derelict shelter tucked into the corner of the horse's field; Bob had previously mentioned it. It had probably been a shepherd's hideout, but it was small and dry, and she knew she could leave the clothing there. She had already stored the brush and bag Bob had given her in this hidden hole. She had one more item that she needed.

Getting a saddle was probably going to be the hardest thing. Hopefully, Bob Brown could help her with that. He knew she was riding Aladdin, but he would question her need for a proper saddle. Preferably, she wanted one with the marquess's obvious monogram on it.

Annie took a quick bareback ride on Aladdin and returned to work. Carrying the large bag had eaten into her time away, and with Mistress Verity lauding over the staff in such a high and mighty way, time off was now precious. Annie had been surprised that her mistress would not feed the child herself but had hired a wet nurse. Sadly, this meant that her ladyship's time was not occupied with the care of her newborn.

For some weeks, Verity demanded to be waited on hand and foot rather than exercise to shift the baby's weight.

The rain curtailed visits to Aladdin for the next ten days, so she would not have been able to ride anyway.

Of the marquess, Annie saw little. Generally, if he entered a room when she was there, she would make excuses and leave. He rarely visited his wife's apartments, and when he did, he left shortly afterwards. A long, lustful glance from him unsettled Annie.

While he was with them, Annie sat silently. He even apologised to his wife if he interrupted her reading or sewing. He would bow, beg her forgiveness, and take his leave. His eyes typically caught Annie's as he turned.

His looks were hot enough to warm the room. Occasionally, she replied with a smile, but more often, she gave an ambiguous gaze to his adoration of her. Sometimes, if Verity were occupied, he would pause when leaving and gaze at Annie to sear her image into his memory.

Two weeks after the incident, Annie put her plan into action.

She began to tempt him by getting in his way far more often than usual. She would appear in a room where she knew he was heading, linger until he came, and then leave.

The scent of violets haunted him. Overall, Oliver honoured his promise not to touch her, though she could tell he wished to.

She managed to brush against him as often as she could. She even kissed his hand a few times.

Behind Verity's back, there would be a touch of a hand here and there, or she'd intentionally move through a doorway as he entered or left. Each contact brought an audible intake of his breath.

At the beginning of the week of Marcus's baptism, Bob brought her a damaged saddle.

Annie had to reveal to him why she was doing what she intended.

Bob was horrified that the marquess had ravished Annie and vowed to assist where possible.

She promised she had no intention of harming him in any way.

Bob had something for her. Annie was thrilled. The saddle had a split in the seat but was still rideable, and it had been discarded rather than sent away for repair. The golden monogram was still shiny and easily seen from a distance. It was perfect for her plan.

Chapter 5   Mirrored Mischief

On the first morning of sunshine, Annie put her plan into action.

Since the birth of her child, Verity had rarely woken up before late morning, meaning that Annie had at least four hours each day to herself. She let herself out the door near the back gardens and headed to Aladdin. She had already tried him with a saddle; today, she would buckle on the new one. She had to don the stolen clothing and then sit and wait for Oliver.

The chill morning air permeated through her thin gown, but her costume would soon cover that. She smiled somewhat wickedly at the thought of what this would do to Oliver's mind. She felt a tiny flash of guilt but quickly banished it.

Aladdin came at her whistle, and she soon had the saddle on his back and buckled up. This morning, she added a bridle and bit to his halter as she needed proper reins to carry off her charade. He stood shivering in anticipation of their morning gallop. Annie dug into the carpet bag and donned her outfit. Knowing how the marquess looked, she was pleased with the effect. Once mounted on Aladdin, she could easily be mistaken for him from a distance. She left her cloak in the bag tucked in its hiding spot. This stone shelter also made an excellent mount, and soon, she was up on Aladdin's back and cantering astride across the field. She had chosen a spot to sit and wait for her quarry to appear. He should soon be out on King's Majesty if his morning went as normal.

Aladdin stood still in the shadow of the large tree that Annie had chosen. He chomped at the bit and pawed at the grass while he waited. He knew she wished him to stay still. He did, but he threw his head a few times and whinnied once until she gave him a pat. The sharp kick he received when he had whinnied made him start a little. She had not done that before. He could feel the tension in her body, and it made him jumpy.

Annie realised her steed felt her anxiety. She patted his neck again and soothed him with calming words. As she did so, she caught sight of her target. "Ready, boy?" she questioned, not expecting an answer. His ears flickered in excited anticipation.

As usual, the marquess was heading out on his regular route. He took the hillside on the other side of the valley.

Annie was waiting. It was precisely where she wanted him. She waited until he reached the top of the hill and saw him stop to enjoy the view as he always did. He would then kick his mount and fly along the top of the ridge. This morning, she would mirror him, but on the opposite ridge. "Okay, let's go." She moved Aladdin into position and watched as the marquess did the same. At the exact moment he took off, she kicked Aladdin to a gallop from a standing start. It was a movement Annie had admired in the marquess's riding.

They raced along the two ridges neck-a-neck. Annie did not need to watch where she was going, as her mount knew the hill well. She watched the marquess' movements and watched him slow as he saw her ride parallel. She slowed Aladdin to match his pace. She also rode astride as he did. She even mirrored the lift of her hand to his head as he did to keep the sun from his eyes.

When he turned to ride down the hill towards them, Annie also turned Aladdin and was soon hidden from sight. From there, she knew she had time to gallop into the shelter of a stand of trees and then head back to his field, which was much closer than the house. By the time the marquess topped her hill, there was no sign that anyone had been there.

Every morning for a week, Annie matched his movements. Each time, she fled before he could get anywhere close. Aladdin soon realised the new routine and enjoyed the hell-for-leather run at the end of the game. The arrival at his field was always a flight over the hedge. He would land perfectly, and then he would have a sedate walk back to the corner where her bag was hidden.

Then, without notice, the marquess went to London, supposedly for a fortnight. During this time, Verity did not require Annie's services as a friend had come for a visit. Most of the staff were asked to bring food or drink but otherwise not to interrupt them. She even seemed to take more interest in the child and brought him to play with the visitor.

Annie had bumped into this man once or twice, and the first time had made her gasp. His greeting of *"Bon jour, mademoiselle"* had revealed his identity. The suave Frenchman made her skin goosebump. The all-too-familiar cleft in his chin had made her eyes fly open.

Annie took this time to return to her usual routine of riding Aladdin where she wished. Since her encounter with the marquess, she had withdrawn somewhat from the other staff. She still ate her meals with them but made excuses to leave and go to her room as soon as possible. Few noticed as many did the same.

In her dealings with the villagers over the years, Annie had learned about procreation and was now aware that having missed her monthly flow, she was probably carrying his child.

The sanctuary of her room had previously been a haven of peace, but now it felt claustrophobic. She needed to be able to breathe, so she spent as much time outdoors as possible. A child was growing within her, and she had no idea what to do. Sick with worry, she knew she had to let him know.

The Frenchman left after a two-week stay. Verity now only called her in the afternoons when she was bored. Annie had to play cards with her, read a novel, or play the piano. It was the last thing that she wished to do. She bit her tongue and did it anyway with a false smile plastered on her face. She knew that if Verity found out about her condition and who the father of her child was, life would become impossible, if not dangerous. She was fully aware of the spite and vindictiveness of her employer.

Annie waited and prayed and waited some more. Still, the marquess did not return. Knowing there had been recent verbal shouting matches between the marquess and his wife, she hoped he had not left permanently. She had no idea what she would do if he had.

~

The fortnight turned into a month before the London carriages were finally seen returning. Annie released a sigh of relief. She could finally tell him she was carrying their child. Her flow had not returned, and she was beginning to feel ill in the mornings. She knew with certainty that she was in an interesting condition. Up until now, she hoped her flow had just been late and her one night of terror and degradation had now materialised into a life of living as a fallen woman. He could not marry her, even if he wished, and she could never return to the rectory. Her disgrace would almost kill her parents, not that it was her fault. She wrote to them and said she was travelling to Scotland and had been asked to attend one of Verity's cousins. The area was isolated, with no mail service. She had asked her friends on the staff to keep her secret of her continued presence in the house.

It took two full days after his return before she could see him alone. Both days, she had taken to shadowing his moves on the hillside when he went on his rides, and she intended to keep doing it for some time. She had heard from one of the old staff members that his mother had died in an unstable state some years after his birth, which reinforced her mother's stories.

Oliver had explained about seeing things after a hold-up as a child. The two things together made her formulate the psychological punishment. He knew that his mother had been affected in her mind, and Annie was aware of the worry this had caused him. He was worried that he may have inherited her insanity. He put his dreams down to this. After he had admitted this to Annie, she decided to play on this story. She made sure her rides were only ever seen by him in what was, in reality, a highwayman costume. He never rode with a groom, and she was out of sight of the house.

The third morning after his return, she was in his office waiting for him before his ride. No one else was around, and she had snuck in and sat at his desk. She heard the sound of his footsteps. She swallowed nervously. She knew she should not be there, but she needed this conversation to be private.

He entered the room with his head bowed, deep in thought. When he entered, he first noticed the scent of violets. His head jerked up, and he saw her at his desk. "Gentle Annie, why are you here?"

Rather than stand, she remained in his chair.

His face shone with delight.

"Can you not guess, sir? You asked me to let you know if something came of your abuse of me; well, it has. I am carrying your child, sir, and I am not pleased. I am now totally ruined and must leave before my condition is discovered."

As fast as his face had lit with delight, it now crashed. This was not what she expected. "Leave! No, you can't! Oh, my dearest gentle Annie, I should say I am sorry, but I would be lying. I will care for you and our child, but you do not need to leave for some months. It has only been eight weeks since our... um, union. You will not start showing for many, many weeks yet. I shall arrange somewhere safe for you to go and... oh my Annie..." he could not finish his words. The delight was reflected in his beaming smile. He walked around the desk and took her hand. "I promised I would not touch you again, so I will not, other than to say I wish you could be mine forever and always. Alas, I belong to another." He dropped her hand as though it were a lump of hot coal and walked away from her to the window.

Then he said, "Oh damn it, Annie, I so wish to take you in my arms and show you the joy I feel." He rested his head on the cold pane of glass, hoping to cool his ardour. She may not have been meant to hear his words, but she did. With a tortured voice, he said, "I may belong to another by marriage, but only you have my heart."

Annie had watched the slow pace at which he walked. She could see that the spoilt, shallow man of just a few weeks ago had changed. She stood from his chair, intending to leave, but the sagging shoulders of the marquess ate at her. She knew that her actions were now getting to him. Her morning rides before and after his return from London were haunting him.

She walked silently to her child's father and lay a hand on his shoulder, turning him. "Sir, I shall not leave without letting you know, but I will not stay the full term of my condition. You will have a hard enough time explaining the child's paternity as it is. Lady Verity will find out I am with child soon enough, but I will hide it for as long as I can."

At her touch, Oliver turned. She saw his eyes were glassy.

Holding her gaze with his, he said, "I never wish you to leave gentle Annie, ever, but I know that you must once your condition becomes obvious. I will provide a safe place for you to go when that time comes." Hope swelled within him as she didn't pull away. He said, "I shall purchase a small cottage where I can come and see our child. I will also arrange a regular allowance so you will never need to work again. I will not abandon you, my darling Annie. I hold you far too dear for that. We can be together there and be parents for our sweet child."

He was now standing so close he could smell her sweet breath. "I want to take you in my arms and kiss you again and again and hold you so very close, my darling gentle Annie, but not only have I promised not to touch you, and I dare not as I will not stop. That move must come from you. My dearest Annie, the consequences could not be any more dire than they are." He wished to kiss her again and hold her close. He knew he needed to share his feelings for this lovely lady who had eaten away at his hardened shell with her care and compassion.

Annie was tempted to put her hand on his chest and accept that invitation of a kiss. The second kiss he had given her when she was hunting for the key had been seared into her memory. She craved more of that heady delight, and guilt swept over her. She turned and left him at the window, aware that he watched her cross the room. The realisation that she no longer hated him washed over her. She returned his feelings in full. She was horrified to realise she had fallen desperately in love with a married man.

A devastated Oliver stared at her as she walked away from him. He was tempted to follow her and crush her to him. Yet she left him. She was more unattainable now than ever. Grief at her going tore through him. His abuse of her had led to this situation.

Annie paused at the door.

When he saw her hesitation, his face lit up. She turned slowly and looked at him, her expression not hatred but adoration. Her delay gave him hope. He crossed the room to be at her side. He fingered away a lock of her hair that had fallen on her cheek. The gentle caress had been done with their eyes locked together.

Annie could no more resist his magnetism than he could withstand her. She placed her hand possessively on his chest. That single movement was enough.

With a groan, Oliver took her in his arms and crushed her to him. The words of apology finally came. "I'm so sorry, Annie, so very sorry." He did not kiss her but buried his head in her neck.

She felt dampness on her neck from his weeping. How long they stood like this seemed endless. Then he gently pushed away from her arms. Annie lifted her face to him; she had decided that one kiss could not hurt. She slid an arm around his neck and pulled him down to her. "This must not happen again, sir."

"Call me Oliver, gentle Annie. My name is Oliver." He lowered his lips to hers. The kiss freely offered and willingly given sent emotions spiralling through them both. Oliver now only held her loosely so she could escape should she wish.

She didn't wish ever to leave the safety of his arms. Annie almost hoped he would ravish her again. The kiss sent shafts of desire shooting through her. Rather than pull away, she stepped closer. Oliver's arms tightened. She was pressed tightly along the entire length of his muscular body. She could feel his need for her rising through the thin fabric of her gown. She had gazed a long time at that part of his anatomy and knew its ability to change size. She knew she was already a fallen woman and he was carrying his child, so she dropped a hand and quickly un-buttoned one side of the front fall of his trousers. She could feel his physical response to the gentle caress of her hand on his manhood. It leapt to attention. Yet her loving action made him pull away.

Oliver gently pushed her from him. Belying his words from only moments earlier, he said, "No, Annie, as much as I'm crying out to lay with you, I will not intentionally break my marriage vows. I was drunk last time, not that that is a real excuse, but I did not realise what I was doing. However, this time, I am sober."

He re-buttoned his flap and cupped her face in his hands. "I will not even kiss you after today, but I find I cannot keep my hands from your very lovely person." He again kissed her reddened lips.

She wanted to sink into his arms again and stay there forever. When he lifted his lips from her, she whispered, "I love you."

Oliver drank in another kiss, prolonging it for as long as he could, and then he stepped away from her. "You must go, my sweet. I do not trust my resolve if you stay longer." He opened the door and gently pushed her through.

Annie was shocked at the about-turn in her attitude. Her abhorrence of his actions toward her was gone, but his rejection of her this time hurt. She had thrown herself at him; she had all but offered to become his mistress and also declared her love, and he turned away from her. Now, she was a fallen woman and not good enough for him to use, even as a wanton. As he closed the door behind her, her tears started to fall. She all but fled to her room to enjoy a fit of weeping. She knew he would still head out for a ride, so after she washed her face and gathered her thoughts, in her anger, she decided to continue haunting the man and playing on his nightmares when a boy, his highwayman spectre would now prevail for as long as she could manage. In a fit of malice, she set her mind on annoying him. He would get his comeuppance; she would see to that. Anger now brewed in her and overtook the love she had for him.

~

Over the next two months, Oliver tried to draw closer to her rather than ostracise her. He knew it was dangerous, but he wanted to be near her. He needed her far more than he thought it possible to want or need anyone. Annie was content to see him, but he never made a move to touch her. He never again attempted to do so. She stopped her silly games of brushing against him, as it was she who became confused with her conflicted emotions. Unbeknownst to Annie, Oliver was fighting with himself. If she gave him the slightest encouragement, he knew he would not refuse her invitation again. He wanted her to be his mistress. He would do her bidding if she gave him a single smile or a tilt of her head. It didn't come.

Now feeling rejected and cast aside, Annie wished to throw herself at him, but she didn't. Having been rejected once, she didn't wish to be hurt again. Unsure of what to do, she showed disdain for him privately, but she spoke about him publicly with such animation that he hardly knew what to make of her. Unable to talk things over with him, she believed he had rejected all she offered. She did not realise her emotions were distorted because of her advancing condition. She found that now she cried over the slightest thing.

Oliver, on the other hand, believed her scorn was well-earned. It made him rethink his life. He was caught in a marriage with a shrew, one he no longer trusted. The one woman he wanted now shut herself off from him. He now saw the rude glances and gestures Annie made to him. For Oliver, the ruder she was, the more she stayed in his mind. He wanted to draw her into his arms and comfort her, but he knew he couldn't. To compound matters, every time he left the house, the mysterious masked image of the highwayman shadowed him. The spectre appeared every time he left his home to ride for five months. On the rare occasion when it did not, he was constantly watching or searching for it. From a distance, all he recognised was the similarity to his horse. Forgetting about the unbroken colt in the far field, he saw his clothing and the portrayal of himself, albeit this apparition was masked. Was this apparition an alter-ego? Or was he seeing himself? Mayhap it is all in his mind?

~

As the months passed, Oliver began to seriously doubt his sanity.

The more Oliver tried to draw close to Annie, the more she pushed him away. Confusion was now written on his brow, as she was the one who had made advances on him. Once, he cornered her to ask her to explain the red flannel. She did, and then the ardour became too much to resist. She all but fell into his arms. Their passion frightened them both. She fled before anything more occurred. Other small incidents occurred when their hands touched. Once, she permitted him to feel his child moving in her stomach. When the baby kicked him, the fire between them nearly combusted everything nearby; such was their passion. He had drawn her into his arms and rained down kisses upon her. They were returned in full. That encounter could easily have ended up on a couch or bed somewhere. The incident ended when they were interrupted. As her condition became obvious, so did her confusion, and then he withdrew from her without notice.

After weeks of the endless emotional tug-of-war between what he wanted and what he knew he couldn't have, there was that damned spectre that haunted him. Oliver avoided her and turned to the only other solace he had at hand: brandy.

Annie began to notice an almost crushed change in his manner and considered calling off the intrigue. Her condition was approaching six months, and although her growing stomach was still not showing much due to the design of her gowns, she knew that with summer approaching, her voluminous winter attire would no longer hide her condition. She worked out that she was due in early May.

Juditty Durham, the housekeeper, cornered her one morning as she was about to leave her room. Rather than condemning Annie, she empathised with her. She had noticed the marquess watching Annie far more than was appropriate. It did not take a genius to add one and one. Annie was carrying the marquis's child, and from her reaction, it was not consensual.

For weeks, Annie had awaited a summons to Oliver's office to discuss the impending birth of their baby, but it did not come. He was now so frequently drunk that she dared not enter his den lest he take her in his arms again. Although she feared his rejection, she was ready to do anything he wished her to do. One glance from him, and she would submit willingly, but it didn't come.

The one morning she did knock on his office door, he was not there. She decided to visit the housekeeper and ask for her advice. However, after visiting Oliver's empty office, Annie bumped into the village midwife returning home.

She drew Annie aside. "Annie, my dear girl, are you interesting?"

Annie nodded. Being close to her room, she ushered her friend inside and confessed all. The compassionate lady, Erminetrude Wilde, took Annie in a comforting hug. "Miss Annie, these things happen in big houses. It is not my position to stick my nose into your business, but let me say, knowing your parents, I understand if you do not wish to return home, and should you need to stay somewhere for a few months, I have a spare bed of sorts at my cottage. My Bobbie mentioned that things up here were not as they should be, but I did not realise it was you that he was talking about."

Annie was beside herself with fear. "Truly, Ermie, I can stay with you? I know I must leave soon, as even Mrs Durham has noticed, and Lord Oliver has not kept his promise to care for me. He's now drinking so much that I dare not approach him again. I have just come from his office, but he is not there."

The two sat together, making plans. "Bobbie can bring your things. He's a good boy, that son of mine. He's so like his papa. Gentle as a lamb, that man was a delight. Not like Mr Wilde; he was a holy terror that one, but because he drank, I got to become a midwife to make some money, so in all, I'm happy. Bobbie's papa died in the carriage accident that took the marquess's grandfather. He was the head coachman here, too. Bobbie took his position."

Annie knew Ermie's story but knew that the dear lady loved a chat. She decided to leave at the end of the week, which was three months before her child was due. With their heads together, plans for her removal were soon set in place.

Oliver had long ago admitted to himself that his feelings for Annie were far more than pure lust. He adored her.

Annie dared not to voice her own emotions again. She would not become his mistress.

He knew his admission to her was too late, as he feared he was losing his mind and, fearing he would endanger someone should he become unhinged; he locked himself off from everyone. He only wanted Annie, and she wouldn't permit him near her. On top of that, the apparition of the mysterious horseman continued to haunt him. He knew he was spiralling deeper and deeper into an emotional morass. No one else seemed to be able to see the spectre but him. He wondered if he was losing his mind as his mother did. He had no one to talk to and no one who cared. He had never had a friend; up until now, he had never missed that companionship. He craved conversation with Annie, but she avoided him. He had hardly seen her for weeks now and was growing desperate. He could summon her but wanted her to come to him willingly. He was unaware that she had attempted to seek him out that week. He was so frustrated that he could no longer talk to her whenever he wished. Worse still was that he had noticed that her condition was beginning to show. He knew he should do something about telling her about the cottage he had purchased for her, but that would mean she would leave. He wanted her close but knew she could not stay. He took another drink.

Sitting in melancholy silence in a pool of misery on his own, Oliver finally broke. He wept for his convoluted and mixed-up life. He had reached the end of his endurance. He did the only thing he had left to do: he prayed. He had not done this for many a long year, not since his nanny taught him to trust God and that God had Oliver's life in His very capable hands.

Oliver wondered. How could he have so magnificently stuffed up his privileged life? Once more, he turned to the delicious amber liquid on the grog tray. The aroma made his mouth water. One drink turned to two... anything to overshadow the scent that invaded his room. Violets!

He hauled himself off the chaise lounge at midnight and dragged himself to bed. Dreams of his gentle Annie sustained him. He thought he had smelled violets in his office that morning but presumed it was his imagination. That occurred often.

In the pre-dawn, Annie and Ermie collected her luggage and went to meet Bob in the courtyard. He and Ermie packed the rest of her things while she stole into Oliver's den to leave him a farewell letter.

Bob was the only one in the house who knew where she was going.

Mid-morning, Oliver woke up with another sore head. Knowing his drinking was getting out of hand, he rolled over with a groan and fell out of bed. Moving was sheer hell, yet he dressed and headed to his den. On entry, he froze. Sitting propped on his desk was a letter. It had just one word on it:

"Oliver." He had seen her writing before and quickly flicked off the unstamped wax seal.

Dear sir,

The time has come, and you have not kept your promises to me, so I have gone. Please make some excuse to your wife about some family emergency. Be assured that I am somewhere safe. I shall contact you in three months. You know why.

Annie

Oliver gazed at the note in his hand, unable to believe she had gone without him keeping his word. He knew he was the father of her child. He knew that he had let her down dreadfully. He had money sitting in an account waiting for her, but she knew nothing of this as he had not had the courage to summon her and explain his provision for both her and their child. He even purchased a lovely thatched cottage and had been preparing it for her and their child. He completed the furnishing only yesterday.

In anger, Oliver grabbed the first thing at hand, a crystal decanter full of brandy. Grasping it by the neck, he hurled it into the fireplace. The amber liquid exploded into flame as it hit the hot coals from the night before. Staring at the flash of fire, he vowed never to drink the mind-numbing stuff again. He stormed out and took the stairs two at a time. He flung the door open and crashed into her room, hoping to find that she had not already left. The room was empty, and the only thing of hers that remained was the heady scent of violets. Oliver slumped onto her bed and wept for his lost love and their child.

Chapter 6   Battle Lines

*R*ather than go home, where Annie risked being cast off by her parents, Annie moved into Ermie's cottage. She settled in quickly, and the following morning, she was ready to continue her haunting rides. Annie now became more diligent in her highwayman activities, rarely missing a day, but she no longer did the wild dashes along the hilltops. Her tactics changed.

Day after day, and week after week, Oliver found the spectre lurking in the bushes or visible from his office window. Every day, it appeared somewhere different; there one moment and gone the next. He was so sure that the sight was of his horse that he checked on King's Majesty in the stables. He kept his eyes on the spectre until he turned towards the stables. By the time he reappeared mounted on his steed and ready for a chase, the apparition had vanished again.

Over the following week, a rider was seen riding sedately along the hilltops. Many thought it was the marquess. Meanwhile, he was again cloistered with his brandy, not daring to venture outside. He had not stopped drinking, as he claimed. He normally had his first drink after his morning ride; now, he, more often than not, was all but insensible. Anything to drown out his pain of loss and the mess his life had become. The heady scent of violets was now missing. While sober, he decided to set traps by stationing the grooms in various places, but none saw anything. Annie made sure she knew where Bob was usually placed, and she sat with him in wait for Oliver. Bob, of course, denied seeing any apparitions as he was fully aware it was Annie. Her expectant condition was now blatantly apparent.

A month after she left, Annie was finally chased by some of the grooms who glimpsed her, but the stallion she was on could outrun any of the horses in the stable, bar the marquess's Godolphin Arabian stallion. At seven months along, the fast riding was vastly uncomfortable, if not a bit painful.

The grooms thought the other young stud horse in the far field was still unbroken. He was cropping on the grass after his exhilarating ride when they reached his field. They were not prepared to draw close to check on him, thinking he was still wild. Annie was hiding behind the stone fence, waiting for them to leave. She controlled her breathing until they departed.

On her return home, Ermie challenged her with the words, "You love him, don't you?"

Annie's answer was a nod and a burst into tears. As Ermie cradled her, she said, "So very much it hurts." Annie wept harder.

May approached, and although heavy with child, she would not give up her vigil. She still shadowed Oliver whenever possible. It was more just to see him than haunt him. When she could not ride due to inclement weather, she knew Oliver could not either. As speed riding was now out of the question, she became more cunning. Oliver's black cloak hid her advanced condition as well as keeping the morning chill penetrating, but she was still never close enough for him to see who the rider was. She was now too cumbersome to ride any distance, but she still managed to outwit Oliver with occasional appearances at unexpected times. Rather than wait until he was out riding, she regularly sat in view of his den window. Often, she tipped her hat to him, then vanished into the woodland.

May arrived, and Annie knew her time was close. She had been having back pain since returning from that morning's outing, and that night, she slept little. The first of her sizeable pains hit her while waiting for Oliver at dawn the following morning; for once, she saw sense and returned the horse to the field before making the trek back to their cottage. By the time she had unsaddled Aladdin and walked a mile home, the pains were now only ten minutes apart. Calling as she entered, "Ermie, Ermie, I need you." Her cries were met with silence. Ermie was not there. Excruciating pain ripped through her. Annie now knew that all her fears of having to deliver the child herself were about to come true. She put on some water to heat and prepared for the birth alone.

The cottage they lived in was tiny. Two narrow beds were in an alcove off the kitchen. Annie presumed this was Bob's old bed. She removed her gown and donned her night rail. Having slept little the night before, she was already tired when the next hard pain hit. She breathed through the contraction as Ermie had taught her to do. As the pain passed, the dear lady entered. The contractions were close.

Without panicking, Ermie placed her bag down and went to Annie's side. "Annie dearest, is it time?"

Annie found it hard to answer as she was in the middle of a contraction. When she was hit with another pain moments later, she nodded. After breathing through it, she said, "Four minutes if that, Ermie; I've put on the water and got the towels. Ermie, I'm scared. It hasn't moved since yesterday, Ermie."

Ermie said, "Oh my lamb, I do this all the time. You are good and healthy, and the child feels to be a nice size. Now, let's get you settled. I have a birthing chair here, and it's much easier using that than lying down."

Only minutes later, Ermie said, "You're crowning, dear; you'll be holding your child soon."

Annie vomited and soon afterwards needed to push. Ermie spoke, encouraging her, "Now, a deep breath and a big push, dearie." Annie did as she was told.

Ermie said, "Scream if you wish, dearie, as it helps."

Annie let forth a bellow and felt a gush between her legs. She waited to hear the squall of a new voice, but there was silence. Annie saw Ermie working on the tiny limp babe. The midwife smacked it and even tried gently blowing into its mouth. The tiny mite remained spiritless. She never took a breath on her own, even though the air Ermie pumped into her lungs had made her chest swell. She remained grey. Annie prayed as she had never prayed before. "Breathe, baby girl, breathe, my little one. Please, for Oliver's sake, please."

The child remained lifeless. Annie reached for her daughter, cradling the dead child to her bosom. Numb with shock, Ermie said she still had to deliver the afterbirth. Annie's baby had arrived late morning on a cold, bleak Saturday on May 5th, 1787. After being in pain on and off for over twenty hours before the birth, Annie was already exhausted, but she had one more thing to do. She was too dazed to weep… that would come later. She refused to release her daughter to her friend. The grief at losing their child ate at her. Could her riding have caused this?

Annie sat up all night cradling her daughter, knowing it would be the only time she would ever have with her child. Her unnamed baby girl's beautiful face was perfect but tinged with blue. The tiny body with her mass of fair downy hair pressed to Annie's chest as she wept over her child. Annie wished to see more of her beautiful baby than her face, so she unwrapped her little body and stroked her perfect tiny fingers and toes, all the while wishing her daughter would move. Tears blurred her vision.

Annie knew she had felt movement in her stomach until the last days, but Ermie assured her that it was quite common for a child to go still before birth. Annie wept and mourned the loss of their baby girl, but it was like a bad dream. Now, she had nothing left of him. Their baby's life was cut short before it even had time to live. Annie had no idea what life would now bring for her, but tonight and tonight only, she had this precious mite to love and cherish, for tomorrow she would hand her to her father, and she would be buried, gone forever, just like her love for Oliver. She gazed at the limp child through her tears. She would leave the child unnamed, just as her love was unfulfilled.

Ermie knew that Annie had to handle grief in her own way. She wrapped her up warmly, stoked the fire, and left her alone with her baby. She knew Annie had her own unconventional plans for the following day, and although she disapproved, she also knew Annie had her reasons. Ermie frequently rose throughout the night to check on her charge, relieved to see Annie was still there and had not snuck off alone.

Annie had dozed but rarely was deeply asleep. She stirred each time the beloved, caring lady checked on her. At dawn the following morning, Annie dressed her daughter in the hand-made embroidered gown she had crafted with such loving care, wrapped her child so snugly that she looked like she was sleeping, and placed her in a small wicker basket bought to be her crib.

Now ready for the final enacting of her plan, Ermie escorted Annie to the field, where Aladdin waited for her. This would be the colt's final appearance as a highwayman's steed. Ermie held the small basket while Annie saddled the horse and heaved herself onto Aladdin's back. She knew Annie was bleeding heavily but understood that she needed to get this done. Ermie tried one last time to talk Annie out of this action. "Annie, you don't have to do it this way; surely the marquess will come if you send a note. I will stay close, and you can hand him the child there." With a final caress to the still-cold baby's perfect downy cheek, Ermie passed the precious cargo to the grieving mother.

Annie said as she took her precious bundle from Ermie's hands, "Oliver would come without a doubt, Ermie, but I must see this to the end. I now need to release his mind. It is over. He must know that it was me. There is no future for us; this is how I must end it. There was far more to this stealth than spite or even vengeance. Oliver has changed, and I need to see this through. He will understand as no other could. Ermie, I love him, and I cannot trust myself to see him alone, but I do not wish him to suffer any longer."

Ermie stood at the hedge, watching Annie and Aladdin saunter away. She knew that Annie needed to do this by herself. She would go home and wait for her return. She at least had Bob to talk to should things not work out.

~

For six weeks after Annie left Bowbelle Hall, Oliver had searched everywhere. Every lead he found took him to another dead end. He tried to follow through with Sir Basil, only to discover he was still overseas. The only Soames family he knew about was the rector; to his knowledge, they had no children. If they did, there was no sign of them. Annie had never mentioned other family, siblings, or even friends except to say she could not return home. Neither his housekeeper nor his butler would admit to more knowledge of her. Soames was not the most common name, but neither was it unusual.

Why had he never asked her? Why would his staff not tell him? Could they not see that he cared? He knew they were protecting her from him. Finally, failing at every turn he took, he gave up and waited. His decision was also accompanied by the determination to stop drinking for good. That decision had occurred after Verity stormed his den one afternoon to find him sitting on the floor sniffing the chaise lounge to see if it smelled of violets. He was wallowing in self-pity at his lost love. Her scorn and ridicule made him realise his life needed to change. However, he banished his wife from his den, wishing he could banish her from his life. That thought made him think… Verity's visit made him realise that he was no use to Annie or their child if he turned into a drunken sop. Within an hour of Verity's visit, he requested that all grog trays throughout the house be removed. From now on, he would have one glass of wine with a meal and one glass of port to follow, but that was it. Verity only drank white wine anyway and now usually ate her meals in her room. White wine was too sweet for his palate, not that he would consider her wishes again.

Oliver left the promised communication in Annie's very capable hands. Her letter said she would contact him in three months, and he knew she would. He trusted her, he always had, and by his reckoning, that time was up this week.

On the last Saturday in April, Verity had patronisingly decided to have breakfast with him downstairs and proudly informed him that they had now been married for eighteen months. She gloated over her title and lauded her position whenever she had an excuse. Oliver realised the staff hated her. He grunted acknowledgement of her statement, thinking that those had been eighteen months of dissatisfaction and discontent for him. He was quite aware that the staff called her Lady Muck behind her back. Her deception and deceitfulness had killed the marriage before it had even had a chance. For the first nine months, he had tried to make it work; then, she threw her son's paternity in his face after the child's birth, and numerous verbal stoushes followed this. He had stormed out after the last one and had hardly spoken to her since. Having recently met Verity's French friend, Oliver knew at one glance who the father of the child was.

Her cackle of delight at his discomfort was the last straw. No more!

He'd had enough! He stood in his place at the breakfast table, sending his chair flying backwards. The knife he held aloft dripped with marmalade. His toast would remain uneaten this morning. The knife clattered unnoticed onto the plate and smashed it. He banged his hands on the table. Everything rattled as the table moved. His anger was raised to a boiling point. Verity could have had everything she wanted, and he would have stayed faithful, but enough was enough."Enough of your cackling, wife! You now have the title you coveted, and your son is unwillingly my heir. There is nothing I can do about that, but from today, there will be nothing else to pleasure you in this house. From today, your life will be vastly different and decidedly unpleasant."

He had decided to live a celibate life after Annie left. He had once contemplated returning to Verity's bed to try to make their marriage work. But now, he knew, he would have no one if he could not have Annie. Verity would not escape; she would also have her wings severely clipped. He then slowly approached her, somewhat threateningly. With a deliberate menace in his voice, he said, "Wife, from today, to celebrate our auspicious milestone, you will find that you will be permitted no visitors unless they are my friends, and I have none. You will no longer be permitted to travel at all except to church with me, and you will have no freedom. As the law says, you will obey me and conform to my will. You wished for a husband, and until now, I have been lenient. No more! I shall have an iron glove on your life. See how you can wiggle your attractive *derriere* in that, my dear. This should curtail your cuckolding exploits. No male staff will be permitted to attend to your whims or your bed. You will have an elderly maid of my choosing to attend to you, and your French modiste will be sent home. Your new maid will shadow your every move outside your room and report to me and me alone. Do I make myself understood?"

Oliver watched Verity's face blanch as he approached slowly. By now, he was towering over her, but he had not, nor would he ever, lay a hand on her. That was not his way. His wife nodded fearfully, realising she had pushed his buttons once too often.

Henry stood silent and unmoving. He was biting his cheeks hard, trying not to smile. Now, he had reason to stop the Frenchman from visiting. He had been itching to let his master know about his secret visits but had refrained. His comments made him realise his lordship was aware that the Frenchman had fathered her child. His master knew he would stay mum about what he had just witnessed, but the onus would be on him to inform the staff they must band together to curtail her ladyship's actions.

Oliver turned to his silent butler. "Henry, see to it!"

Henry still didn't move. He knew that any male staff member caught with his lordship's wife, let alone in a compromising position, would receive instant dismissal and no reference. "As you wish, sir." Henry gave a bow but remained stationary as Oliver made his way to the door. The door crashed open, and the paintings on the walls shook as it slammed shut behind Oliver. Henry knew that an explosion from his mistress would follow his master's departure. He wondered what she would throw this time. He was getting used to sending in a maid to clean up her messes. As predicted, the explosion occurred, but all she had to throw was her favourite dinner service, which she had demanded they use this morning. For once, she was beaten. Although Oliver had broken a plate, she would not destroy this gift from her Frenchman.

~

Within the hour, Bob Brown made sure no groom was prepared to break the marquess's rules. He only had the new coachman to speak to. He would be arriving tonight. He knew the reason for Annie's reaction to his master but had no idea that the Frenchman who had visited had been the wedge that caused the break. He had not yet seen the child her ladyship had born, but there were rumours that it resembled the Frenchman more than the marquess. He had wondered why Annie had not left directly after the incident occurred, but he saw the compassion written on her face. The revelation finally hit him. "She loves him." She may not even realise it, but he could see the softening of her frown and the smile that teased her lips when she talked about him. He had noticed the same in his lordship, but he was married.

For the next few days, Verity's animosity toward his lordship was obvious to everyone in the household. Oliver ignored his heir, the child he must acknowledge to the world as his own or be scorned for being cuckolded before his marriage. He would have nothing to do with the boy but would ensure Verity didn't either. Her son would be kept in the nursery, and she would be banned from seeing him. A sound caught in his throat and became almost a choke. He then thought, "Verity is as stuck in this distasteful marriage as much as I am, but this is of her doing." Oliver wished she would leave; he would risk the disgrace of approaching Parliament and having the marriage annulled. He wanted his gentle Annie, not this viper. He intended they would live separate lives at home, rarely even eating together unless they had visitors. Even then, they were to be seated at either end of the huge banquet table. Thankfully, it was so large that he could hardly see her past the numerous centrepieces he insisted would be placed amongst the floral arrangements down the centre of the spread.

Verity was the perfect hostess; she acted the perfect marchioness and was a good clothes horse, as she looked magnificent in everything she wore. His father had chosen a pretty face, and that's all she was. She was cheap, shallow and conniving, and underneath was a scheming shrew with little substance and no goodness in her character. She was exactly what society admired. Oliver just wished she wasn't his marchioness. He wanted her gone and replaced with his gentle Annie. Verity, on the other hand, was as evil and nasty as a woman could be. She undermined him at every opportunity that arose and belittled him to the staff, not that they listened. She took great glee in flaunting her good looks to him and the male staff, often mincing around the house scantily clad in an almost transparent night rail.

A week later, after breakfast, Verity walked towards the library. Once there, she paced and stormed but realised she was beaten. It had not taken long for her to realise that the footmen now looked away from her when she appeared, no matter how scantily clad she was. Previously, her diaphanous night rail was enough to entice any male to do her bidding. Now, they moved aside and let her pass. Her ire was severely raised when she wished to resume her social life.

Unaware she was in the library, Oliver entered to collect a book. If last week's clash over breakfast was loud, the explosions that followed were worse. He put his foot down. She could not visit anyone anywhere unless he accompanied her. Church outings with him beside her were the only ones she was permitted unless he suggested it. Her father may visit, but she could not return to Scotland with him. Most of her gowns were to be destroyed, and she would be permitted to retain only the bare minimum of clothing. The fabulous jewellery collection would be held under lock and key to which she would no longer have access.

Many of the staff heard the string of foul expletives that oozed from her ladyship's pretty mouth. They had gathered outside the library door to listen to the volatile relationship come to a final stalemate. Lady Verity's wings were clipped, tied, and severely impeded, and she knew it. The staff jigged with glee.

Her ugly words were like water off a duck's back for Oliver. Her vitriol could no longer hurt him. Her shrewish and sluttish ways had brought her position in life but little else. The more she railed at him, the more he would reduce her activities. This morning, he cut her clothing allowance to a minimum. Oliver said, "As you will not be going anywhere, you will not need new clothing." When he left the library, he dismissed her dressmaker with severance pay, making her count her blessings. She could now open her own shop with the money he gave her.

Oliver had no way out of the marriage but didn't have to live with his wife flaunting herself to every male within her eyesight. As her husband, she must do what he said and be where she was told to be. This was the lot she had chosen, and now she must conform to the life she must lead. Even Nanny knew she was now forbidden entry into the nursery. She would not taint the child with hatred for him, as he was Oliver's heir, like it or not.

Meanwhile, Verity's loathing for her husband grew. Cuckolding him was not enough. She hunted for another way to hurt him.

Oliver fully reciprocated. He held her responsible for all that had occurred, and he was not wrong. Of his heir, he saw as little of him as possible. Oliver had forbidden him to be brought into any room he occupied. He wanted nothing to do with the little boy. However, Oliver knew the child was now nine months old because he had been counting the weeks as they passed, as he was aware when he abused Annie. Oliver's one concession to Verity was they would attend church together once a month. There, under his watchful eye, she could do no harm. Oliver wondered if the minister was related to Annie as they had the same surname. Considering what he had done to Annie, he had never plucked up the courage to ask his vicar. Oliver thought deeply about the faith that Annie mentioned frequently. He had never thought much about what he believed before their conversations, and now her words brought back some of his father's teachings. He was sure that if Annie had returned to her family, he would have heard of her presence and condition; he would have been ostracised. Therefore, for the sake of the entire village, the big house family put on a happy face. Not all marriages were happy, and his certainly was not.

Verity avoided holding on to his arm by carrying Marcus. It was the only time she saw her son, and they tried to put on a happy family front. Oliver was anything but happy. The words of the sermon flew over his head. He stopped listening when he heard the rector's title, 'Forgiveness and God's endless patience.' Oliver couldn't sit and listen to the words he really needed to hear. Knowing he could not leave the building, he would rather tune out and wallow in the grief of his own making. He thought back to Annie's remarks the morning after he violated her. He had finally acknowledged that this was what he had done to her. She called him out, and he had taken her chastisement like a lamb. She had called him many names: spoilt, shallow, self-centred, egotistical, poor-little-rich-boy who had never been crossed. He was conceited and stubborn, yet the only term he had responded to was the least important of them all; her final insult had been that he was cheese-paring. Well, he had fixed that immediately, and she had actually thanked him on behalf of all the staff. They all had their salary doubled at least, but the lowest paid ones found that they were now quadrupled. He still found it amazing that someone could possibly live on a mere four pounds a year, but somehow they did. He also permitted access to supplies from the house and increased the provision of food allocations for their family use. He fixed their cottages and sorted individual rooms for all the staff who wished to live in the big house. He would never again give the women in his household red flannel after Annie explained why it was such a hated gift.

For the rest of the insults she had thrown at him, he knew he deserved each and every one of them but didn't know how to be any different. He could have even added a few more. From the time his mother died as a small boy, he had stood alone and aloof. He had no friends and knew no different. His father had never married again, and he grew up a very lonely but spoilt child. Born as an earl, he had never had his will crossed and rarely had been held responsible for his actions. Only Annie had called him to account and question his behaviour. Only Annie had dared to pull him down a peg or two. Only Annie had crept beneath the shell he had encased himself in to find the real living, breathing, hurting and lonely man. Yes, he was all the names she called him and many more, and he loved her for challenging him as no one else dared to do. As he wiped an errant tear from his eye, he realised the sermon had finished. They sat together in the family pew and put on a united face. As usual, little Marcus joined them under the care of his nanny. The child looked nothing like him and not much like his mother, except he had her dark colouring, and his skin was darkening, too. Oliver fobbed off the rare comments by saying he took after his mother's Scottish side of the family. As no one had met Verity's parents, they could not comment. He had dreamed of having an heir and many spares until the day the child was born. One look at the baby and Oliver knew his wife had cheated on him. Verity had confirmed his suspicions and laughed at him, explaining that she had spent the nights two weeks before her wedding in the arms of another man. Oliver's answer to that had been to get drunk, and that had led to his abuse of Annie. His guilt and anxiety for that knew no bounds.

Knowing that Annie would choose an unusual way of reaching out to him, he half expected her to be in church that week. She wasn't. Sitting in the front pew, he took every opportunity to check the rest of the congregation when he turned to sit after each time they stood for a hymn. His eyes raked the congregation, especially checking the back seats. Nothing! At Holy Communion, he eyed every recipient. The only one he noticed missing was his housekeeper's friend, the jovial midwife, who was frequently called away for a birth. She was a happy soul whom everyone knew and loved.

After the service, he followed the rector and his wife as they left the church. He concentrated on greeting the many villagers as they left the building. Releasing a frustrated sigh, he knew he must continue to wait. Verity made her excuses and went directly to the carriage with the boy. Oliver waited until most of the congregation had left before finally leaving. He hoped that Annie would appear somehow.

Annie watched her parents and Oliver after the service, unseen from the woodland edge. Her mother stood chatting happily to Oliver, not realising what he had done to her daughter. Sitting in the shadows, Annie waited for him to walk to his carriage. Happy that she had confirmed his presence and knew his timing, she would make her final appearance as a highwayman today. She was tired and looking forward to sleeping for a long time. Her precious bundle was sitting carefully on her lap. She was feeling lightheaded, but she was determined to enact the final scene. Today was to bring closure and peace to Oliver's mind. She would release him. He had made it clear that he would not willingly break his marriage, and Annie loved him even more for that.

Chapter 7 Stand for Delivery

*T*o date, Verity had not realised the situation between her ex-companion and her husband. She had been so obsessed with secreting her lover into her bedroom suite that she had not noticed Oliver's apparent withdrawal. She knew he was moody, but at least he wasn't drinking so much. Lately, she had noted that her husband had become even more withdrawn and distant, even to the point of morose. Still, she had put that down to discovering he had been cuckolded and having to acknowledge a child that was not his. In the weeks since she invaded his library, he had stopped getting drunk each day. Verity had no time for a man who turned to the bottle with so little cause. However, yesterday's outburst over breakfast and then their harsh words made her somewhat fearful of what her life would now be like. Until recently, she had been content with how her marriage had turned out; at least he didn't hit her as his father had taken to her mother. Francois cherished her; he always had, but he was French, and in England, he was considered an enemy. He had seen what her father was like and had come to her rescue. Her mother's death at her father's hand had given Verity little option but to do what the angry Scotsman said. She would not have been surprised if her father took to her with his riding whip as he had done regularly with her mother. Thankfully, Oliver didn't have a temper like that.

Unbeknownst to Oliver, for the months he had been distracted with Annie after the heir's birth, his absences and distractions had allowed her dalliance with Francois to continue. She had been careful to be reasonably discreet. She had been in love with him since she was young, and her father had not permitted them to marry. She was aware that when she married, there was already a possibility that she was carrying his child. Francois had snuck into her room each night for the two weeks before she married. Prior to that, she had resisted his suggestions to sleep with him. They had two weeks of unbridled passion.

After Marcus's Baptism, when Oliver was away, Henry discovered them in the orangery more than once. Still, thankfully, they had only been sitting talking at the time, having already taken their pleasure with each other before the butler's untimely entry.

When Marcus was born, and he had Francois's cleft chin, she realised she had been correct; she had indeed been with child when she married. She had been due for her flow the week before the wedding, and it had not come. Francois had returned to France for a few months. Verity was determined that she would put Oliver's rules to the test once he came back. Francois had seen his son a few times while Oliver was away, but now Oliver never left the house, and Francois would be unable to arrange secret meetings. The big glitch now was that the staff had been told to forbid his entrance. She sat glaring at her husband, who was seated beside her in the new coach. She knew she had pushed him too far yesterday morning. She bit her cheek, wondering what her next step should be. Would an apology work? She knew that if she fell with Francois's child again and had not slept with Oliver, he could send her away or, worse, he could still follow through on his threat to lock her up in Bedlam Hospital. She glanced at him and saw he was looking out the window.

Oliver gazed out the window of the carriage. The drop glass openings were a blessing. The open window let his wife's cloying perfume out of the cabin. The scent was nauseating and very unlike the fresh perfume Annie exuded. He rested back on the comfortable squab seats of the new travelling carriage he had ordered from Newcastle-on-Tyne. Lancelot Usher was a new name in the business but one that Oliver had decided to patronise. He would certainly purchase again from him. The man knew his stuff. This vehicle was well-sprung and comfortable. He liked the blue leather upholstery in this carriage and thought that he must tell Bob that he approved of how his vehicles were turned out. Up until Annie, Oliver had never thought of staff as people. She had told him how proud each of them was of him and his achievements. Each speech he made in Parliament or action he took on the farm or in London spread throughout the house like quicksilver. She told him of the below-stairs discussions and how a single word of praise from him could lift the mood of the entire staff for a day.

Oliver had set about treating them as people. He had thought most of the footmen were named John, as his father called them. Andrew, Keith, James, Michael, Robert, and, of course, Henry, were now called by their given names, as were the others except his housekeeper. Juditty Durham treated him like a leper, and he realised that she knew what he had done to Annie.

He was deep in thought again; up until two days ago, the spectre had still shadowed him. He had wondered if it were Annie as he knew she rode as well as any man he knew, if not better. But as the rider continued to appear after she left and the person was definitely not riding sidesaddle, it must not be her. The rider on the horse wore breeches and top boots the same as his. His visions now assured him that he was going to lose his mind.

About a month ago, his head groom was with him when the rider appeared before them both. Oliver asked the man what he saw. "Bob, do you see that spectre riding over there? Is it me, or am I dreaming?"

Knowing it was Annie, Bob replied honestly, "I see no spectre, sir. I see rolling hills and a lovely vale but no spectre, ghosts, or mystery horsemen."

This had been what they had just discussed.

Bob waited until Oliver's back was turned, then waived for Annie to go. She walked into the shadows and vanished. Oliver slumped in the saddle and became even more depressed. He missed the flash of anger that crossed his servant's brow. Bob looked at his boss and felt sorry for him for a fleeting moment. However, his boss deserved what she was doing to him. How dare he abuse her?

Annie had taken a shortcut from outside the church and was waiting for the coach to turn the corner on the road to the house. Dressed from head to foot in her black highwayman garb, she rode to the middle of the road and called for the coach to stop. However, the words she cried were somewhat unusual; instead of calling the carriage to "Stand and deliver," she cried, "Stand for delivery."

As the coach and four horses approached, she remained unmoving. The new coachman, faced with a mirror image of his employer but wearing a mask, jolted the vehicle. He tried to ascertain who the rider was, as he knew his employer was already in the carriage.

Annie leaned down and pulled open the coach door. Oliver jumped to his feet as soon as the carriage slowed. Rather than rob the coach of its valuables, Annie leaned down to him and carefully handed Oliver her precious cargo, saying, "Do with her as you wish, Oliver, for she is of your blood. As yet, she is unnamed." His hand touched hers as he reached out for her gift. Annie felt as though his touch burned her skin. She wished to throw herself into his arms, but she had to say farewell instead. Annie heard his almost breathless voicing of her name.

He murmured, "Annie, my love." His words were not soft enough. Recognising Annie's beloved voice, Oliver reached out and accepted her cherished gift with a broad smile. "Thank you," was all he managed to say aloud. He was thrilled to find that Annie was alive and well. He glanced down, expecting the babe to cry at the manhandling it received; he cradled the small basket lovingly and carefully.

She reluctantly released his hand. By the time Oliver looked up to speak to Annie and thank her properly, she had vanished. With her job now done, Annie turned Aladdin and rode away.

The coachman watched as the trees swallowed the mysterious masked rider. Verity's mouth dropped open. She knew that voice well and heard Annie's words and Oliver's soft and loving reply.

Oliver was relieved to see the spectre up close, and he recognised her instantly. Finding that it was Annie all along, relief swept over him. He thought back to when the sightings started and realised the time tallied to his violation of her. He had put it down to his guilt and sleepless nights. Oliver was oblivious to Verity's anger; he expected the child to be whimpering or even to hear her breathing, then he realised why the babe was quiet; it was cold, so very cold and still that it could only mean one thing. He pulled back the flap of the blanket and released a howl of grief when he realised their baby was not breathing. Their child was dead. Taking the blue-tinged infant from the basket, he slowly unwrapped her and saw the beautiful smocked gown and blanket she was dressed in. He counted her fingers and toes, then traced his finger over her unsmiling rosebud lips. The fair fuzz of her hair was just like Annie's, and it was that that finally broke him. Guttered and utterly miserable, he howled again with tortured grief as he cradled their child to his chest. She, too, smelled of violets.

Sometime later, with just a tap on the roof, the carriage moved forward and travelled home. With the spectre now unveiled, Oliver revealed all to his astounded wife, who had thankfully remained silent until now.

Verity smiled in an evil way at the revelation. Though she was livid that Annie had given birth to her husband's child, she could not see the duplicity of her behaviour. She silently vowed to get revenge on the girl. Verity watched her husband sobbing over a dead child. "Control yourself, husband, or I shall say you are not of right mind."

The look Oliver gave his wife was one of seething anger. With a harshness she had not witnessed before from him, his words stung her. "Watch your tongue, you shrewish wife. I do not care what you think, now or ever. You are the one who is in jeopardy of being incarcerated. There are many reasons for having you declared insane. Cuckolding is the very least of these. Would you care for me to list them? I could send your bastard son to join you and kill two birds with one stone. Then I could marry Annie."

Verity fell silent. She knew that with one word from her husband, she would never see Francois again, let alone their son. A word was planted deep within her…revenge.

~

After delivering their daughter to Oliver, Annie decided to return to her Uncle Basil's house rather than Ermie's cottage. She knew there that she could recuperate in peace. Bob could bring her things over later.

Aladdin noticed that Annie was not her usual alert self. The route she took was not back towards his field.

Annie was now feeling very faint, and as she was weeping uncontrollably, she had taken the wrong path through the forest. Oliver had said nothing as he took the child from her. He had not tried to stop her departure, and her heart felt like it was breaking.

After turning Aladdin from the coach, she was blinded by her released emotion. She headed away from the carriage but had no idea of her direction due to the tears cascading down her face. Ermie had told her not to ride, but she knew it was the only opportunity she would have to have access to Oliver outside the house. She had not wanted him to know of Ermie's involvement. She held on to the pommel while Aladdin walked along the unknown pathway. Needing to rest, she leaned forward momentarily onto his neck. Aladdin plodded on with her now dozing on his back. Weak from blood loss and exertion too soon after the birth, Annie passed out. Her arms fell limp and were now draped down either side of Aladdin's neck, and her legs hung from the saddle. She was still dressed in her male highwayman garb and had not even removed the silk mask.

Feeling her knees at his side loosen and the reins go slack, Aladdin realised something was wrong. However, he kept walking down the path she had set him on rather than turning and heading down the road that led back to his field. He continued down the shaded trackway.

Unfortunately, this road led to another village rather than where Annie and Ermie lived or to her uncle's house. Having never seen the many smoke-exuding buildings before, Aladdin whinnied with fear and drew attention to his unconscious, masked, cloaked rider. Seeing the rider's garb, he was soon surrounded by a posse of angry villagers. Without checking for identity or injury, Annie was bundled off the horse and dumped unceremoniously, still unresponsive, on the cell floor of the local lock-up.

Startled by how Annie was abruptly dragged off his back, Aladdin was now stressed. Some of the village men manage to remove his saddle; however, while attempting to stable him, he broke away. Once the saddle was gone, he started bucking and rearing with fear. Now wearing only his halter, he took off through the village, snorting and rampaging in terror. He whinnied in panic, and he reared up on his hind legs, then released a long neigh and took off at full gallop. The villagers, now knowing that trying to capture the beast was impossible, watched him leave. He was last seen galloping down the cobbled roadway in a state of alarm. His wild ride saw him on familiar ground, and he sailed over the hedge and back into his field. His black coat was now shiny with sweat, and he was shivering in fear about what had happened to Annie.

Although slightly worn with a repair, Aladdin's elegant monogrammed saddle was kept as evidence of the horse thief's crime. The town elder wrote a note to the magistrate informing him that they had captured a villain. No one had checked on Annie for some hours.

Annie's captors were entirely unaware of the grave error they had made as her post-birth bleeding continued unabated. The masked, so-called horse thief was a gravely ill lady.

Late in the afternoon, the magistrate organised her transfer to his house and the secure cell he had there. Annie, now weak from loss of blood and lack of sleep, hardly even noticed when she was removed from the lock-up and taken to the magistrate's house. Having not slept for nearly forty-eight hours and still bleeding, her condition now was perilous. She needed food, drink, and medical attention. Only after she was thrown in the magistrate's cell did the pool of blood under her body elicit further investigation by a maid, and finally, her gender was revealed, but the state of her health was now dire. The prisoner was still completely unresponsive.

Meanwhile, Ermie was in a state of panic. Annie had not returned, and she had no idea where she had gone. Knowing she could not do more than visit where she left her, she arrived back at Aladdin's field only to find the horse in a lathered state. He was throwing back his head and still snorting. Knowing little about horses, she didn't recognise the stallion's actions of his high tail prancing and head throwing as stress. Of Annie, there was no sign. She dared not ask to see the marquess, but she told Bob, and he attended to the sweating horse. He also had no idea where Annie was. Ermie was unable to do anything more, so she returned to her cottage to wait.

~

When the carriage returned from the church after the holdup, Oliver realised that the one person who seemed to link the black horse and the monogrammed saddle he saw Annie riding was his head groom.

As Bob opened the carriage at the door, Oliver said, "Meet me in my den in ten, Bob. We need to talk."

"Certainly, sir," Bob replied cheerfully. Hopefully, he could set the marquess straight on a few things. Annie had never sworn him to secrecy as she had never seen the need to, as it was doubtful he would ever be questioned. She had confessed more than she needed to her trusted friend. Now was the time for him to reveal his knowledge of her affection to his master.

Oliver had not said anything to Verity since his outburst. He did not even wait for her to alight before he carried his precious bundle indoors. When he arrived home, Oliver locked himself in his den with his dead child. Not that Verity wished to talk to him, but for her to be locked out irritated her. When Bob arrived, Oliver let him in, and the story unfolded. Oliver realised that because his daughter had not ever taken a first breath, and therefore, she was not baptised; as such, she was not permitted a funeral of any sort. He knew that, but the knowledge did not ease his hurt. That fact would not stop him from honouring her. She was the flesh of his flesh and bone of his bone, even more so than his living heir was. However, he had the perfect place to lay his tiny daughter for eternity.

At dawn the following morning, he and Bob Brown, his now trusted groom, would place the small child in her final resting place. His daughter would be safe and at peace and would probably never be discovered. However, that must wait until the morrow. Bob revealed he had known all along what Annie was up to and what had occurred to her, but he refused to reveal more to the marquess other than to say Annie had never meant to harm his lordship.

Oliver understood what her reasons were and that her method was certainly effective. He was beginning to see other people as people, not chattels. It had been a hard lesson, but he swallowed willingly now that he knew the truth. He loved her all the more for it.

Over the weeks and months, Oliver found Bob was the one he turned to for companionship. He even asked if he could accompany him on his morning rides. Oliver had found a trusted friend for the first time in his life.

~

The magistrate recognised the monogram on the saddle and wrote to the marquess explaining the capture of a horse thief. Sadly, the note was intercepted by the marchioness. Verity wrote back to the magistrate that her husband was unavailable, so she would attend to the matter herself. She quietly arranged for their new coachman to take her to the magistrate's house to view the prisoner personally. Knowing she was breaking a direct order, she snuck away through the servant's entry. She was fully aware of whom she would find when she saw the rider. The new coachman from the holdup also could bear witness to the incident. Unaware of the reality of the situation, the coachman was only aware that the marquess's coach was bailed up after church. He had no idea if anything had been taken, but he took a good look at the highwayman's outfit.

Henry objected to her leaving without the marquess, but he also realised that he could only stop her departure by personally holding her or locking her in a room. He instructed her to return immediately after meeting the magistrate. The coachman acquiesced, and they took a trusted groom to hold the horses.

Verity insisted she comply with the magistrate's request and that her coachman was a second witness to the heinous crime. Both she and the groom could identify the saddle and monogram. Out of spite and jealousy, Verity decided to get rid of Annie and laid false charges while Annie was still unresponsive. Verity viewed her previous companion's prostrated form and identified her as the person who held up their carriage. The coachman just saw the outfit and confirmed her identification. He had no idea who the person was. Verity's revenge was complete. She grinned with delight. Annie's fate was sealed without her even being aware of her crime. Oliver's beloved whore would be banished. While not even able to respond for herself, Annie was charged and sentenced to seven years for highway robbery rather than horse theft, as the horse had vanished. For a week, Annie lay at death's door. As no one had told them any different, all the villagers still thought the horse thief was a man.

Stories of the arrest of a horse thief filtered back to the big house, but no one knew who the mysterious criminal was. No horses were missing from their stable, so even Bob did not connect the incident with Annie's disappearance.

For the magistrate, the marchioness and coachman identified the prisoner as the highwayman who bailed them up. The coachman had vouchsafed that it was indeed the right person. He, too, had not been told about the person's gender. He knew the rider was astride the horse, so he also presumed it was a man; he had no reason to question the marchioness.

In the meantime, Oliver was occupied with his daughter's burial arrangements. After a few prayers, he and Bob laid the tiny mite in his mother's arms in the family crypt. Then he got drunk, very drunk.

Over the following weeks, Bob kept his eyes and ears open for news of Annie, but she had just vanished.

Chapter 8   The Lady Penrhyn

$\mathcal{A}$nnie hovered between life and death for many days. She stirred to drink and then fell back into her semi-comatose state. Her exhaustion was not just post-birth but an amalgamation of the stresses from the past months.

As yet unaware that her life has taken a horrific turn for the worse, she slumbered on. She was aware the light was dim, but the arm that held her was gentle and caring. She liked the calming voice of the person speaking to her.

Annie swallowed when told to and felt someone washing her all over. Delirious, Annie thought she was at the cottage. Mayhap Ermie was caring for her, but it didn't sound like her. She cared little for anything in her life.

Oliver was gone from her, and their child was dead. Her parents could never know what had occurred, thinking that she was living in the wilds of Scotland. In her stupor, Annie wept with all the losses in her life. Now, she was a fallen woman, and even Oliver had rejected her advances. She would have willingly become his mistress if he had asked her.

With the loss of reputation, loss of her family, loss of Oliver, and now the loss of their child, Annie curled into a ball and hid her head under the blanket. In the rare moments she was awake, she wept.

For days, she woke, drank, ate soup, and slept again.

After some time, the caring arms that held her shook her awake, and Annie finally roused enough to listen.

The kind but uneducated voice pleaded with her to wake. "Miss, you must awake. You is being shipped out to the Antipodes and must get up and get ready."

Annie stirred herself to sit on the cold pallet bed. The room spun. She opened her eyes and desperately tried to focus on the girl's face. The girl was not familiar to Annie or her surroundings, and she saw the frown that settled on Annie's brow.

The person who had been assisting her was a maid dressed in a mob cap and clean uniform.

Annie looked down at her own attire. She had no recollection of anything bar her deep sadness after passing their daughter to Oliver and hearing his yell at the discovery that she was dead. After that, everything was a blur.

The nice maid sat next to her and held her upright with a comforting arm along her shoulders. "Miss, are you all right? They will be here to collect you in two hours."

Again, Annie looked down at her clothes. She wore a dress that was similar to the girl's. "Where am I?"

The maid kept her arm around Annie, steadying her. "You is in the magistrate's cells, miss. You were brought here nearly a week ago after her ladyship identified you as a highwayman what held them up, miss." The maid was in awe of this girl. "T'was me that did discover you was a girl, and I figured you has just recently had a babe from how you was bleeding like."

Annie nodded. Whomever the girl was, she was nice and clean. "Did you say I've been here for nearly a week? Truly?" She knew Ermie would be panic-struck. "Will you get a message to a friend for me? She delivered my baby and must be upset at my vanishing. I wish her to know I am alive and well but don't tell her any more. At least, I think I am well."

The girl nodded. "You will be, miss, now. But I was a bit worried for a while. You is good now but! And yes, of course, miss, I'll send word. You jus' tell me, and I'll make sure the lady gets the message. I can't read or write, but I can remember real good."

Annie gave the maid Ermie's direction and then asked, "Did you say I am a prisoner?"

The girl explained. "Yes, miss! You was arrested and tried while you was sick. You was in full highwayman garb, missy, so they say you was catched all but red-handed, miss. Her ladyship came from the big house and said you did hold up their coach. Did you really do that?"

Annie swallowed, typical of Verity. Annie realised she would have been unmasked by then; Verity knew precisely who she was banishing. She nodded, accepting her fate. At least she would not have to make decisions for herself for some time.

She said, "Yes," but her reply was so soft that the girl barely caught the word.

The girl's raw language grated on Annie's ears. She shook her head as if to clear it. "Did you say I'm being shipped out? Where to?"

The maid's face showed fear. "Miss, we just got the word you is to fill a berth on a ship to the Antipodes. You is to go to Portsmouth this afternoon, and then, as soon as you is there. You'se gotta be on the ship what is setting off as soon as you is on board."

Annie was stunned, "The Antipodes? Do you mean the Americas? I didn't think they sent people there anymore."

"No, miss, you are going to a new colony. I heard it's called New Holland, but there's no towns there nor nuffing. You has got to build the place yourselves."

Horror shivered through Annie. She had heard about the discovery of a great land in the south of the globe. Her father had followed Captain James Cook's travels and heard that a trip was proposed to send a fleet of convicts to the new land instead of the Americas and plant a new English colony. A wave of dizziness swept over her. "Two hours, you say? Is there any chance of a bath? Or a wash, at least?"

The maid pointed to the pitcher of hot water and a big basin. "I have washed you a few times, miss. After my mama had a babe, she bled a lot too, so I cleaned you up as best I could; there are more clean flannels for your flow, but I don't have no more clothes for you." The girl was a shade embarrassed. "I managed to keep your warm cloak, but they took the other clothes as what they called evidence."

Annie took her hand. "Thank you," Annie didn't even know her name, so she asked, "What's your name, please? Mine is Annie."

"I is Julie, miss," she volunteered.

Annie smiled. "Then thank you, Julie. Can you assist me, as I'm still as weak as a kitten?" Annie fingered Oliver's cloak; that was all she had of him now. She would guard that with her life.

Julie made Annie eat some beef broth, and then Annie had another long drink of cider.

The alcoholic beverage went straight to her head.

The two girls set about preparing Annie for what lay ahead of her.

Before she was collected, Annie had a bowl of thick stew. It tasted and felt so good after having nothing solid in her stomach for a week.

~

The vehicle that collected Annie was a black box-like carriage with barred windows. Annie owned nothing but what she stood up in, which included Oliver's warm black cloak, which thankfully the girl had saved, and she wore that. She was roughly bundled into the back door and shoved inside. She clutched the bundle of clean flannel squares under the cape.

Shortly before she left the cell, Julie handed her six clean flannels, and Annie hoped she wouldn't need them all on the journey. Thankfully, her bleeding had eased somewhat after ten days.

The only opening in the carriage was a six-inch grill in the back door. There were no seats, just an empty box. She had no luggage but the cloak and flannels. As she was still weak, she rolled her possessions into a ball and used it as a pillow. She may as well sleep while she could as she had no idea what lay in front of her.

She must have slept as she woke to the sound of cobbled pavement. Rolling on her back with her legs bent, she wondered where they were.

The door opened, and food was shoved towards her. It was a hunk of dry bread and some cheese. The tumbler of ale was consumed greedily. The carriage was soon on its way again. This was repeated at the next stop, but the bread was so hard she could not eat it. She nibbled at the mouldy cheese.

The trip to Portsmouth took hours.

The horses alternately trotted over the rough roads or walked along particularly rutted sections. The trip was very uncomfortable.

Annie was permitted out of the carriage twice to relieve herself in the bushes. Each time, she was given a drink of flat cider. With her thirst quenched, she was again loaded into the black hole.

At dusk, different sounds permeated the grill.

Annie crouched up and gazed through the bars. They were in a large town, and she could smell the sea. Her parents had taken her there when she was little. Her father had to visit a bishop, and they had spent a few days by the sea.

The odour that met her nostrils was not the clean smell of salt but of grime. She figured that this must be her destination. She grabbed the door bars and looked at what surrounded her.

A uniformed man approached. "Get back, lady; I don't want no trouble from you."

Annie had no intention of giving any trouble. "I will behave, sir. Is this Portsmouth?"

She moved to the back of the carriage and waited until the door opened. He unbolted the lock and flung open the door.

In the dim light, she saw the man nod. He said, "It are, miss, and that thar are your ship."

The chill of the evening bit, and she wrapped Oliver's cloak around her shoulders. She had been unable to stretch out her legs for hours, and as she sat on the back opening of the cage, she asked for a moment to get her balance.

The ghostly silhouette of a three-masted ship sat alongside the wharf.

As she stood, she wobbled.

The man grasped her arm to balance her. "Sorry about the rough trip, but you set sail tomorrow, and we only just made it. You is a special addition to the passenger list. We got paid double to bring you." He gave a nasty chuckle. "I believe you is a highwayman, miss; you don't look like a nasty rough type."

Annie refused to reply. Telling her story would not ease her situation. She would only tell those whom she deemed needed to know.

The man marched her down towards the dock.

The gangplank was still down, and she could see people moving on board.

As they approached, a man walked down the gangplank to meet them. Behind him were two soldiers.

She noticed that the rickety board bounced unsteadily as they walked. The bouncing movement made her head spin.

Annie was escorted by her captor directly to the foot of the gangplank.

"Here you go, Doc, the last one." He gave Annie a shove, and she stumbled slightly, grabbing onto the sick-looking doctor to stop herself from falling.

Holding the doctor's arm to steady herself, she stumbled slightly, grabbing the sick-looking doctor to prevent herself from falling. She said, "Oh, sir, I am so sorry."

She turned and gave her captor a dirty look. "That was unnecessary, sir."

The doctor shook her from his arm. "Highwayman is what your record says, but only a first name is given. Annie, what, miss? What's your moniker?"

Annie lifted her head; she'd had some time to think about this exact question. She didn't want her parents' name sullied with her criminal record. She knew exactly what name she would choose. She was here because of Oliver. "Gentle, sir, Annie Gentle."

The doctor said, "Well, Annie Gentle, we set sail tomorrow. You are considered a criminal now, so you better get yourself settled tonight. Someone should bring you food and a blanket. Are there any medical situations I should know about? The clap, crabs, or any infectious conditions?"

Annie was indignant. "No sir, none at all, but I lost a child last week and am in a somewhat weakened condition."

The doctor jerked his head. "Oh! So, still bleeding?" He nodded and marked that down. And the child's father?"

Annie knew her next words would be true as Oliver had said he would take care of her. "He's burying her, sir. I have not been with any other man, so I have no other conditions."

The doctor noted, "Stillbirth then?"

Annie nodded and replied softly, "Yes." She was close to tears just at the thought of their daughter.

The doctor nodded and thumbed towards the soldiers. "They'll take you on board. You're number one-hundred-and-nine, miss. So it's a bit cramped below decks until we set sail."

Annie swallowed. Over one hundred others would be confined with her, and as an only child, she had never been required to share anything in her life. Even at the Hall, she had a tiny room by herself.

The two soldiers each took an arm.

She didn't mind as she was again feeling light-headed.

"You're lucky, luv. Some of them bunkmates have been here for over four months. We set sail on the tide, so settle in quick like. We'll bring a lamp until you get below decks, then you be on your own, miss."

The other soldier said, "It's nearly dark, miss, but once we get on deck, cover one eye; when you get below, you'll be able to see easy like. Privateers and pirates do that; it's why they wear an eye patch."

Annie was roughly bundled up the gangplank and onto the deck of the ship.

Various uniformed men stood watching her.

The soldiers almost dragged her towards an official-looking gent.

The first soldier said, "Here's the last prisoner, captain; says her name is Annie Gentle, sir."

The uniformed soldier he addressed was obviously the captain of the guard rather than the ship's captain. He looked over at Annie and asked, "Charge?"

He was frowning as the look of this seemingly well-behaved, petite, fair-headed lady did not match her supposed crime. But then again, another below was similar.

Annie only knew what Julie had told her. "Highwayman, I believe, sir."

The man nodded; it seemed to tally with his records. "So my list says. Seven-year sentence. How long have you served?"

Annie had no idea what day it was, so she asked, "What day is it, please, sir?"

"The sixteenth of May, why?" The captain frowned again, noting that it was a strange question to ask.

Annie answered honestly, her gaze not wavering. "Then, sir, I guess I have served about ten days. I gave birth to my daughter on May 5th. I was charged the following day, I believe, but I have been insensible for over a week."

The captain's frown deepened. "And I suppose you are innocent?"

"No sir, guilty as charged, I suppose, but I did not rob; I gave. They didn't like what I gave them. Sir, I passed my dead daughter to her father. I believe his wife charged me out of malice. Of that, I willingly admit, and I was dressed as a highwayman when I was arrested but unresponsive when charged."

Annie found it hard to believe so much time had elapsed since she gave birth. She was still too numb to grieve or process what had happened.

The captain screwed up his nose. "Really? You passed in a dead baby?"

Annie nodded. Her legs were going to give way, and she swayed. "Please, sir, I need to sit."

The captain thumbed her away. "Take her to the cells. Annie Gentle, they are a rough lot below. I don't know how you ended up in this mess, but now that you are here, you will have to cope as best you can."

Thankfully, the two soldiers behind her grabbed her arms.

Her legs buckled as they did so. "May I have a moment?" she pleaded as she sank onto whatever was beside her.

A kind voice spoke from behind her. "Head between your legs for a moment or two, lassie. Leave her to me, gentlemen; I will see her below."

The first soldier willingly handed his charge over to the crew's surgeon. He had other duties to perform.

The other soldier stayed beside her, along with the doctor who was to attend to the crew and soldiers.

The kind voice spoke again. "Did I hear you say you have just had a child?"

Annie was feeling a little clearer. With her head still down, Annie murmured, "Yes, sir."

"When?" shot back the question.

"Saturday, last week, sir." Annie slowly sat up. The deck was still spinning. "I'm still not feeling too good, sir."

The nice man felt her brow and saw she was somewhat hot. "Have you been ill?"

Annie nodded. She was feeling quite that way now, but at least the area around her was calming. "I don't remember the last ten days, sir."

He was now squatting beside her.

The concern on his face nearly made her weep again.

The caring man stood and said, "Come on, we'll get you below deck and get you settled. Soldier, take her other arm. She has nothing infectious and nothing that rest and time won't cure. You will have plenty of that on board, missy."

With a man on each side of her again, each slid an arm around her waist and assisted her to the dark opening leading below decks. Her weakened legs were not quite able to hold her weight. She had not eaten a proper meal since before she had the baby. Julie had fed her a small bowl of thin stew, but that was many hours ago, if not the day before. Time blurred.

Her stomach rumbled from hunger. Over her head, she listened to the two men discussing her accommodation.

The soldier addressed the friendly man as Surgeon Bowes-Smith. He said, "She's to go in with Gaskins and Frownes, doctor, as there is a berth in there. They are also a little less rough than the rest of the animals below."

The surgeon replied, "Good, at least they don't have anything infectious either. Gaskins sounds like she's a bit better class of girl. Being somewhat older than the rest of the rabble, Margaret Frownes should keep them in order."

Annie was still feeling a little dazed; he had a nice voice, and she told him so. He also smelled clean. She mumbled, "I like your voice, sir; you sound just like Oliver."

The surgeon smiled. "I have no idea who your Oliver is, but thank you."

Unaware she was babbling, she murmured, "He is my daughter's papa." She gasped at her words. She thought about what she had said, then corrected herself. "No, he was. She's gone, and he no longer cares."

Tears blinded her eyes again as she stumbled down the darkened walkway.

This surgeon who was with her now was the crew's surgeon. She discovered that the sick-looking man she had first met was Doctor John Turnpenny Altree, the convict women's doctor.

The doctor, with a kind voice, said that Doctor Altree had been ill and was slow to recover. He was now back on his feet again. He had his hands full before they even set sail. "Lassie, I'm the crew's surgeon, Arthur Bowes-Smith, by name."

He had been twiddling his fingers above deck while his colleague was overworked below with the convicts. Thankfully today, his offer to assist in getting the prisoners ship-shape for sailing had been willingly accepted. Now done, Arthur would step back and allow the younger doctor the space he needed once they left port.

As a naval doctor, Arthur was employed to look after the needs of the passengers, crew, and soldiers. He expected to have little to do. Doctor Altree was a civilian doctor, and Arthur wondered how the inexperienced young man would cope with the journey and trials ahead of him. He would offer his assistance again if required.

Weeks earlier, the vessel had set sail from Deptford in the Thames River to stand by at Portsmouth.

This would be the *Lady Penrhyn's* maiden voyage; she was an unknown quantity when it came to the sea. If the short journey to Portsmouth was any sign of her capabilities, it boded to be a very long trip to the new colony. It seemed that the *Lady Penrhyn's* so-called sleek lines belied the sluggish speed at which she sailed. After eight weeks at Portsmouth, the open hatches exuded an unpleasant odour of unwashed bodies, excrement, and stale urine.

Annie dry retched with the stench.

The soldier half-laughed as she reacted. "Sorry about the conditions, miss, but all the upper-class cabins are taken."

The doctor gasped at his rudeness. "Leave her alone, soldier."

Annie was taken to a cell at the back of the deck.

The soldier now carried a lantern and held it aloft. He fumbled at his waist for keys and unlocked the barred cell door, and the two men showed Annie her wooden pallet bed.

The soldier chuckled, gave a mock bow and said, "This will be your berth for the duration of your cruise, madam, so settle in as best you can."

Ignoring the doctor, he gave another rude, mock bow and went to wait outside.

The nice doctor looked around at the faces. He presumed they were probably waiting to pounce on her to see what possession she had on her.

He shook his head, knowing there was little more he could do to help her. He followed the soldier out and left her to settle in.

Annie was unable to think straight. She wanted to die. She thought it would seem preferable to what was ahead of her now. Her eyes were adjusting, her head still swimming and her stomach roiling at the stench.

A woman approached her.

Annie recoiled in horror at the hagged-looking woman.

Before the lamp had left with the doctor, she saw that the woman's teeth were blackened, and two were missing.

The woman squatted beside her. "I heard you got done for highway robbery too, dearie? So did I! My name is Margaret Frownes, Maggie to me friends. A gel's gotta do what a gel's gotta do, don't we, dearie?"

Annie knew she had to share a cell with these women for a long, long time. "Yes, ma'am," she replied in a forlorn voice.

Despite her scary appearance, the woman sounded friendly. She wondered if it were an act.

The woman seemed nice enough, and she continued. "Let me introduce you to your bunkmates, dearie. Anne and Mary Fowles are over there; Mary is the kiddie. Mary Gabel is the one sharing your bunk. Olive Gaskins is over there in the bunk next to you; I share with her, but she's head to toe with you." The rest she pointed to as she spoke. "Ann George, Ann Green, Mary Greenwood, Elizabeth Hall, and that one is Sarah Hammond; she is the last one over there. Mary Love and Winifred Betty Bird are in the next cell, but everyone calls her Betty."

Annie replied in a hushed tone, "I'm Annie Gentle."

A groan was heard from the top bunk. "Another blooming Ann; why couldn't you'se have been a Jane, Amelia, or somethink like that?"

Annie shrugged. "Sorry, but that's my name. I suppose you can blame my parents." She didn't feel like laughing, but she sometimes hated her very common nickname, even though her real one was Annabella.

Maggie said, "Settle in, dearie, we already have." She gave Annie a gentle caress on her forehead. "I don't suppose you got no more clothes? They are a bit in short supply down here."

Annie shook her head. "No, sorry, I don't even own the ones I wear." She wrapped Oliver's warm cloak around her tightly. She didn't wish to lose the last thing she had of his.

Annie and Mary Gabel sorted their shared bunk out. Mary had claimed the blanket, and Annie wondered if she would be given one later. In the meantime, she only had what she had arrived with. She was hungry and thirsty and now needed to use the privy.

Maggie had returned to her own bunk, so Annie asked Mary, "How does one use a privy here, Mary? I need to go." Mary, as yet, had not spoken to her.

A raucous laugh greeted her question. "The lady wants a privy." She set off in a peal of laughter. "Luv, see that bucket, that's your privy, and don't kick it over 'cause it stinks as it is."

A coopered pail sat in the corner of the small cell. At least, with her skirts held down, she could have a modicum of privacy. Having eaten very little for over a week, her stomach was rumbling, and her head was still spinning. But it meant that at least she didn't have to worry about adding to the near-overwhelming stench of bodily waste from over one hundred convicts.

Annie managed to relieve herself and return to her bunk. She had taken one clean flannel with her and had changed that. The one in her hand was now well blood-soaked. She had used three on the trip; soon, all she had was four fouled rags.

In that short time she had been gone, the other clean flannels she had left on her bunk had vanished. As she looked around for them, the last lamp was extinguished for the night.

No blanket or food was forthcoming for her.

She now had nothing but used rags to sop up her blood. It was the last straw.

Annie sank onto the wooden bunk and let the silent tears flow. She tried hard to keep from making a noise, but a hand reached out and took hers comfortingly.

Olive whispered, "Here, have one of mine." In the darkness, she felt for Annie's hand, and she was given a flannel square. "You can wash them in the morning, but after a few months here, you probably won't need them anyway. Lie at this end, and we'll chat."

The voice that spoke sounded kind. Annie knew it belonged to Olive, who was in the next bunk. "This is post-birth bleeding, not my monthlies."

Her accent was not one she expected to hear on a convict ship. Although it had a hint of Yorkshire in the dialect, it was one that could have been heard in the best drawing rooms in London. Annie at least found one girl who was somewhat friendly.

Chapter 9   Anchors Aweigh

*T*he pre-dawn light brought unusual noises from the deck. A tin whistle played a tune, and the stomping of many feet showed activity. Annie stirred, as did many of the other convict women. Olive touched her arm. "We're setting sail today, and that's the crew raising the anchor. I don't know what's before us, Annie, but at least we have each other."

In the hours before the two girls slept, Olive and Annie had shared some of their stories. Even saying her new friend's name brought tears to Annie's eyes. However, Olive admitted she was not using her real name and had been caught red-handed in a robbery. She was cast off by her well-to-do parents and told that as she had done the crime, she now had to do the time. "Annie, I did not want to be paraded around in London and sold to the highest bidder. There is far more to life than that, and I refused to play their game. Papa was right about one thing: I'm certainly reaping what I sowed." She gave a long sigh. "What about you, Annie?"

Annie gave Olive a brief description of what had happened. "Olive, I was abused, but I fell in love with him. When I found I was carrying his child, I offered myself to him and was rejected. I began to seek revenge by dressing as he did and mirroring his riding. It had been a nightmare of his when a child and I played on disturbing his mind. On the day I was arrested, I was dressed again as my alter ego, complete with a mask and delivered our dead child to him as he drove back from church. Although we barely spoke, he realised it was me, and I could see he was not angry. However, I'm sure he understood my reasons. It was because of that hold-up that I was convicted. I passed out. His wife laid the charge of highwayman rather than highway robbery. I only received seven years instead of life. Considering I was in my full masked outfit when found, I had no case to answer, but I was not caught in the act, and no one had reported a theft. I was convicted and sentenced while still insensible." Olive gasped.

Annie retold her tale as though it had occurred to someone else. "Olive, all that was only last week." She gave a sigh of resignation.

"Oh, Annie, that's so sad." Olive grasped her hand to comfort her. "We'd better get some sleep." Olive lowered her voice and said, "Annie, if you hear things, well, certain sounds at night, ignore them. Some girls have already made friends with the crew and soldiers." This time, Olive heard Annie gasp, but the two girls settled down to sleep.

The morning noises that awoke them were the grating of the anchor chain being hauled on board with the crew turning the giant capstan. Through the bulkheads above them, feet were heard moving above. By now, Annie had not eaten anything for nearly thirty hours, and as she was still losing blood, she was feeling decidedly ill and even more light-headed.

A hatch opened as the ships prepared for departure, and light flooded in from above. Her hand quickly covered her eyes to ease the blinding light.

Olive knew it would be the doctor coming to check on his patients. "Annie, Doctor Altree is here; tell him you need food."

Annie groaned but nodded. Her head throbbed, and her eyes hardly focused. She could barely sit up. The doctor did his rounds checking each of the cell blocks, and when he reached their cage, he noticed Annie still prostrated. "Is she ill?"

Annie tried to rise, but Olive kept a hand on her shoulder. Olive answered, "No doctor, just hungry; she has not eaten for nearly two days after having a baby."

"Damn," The doctor's expletive made many chuckle. "I told them to bring her food last night. Didn't they?"

Olive shook her head, "Nor was she given her convict allocation of vitals. She has no blanket or utensils."

The man looked as ill as Annie, and Olive felt he was actually in need of medical attention himself. The doctor turned on his heel and went to source some sustenance for his patient. One more ill person would not be good. He had enough to do as it was. Far too many had already fallen sick in the weeks they had been on board. One had already died even before they set sail; he was not happy that his orders had not been followed. He was determined that the ship would not mimic the *Alexander,* which was anchored near them and had multiple deaths already.

After two days, Annie was finally given the blankets and eating implements other convicts had received. She now had her own bowl, spoon and various other items required for the long months of shipboard life ahead of them. Within minutes, a bowl of gruel was brought for Annie's consumption. Olive sat her up and held the bowl for her. "Eat it slowly, Annie. We'll get some porridge in about an hour, but at least you will have something in your stomach to throw up."

This meal ended up being more of a hindrance than a help. The ship was barely an hour out of port when the seas decided to dance to a different beat. The calm waters of the Portsmouth harbour were well behind them, and the *Lady Penrhyn* was not a steady vessel.

Annie's constitution was already weakened, and soon, her scant meal was in the slop bucket. She was not alone in her stomach condition.

When the porridge was served, many were too ill to eat. As her cabin leader, Olive insisted that their cell occupants eat anyway, so at least they would have something to throw up. The stench below deck was overwhelming. With the hatch above them still open, at least some breeze circulated, but very little fresh air made it back to the cell where Annie lay groaning.

~

For a week, the seas remained angry. Many were too ill to leave their bunks and vomited over the edge onto the floor or fouled their beds, being unable to use the slops bucket. Mary Love had fallen and broken at least two ribs. No one had their sea legs, and few were not ill. It was not long before the overfull slops buckets tipped over, and the cell floors ran with excrement, vomit and urine. The food that was served was minimal. Porridge and gruel with dry bread were consumed and brought up again. Ships biscuits were doled out, and Olive was the one who insisted that they all nibble at this dry tack.

The sluggish vessel sloughed through the big seas and tried to keep up with her sister ships. The eleven ships of the fleet sailed southwards, away from the motherland. Each nautical mile took the seven hundred and seventy convicts away from all they knew. They were banished, no, stolen, from their homeland, and probably few, if any, would ever return; they were a stolen generation of petty criminals. They were sailing away from home and into an unknown world that they were told they had to build from scratch. Most were petty criminals who normally would have been released in just a few years. Some were to serve life sentences. All were now aware that there was no settlement of any kind where they were heading. There was no food to purchase or shops to obtain supplies. Already, some seedlings were being grown on board, and these were tended with great diligence. Hopefully, they would be able to keep them alive.

The convicts on each ship were told they would starve if they did not work hard and grow food. However, most on board had never produced a thing before, let alone know how to tend plants. Most were city folk who knew nothing of farming. Few had ever done an honest day's work. Fewer still had tilled land and grown plants for sustenance. Annie had loved gardening, but growing strawberries and flowers was all but useless.

Olive had filled Annie in on the past months in the dock while they clung to their berths. With nothing in their stomachs to bring up, the girls below decks wallowed in self-pity, wishing the journey ahead of them was already over. The stench was overwhelming, and the rolling movement of the sea made it worse. All knew there was much more to follow. When they woke on the morning of the eighth day at sea, they first noticed that the sea's motion was more settled.

The hatches and portholes were thrown open, and the doctor waited until the worst of the foul air from below deck had been evacuated before he descended into the filthy cells and started to make his rounds. Their deck was awash with excrement and unknown detritus. The doctor's cheery disposition belied the conditions below. "Good morning, ladies; today is a great day for you. Your fetters and restraints will be removed so you can clean your quarters. Food will be served shortly, so get moving. Washing facilities will be available for those who wish. Preferably, that will be all of you, as you all need it."

His voice didn't carry to the back of the cells, but word soon spread.

The gun ports were soon opened, and the excrement flushed from the deck floor with buckets of seawater. Annie's legs were caked with blood, and she felt filthy. Her flow had certainly lessened, but she was still bleeding. The spare flannels had not reappeared, and the few she had were inadequate. She had reused the dirty ones once they had dried without being washed. The little fresh water they had access to was to drink, so her state of uncleanliness was far more than irksome to her. To top it off, she had also vomited down the front of her gown as she had been unable to make it to the bucket. In her stupor, she had fouled her drawers. Like every other convict, she stank. Goodness knows what her hair looked like. It was always a fight to restrain her riotous curls.

Cellblock by block, the locks were removed from the grill doors. Barred doors were swung open, and freedom of sorts was permitted for the prisoners. They could now roam their deck as they wished, but that meant pilfering was rampant. Annie kept her remaining rags in her pocket.

With nearly everyone now resigned to the conditions, they set about cleaning the deck of the effluent. Mops and buckets were produced, and the prisoners were informed that food would be brought after they had cleaned their living quarters.

By eight o'clock, the worst of the bodily emissions had been removed, sloshing the muck through the open gunports. The odour remained, but the cells were as clean as they could be with the implements they had access to. With the hatches above open, the pure salty air slowly permeated to the back cells.Eventually, a barrel of water was lowered to their deck. Hot porridge and more buckets of water were supplied for consumption. With the rough seas, the meal routine had not quite been organised. Now, with the calmer seas, the female convicts were arranged into messes, and from each group, a convict was chosen to serve the food.

~

The new routine fell into place on the *Lady Penrhyn* in a matter of days. With little work to be done, the convicts rose soon after dawn and set about cleaning their cells. Of her cabin mates, Annie had also made friends with Margaret Frownes, whom she had met when she first arrived. Olive Gaskin and Mary Gabel, with whom she shared a bunk, had already shared their stories, but Maggie's kindness and care drew Annie.

Margaret and Olive had been bunkmates, but the women were permitted to spread out where they wished when the cells were unlocked. Doctor Altree decided that all the mothers and children would be better off in a section to themselves and moved them to some empty cells. Elizabeth, Sarah, and Ann George also moved out, and the remaining women spread out.

With room to move and the freedom to walk around below decks, conditions eased somewhat, as did tempers.

On one of his first visits, Doctor Altree chattered about the ship: "You women should count yourselves lucky. This ship was built as a slave ship, but this is its first voyage. It was designed to hold over two hundred and seventy slaves. With less than half that number, you have plenty of room to move around."

Annie was horrified. Was she on a slave ship? Maggie and Olive had filled her in about their stay to date. She was pleased she had come on board when she had.

Maggie said, "Dearie, you are lucky in one way, as you only arrived on deck the day before sailing. Many of us have been on board since December. Trust me, dearie, December on the Thames River is not pleasant. If you think this is bad, the hulks is worse. The rats that shared our accommodations there were as big as cats. Oh dearie, them hulks was real bad. They leaked and stank something bad. Then we got sick. A few died, and they just threw the bodies into the river. I heard that the men on the *Alexander* got sick, and it spread below decks something horrible. Many died even before we left London."

Olive joined in. "I was only on board for a few weeks before we sailed to Portsmouth in March. Thankfully, I missed most of the time in the hulks, but I agree with the size of the river rats, Annie. Fearsome beasts they were. Food was in such short supply on the hulks that we caught them and ate them roasted over the fire. They came in through the gun ports at night."

~

The women had little to occupy them, and Annie and Olive decided that if they could find some chalk, they could teach the children to read. Both girls realised that they would be inactive for many months. Although both had many handcraft skills, they had nothing to work on. Teaching the children and any of the women would at least occupy their time. Doctor Altree arranged for one of the empty cells to be used as a schoolroom. He found some chalk for them, and they set about teaching the children their A, B, and Cs by writing on the walls as a board. Annie remembered learning with a rhyme and soon had the children singing the ditty.

Olive and she were permitted to bring other children into the classes, but they were moved above deck, and the two groups of young people sat learning to read and eventually write. As more children of the soldiers wished to join the class, the many children were soon broken into two groups.

Olive took the older ones and Annie the younger ones.

The lesson time was a blessed relief to parents, both above and below decks.

Both girls had taken the opportunity to have extra space and access to as much seawater as they wished and washed themselves from head to foot. They had even managed to wash their gowns. Olive had a spare one, but Annie only had Oliver's cloak. She wrapped herself in this with only her camisole and stockings underneath. Annie washed everything she could, and Olive took her gown and undergarments and hung them out to dry. Annie remained in their cell until she could once again don her garments. They were returned two hours later, stiff with salt but clean. Olive had sat guard over them so they didn't get stolen.

The weather was now fine, and the convicts were permitted to wander around their cell deck for some exercise. Down below, many would try to stand in the patch of sunlight under the open hatches to get sun on their faces.

Annie and Olive had been permitted to move to the quarterdeck with the children and sat out of the way of the soldiers and crew as much as possible. This was a privilege that none of the other convict women enjoyed at this time. The girls often caught sight of one or another of the vessels as they taught the children. They knew their ship, the *Lady Penrhyn*, was one of eleven ships that had set sail to find the new penal colony, but they didn't know if the other ships remained close by. The nice doctor had told them how to identify each vessel.

Surgeon Bowes-Smith sat and watched as the two girls taught their students. He was finished with the few patients he had, and being at a loose end, he volunteered to oversee the education of the young ones. As before, the combined group were separated into older and younger ones. He knew that some of the more disreputable convict women were currently isolated due to their behaviour. He had been horrified when the captain of the guard ordered them to be manacled again. Their punishment consisted of thumb screws and iron fetters, and in some cases, they were flogged with a cat of nine tails and their heads were shaved. He was unable to do anything to assist them, but thankfully, most of the women were not like those poor wretches. He understood why such wretches like them had been imprisoned, but his anger boiled when he realised girls like Annie and Olive would receive the same treatment.

Now that she was teaching, Olive found that some subjects were sadly lacking in her education. Knowing she had been brought up in a rectory, she pleaded for help from Annie. She said, "Annie, I've been told by Reverend Johnson I have to teach the children their Catechism, and I have no idea where to start. Your papa was a minister. Could you take over that class while I teach the little ones?"

Annie had not held back any of her private details from Olive. At twenty-four, Olive was more worldly-wise than Annie but admitted she was a rebel.

Olive continued, "Annie, I studied what I had to until I turned eighteen.

Then, I was presented in a Drawing Room, curtsied to the King and paraded in front of the stuck-up aristocracy like a horse in an auction. I'm surprised some peers did not check my teeth as they do with a broodmare. I hated it. My parents planned to pass me on to the highest bidder, and I was not going to have a bar of that. I rebelled in a big and foolish way, and look where it got me. They ended up getting my term reduced from a life sentence to seven years with transportation; then they wiped their hands of me. My father was a Chief Magistrate, so you can imagine how my behaviour went down." She had shrugged in resignation. "The lessons I did, well, I only listened to what I liked, which wasn't much. I like to read, so the literature was good. History and geography were my brothers' favourite subjects, and I was not supposed to be listening to them, but I loved them. I'm not much of a dab hand at watercolour painting or embroidery, but I can shoot a gun and aim a bow and arrow as true as you please." She had the courtesy to blush, and she screwed up her nose. "Religion was not one of my favourite subjects. So, I have no idea what teaching the Catechism entails."

Annie chuckled. "I hate religion too, Olive, but that's not what my Papa taught. He said what he teaches is Christianity, not religion. He explained the difference to me many times before I understood. Papa taught about Jesus' love and forgiveness, not about the laws mankind has made, which makes it impossible for us to keep any of them. God is loving and forgiving, but He gives us guidelines to live; that's the Ten Commandments. Sadly, we are not taught that way. We are given a list of do's and don'ts as long as your arm. When I see how people are treated in the name of Christianity, oh, my blood boils, Olive. The way Papa taught it made believing in Jesus easy. In religion, Jesus is hardly even mentioned."

Olive screwed up her nose. "So you don't like religion either?"

Annie shook her head violently. "No, and what I see done in the church's name makes me cringe. What's more, I know Jesus hated religion, too. He chastised the Pharisees often."

Surgeon Bowes-Smith overheard her comment and gazed at her in admiration. The two young women had come under his authority as they oversaw the education of the passengers and crew's children. Therefore, they were under his careful watch rather than Doctor Altree's while above deck. Her comments made him decide to keep a careful watch over her.

~

Under the watchful eye of both captains, the classes meant the children were safe and out from underfoot. They were also given free time for play, but the convict's children were sent below deck to their mothers as soon as lessons finished. Sadly, Olive and Annie had to accompany them.

Seven weeks since leaving Portsmouth, the women below decks were still recuperating from their various illnesses. One baby had been born, and many women were still suffering from the effects of venereal diseases.

Doctor Altree's only option for the treatment of most illnesses was mercurial salts, bloodletting or cupping. He felt so ill that he needed most of these treatments himself. The poor man was still battling with the effects of his sickness. He was thankful he had not died. However, by the time the ship reached Tenerife, Doctor Altree had succumbed again to his illness. Rather than now being the convicts' doctor, he became one of the patients.

Doctor Arthur Bowes-Smith had no choice but to take over.

The two captains, Captain William Sever, the *Lady Penrhyn*'s skipper, and Captain James Campbell, the commander of the marines on their ship, consulted over the matter and sent word to Captain Phillip.

While at Tenerife, the governor announced that the medical care of the entire ship had been consigned to Doctor Bowes-Smith. Doctor Altree was relieved of duty, and full care was handed over to the more senior naval surgeon. Doctor Bowes-Smith knew the convicts, as well as Doctor Altree, did, and the transition of roles was smooth.

The new doctor had set a daily morning clinic schedule within a day. Crew and passengers would be seen first, followed by any of the convicts. Emergencies would be dealt with as required. Having not been handed this role before leaving London, his clinic was unprepared for the requirements of the ill passengers. Supplies had not been estimated appropriately by the inexperienced civilian junior doctor, and he had to make do with what he had. On the other supply ships, there may have been what he required, but that was for use in the new colony. He would try to obtain more medicines *en route*.

The stay in Santa Cruz harbour at Tenerife kept the crew on tenterhooks, as there was only safe anchorage for one ship. The other ten vessels had to stand at anchor and be ready to set sail with hardly any notice should the winds turn. The benefit of this stay was that all the ships could stockpile fresh fruits, vegetables, and poultry. Doctor Bowes-Smith was able to obtain some but not all of the requirements for his clinical work.

Classes for the children were suspended while the ship was near land, and once again, the convicts were locked below decks. One of the convicts had attempted to escape from the *Alexander*, and one of the crew jumped ship shortly before departure.

To the delight of Annie and Olive, the captain was able to secure fresh corn, bananas by the bunch-full, watermelons, almonds, figs, cherries, mulberries, and pears. They were also able to purchase some goats, fowls, ducks and geese. The girls watched through the tiny side hatches as the stock and produce were brought to the vessel by long boats.

They knew they already had some stock on board, but with nearly two hundred passengers to feed daily, the vittles' consumption quickly diminished the supply. The goats could also supply fresh milk, but they also needed their own food. Bales and bags of feed were also brought on board. The poultry would be dual purpose; with the excess cockerels being eaten by the cabin passengers, the carcasses would be made into a tasty broth for the convicts. The numerous chickens provided eggs for consumption, although some were left to hatch under broody hens.

All the live produce would now have to be cared for. Food for the animals needed to be sourced and enough supplied for the trip, and some of the unused slave cells on the lower prison deck would serve as cages, thus adding to the stench below.

Annie watched, intrigued by how the long boat barrels were filled with water from a hose on shore and then ferried full barrels back to the various ships. This was a long and tedious chore but one vital to the well-being of the entire ship's complement. Each ship also had methods of catching rainwater, but this was only useful if it rained. It also meant that a good sail had to be used, and sometimes, the weight of the water tore the precious fabric.

After a week in port, the fleet once again weighed anchor and set sail. Doctor Bowes-Smith mentioned they would have to add another stop to the voyage. "We could not get enough fresh fruit to my liking, and I have requested that we attempt to obtain more or risk scurvy. Port Praya will hopefully be our next stop; if not, we must make it to Rio de Janeiro with what we have on board."

The fleet sailed on from Tenerife with favourable winds behind them, heading southwest to the next destination. The women were getting used to being locked up each time they were near land.

They passed the first milestone of a month at sea only days after leaving the last stop. Each fleet vessel was in sight of at least one other ship at most times, so they had been able to stay reasonably close to each other.

Annie had learned to recognise the sounds of various sailors coming to collect their girls. Ann Green had revealed that Captain Sever regularly called for her company; others also succumbed to the tantalising offer of better or extra rations for their favours. Various other girls were offered the duties of milking and caring for the stock.

Annie and Olive kept their heads down and concentrated on the children. Neither wished to become bedfellows of any of the men on board. With good educations behind both of them, they put them to good use. At least this meant they were permitted on deck when many of their cellmates were locked below.

During the time at sea, many of the other women were permitted an hour or so in the sunlight. Rotating the roster of the convicts until all but the few who had been again put back into chains had time in the open air.

James Duncan Campbell, the marine captain's young cousin, whom Annie named Jamie, joined her class. This left the soldier free to do some fishing. This was a beneficial pastime for many of the crew and soldiers on board, but rarely was anything of interest or use caught. Shark after shark attacked the occasional fish that was hooked, but the half-eaten fish were trimmed and added to the stock pot.

One class was interrupted when Captain Campbell hooked onto a large fighting fish. Young Jamie was the first to watch the battle at his cousin's side.

For once, the conflict between man and fish was not interrupted by a shark, and Captain Campbell landed a huge bonito. It was big enough to feed the entire ship's company in one way or another, from bonito steaks for the marines and senior crew and fresh fish soup for the convicts. The change from salt beef or pork stew was a delight. After this catch, more troll lines were left at the back of the ship. Once, a huge fish with horns was caught, with sucker fish attached to it. It was kept overnight before the decision was made not to attempt to eat it. Other fish were caught and eaten with delight, but sadly, these events were few and far between.

Towards the end of June, the fleet was heading to Port Praya. The winds dropped completely two days in front of the Port. Although within sight of each other, they could not get close. Becalmed! For three days, the fleet sat at the mercy of the wind. All took the opportunity to clean and fix whatever they could. Hatches were left open for the convicts, and what little breeze there was helped ventilate the cells below.

Sleeping in the calm waters was pleasant, but at three in the morning on the third day from the port, a storm rose from almost nowhere and hit the fleet. For two hours, the violent tempest buffeted the ships. Lightning, thunder, and torrential rain tore at the previously luffing sails. The crew were all called on deck to erect the rain sails and catch water. The crew set up the rain-catching sails in the middle of the gale and filled the empty water barrels. Although the ships were caught unprepared, they weathered the storm. By dawn, the gale had all but vanished. They once again set sail towards the equator.

For the next week, the winds rose and died equally fast. Empty barrels were left on deck to replenish with the now frequent nighttime cloudbursts. Many took the luxury of washing in the semi-clean water from the first flush of the sail collection.

Finally, they made it to the island. The ships heaved to and dropped their sails. First one, then another, tried to anchor only to find the winds were gusting and swirling. It would hit one ship one way, curl around a headland, and buffet a sister ship from the opposite direction. Acknowledging the danger to the entire fleet, Captain Phillip made the captain's call to abandon the anchorage and sail directly to Rio de Janeiro. So, only two weeks after leaving Tenerife, the fleet now had no more ports in the Atlantic Ocean as an option. They set sail for South America. With rations of fruit and vegetables cut again, the danger of scurvy was now real. Vinegar and preserved cabbage were soon the only way to ward off this condition.

Chapter 10   The Circle of Life

One of the convicts near Annie was Elizabeth Colley.

She was expecting a child, and Annie and Maggie kept a watchful eye on her. In the early morning of July 4th, Elizabeth went into labour. With few facilities to assist her, they had to wait until the doctor came on his rounds.

There was not much they could have done other than walk her, which they did. By late morning, the birth was imminent.

Maggie assisted the doctor, and Annie stood by if required.

Sadly, like Annie's own daughter, the little boy never breathed. The tiny infant was buried at sea later that day.

After the short service, Elizabeth turned to Annie for comfort. Knowing how the loss of her baby had hurt her, Annie was able to comfort her.

Annie escorted her back to her cell and encouraged her to rest. She now spoke to her friend the words that she had needed to hear herself. Annie stood next to her and cuddled the grieving mother as Ermie had done for her.

Things she had heard her mother say now came to her. "Elizabeth, I heard my mother tell others that even though a child never breathes, God still loves it. It's not a punishment or a chastisement to you but a release for the child. These things happen because of something that occurred long ago."

Annie didn't notice the hush that fell around her as she spoke. "I'm sure you have heard about the Garden of Eden?"

Weeping softly, Elizabeth nodded, wondering what the Bible had to do with her dead baby boy.

Annie continued; her parents' conversations came back to her as though they were beside her, telling her what to say. She took a deep breath and asked God to help her say her words in a way they would understand. "Sit down, and I'll tell you."

She took a deep breath and started. "Back when God made the world,

He made it perfect. Everything was ordered, and as it says in the Bible. 'It was good.' Then he made man, Adam, but soon saw he was lonely. I won't tell you the whole story, but He made Adam a partner, a woman. That word, 'wo-man,' means 'from a man.' Anyway, they lived in the Garden of Eden, where there was no death, no sickness or illness because God made it good. That also means pure and sinless, but God had also made the angels. Now, one of those angels decided he was as clever as God and ended up being cast out of Heaven because of those beliefs. That was the first sin. A third of the angels followed that angel who was named Lucifer, who we know as Satan or the devil, and they were banished from Heaven with him."

Annie swallowed; she knew she had to set the background to make her understand.

Elizabeth's gasp was not the only one Annie heard. She realised that many others were listening to her words. She had not been speaking softly, as the noises below deck were often loud.

Annie continued talking at the same level. "Satan is wily and seeks many ways to trick and deceive us. We are all here on this ship today because of his actions. When he tricked Eve into giving Adam the fruit, the snake lied, of course. Adam had been told that he could eat from any tree in the Garden of Eden, including the Tree of Life, and he could have lived forever if he had done that. God gave him just one rule. One tiny rule…" she paused, now realising others hung on her next words. "That rule was, '*Do not eat from the Tree of Knowledge.*' One rule, one tiny rule, and they broke it. All of us are here because we broke all sorts of rules. But God gave them just one. Well, of course, God knew what had happened and called Adam and challenged him. But…"

Again, she paused and looked around at the many faces listening. She nodded to herself before continuing with her explanation. "But God didn't kill Adam and Eve as Satan said; He banished them but promised that He would make a pathway back to Him. They just had to trust Him."

Annie swallowed nervously, realising that she should shorten her story, but too many were now listening. However, she said, "Skip ahead about two thousand or so years, maybe more, to Jesus's birth. A lot happened on Earth in that time; that's what the Old Testament tells us about, but for God, it's the blink of an eye. God was just about to set the pathway in place to bring us back to Him. Up until now, He had just been preparing us. That pathway is God's son, Jesus. His life is retold in the New Testament in the Bible. God sent His own son to be born of a virgin, that is Mary, to live as a normal child, to grow to be a man and then to die on the cross, taking all of our sins with Him. On the day Jesus rose from the grave, He won the battle that Satan still thinks is yet to be fought. My Papa said our sins were forgiven on that day, wiped clean like chalk washed off a slate with water, not a duster. Only it was Jesus's blood that washed away our sins. He took them on himself, and they died with him on the cross. After that happened, Jesus descended into hell and defeated

Satan. So, Satan has already lost the fight over us; however, even today, he doesn't realise that. But our God is a loving God; oh yes, He's angry at times, too, but loving and kind. He doesn't kill babies or make sickness; He doesn't make diseases, or storms, or floods. Satan does all that. Satan's rebellion against God brought sin and sickness into the world. Sin made God's perfect world out of balance. Yet, God still gives us choices in our lives. He doesn't push us against a wall with a finger on our chest and say, 'Now choose'; no, He gives us free will. But our rejection of God is sin, and we fall back into Satan's very willing grasp."

Again, Annie paused, letting that sink in while gathering her thoughts. Were they even listening?

Elizabeth prompted, "Go on, Annie; what happened next?"

Annie gave her hand a gentle squeeze. "Like Adam back at the beginning in the garden, we have one and only one decision to make. Adam's choice was to *obey* or *not obey*. We still only have that one option: either follow God and trust Him or reject Him and follow Satan. There are no other choices, not one single one. Every decision we ever make comes under one of those two headings." Annie sighed with relief.

A teary Elizabeth asked, "But what about my baby? Did he sin?"

Annie hugged her. "No, Elizabeth, and neither did my baby. They are part of what's called 'the fall', caught up in the consequences of mankind's wrongdoings. The fall has made the earth go out of kilter. The storms, fires, earthquakes, and even death were not what God wanted for us. He wanted us to have peace, happiness, love, joy, and to have a long life. Remember, Adam could have eaten from the Tree of Life and lived forever, but he chose not to. When they were cast out of the garden, access to the Tree of Life was also barred to them. Sin, evil, and disobedience to God brought death, destruction, hate, and wars, and the earth itself got out of balance. We must ask God for forgiveness for the sins we have already done, then try not to sin again. That's called repentance. If we do, He will forgive us for them, too, but it's up to us to try to be good."

Elizabeth rasped. "So I didn't do nothing wrong?"

Annie shook her head and cuddled her grieving friend. "No, dearest Elizabeth, at least not about this, but we each need to respond to God's question for ourselves. God wants us back following Him. Papa used the term 'In unity or oneness' with Him. God wants us at home, His home, and that is with Him in Heaven. It's where both our babies are, Elizabeth. However, my mama said that a dead baby isn't a baby in Heaven; it's a perfectly grown person in perfect health. One day, I wish to join my daughter and see her all grown up and beautiful. I can only do that if I get to Heaven, so my choice is, 'Yes', I'll follow God. I'll do what He wants and live the way He wants me to. The other choice is to reject everything God offers us and to live our own wilful way."

Annie had no idea her face shone with a radiance of love. A soft shaft of light from the deck above illuminated her for all to see.

She had faithfully spoken words she believed, and they came from her heart. It had been well over a year since she had seen her parents, but their teachings had never left her.

A voice came from the darkness. "Well, luv, I don't believe in your God. He makes bad things happen to good people. I still say kiddies die for no reason, sickness happens, and people die from starvation, so I blame your God for all that."

Annie chuckled at the comment, which was not the answer the woman expected, and she heard the gasp of astonishment.

Annie explained, "It's funny, isn't it, that you say you don't believe in God, but in the next breath, you blame Him for things that have happened to you. I'm sorry, but you can't have it both ways. I told you God didn't 'make' sin. Sin came about by our own disobedience and us each rejecting God. Us, that is you and me. God doesn't want us to be sick or die. God does not wish us to be hungry. God wants us how He made us: perfect and in good health." Annie knew she didn't have all the answers.

Elizabeth still needed reassurance. "So, if I say I'll follow the God being, I'll get to see my son in Heaven one day?"

Annie nodded and said, "I don't understand Heaven or in what form it is, but yes, I believe that. I'm not going anywhere, Elizabeth, so I will answer any question you have whenever you want. There is more to talk about, but that's enough for the moment."

She had just delivered a heavy sermon to everyone. Also, Annie had just seen Doctor Bowes-Smith sitting on the step listening to her. He was sitting just out of another shaft of sunlight, but she could see his grin. She gave her friend another big hug and returned to her bunk.

Once more, the babble of chatting voices rose in a crescendo.

Annie lay on her bunk and thought of Oliver and their daughter. She had so wished that she had lived. She wondered what Oliver had called her. Her mind's eye saw her blue-tinged but perfect face, and it was seared into Annie's memory. She lay on her bunk for a time and gently wept at her loss. Her parents had never even known she had given birth to an illegitimate child. She had just vanished from their lives, telling them she had gone to Scotland. On the few days of leave she had received, she spent them with the horses, then later shadowing Oliver.

Guilt for her neglect of her beloved parents swept over her. She missed them dearly, and now it was too late.

The doctor did his delayed rounds, and when he came to her cell, he said softly, "Annie Gentle, that is the best explanation of what life is all about that I have ever heard. I wish I could have recorded what you said and played your words to so many of my patients. You summed up the past four thousand or so years perfectly."

Annie jumped up at his entry and bobbed a thank-you curtsy that was not at all rude, just appreciative. She said, "I try to live the right way, but I'm here today because of my choices, sir." She knew that what had occurred had not been her fault *per se*, but the consequences of her actions still fell on her shoulders.

With a kind voice, the doctor said softly, "Annie, if but one person changes today because of your words, it will have been worth what you have put up with. But somehow, I think many will think deeply and hard about your words. For many, it may take years for that seed to germinate; it may even take a tragedy or loss in their lives, but today, you have planted words in fertile soil. I think your captive audience will one day thank you."

He saw a glow of happiness appear on the young girl's face. Her words were certainly personal as her tear-stained face tore at him. She and Olive were two convicts he knew he did not have to worry about.

~

Days of intermittent breezes passed in the relatively calm passage of the fleet.

Throughout the night of July 11th, one of the oldest female convicts, Elizabeth Beckford, had a fit of apoplexy and died in her sleep.

Annie only found out after her death that she was eighty-two.

The older lady had kept to herself somewhat, but Annie was sad that another body had now to be committed to the deep.

Soon after dawn, Elizabeth Beckford's bunkmates, plus Olive and Annie, were permitted to attend her burial service, held by the third mate, Mr Ball. It was short, and the sound of the body hitting the water made Annie jump. She wondered if this Elizabeth had heard Annie's story just a few days before. She hoped so.

Annie was in a melancholy mood, and she was thankful that lessons were cancelled for the day.

Much activity was happening on deck, as a school of tuna had circled the ship, and many of these delicious fish were hauled on deck with gay abandon and much excitement.

The children's classes would have been in the way of these enormous flapping fish.

To keep the young people safe, Annie and Olive had the children of the marines watching the proceedings on the uppermost poop deck and well out of the way.

The day descended into a dark, still night.

~

Annie and Olive were settling down to sleep when the doctor quietly came down and told them to follow him.

It was so hot below deck that neither had been asleep, so they crept past their dozing bunkmates and followed him into the cooler night air.

Once on deck, he said, "You two have behaved extremely well, and as a reward, I thought you would like to see one of God's miracles being performed. We are only days away from the equator, and on still nights, this is an occurrence that occasionally occurs, and it can only be termed a miracle. The sea comes alive with the most amazing sight. These luminous bodies light up the waters. Hold tightly to the side rails and carefully watch the bow waves breaking."

Both girls did as he said; what they beheld was an awesome sight. In the inky blackness of the night sky, the waves were alive with glowing lights.

Each bow wave and splash was filled with vibrant showers of glorious blue-white lights.

The doctor, marines, crew, and even the two captains joined them at various times over the following hour.

The coolness of the moist water was a delight.

The doctor once again escorted them below.

As they reached the entrance to their dungeon, Olive preceded Annie and vanished into the gloom.

Annie turned to the doctor from the top step and said, "Thank you, sir, so very much for that experience. Sometimes, I'm so busy looking upwards for God that I forget that He is all around us in all things."

Without another word, Annie headed down the steps, which she had long since found was called a ladder on a ship.

~

Three days later, they were crossing the equator.

The seas were still calm, but a violent vomiting illness swept through the convicts.

Annie had wondered about the state of the meal the evening before. She was getting used to the weevils, maggots, and slimy food, but yesterday's stew smelled disgusting. She managed to eat only a mouthful of it before putting it aside. One other greedy woman snatched her bowl and poured the contents into her own. Knowing she had no intention of eating it anyway, she didn't complain. She ate some dry ship bread and crept into her bunk to reflect on the magical sight of only a few days before. After retiring to her bed that night, she had lain awake for some hours thinking back on the beauty of the sea.

Tonight, the snoring of the bunkmates was rhythmical and somewhat soothing. She had quickly grown used to the noises surrounding her, and soon, the sloughing of the waves against the hull lulled her to sleep.

Sometime later, the noises and smells surrounding her were enough to wake her, so she called the guard and got the doctor. Most of the women were violently ill.

The slop buckets were soon overflowing, and the overwhelming stench of vomit assailed Annie's nostrils.

Olive and Maggie were ill. Annie realised that the stew must have been off and was thankful she chose to go hungry rather than throw up. As the cells remained unlocked, Annie was able to get water and bathe their faces. Others who had abstained from eating were doing the same to their friends.

Soon, the doctor came, the lamps were lit, and those who had refrained from eating the toxic meal attended to others.

Annie managed to catch the doctor's notice and inform him of the state of their food.

Relief flooded over him. "Oh, I say, as sorry as I am about this, I'm glad it's not an infectious malady. I shall have a word to Captain Campbell and get something done about your food."

Daylight brought a big clean-up below decks again.

Most of the women who had been ill were still prostrated on their bunks, and many of them were still asleep.

A bland meal of porridge was passed out in bowls, and even the ill were encouraged to eat some sustenance.

The day passed without further incident. Thankfully, the seas were calm, so *mal de mer* was not a problem. The scuppers and hatches were all open wide to flush the stench from the deck, and the deck was once again doused with cleansing sea water.

With the continuing calm seas, the barnacles had enjoyed a free ride, and they were now adhering to the hull in such quantities that the ship's speed was affected. The small side hatches, gun ports, and lower scuppers were all open, and Annie could see the sailors hanging over the sides on ropes, scraping off the offending critters.

As promised, the doctor insisted that the food for the convicts be better supervised. The stew must now be served as soon as it is cooked rather than let it ferment. The food had been left to spoil in the tropical heat.

Two days later, a pig, a sheep, and a goat were slaughtered to bolster the food supplies. Fishing lines were again set to catch what they could.

The heat below decks was sapping. Most of the women peeled off their scant clothing and lay virtually naked on the floor of their cells to ease the heat. Barrels of water were consumed in vast quantities, and water kegs were exhausted in a day rather than over the normal three days.

All the hatches were opened as wide as possible, and small torn sails were set up on deck to funnel air through them.

The sluggish ship had by now fallen behind the rest of the fleet. The sails of the other ships were but dots on the horizon. Captain Sever was doing all in his power to catch the leading vessels.

Annie and Olive were sitting under the shade of a sail teaching when a call of "Whale ho" was made from the crow's nest.

With permission from the captain, the children were permitted to watch the giant creature rise less than twenty feet from the ship's side. It released a spray of water from a hole in its head, making the children squeal with glee as it washed over them.

The beast swam alongside for some time, eyeing the ship and people on the deck. It rose majestically, then, with a flip, turned upside down and descended to the deep.

Shortly afterwards, three more appeared. The vast size of the animals amazed everyone.

The doctor joined the girls at the railing, watching the sight until they vanished below the briny ocean again.

Within hours, all were driven below decks as a squall set in. As the shade sails were already up, every raindrop was collected and filled the barrels.

Rain and wind set in, and the storm grew wild, but the hatches were left open as the humidity below deck was still almost overwhelming. The rain was like a shower to the parched women, and many stood naked in the cool drops to ease the stickiness.

With the cleaner hull, the skill of the crew saw the *Lady Penrhyn* slowly catch the fleet. Soon, the *Alexander* had fallen behind them, but it was because they had to drop sails to find a person overboard. The storm raged for over a week, with the *Sirius, Golden Grove,* and *Alexander* all losing mainsails. The *Lady Penrhyn* lost its foremost topsail but continued to press onward through the growing seas as another storm approached.

Over the next week, Annie heard calls from above of more whales sighted. Lessons during the storm were cancelled, so the two girls once again had little to do but lie on their bunks and hold on. The water barrels were secured, but the slop buckets had yet to be. The stench below decks once again became horrific.

Up on deck, the fishing lines were still towed behind, and two colossal albacore tuna were hauled aboard, much to the crew's delight. Fresh fish would be a welcome delight to everyone, and these two fish were so large that everyone ate well for some days.

After another few days, the storm abated, but the fresh breeze kept the ships on track towards South America. Communication between ships by flags meant that sad words of losses overboard during the storm were shared. Annie discovered that ships used flags of various colours, shapes, and patterns to communicate messages. Each flag or combination of flags represented a specific letter, number, or predefined message. By hoisting and arranging flags in specific positions, ships could convey messages over long distances.

At least two were drowned from the *Sirius,* and they knew that one also had fallen from the *Alexander.* They had seen the ships set to and had wondered why. The loss on the *Alexander* was distressing because they had lost over thirty due to illness in the weeks before sailing and the following two weeks at sea. Other ships may have suffered a similar fate, but rather than heave-to to find out, they sailed on, knowing that the next port was close.

Ships leaving port were seen, and messages were passed by flag signals.

Rio de Janeiro was now only days away.

Whales abounded nearby, and the cooler weather eased the tensions and heat below decks. The calls of birds that landed in the rigging were heard from the convict cells. A masked booby and numerous gulls alighted. The large booby bird, or gannet, was caught, despatched, and sent to the galley. Lines were set behind the ships nearly all the time.

Although mountains could now be seen from the crow's nest, the wind dropped, and the ships, once again, were almost becalmed. By a light up the mast, a signal went up from the *Sirius* to draw the fleet near to it. With the light winds, the vessels made what effort they could to obey the order. Rio was so close, but the lack of wind meant it took another four days before the harbour was in sight. More boobies were captured, and their fresh meat again enhanced the ship's menu.

The wind once again failed, and within sight of the harbour, the order was given for the longboats to be let down and tow the ships to the port.

On August 6th, the fleet finally limped into the harbour. As the sails were being furled, a scream echoed past the side hatches, and the running footsteps above signalled that a sailor had fallen from the rigging. The women found out later that afternoon that he had fallen on his head, which smashed on the still water. The man was somehow still alive, but his skull was crushed to almost a pulp.

Once anchored, the rest of the long boats from the supply ships were lowered to ferry stores. One boat from the *Lady Penrhyn*, carrying Captain Sever and Captain Campbell, was sent to meet Captain Phillip on his ship to get fresh orders.

Once in port, Doctor Bowes-Smith instructed sourcing fresh produce, especially citrus fruit. Long boats from the supply ships set about securing oranges and lemons. No sooner was it brought on board than he doled it out to waylay the scurvy that was beginning to show amongst the convicts.

Other produce came in by both canoe and long boat: bags of yams, more oranges, bunches of bananas, some ripe but many green for future consumption, guavas, limes, lemons, lettuces, and other fruits and vegetables.

By watching through the small side hatches, the girls saw the arrival of every kind of food possible, plus crates of poultry, barrels of preserved meats, and other goods.

One or another of the women would call out to inquire about what the long boats carried. More often than not, the sailors replied.

After being anchored in port for a week, soft, mournful sounds of singing awoke the women. During the night, another foreign ship had anchored nearby, and the dawn light and gentle breeze carried the sad sounds of mournful and melancholy singing from a slave ship. Mid-morning saw the unloading of the shackled black men as they were slowly ferried ashore to the slave market.

Annie watched from the small hatches in their cell. She wept at the sight, and Olive finally pulled her away from the opening as she became increasingly upset. Annie stomped angrily back to her bunk before exclaiming, "Olive, no one should own another person. It's so wrong. It's bad enough being a convict, but we are not owned. One day, most of us will be free. But to be sold in a slave market in a foreign country is horrific. God didn't make us for that; He gave us freedom." She plopped herself sulkily on her bunk and dropped her head in thought. "Life is not fair sometimes." She lay on her bunk and thought over her short life so far. At nearly twenty, she should have been enjoying the sights and sounds of London and possibly even a second season doing the circuit of balls and dances. However, since her Aunt Violet's accident and subsequent death, her life had radically changed. Now, because of her determination to get a job, she was here on a convict ship sailing halfway around the world from all she held so dear. Torn from the loving arms of her family and Oliver. Oliver... even to think his name still hurt. It was nearly six months since the birth and death of their child, but the love and affection for him had not abated. He was beyond her reach, and she knew she must release her feelings for him, but she could not. She did not wish to; she loved him.

After a month locked below decks, the rattle of the chain on the capstan woke the women. This could only mean they were again setting sail.

Excitement mounted below decks. The cell doors would again be unlocked as soon as the ships were at sea. Cramped as the women were, there had been little trouble from those below decks. They had been fed and watered, and there had been no illness while anchored.

One of the guards mentioned that an infuriating crewman had jumped ship the day before. Most of the crew and the captain seemed pleased that the troublesome man was gone and made no effort to find him.

Only days after leaving port, the first of the water barrels that were sourced from their last stop was opened and found to be poor-quality water, if not horrible to drink. On further investigation, the flour was found to have weevils, and many of the bananas were found to be ripening very quickly. These were doled out in plenteous quantities to all who wished to eat them. Most did.

After a peaceful time in the harbour, the weather again turned, and another week of storms hit. The rain catchment sails refilled the barrels. Life on board the ship settled back into its routine until the next one hit. The sound of tearing sails and creaking spars was accompanied by shouts. Fearing the encroachment of waves, the hatches were all barred shut. The lamps were extinguished, and the cell deck became a fearful black hole again. Fearing for their lives, the women stayed in their bunks, hanging on as tightly as they could. Unfortunately, Captain Campbell's young cousin was in the wrong place at the wrong time, and Jamie was caught under a cage of chickens that had broken loose. It was soon discovered that the poor boy had broken his thigh bone. His teacher, Annie, was called in to bring comfort to the lad while his cousin was on duty.

One blessing from this last port of call was that their stop had meant purchasing every kind of fabric possible. With needles, pins, and other notions now available, the women set about sewing in the dim light below deck until the storm reached a ferocious crescendo. Knowing that the fabric she had been able to source from Rio would probably be stolen in her absence from the cell, she shrugged in resignation at what again befell her. This duty meant she was able to get clean.

Captain Campbell insisted that she have a saltwater bath before entering their cabins. She complied willingly. Below decks, they rose from their bunks only to drink, use the slop buckets, or grab some dry food to eat. For a week, the hatches remained closed. The gunports that drained the effluent from the bottom of the cell floors were also closed as the waves were oozing in the leaking openings, setting all the cells awash. For days, the storm seemed to follow them. However, the rain brought plenteous supplies of fresh water. They were able to replace all the stagnant supply from Rio. They collected every drop possible in the remnants of some torn sails. After days of heavy seas, the relative calm after the storm brought relief.

Soon, the hatches were opened again, and fresh air flooded in once again. As they had done many times before, the cells were sluiced through the once-reopened gunports, and the cell deck was cleaned and aired.

Word was sent from the *Charlotte* that one of the convict women had been lost overboard in the storm. Annie heard of others lost overboard in storms and grieved for each one. There had been no chance that any of them would get rescued.

A feeling of melancholy settled on the convicts, but they wondered why she had been on deck. It could easily have been one of the women from their ship.

Again, the ships had a fair breeze behind them, and soon, the fleet was nearing their next port. The Cape of Good Hope was now only a matter of days away. They all knew this would be their last port to resupply before their final destination. The longest leg was yet in front of them.

On October 13th, they dropped anchor in Table Bay at Cape Town. Once again, the women were locked in their cells for the duration. After the restocking, some of the better-behaved women were permitted some time on deck. This was a rare privilege at the best of times, but to be permitted above deck in port was extraordinary. Maggie and a few others accompanied Annie and Olive.

Once anchored, word came that disease was spreading through the *Alexander* again.

The following day the *Charlotte* also dropped anchor, and her doctor reported that dysentery had taken the lives of thirty of the prisoners on board, and many more were ill.

To top it off, some of the convicts on the *Alexander* were chained to the decks after discovering a whisper of mutiny. Having only been in the bay one day, the second mate from the *Friendship* had imbibed too freely and went overboard; he never surfaced.

Only two days later, more women were permitted to spend some time on deck. Phoebe Norton, along with many others, was watching the boats come alongside when she overbalanced and tumbled headfirst into the ocean.

Thankfully, men in the longboat dived in and rescued her. This stay in Cape Town was once again for a month.

By the time they set sail in mid-November, they had already been at sea for six months.

Chapter 11   The Final Furlong

Shortly before departure from Cape Town, to Annie's delight, the *Lady Penrhyn* was loaded with special stock. The arrival of the female convicts from other vessels had been preceded by a juggling of the convicts.

More female convicts had arrived on their ship from the *Charlotte*. They were clearing out the hold to fill it with supplies, and the female convicts on board were distributed to three other vessels. The cramped conditions were worth it when Annie saw what the *Lady Penrhyn* was allocated to carry. Her heart started beating faster when the sounds of horses roused her from her morning slumbers.

One flighty stallion, three mares in foal and three colts were brought on board along with sheep, goats, cows, and poultry. The horses were for Governor Phillip's use in New South Wales.

Annie's cell was unlocked while in port, as they had proven themselves trustworthy. The seven women were permitted to do the work required for the animals. Annie watched her new deck mates be led into the prepared cells. She had known stock was coming but presumed it would be cattle or sheep. Her heart was beating a tattoo with excitement.

The lactating goats and cows needed milking, and the animals all needed feeding and attention. While the crew and marines were seeing to repairs and stowing the new supplies, Annie's cell group of select convicts proved their worth by caring for the new stock. The stallion, in particular, was unsettled, and Annie intended to befriend it. The magnificent beast did not like his new unsteady quarters, and the crewman in charge of the stock was at his wit's end as to how to handle the flighty horse.

Some of the marines tried to assist, but Annie went directly to the roaring beast and soon was permitted to try her hand at soothing it. When the crewman saw how the stallion responded to Annie's gentle touch and approach, she was permitted to befriend the beast.

Only a matter of days after its arrival on board, the stallion whinnied when she approached. Annie had no access to apples, but she rarely came empty-handed. From a small fist full of chaff to a corn cob or a handful of dried peas, the beast slowly calmed and soon permitted her to enter his cell and brush him. She discovered his breed from the crewman and that, unlike Aladdin, who was a Godolphin-descended Barbary Arabian stallion, this beautiful beast was a cross Barbary Spanish horse. His shoulders were not set as far back as Aladdin or King's Majesty. He was, however, a bay like the first Godolphin stallion had been. This horse was as flighty as Aladdin was when she first saw him. The day Annie first entered his cage, she was admittedly very fearful. Her unusual technique had already won over other horses. They were used to being whipped and chastised, so Annie's loving and gentle approach was foreign to them, but they responded to her compassion and care. Annie now had a second responsibility besides teaching, which was suspended while anchored, and that was caring for the horses.

The crewman oversaw her initial interaction with the big bay beast, and he expected that she would ask for a whip or at least a rope for him. He was stunned when she requested that he stand back and watch.

She said, "Please, sir, I've done this before to unbroken colts. I'm quite safe, but I need you to stay well back and as still as you can."

The man would much rather tackle a huge sea than care for a horse. Not being a landlubber, he'd had little to do with these highly strung animals. "Luv, I've gotta care for him."

Annie turned to him and quietly said, "Please, sir, I do know what I'm doing. Just stand still and stay silent, very silent."

He shrugged his shoulders and left her to it. He watched as Annie gained the trust of the ferocious creature. He opened his mouth to say something, then remembered her request to remain silent and shut it again. He folded his arms and leaned against the bulkhead as she requested. He was in no hurry to head up on deck as enough hands were there to do the work. He was, however, stunned at her approach as she did absolutely nothing.

Annie stood with her hand out to the horse and remained silent for most of the time. Occasionally, the words "Good boy" or "Come on, you beautiful boy" were heard softly spoken. As the horse took a step towards her, she turned her back to him. Again, the crewman was about to say something when her hands went to her lips, shushing him. She was listening to the horse approaching her. As the flighty animal approached, Annie moved a small step away from it.

The sailor was puzzled; this was not what he expected. He was now spellbound. He would not have left even if the captain had ordered him away. He saw Annie smile; she obviously realised that the beast was standing right behind her. The horse was sniffing her hair, then soon nuzzling her neck. She stayed absolutely still for some minutes, then slowly turned towards him. The flighty beast raised his head like he was nodding but did not step away. Annie knew she had broken through. She held a small section of a dried cob of corn from the fresh produce. As the stallion was already broken in, it was just a matter of gaining his trust. He would now be approachable for her when she wished. As she was now talking to the remarkable beast, the supervising crewman softly muttered, "Well, I never! Cor miss, I know's nothin' about them horses. I hopes you don't mind, but I'm getting you assigned to looking after these beasties with me."

Annie was overjoyed. "I don't mind at all, sir." She hid her big grin against the warm neck of her new friend. This was exactly what she wished. As she wrapped her arms around his neck, the stallion almost hugged her in return by wrapping his head around her.

After breakfast each morning, the fair head was seen pressed against the flank of the quivering stallion while she groomed him. The sight of the young convict girl and the big bay horse was quite one to behold. Often, she would hear something and turn to find a few crew members or marines watching her in awe. The stallion's nostrils would flicker and quiver in anticipation of her arrival. At first sight of her, his snort and whinny would echo down the cells. If she was late for some reason, he could be heard pawing at the deck and neighing. Annie would clean his stable, moving around him with ease, then replace the straw; then she set about giving him a brush down. This was more to calm him than for any other reason. With his tail held high in the air, he would stand with his legs well apart, bracing against the movement of the often tossing ship. Once done, his head would nod again as though he was saying thank you to Annie. She would wrap her arms lovingly around his neck and give him a hug, then go about the rest of her duties.

Olive was not to be left out of the special privileges; she was one of the convicts assigned to care for the new garden, plants, cows and goats. Others in the small group were also awarded special privileges and joined her. Elizabeth Colley had stayed close to Annie since the loss of her baby. She was friends with two other Elizabeths, Lees and Hipley, and another girl Olive had befriended, Ann Inett, who had been convicted of theft. The six well-behaved women were given much more freedom than other less well-behaved convicts.

Very early on in their journey, Annie realised that Olive's warning about nocturnal sounds was far too accurate. Many of the convict women had discovered early on the benefits of offering their services to both sailors and marines for various privileges and increased rations. Rarely did they ask for fresh food as they wanted grog. Sighs and groans of delight were often heard from the cells of the chosen women.

Quite a few of the convict women were now with child, and some had no idea who the fathers of their babies were. Others like Elizabeth Dalton, Sarah Bellamy, and Catherine Hart had formed regular liaisons on board and knew the paternity of their children. Most of the women had found their monthly courses had ceased.

While many of the women were busy occupying themselves with the crew and marines, the group of specially chosen friends were quite content in their more passive occupations on board. They all now shared the cell with

Maggie Frownes, who, at forty-five, was much older than the majority of women, although Betty Bird was nearly sixty and also in fine health. The two attempted to keep order below decks. Sadly, they had little success. The six girls knew how vital the provision of fresh food was to all on the ship. Unlike many of the London-bred convicts who knew little about where food came from or how it was produced, these girls did. From Captain Sever, whom Annie had discovered was also part owner of the vessel, to the newest born child, all needed the fresh vegetables. Sadly, no matter how much food they grew on board in their tiny portable vegetable patch, it was a drop in the bucket of what they required.

Olive especially realised that growing their own food once they arrived in the new settlement would be vital. She learned all she could, including how to milk cows and goats. Betty Bird joined her in this.

Annie knew how to sew, but spinning, weaving, and cooking had not been included in her education. At home, she had loved their flower garden, and now, being hands-on while still on the ship, she set about educating herself about what was ahead of them. Governor Phillip had purchased many young fruit trees and assorted seedlings in Cape Town. Olive loved the chore of caring for these. She and her friends set about watering the plants using water from various sources. This was also a good way of keeping well away from the majority of the undesirable women.

The doctor mentioned in passing while doing his clinics that the reverend and his wife on the *Golden Grove* had also stocked up on many fruit trees. Not being permitted to store them in the hold, the Johnsons' had placed them in their cabin. He had laughed about this, knowing how small his own cabin was. Lettuce, cabbage, and cauliflower were grown on board and eaten regularly. The cabbages were specially grown in vast quantities and then pickled in vinegar. This was doled out to ward off scurvy at the doctor's insistence.

Before the next storm hit, Annie had been thinking of a way to keep the horses safe. She wondered if they could erect a sort of sling under the horses' stomachs to prevent them from endangering themselves in the bigger seas. With one of the torn sails, this feat was achieved relatively quickly. Within a week after leaving the port of Cape Town, the carpenters had finally finished converting part of two cells to safe stalls for the horses and larger stock. Having been through some big swells on the trip already, Annie knew that the horses, in particular, would need narrow padded confinement for when the storms hit, knowing that a horse would need to be shot if it broke its leg.

With knowledge of more storms ahead, Annie needed the converted area to be ready when required. She would assist with the move from the larger cell to the new tight stalls when required. Word had come through that a big storm was brewing as the barometer was falling fast. Annie moved fearlessly about the stallion and soon had his stomach barely an inch above the sail cradle she had invented. If he fell now, he would not injure himself. The mares, colts and even some cows received similar treatment. All should remain safe, although they would be unable to walk around at all; however, in a storm, that was not advisable. Annie had also had their water buckets put on a double pivot so that even if the waves hit and the ship heeled over to such an extent that the normal buckets spilled, they would still have access to water. The cows received similar treatment. Thankfully, they were in calf and did not need to be milked.

~

Two weeks after leaving Cape Town, the next storm hit the fleet. Sadly, the sheep and goats did not fare so well. Five died in the first week of the storm. The larger plants occasionally tipped over but were easily righted, so they fared reasonably well as they had been adequately secured.

Shortly before this storm hit, the first water barrels were tapped.

"Oh, that's disgusting!" came the report from a marine, followed by a sound of spitting out the vile brew. He had been about to dole out the supplies to the convicts. The same thing had occurred after leaving Rio de Janeiro, and they should have been checked. At least if it rained, they could replenish the water. However, the wind was too strong to hoist the rain sails.

The two captains were notified, and all the new supplies were checked. The water was stagnant, and the barrels of food were not as requested, as the fruit was again too ripe to keep for long. The life-giving water was worse than stagnant creek water and almost unsuitable for drinking.

One of the sailors had heard of running water through sand or soil to help clean it, so they tried catching it after watering the plants. This helped, and the water was earthy but drinkable. The plants could use it, but nothing living could, in case it caused dysentery.

The doctor had long since known of this condition as the *flux*. Water rations were cut to three pints per day per person, which included all cooking. Washing in freshwater was forbidden. Seawater was the only means of washing anything. The result was that everything washed was salty and stiff, not that the convict women washed often anyway.

When the wind calmed, a torn rain sail was erected in the hope that the supply of water could be replenished before they ran out of the remaining good drinking water. Although normally reluctant to use a good sail for water catchment, they knew that a sail was no good to them if they were dead from thirst.

The stock consumed more precious commodities than expected, and all knew the situation could become dire if they didn't catch the rain.

Just as the storm hit, another convict, Jane Parkinson, died. Her body was quickly consigned to the deep before it became too dangerous to do so.

Annie had shortened her lessons so the children could be secured below decks and out of danger.

Jamie Campbell told Annie that Governor Phillip had notified the fleet's captains that he was transferring from the *Sirius* to the *Supply* and would run ahead of the flotilla to see if they could scout out a settlement site for the new town. Jamie was full of news about who was moving around in the various longboats they could see. Seaman Thomas Webb was transferred along with the Governor, Lieutenant Phillip Gidley King, and five others.

New orders were received while Annie was still on deck. She overheard the instructions issued from Captain Campbell to Captain Sever. These were that the fleet would split, and the *Supply*, *Alexander*, *Scarborough,* and *Friendship* would sail on to select and clear the area for the new settlement. Major Ross also left the *Sirius* and went on board the *Scarborough*. Captain Hunter remained on board the *Sirius* and was now left in charge of the remaining seven ships of the fleet. The governor gave him the necessary instructions in case the *Supply* did not complete the voyage.

Only thirty minutes after the transfers were completed did the expected second wave of the heavy squall hit. Headway became nigh impossible as the wind drove straight at them. Tacking was ill-advised, so with their sales lowered, the flotilla again sat at the mercy of the waves and wind. The ships weathered the storm as best they could.

~

As New Holland drew closer, tempers flared below decks. The ship had endured storms, tempests, and periods of being becalmed, but this one gale seemed to be mightier than them all. The rolling waves saw ships within hailing distance vanish from view, but the shouts of sailors still could be heard from the next ship. Amid this ferocious sea, one of the braziers below decks had not been extinguished, and Margaret Burnett's legs were on the receiving end of a pot of hot water. The burns were excruciating, but little could be done to soothe her wounds other than dousing them in seawater to cool the burns, so they sat her in a barrel of salt water.

The storm finally abated, and the situation below deck was horrendous. Some even wished they could jump overboard rather than endure such torture again. The convict women had become violent and abusive to the extent that they ripped the scant clothing from each other's backs. Some were naked to the waist as they now had nothing to cover themselves. Others were so violent that they were separated from their cellmates, brought up on deck and chained in leg irons. Of this group, some were flogged, and those not willing to stay silent were gagged. Betty Bird started praying, being nearly sixty, as she was too old for such an experience. She had befriended the cows in such a way as Annie had with the horses.

The storm and water problems had caused much grief with the stock. Despite the best attention possible, many of the new stock had perished. Only twelve chickens were left alive on the *Lady Penrhyn*. Some sheep and cows died because they could not find purchase on the slippery decking. The cradled horses, however, remained alive, well, and uninjured.

With Christmas nearly upon them, all thoughts of a celebration were cancelled when some two thousand nautical miles off the coast, the swells and sea became so large that the waves towered over the masts. Even Captain Sever said the previous storms had seemed like a slight breeze compared to what they now encountered. He was fast beginning to run out of words big enough to describe the seas. The chunks of sea ice did not help. The one blessing of the large waves was that they were going in their direction. The small wooden ships bounced like corks in the violent rolling ocean. The waves were no longer blue or green; they were seething with white foam like snow, which also landed on the decks, making them slippery.

Christmas came and went unnoticed. The swell did not abate. The *Lady Penrhyn* had somehow survived being sunk, but the storm had not had its final fling. They had merely entered the eye of what was now being termed a hurricane. While the seas did not lessen, much of the wind died. Annie's slings for the stock were working brilliantly, but the care for all the larger animals had by necessity been neglected. These precious beasts had access to food and water but nothing else. It was just too dangerous to be near them. Annie dared anyway. As she had just finished replenishing the water in the stallion's bucket, the ship was caught by a rogue wave and pitched sideways. The gun ports along the length of the deck were forced open by the pressure of the giant wave. The holes started spewing seawater onto the already foul-smelling decks. The effluent and excrement from the animals made the deck as slippery as ice skating. The excess of salt water now oozing in exacerbated the danger.

Annie, along with everything not tied down, went sliding. She knew the instant she hit the bulkhead that she had broken her arm badly. Waves of pain shot through her, nearly making her pass out. No one was within call, and even if they had been, the noises overhead would have drowned out her yells. She knew it was too dangerous for the doctor to be called out on deck to see her. Her arm hung limply by her side, and she realised that she had also injured her leg somehow; she hobbled back to her cell. The only blessing was that she had finished attending to the horses.

Her arrival back at the cell was met with shock. Through the pain of her injury, she did not realise that the cells themselves had become flooded with that last wave. Every bunk and cell was awash with seawater. Quite a few others were wounded, some with similar injuries to Annie. Screams of panic and fear were tumultuous, and all the girls in Annie's cell were on their knees beside their bunks, praying for a safe deliverance. Others in other cells soon joined them, and in her own agony, even Annie added her pleas to the good Lord above to spare them from a watery grave. All were sure that this time, the ship would sink.

Elizabeth Colley said, "Blooming heck, Annie, that God of yours certainly knows how to test us gels." Then she saw Annie's arm, "An' wot you done to yer arm? It's hanging loose like, at yer side."

Another two Elizabeths had drawn a little closer to the cell group; they, like the others, awaited Annie's answer. Elizabeth Anderson and Elizabeth Bruce were friends who had been convicted together in London for theft.

During the trip, many women juggled bunks as personalities clashed and settled. These two women stuck together but were now more often seen with Maggie than affiliating with the more rebellious women. They now lay together on a bunk, weeping softly and praying that death would come swiftly.

The seas raged on as the terrified screams of the women below echoed through the bulkheads. Another rogue wave hit; somehow, the ship righted itself again and was ploughing through more of the leviathan seas as they all waited for Annie's answer.

Annie's reply stated the obvious: "My arm is broken, Elizabeth; that big wave knocked me off my feet and sent me across the deck. Thankfully, the slings are holding the horses fast. They are fine."

Elizabeth Anderson half yelled, "And which particular 'big one' would that be, Annie? I've lost count of those."

One of the other girls spoke, her voice dripping in fear. "I got no idea how this bobbing cork even makes it over each liquid mountain."

Olive swore. "Damn the horses, Annie, you could have been killed." She was weeping in fear while holding on for her life. "We may all yet die, Annie."

She replied to her friend. "They have to drink, Olive, just as we do." Annie made it to her bunk and held on for grim death. She totally agreed that there was a strong possibility they may not survive. The waves of pain swept over her, and each jolt grated the broken bones together in her arm. She took a quick look and noticed they were not sticking out. With a sigh of relief at that, she still had Oliver's cloak and wrapped herself in it to immobilise her arm. If the ship sank, she knew she would be unable to swim anyway, so if she died with his cloak wrapped around her, at least, that would be something. She could get the doctor to set it if the sea calmed soon. She lay on her bunk in agony, not caring if she lived or died. She, like all the others, held on for grim death. Olive lay head to head with Annie, and they quietly prayed as each wave succeeded the next in size. With each crash of the ship, Annie screamed in agony as it landed in the trough.

Annie was lying on her berth trying hard to stop from moving when Olive said, "The miserable have no other medicine but only hope: I have hope to live and am prepared to die."

The randomness made Annie say while groaning through her agony, "What?"

Olive said, "William Shakespeare wrote that in 'Measure for Measure,' it seemed sort of apt."

It took another day and a half before the sea calmed down from this storm. The doctor came down to check on the convicts late that evening. The moans and groans he heard as the hatch was quickly opened for him boded much work ahead. He had brought many supplies to fix cuts and wounds, but the broken bones he found were unexpected. Annie did not even call for his help, but the others in her cell demanded he come and see her. His fingering of the floppy arm was enough to make her finally pass out. Both her bones were broken in the lower part of her arm. While she was unresponsive, he quickly set the bone as best he could in the poor light, bandaged it thickly, and then tied it to her chest. He had no splint on him and dared not make another perilous journey on deck to get one, or, as he looked around the cells, more than ten others were required. The carnage that one wave had caused was dire. Not realising that she had also injured her leg, he left to attend to others. Olive was holding fast to her bunk but said, "Thank you, doctor, for making us all move the plants into the cabins. I hope they have fared better than we have. The gunports sprung open, and we had no hope of stopping the salty deluge. Annie said the horses somehow were fine. Her slings seem to be working."

The doctor answered her as he was treating Annie. "Thankfully, they are fine, Olive, but I'm not sure the plants were anchored well enough to stay as safe as they should have. We'll deal with them later." Knowing he had more patients to see, he asked, "Make Annie stay in her bunk, will you?"

Olive gave a half laugh and said, "She was up at that beloved horse of hers. She was just about to head back when that rogue wave hit us."

The doctor gave a nod, "I should have guessed. Well, she won't be doing much for some time."

Once the storm finally eased, the reports of the distances travelled astounded those who heard. The fleet had been blown over two hundred nautical miles in just one day. As the storm had lasted over a week, they were now off the south of Van Diemen's Land. Hopefully, South Cape would soon be sighted, and they could finally head northward. The bilges were constantly being hand-pumped. Many of the barrels of supplies had come loose, and some of the stores were damaged. Fodder for the animals was spoiled and now unable to be eaten.

Thinking that they had seen the last of the enormous seas, they were thrilled to see the land. South Cape was finally sighted. They had a reprieve, and Doctor Bowes-Smith went about setting the various breaks properly. Annie had her arm now splinted, bandaged and tied up in a sling made from a torn sail. Her leg injury was treated, and a large splinter was extracted and doused with rum. Knowing it could yet infect, he told her to keep an eye on it. Thankfully, the break was to her left arm, so she could still do some things for the horses. Teaching was cancelled until the colony was reached, as the seas were unknown and still wild. Again, all eleven flimsy wooden vessels somehow made it through the horrendous conditions. For three days, the fleet had a reprieve from the enormous waves. Then, they resumed their journey north on January 8th. They all wished they had taken refuge in anything else than a boat.

If the previous seas were huge, enormous, or even gigantic, then what they now faced was immeasurable, as the herculean waves crashed over every deck of the ship. More than one of the vessels turned ninety degrees sideways before somehow righting itself upright again, before being hit by the next liquid mountain. How they didn't flip right over was a miracle. Each ship was truly rocked to the scuppers as the water gushed in from the openings.

Worse was yet to come. The call of "Brace, brace, brace" was heard from above. With the force of the approaching wall of water, the gunport covers were again blown open all along the sides of the vessels, and the water poured in on all decks. How no vessels sank was a miracle and showed the mighty skills of the crew who sailed them. The Almighty above certainly had His hand upon the ships protecting them. Somehow, the almost-stricken fleet made it through two more days of hell on the high seas.

The remaining animals were now short of feed, as the seawater had ruined the hay, grain, and other food stores. They had only one day of edible stock food left on board. As they headed north, the seas abated slightly, but the storm continued to rage overhead. Lightning and thunder fought a battle royal above them. Below decks, the hell let loose amongst the women made the storm outside pale into insignificance. From the praying women of only a short time ago when the seas raged, the cells rang with such vile abuse that the hardened sailors were put to the blush.

The fleet seemed to find a lull in the storm, and when finally the *Lady Penrhyn* came within sight of the *Sirius*, they discovered that most of their stock on board that ship was dead. As they now had little need of the feed, a bag of barley was carefully transferred on board the *Lady Penrhyn*. The captain had been back on board less than half an hour when the storm returned with a vengeance. The *Lady Penrhyn,* being caught a little unprepared, nearly hit the *Fishburn,* which had drawn up close. Once more, the ship was nearly flipped over but somehow righted itself. The horses remained in their cradles and somehow managed to survive unscathed. The fleet hobbled northward until the storm finally dissipated. All ships but *Sirius* and *Lady Penrhyn* sustained structural damage. The *Prince of Wales* lost its main yard sail, topmast, and mainsail, the *Charlotte* lost her mainsail. The *Lady Penrhyn*'s only problem was a jib, which had a small tear that took less than half an hour to repair. The *Borrowdale* lost her foretop sail; the *Fishburn* had her jib split in two; the *Golden Grove*, with Reverend and Mrs Johnson on board, lost her foresail and mainsail. Somehow, no one had died.

It took three days for the seas to settle back to anywhere like normal. By January 13th, Annie refused to stay in her bunk. One of her beloved mares was ill. She knew the cows had flux and figured barley was not as good as stock feed. Thankfully, she knew there was not that much left of that. The bag of grain had only lasted for four days, and now the stock had nothing left. With pleading and begging, Annie got some dry bread and peas to feed the hungry animals; this, thankfully, did the trick. With something now in their stomachs, the stock settled. They still had over five hundred nautical miles to go. Three days more sailing and the food was nearly all ruined or eaten; even the crew were now hit with diarrhoea… yet the ships sailed on.

Chapter 12   *That Fatal Shore*

*T*he weather became so hot that many braved the rain squalls to get drenched rather than sweltering in the overheated bunks. The barometer started dropping most evenings. Lightning shows often hit during the night and were gone within a matter of hours.

Doctor Bowes-Smith informed the convicts, "If you all think you were hot last night, you were correct. The thermometer didn't drop below 76° Fahrenheit. I checked it at midnight." He stifled a yawn as he spoke.

The land was now visible to the port side of the vessel. They had been sailing up the coast for some time but had kept well off the land, and by Captain Sever's reckonings, they should be close to Botany Bay. They had Captain James Cook's maps and found them to be accurate. Annie was permitted some time outside in the morning sun. Each of the women with such injuries was relieved of their duties until they healed. Annie, however, insisted on visiting the horses. She kept a handful of peas for the beloved stallion. She had never dared name him as she had no right to do so.

They were on deck in the sunshine when the entrance to Botany Bay was sighted on January 20th, 1788. A few of the women and marines watched in mixed awe and horror at the sparsely vegetated, uninteresting landscape before them. Annie said, "How are we supposed to carve a settlement out of such terrain?"

As the *Lady Penrhyn* entered the bay, five other ships sat at anchor. Later, they found that the *Supply* had only beaten them by two days; the *Sirius* had arrived at four that morning, and the *Scarborough* was four hours behind. The *Scarborough*, *Friendship*, and *Alexander* rode at anchor nearby. Considering the *Lady Penrhyn* had been considered one of the slowest ships in the fleet, she had come in sixth out of eleven vessels. Hopefully, the other five would make it safely. They did.

Once all the fleet arrived, the various captains met with the governor and reported in. Of the entire complement, only forty-eight persons had died *en route*, not counting those who died before departure. Some were marines or their family, but the majority were convicts. The *Alexander* had the most fatalities due to sickness, with over thirty deaths. However, half of them had succumbed before leaving port in England due to the bilges not being pumped out. Fifteen more died within a fortnight of leaving Portsmouth.

It took Governor Phillip only a short time to realise that Botany Bay was unsuitable for the new settlement. He had apparently gone ashore and reconnoitred the area before the fleet joined him. He had met and befriended the natives and made some trades with them. In the short time they had been on shore, the land to the north of the bay had been investigated and found to be nothing but black sand to some depth. Crops wouldn't grow there.

Annie watched the official group meet with the natives of the land and was greeted with inquisition but in a friendly way. From the deck, she could see that the indigenous peoples were tall and slender with very dark skin. From her elevated vantage point, she could see they were not as dark as the negro cook she had seen on one of the other ships; although their hair was curly, it was not in tight spirals like the cook's. When one of the ship's company who had been ashore returned, he reported to the doctor that each of the men had a top front tooth missing and a six-inch stick through the nasal bridge of their noses. They were close enough to see that the men's chests were covered in tribal scar ridges and had a bone or stick through their noses. Although they looked fearsome, the newcomers were welcomed ashore, and goods were traded.

Doctor Bowes-Smith went ashore the following day and checked the ground and bushland for himself. He wandered off from the group and ended up lost. After some time, he stumbled on a small cluster of shanty-like huts that was obviously an indigenous encampment. For a while, he hid and watched these people's peaceful lives. He snuck away and, after some time, found his way back to the shore.

The northern side of the bay proved not to be fertile, and the soil to the south was tested and found to be not much better. The winds howled through the open mouth of the expanse of the low headland, and Governor Phillip, knowing that Captain Cook's maps mentioned other bays further to the north, set sail to explore another bay as a possible site.

In the time spent on board, Annie, Olive and some of their cell block had spent some time pumping the doctor and others about the land to which they would make their home. To their delight, they found he had read Captain Cook and Joseph Banks's journals. From them, he was able to extract a fair amount of information.

Doctor Bowes-Smith had read the two books, and both mentioned the curious animals reported. One was a bouncing animal that carried its babies in a pocket on its stomach. He had suggested that the girls watch out for these creatures. While on the deck watching the interaction between the natives and the deputations from the ships, some of these bounding jack-in-the-boxes were seen springing across the short grassy land and then stopping to graze.

Excitedly, Annie cried out, "Look, doctor, over there! They must be the kangas-roos you spoke of. I had not realised they would be so big."

The doctor, who was standing nearby and watching his injured convict charges, replied, "Neither did I, Annie; I had expected the descriptions I read to be somewhat exaggerated. It seems that they were quite accurate."

They watched a group of about twenty unique creatures move along the foreshore grazing. Annie excitedly exclaimed again, pointing to one small one she had just seen appear, "Oh look, one has a baby. It must have been in the false stomach you mentioned, sir. I presume it's some stretchy pouch."

The miniature version of the larger creature had emerged from between its parent's feet. It was somewhat wobbly on its spindly hind legs but set about nibbling the grasses close to its parent.

Mary Love, Betty Bird, and Maggie joined them at the railings.

"It's so sweet," came a call from one of the other girls nearby.

They stood watching the strange sight until the sun's heat drove them to seek shade.

On the morning of January 22nd, Governor Phillip returned and announced that the fleet would be moving to Port Jackson. Broken Bay was another option if Port Jackson was unsuitable.

The ships readied to leave the open bay when unexpected sails were seen on the horizon. Knowing that all eleven of the English fleet had arrived safely, they wondered what country these vessels belonged to. They could have been from anywhere, Dutch or Spanish; they just hoped they were not French. Relations between the two countries were already tense.

While the fleet still lay at anchor, the two new ships drew closer.

As the winds once more played havoc with the sailing ships, it wasn't until January 24th that the two ships came close enough to see that they were indeed French vessels. They came and anchored in the bay, having seen other ships at anchor. A longboat was sent to greet them and place the English claim on the land before them. A near calamity occurred as the English fleet was waiting for favourable winds to leave Botany Bay. The fleet had weighed anchor and were waiting to leave the bay. The wind was swirling to such a degree that the *Charlotte* nearly ran aground, and then the *Friendship* and *Prince of Wales* nearly rammed the *Charlotte*. The *Friendship* received superficial damage with the loss of the carving at the front of the vessel. All three ships lost sails due to the incident and inclement weather. To have come so far and then to nearly lose three ships within sight of the final destination was a near catastrophe. What the French thought, no one knew. The situation could have been dire; had the three ships been lost, the settlement may have been unviable.

~

On the morning of January 26th, on the third attempt to leave their anchorage, the fleet finally exited Botany Bay and headed northward. The wind was still gusting from various directions in the almost circular bay, making sailing difficult at best. They had to leave with the outgoing tide. Following the bulk of the fleet, the *Lady Penrhyn* finally reached the immense headland of the Port Jackson entrance. Annie, Olive, and the others from their cell were permitted on deck to view the passage towards their new home. The military was not fearful of the women absconding as there was nowhere for them to go. The evening meal had been served, eaten, and cleaned up while sailing. The chosen group of women were escorted on deck as a reward for good behaviour. Annie's entire cell block and the injured women were some of the prisoners included in this privilege. The sun was a few hours from setting as they reached the towering cliffs of the heads.

Annie and Olive had been told by Doctor Bowes-Smith that the journals he had read described the most amazing opening of the harbour. They stood at the gunnels and watched the ship tack towards the cliffs. As they sailed by, they saw small beaches with crashing waves. Now that the ship had tacked, they were heading to what looked like a recess in the cliffs. As they drew closer, they saw that the wall was, in fact, three distinct headlands. The cliffs were sheer to the north and south, while the central headland in front of them had a bushy shrub nearly reaching the waterline. It was indented with various bays, but they sailed past that promontory, turning southward again.

As their ship entered the expansive harbour, the myriad of bays and headlands brought gasps of amazement and awe. The fleet's main vessels, having left a few days earlier, were already anchored, and the crew dropped all but one sail and moved to meet their sister ships a few miles further into the bay. They now proceeded westward at a much-slowed pace.

They could now see all the other vessels moored to the south of the huge harbour in one of the many bays. Some of the ships were so close to shore that they had tied up to the trees and anchored them at the stern. They had been hidden from view until they drew close.

At dusk, the *Lady Penrhyn* took its allocated place amongst the fleet. It was one of the closest to the shore. It dropped its anchor in the bay, and the stern was tied to the trees on the shore. Knowing their cargo of women would be some of the last to land; they were surprised they were not sitting a little out from the other ships. Unloading the horses and stock would be problematic, but with access to the native grasses collected at Botany Bay, they now had fodder for them. Few other ships had managed to keep their stock alive.

Annie and the crewman discussed the possibility of constructing a makeshift jetty to offload the stock, but that would take time. She was concerned with how the horses would be landed and wondered if they would be lowered in nets and swum ashore, for she could see no other way of removing them from the ship. With her arm still immobilised, having been splinted, bandaged, and then placed in a sling, she found that her activities were limited. She was permitted to sit with the children on the quarterdeck and conduct classes of a sort; this also permitted the parents more freedom than they otherwise had.

On the 27th, the morning after anchoring, the first of the convicts were sent ashore from *Scarborough*. They began clearing the area chosen for the construction of the new town. Trees were required for tent poles and others for firewood. Clearing the selected area would require much effort before erecting any structures or even tents.

Olive had taken one look at the raw state of the area, and Annie had found her weeping on her bunk that night. "I can't do this, Annie; why did I ever reject my comfortable home where everything was provided for me? My papa told me that I had made my bed, now I have to lie on it. I had no idea I would have to make everything from scratch, including the damned bed upon which I was expected to lay." Her weeping was so pitiful that Annie was gutted. She, too, knew the comfortable life she had before her desire to work had been approved by her parents, but that did not appease her much. Because of that, her world had also been turned upside down.

Over the following days, Annie and Olive watched the site's progress. On the third day after arriving, the first gardens were dug close to the settlement but in the next bay to the east. Soon, a large pile of fallen trees were stacked, awaiting later use. More and more men were sent to work to erect shelters. Also, a start on building a small wharf was begun so provisions, stores, and stock could be unloaded. Annie still tended to the horses, once again released from the narrow stall and left now to wander about their cells. Fodder was sourced from shore and brought aboard. The long grasses from the settlement site had not been wasted. When scythed, they had been bundled and supplied as stock feed to the ships before digging the area into garden beds. Ticks and snakes abounded, but no one was bitten. The convicts were all aware that various meetings had taken place to determine their futures.

On February 5th, after returning from a meeting, Doctor Bowes-Smith and Captain Campbell called Olive, Elizabeth Colley, Annie, Elizabeth Lees, Elizabeth Hipley, and Ann Inett onto the deck. Wondering what trouble the group could possibly be in, they approached with trepidation.

Captain Campbell had come to know Annie quite well because she had nursed his young cousin when he had broken his leg. The lad had fully recovered, but he noticed his cousin still sought Annie out when possible.

Annie saw that Captain Campbell looked at her with a frown plastered on his brow. Tearing his eyes from her worried countenance, the captain said, "Ladies, our instructions shortly before leaving London was to colonise Norfolk Island to stop the French from claiming it. With them so close at hand, this has become a priority. We know that there was, at some time, an ancient settlement on the island, as previous visits have discovered evidence of this; however, it is now deserted. It is cleared fallow land, and it is ready for cultivation. The extra food produced from this venture will supply this infant colony in Port Jackson with desperately needed food." He paused, looking at the women standing before him. He released a long sigh. "So, those chosen will need to put their hands to many new skills. I have selected you all as being the best-behaved women on the ships. Annie Gentle, with your broken arm, you are, unfortunately, currently ineligible, but I know of your friendship with these ladies, and I wish you to hear for yourself what they are being offered. Mary Love and Betty Bird will remain in the colony with you as they both have some farm skills, and we will need them as teachers. It's why they have not joined us."

Annie nodded understanding. She felt Olive seek her good hand and cling to it tightly. She knew Olive would go. She had been almost inconsolable when she saw what was before them. Norfolk Island gave her another option. At least there, the land was already cleared. Annie looked at Olive's face and saw her smile. Yes, Olive would leave.

The captain continued, "Ladies, it is proposed that those willing to accept this offer will be encouraged to marry and settle down on the island. Initially, there are to be six convict women of good standing and a few more hand-picked male convicts, but no more than ten. Marines and a few free settlers will accompany them." Again, he paused, looking at them. He could see Olive's grin, so again, he continued. "You have been selected, but this is a voluntary trip, and you may refuse to go. However, once there, you will be expected to work hard and settle down to make new lives for yourselves and, as I said, marry and have children."

Olive released Annie's hand and stepped forward. "I'll go, sir." Her friend Ann Inett joined her with the three Elizabeths, also volunteering for the work ahead on Norfolk Island. All had accepted the offer.

Annie knew that would leave her all but alone in the new settlement. However, she had no wish to marry. She was left standing by herself with the volunteers now to be escorted ashore to join the governor for further instructions. That five well-behaved women chosen from his ship made the doctor smile. He knew that only one of the women from the *Friendship* or *Charlotte* could now be offered to join the party. He knew that a convict by the name of Susannah Gough had had her name put forward. As the group disembarked down the rope ladder, the doctor tagged along with the chosen women and stood in the primitive camp, waiting for the arrival of the sixth girl. He was sure that Susannah would accept the offer. He was correct; she joined them soon afterwards.

Annie stood on deck watching the departing long boat with all her friends on board. She knew they would return after the meeting, but she was grieved that she would be all but alone. Although she had Betty Bird and Mary Love, they were much older than her, and she was not as close to either of them. Tearing her eyes from the meeting, she glanced upward to see clouds gathering once more. The weather was simply awful, and it fitted her mood. February at home was cold and bleak. Here, the sweltering days and violent storms at night made life perfectly miserable. Her sad mood had made her rethink her injury, and it brought her up short. But for her arm, she would have been offered a place, and she would have had to refuse as she refused to marry. Annie was pleased she had a broken arm as this released her from the possibility of being sent ashore with so many of the male convicts now wandering freely around the cleared area. Only that morning, she had seen the British flag raised, but the doctor had told them the proclamation had not yet been read to claim the land. The flag was now fluttering in the stiff breeze as it had done in Botany Bay. A group of red-coated marines were standing guard. Knowing their red coats were made from thick wool, Annie knew they would be feeling the heat terribly. As she watched, she felt the presence of young Jamie Campbell at her side.

His pubescent voice said, "Cousin James tells me we must go ashore soon, miss. I don't want you to leave me." He stepped close to her, and she slid her good arm around his shoulders. He was at that awkward age when he was caught between a boy and a man. That he still sought her out spoke of the closeness that had grown between the two, but he no longer sought to hold her hand as he initially had. She would not even be permitted to touch him soon. Annie saw that the young boy he had been on embarkation had now become a young man. At thirteen, he now stood at eye level with her. His voice had broken *en route,* and he had shot up since his leg had healed.

His words were almost an answer to her prayers. She felt that her work with the children may be what she was meant to do. It was important to keep them safe and educate them. "I'll be staying in the colony, Jamie, so I'll be here with you. With my broken arm, I may even be permitted to continue the lessons rather than work in the gardens. Let us wait and see what happens. I'm sure God has everything planned just right." She saw the head nod at her words. She gave him an extra squeeze. "Jamie, ask your cousin; he will know more than us both." The man-boy gazed adoringly at her. He missed his mama so much and had sought comfort from this convict woman who reminded him of his mother's loving care. To him, she was someone who he both liked and cared for, plus he trusted her.

The group returned after a few hours on shore.

Olive was deliriously happy. "Annie, we're going. The governor told us what the reports of Norfolk Island were like, and it sounds almost like paradise compared to here. I met some of the chosen men, and one has already caught my eye. His name is Nathaniel Lucas. Nate later sidled up to me, and, well, we got talking. I like him, Annie; I like him a lot." Olive released a long sigh of what could almost be called contentment.

Annie realised their departure would leave her, Maggie, Betty, and Mary Love alone in the raw settlement. Maggie had not been chosen because she had been somewhat unwell. Plus, she was too old at forty-five to marry and have children. Betty and Mary had farm skills, and even though they were older than Maggie, they could teach the others. Their age and skills precluded them from selection. Annie was really thrilled for her friends but sad that they were leaving; as she had said to Jamie, she knew God had another plan for her life. The look that Captain Campbell had given her made her wonder if he wanted her to remain close to him or to Jamie. She was already determined not to permit an illicit relationship of any sort. Although Oliver had taken her by force, she realised she was more than half in love with him even then. When he kissed her the second time, she responded very willingly and enjoyed feeling his muscular body through his linen shirt. She knew it was wrong, as he was already married to Verity. Later, his refusal of her offer confused her.

Throughout the entire journey, Captain Campbell was the perfect gentleman and did not make a move on any of the women. Annie's care of Jamie had been a delight for her. He was the oldest of the children on board, and she had also given him some Latin grammar lessons. Her father had studied classics while training for the ministry; therefore, she knew a few languages, and he encouraged her to learn what she wished. Latin, Hebrew, French, and a smattering of Ancient Greek were not the usual skills of a young girl. However, her mother has seen to her other talents that a young lady was required to have. She played the piano well, not that there was one in the new colony; she could sew and paint a passable picture. Few of those skills could now be put to any use at all, and little more had been required of a society lady but a pretty face, a good family tree, and the ability to have babies. She had them all. Sometime after they had started teaching, Jamie agreed to do some Latin and French, but the rest, he downed his chalk and shook his head, replying, "I'm unlikely to need those as a soldier miss. I want to follow in my cousin's footsteps and join up."

Annie stuck to Latin and French lessons quite happily as she had no books other than the Captain's Bible. Her French was good enough to follow a conversation easily. She had been able to understand Verity and Francois's conversation and, therefore, knew just how inappropriate it was for a married lady to speak so intimately to a man who was not her husband. In the time that Jamie had been waylaid with his broken leg, his spoken language skills had improved dramatically. She also described the various skills that a soldier would require. Realising he would need to write reports and journals, he reluctantly added drawing lessons to his curriculum.

After over a week on board while at anchor, and with most of the cell block of six already assigned to the trip to Norfolk Island, Annie and a few others still carrying broken limbs were soon all that would remain on board the *Lady Penrhyn*. The rest of the convict women were told they would go ashore the following morning. Throughout the night, there were catfights among the women over who owned what articles of clothing; the evening also brought another storm.

The dawn light saw the bedraggled group of women assembled on deck for landing. Many longboats were filled and loaded with filthy females. As soon as one filled, another loaded. Soon, the ten longboats were all heading for the shore to fight over who would settle in which tent. Betty and Mary hugged each of the remaining girls farewell.

Annie and her friends stood waving to the women as they landed. None were really sad, and the majority had gone. The deck below fell strangely silent, with over ninety fewer bodies to share their quarters. When the final group of girls had gone in the last long boat, she turned to go below to tend the horses when they heard the doctor gasp and shout.

"Oh no!" The doctor was shouting for the marines' attention but soon realised that they were fully aware of what was occurring and they were turning a blind eye. The girls turned to view the most horrific sight. Before even the last boatload of the women reached the relative safety of the women's tents, many of the convict men had grabbed them and tore the last remnants of their clothing from their bodies. The rutting that soon occurred throughout the clearing was horrific. One by one, the men egged each other on, each taking turns using their chosen woman. The poor girls were lying pinned down and violently abused. A few women were seen to encourage the men and offer their services with little resistance, but the majority were unwillingly violated. No one was exempted.

After living with such women below decks for so long, the girls remaining on the ship knew just who would be the ones to encourage the men to slake their lusts with them. However, they also knew of other young ones who had never been with a man. They stood witnessing the most abhorrent scene. All the long boats from their ship were ashore. Watching for a few minutes and realising there was nothing they could do, Annie and Olive turned in disgust and went below deck. Even the crew now on shore seemed to have turned a blind eye to the activity going on around them. Some may well have joined in, but the girls didn't stay to watch their friends get violated.

Annie had not long returned to her bunk when the brewing storm broke. A rumble of thunder made her jump. She smiled, thinking that this deluge would send the abusive men scuttling for cover. The remainder of the girls from on the ship soon joined her. They set about checking the now-empty cells for forgotten items. However, every bunk had been stripped bare, but they noticed that the slop buckets had not been emptied that morning. To while away their time, the girls emptied the buckets from the cells and sloshed the floors with seawater from the standing barrels. Their remaining days could at least be spent in a relatively clean area. They had all become far too unheeding to the stench of the excrement and the filth in which they were required to exist. With few women now below, Annie decided to wash. The drinking water barrel was nearly full, and her desire to be clean was suddenly vital. She remembered the thorough wash she had wanted after Oliver had abused her. She now felt that shame again, not that it had happened to her, but witnessing the violation of the women on shore brought back that night's actions. Today, the smell hit Annie as she went below deck. The scent of some exotic tree on shore smelt clean and fresh, and the heat of the sun seemed to intensify the odour. The girls had just finished their chores when what sounded like an explosion made them all jump. The storm seemed directly overhead, and the lightning bolt that hit seemed very close as the thunder growled simultaneously. Annie went to check on her precious horses. They had not yet been unloaded as there were no stockyards for them.

Running footsteps on the deck above soon brought the crewman in charge of the horses. His duty of care for the beasts had seen him descend below to check on the well-being of his charges. Annie, of course, was already there, calming them.

"Cor, miss, that was a close call. The sheep pen in the middle of the settlement got hit by a lightning rod directly from above. It was like a punishment for the camp for the actions we had just witnessed. Miss, the tree in the middle of the stockyard is smoking, and I can see some beasties lying nearby. Five by my count, but there could be more. I'm so glad the horses ain't been taken ashore yet." The crewman set about helping Annie settle the startled animals. They had long since used the chaff and now had to use the local grasses and rushes for the floor of the horses' cells.

When the storm passed towards dusk, the doctor came below deck. "Annie, Olive, ladies, I need a quick word. For some reason, the captain has permitted the crew to make free with some grog tonight. I suggest you lock yourselves in your cells. After what we witnessed onshore, I dare not put you all at risk by their behaviour." He locked the cell door, and then, amazingly, he handed Annie the key. "Let yourselves out when you wish, but be careful. I imagine there will be quite some party on deck tonight. My suggestion is to stay well clear." With those words of advice, he left them locked in their safe cell. Having been fed, the girls settled into the now silent night. Noises from the shore were not too edifying, and they presumed more carnal activities were occurring. They were all pleased they were not there. Knowing they were safe and locked into their cell, they settled down to sleep.

Annie's arm ached, but before she slept, she thanked God for it; otherwise, she would have been violated like their friends. She smiled, then turned over and slept. As the doctor predicted, they were roused from their slumbers by some of the now-drunken crew attempting to reach them. Knowing they had the keys, they silently thanked the doctor for his forethought. The revelry on deck grew to a crescendo, then quieted as the men fell down drunk. A few had come and rattled their cell door, but the girls were left in peace.

Had any catastrophe occurred to the ship, the drunken crew would have been useless in attempting to save it. Thankfully, the night passed in relative quiet. The storm's return overhead once more disturbed their slumbers for the remainder of the darkness.

The dawn light saw Annie unlock their cell and quietly go and check on the horses. They would need attention, and even with one hand, she could see to their needs and refill their water buckets. The other girls roused as she opened the barred door. With no battle over food and no catfighting, the early morning passed in an unusual calm. The fresh air filled their lungs, and the sun shone through the open hatches. The occupants were unfamiliar with the absence of the rabble's noises below decks, and the silence had woken Annie in the pre-dawn light. She had just returned to the cell when the doctor's steps were heard descending to their deck.

The doctor's question, "How did you fare last night, ladies?" received replies of thanks from the two cells of girls.

Annie was approaching but heard her friend reply. Olive said, "But for you, sir, we would have received the same attention as those so recently landed. The crew were so inebriated that they could not work out how to unlock the doors." She chuckled at the fumbling attempt the various crewmen had made while the girls feigned sleep.

He nodded. "I figured they would try that. After yesterday's shenanigans, I have come to tell you that Governor Phillip called an onshore meeting. I am to accompany you all. Those injured will also be given light chores, even if it's looking after the children. Each one of you will need to pull their weight." He retook possession of the key and escorted the girls on deck. "You will eat your breakfast onshore with the other women. I'm not sure if you will return here, so pack your possessions and bring them with you, just in case."

Annie's heart sank. She knew the horses would be left on board until the small jetty was complete. Hopefully, that will be quickly finished. She had watched the sheep pen construction, and the cattle and horse yard were nearing completion. As they landed some thirty minutes later, she saw the remains of the tree in the middle of the yard. It was still smoking and split asunder. The dead sheep had been removed, and as they had died in such a way as they had, their carcasses were butchered and consumed. A pig had also been caught in the blast, and it was also in the process of being hacked up.

Governor Phillip instructed all fifteen hundred members of the fleet and as many crew as possible to be seated in a large circle, with the women and marines towards the outside and the six hundred or so convict men sitting in the middle.

The angry governor then issued his orders and told of his commission from the king. "After the disgusting exhibition that occurred yesterday after the women landed, no man shall be permitted in or near the women's tents, or they will be fired upon. With the supply of food so low and the death of so many of the stock *en route*, stealing stock or provisions will be a death penalty. Be warned, do not take my direction lightly. I will also say that death may not be by hanging or even firing squad, but banishment from the settlement. With no provision of food, you will be as good as dead. We are halfway around the world from England, and as you have all realised, returning home by foot is impossible."

It was on the 7th of February, 1788, the governor inaugurated the colony of New South Wales. Towards the end of his speech, he said, "The laws of our country, England, will, of course, be introduced in New South

Wales, and there is one that I would wish to take place from the moment His Majesty's forces take possession of the country: That there can be no slavery in a free land, and consequently no slaves."

Despite these words, he instigated severe punishments to the point of death for what seemed like small issues on paper.

Everyone knew full well that stealing provisions from their stores could bring down the entire project.

Annie knew that many would still try to take what belonged to everyone.

The large group sat on the foreshore, listening to his speech. Life ahead of them would be hard, but for many, even this was better than they had been in England. Nothing the governor said was a surprise except that anyone stealing food or stock would be executed or banished, which amounted to the same thing. As the doctor expected, the women did not go back on board the *Lady Penrhyn*. They were allocated quarters in the newly erected women's tents.

The tents were relatively safe as they were near the reverend and his wife. They settled in as best they could. At least on the ship, there were bunks of sorts; here, they had little comforts.

Annie tried to educate the children. There looked to be about thirty children of teachable age and about twenty too young to learn. She had no idea how many were children of the marines or how many were convicts. The large group of settlers were told to make friends with the natives but not to give them tools as they could not be replaced.

The doctor came and sat near her and filled in some information for her. "Annie, I have discovered that we are not all English. There are over three hundred and thirty-five non-English folks here. One hundred and thirty Irishmen, two from the Channel Isles, thirty-three from Scotland, and nine Welshmen, plus men from other lands, but they are not all convicts."

Annie nodded. "I saw one of the ship's cooks was a negro man."

The doctor said, "Yes, true, there are twelve Africans, West Indians or Native Americans plus fifteen others from Madagascar, West Indies, Holland, France, Germany, Norway, Portugal, Jamaica, Sweden, Bengal, and India. However, there are also some different religions. The reverend said there are nine Jews, and I presume most of the Irish will be Roman Catholics. However, many of these folk are not convicts; some are crew, and others are militia. Only one man has come free, and the governor is wondering what to do with him. There is talk of giving him the role of policing the rules. His name is John Smith and the governor has made him a constable."

Annie said, "Do you know how many children there are?"

The doctor smiled and chuckled at her question. "I wondered if you would keep teaching. I believe there are fifty, but about half of them are too young to learn."

Chapter 13   New Life Begins

$\mathcal{T}$he injured women had to be checked by the settlement's doctor.

Most were able to head down directly, and many were allocated jobs of watering plants or caring for the tiny children while their able-bodied mothers worked. At least on the ship, there were bunks of sorts; here, they had little in the way of comforts.

Reverend and Mrs Johnson visited the women. Mrs Johnson sought out Annie and Olive and thanked them for their work on board teaching the children.

Unbeknownst to Annie, Jamie Campbell had spoken in glowing terms of Annie's skills. When the lad was told of no further classes, he asked if Annie would be teaching while her arm healed. The education of the many children of both convicts and the marines was something they had not considered.

Mary Johnson didn't think she could handle twenty-five children by herself. As Annie was currently incapable of doing much physical work, Mrs Johnson sought her out to ask for assistance. Only she did so by approaching the official officer. Jamie's cousin then spoke to Reverend Johnson, who took it upon himself to notify Annie.

The Johnson's tent was close to the women's tent, and with encouragement from his wife, he set out to find this educated girl. Upon entering the women's tents, the reverend gentleman said, "Annie Gentle, please come forward."

Within minutes of meeting Reverend Richard and Mary Johnson, Annie felt that once more she was with loving people like her parents. She discovered that being literate and injured, she was now officially assigned to Mrs Johnson to assist with teaching the older children.

Olive had hoped to join Annie, teaching until she was to leave, but she was sent to the new gardens to learn how to farm and grow things. She didn't really mind this, as she needed to learn how to care for the plants. Olive was also required to attend various meetings for what was required at Norfolk Island, but these were a delight to her as she was permitted to see Nathaniel and encouraged even to spend time getting to know him. Choosing a marriage partner was not something she would have had in England, and she liked Nate a lot.

Betty Bird and Mary Love were now giving instructions on the little they knew about gardening.

~

Alas, despite the governor's warnings about the consequences of rule-breaking, less than three days after the warnings, a man was caught in the women's tents and marched out of camp with his hands bound behind his back. The soldiers returned without him, and Annie presumed he had been set free into the bush as they had not heard a gunshot. Annie did not know if he was unbound when he reached the edge of the settlement or if he had been killed. She dared not enquire.

With the temptation of women so close and many of the women quite wonton in their morals, the following day, the carpenter from the *Prince of Wales* repeated the offence. He, too, was quite literally drummed out of camp. His hands were tied behind his back, and the marines marched him to the outskirts of the camp with the fife and drum beating their tune. He, too, was banished to his own devices. He was given no supplies or water. Annie wondered if he would sneak back on board.

Later that evening, a third man, a convict, attacked and struck one of the sentries. Annie did not know if it was a sentry of the women's tents or the food store room. She heard a yell and heard that the guilty convict was soon arrested. He was sentenced to one hundred and fifty lashes. The man's punishment seemed harsh, but the governor knew he had to set hard penalties, or the infant colony would not survive. The greed of just a few could endanger them all. Annie had no idea how much food they had, but Mrs Johnson had mentioned that much on their ship had been spoiled on the journey here. She was aware the situation on the *Lady Penrhyn* was similar and presumed other ships were much the same.

~

Two days after the governor's charge to the new colonists, the captain of the French ship *Astrolabe*, which was still anchored in Botany Bay, and two other French officers came to visit Governor Phillip.

They brought despatches for France that were to be sent back with the returning English ships. The French vessels would continue their voyage of exploration at some future date. During the course of their conversation, they reported their activities to Governor Phillip. They breezily mentioned that they had a run-in with the natives and had shot some. The governor had spent time with these gentle people and had traded with them. The interest of the indigenous men in the clothing and tools had endeared them to the Englishman. Hence, reports of some twenty or more of the Aboriginals being killed for attempted theft horrified Governor Phillip. He delicately questioned the Frenchman to get to the bottom of why the tribal men should attack. Only then did French officers admit that they had shot at them to keep them from disturbing them as they continued to pilfer the supplies they had.

Governor Phillip picked up on a single comment that perhaps one of the French crew members may have acted in an untoward manner toward one of the natives. He wondered if one of the Frenchmen had accosted one of the native females, as he was sure the tribal men he had met would not have permitted such a dalliance with their women. The females had not even been in evidence during their meetings with the tribe. Maybe they didn't realise that the ships there now were not the friendly Englishmen.The governor knew they had been no danger to the French at all. The Aboriginal men merely wanted to trade as they had done with the English.

Although, during their first meeting, the French captain agreed that they had no intention of making trouble with the natives, this was exactly what had occurred. On this visit, Monsieur De La Perouse also reported that they now had a strong fort and three big guns mounted for the protection of their possessions. The French captain went on to describe a hail of stones pelted at them and that some of his crew had received injuries. After their experience in Samoa, the Frenchmen had built a mini-fort to protect the boats they had come to rebuild or repair. They must have done this quickly, as it had only been days since the English had set sail from Botany Bay. Governor Phillip knew that few such stones were in evidence in the area, although they had seen large cockle shells in the sand. He listened without interrupting and grew increasingly angry. Knowing this boded ill for the English colonists, the governor was not impressed. His ire at their actions was barely held in check. He had befriended these lovely people, and even the king had issued orders to make friends with them. The natives would not understand the difference between the two groups of white people, and Governor Phillip knew that reprisals would soon occur.

The three Frenchmen were escorted to the edge of the English camp, and Governor Phillip watched as they were absorbed into the bushland. Once they had gone, he ordered that the soldiers not fire on the natives without undue cause. Usually, their men pilfered food, and the law would fall on them severely.

Over the next few days, various convicts were reported missing. As there was no possibility of escape, no great effort was made to find them. They were sure they would return in good time. Thirst and hunger were their enemy, and both would be enough enticement for the escapees to return. Flogging was an apt punishment for the meagre supply of vittles. He didn't even care if they had joined the French and absconded; the fewer troublemakers that remained, the better.

~

Annie and Olive received word about the expected departure date for Norfolk Island. It was to be only three days, on February 14th.

Now well again, Doctor Altree was sent as the medic with this expedition along with another young doctor who would be his assistant.

The farewell between Olive Gaskin and Annie Soames was hard. Olive hugged her friend carefully, but her excitement was infectious. She said, "Annie, I feel as though this will be getting my life back on track. With a new start, I think I will return to my real name, Olivia Gascoigne. I did not correct them when it was recorded as Olive Gaskin, but now I shall."

Annie found talking hard, as the lump in her throat made it difficult. With a false smile, she hugged her friend farewell and managed to say, "I'll pray for you, Olivia Gascoigne; please do the same for me but as Annie Soames."

Olive nodded and turned to join Nathaniel, who stood waiting for her. Hand in hand, they set off on their new life together. Annie caught a smile they gave each other on meeting. It made her gasp. Olivia had fallen in love. The young couple were starting their life together, but seeing them so happy made Annie miss Oliver even more. She would never have a happy ending like her friend. She would, in all likelihood, never see Oliver again. Annie thought that it was unlikely she would make it out of this place alive; even if she were permitted to return to England, her life there was over. Sadness overwhelmed her.

The bitter-sweet departure of her friends left Annie somewhat lost as the ships raised their anchors and were towed out into the channel by longboats. Annie sank to the ground in despair. She had managed to hold back her tears so she would not dampen her friends' joy of what lay before them, but she watched, almost unable to breathe, as her friends sailed out of sight. Grief overwhelmed her. Her own resolve, however, was not as strong as she wished. With her broken arm aching terribly, she knew that she needed to have the doctor reset the bones. As such, there was little she could do for work. Even making her bunk tidy was somewhat of a chore.

Annie was enjoying a fit of melancholy when she felt Mrs Johnson's gentle hand resting softly on her shoulder. Annie turned her tear-stained face to see that the minister's wife had come to her side.

Mary Johnson cleared a few twigs from the grassy bank and then took her place beside Annie. "Dear, parting in such circumstances is such sweet sorrow, as Juliet said to her Romeo, for we know that Olivia Gascoigne, as I believe that is her real name, is going to what she desires. I feel she and Nathaniel will make a fine pair, but that leaves you bereft of your friends."

Annie knew that. Her gulping sobs showed her distress at being left behind. She was so far from all those she loved, and the aloneness of this place was now setting in. As an only child, she had never been lonely, but here, surrounded by so many, she had never felt so alone in her life. After a few more minutes, her weeping eased. An occasional sob still escaped her, but Mary Johnson seemed to understand.

As the top of the ship's mast vanished behind the headland, Mary drew Annie onto her shoulder. "Annie, I need your assistance far more than I realised, dear."

Annie looked at the kind lady and wondered what she meant.

Mary smiled and continued, "You have a champion in the camp, a very young man named James Duncan Campbell. He tells me your papa is a clergyman, too."

Annie nodded. She sniffed in a very unladylike manner. She had nothing to blow her nose on, and she absolutely refused to wipe it on her sleeve, so she sniffed.

Mary smiled again and passed her a lawn handkerchief. "You can return that when clean, dear."

Annie blew and gave her a small smile.

Mary spoke softly, saying, "Doctor Bowes-Smith said that as you are injured, as you know, you will remain under my care until you can work in the gardens. In the meantime, I am a friend and a shoulder to weep upon."

Annie turned into the caring woman's shoulder and did just that.

Once more, Annie gave way to her shattered emotions, only this time with a hint of happiness.

With her life now given a little direction, Annie set about making the best of what had become her lot in life. Mary Johnson was so like her mother in how she approached people that Annie could not help but love the woman she was now assigned to help.

Only days after the departure of the ships to Norfolk Island, Reverend Johnson held another church service. He was determined to build some form of a church; however, God's provision of an open-air area must suffice in the interim. He had been permitted to have glass squares brought for the windows of the proposed building, and they sat in the storeroom awaiting the construction of a suitable edifice. Being industrious, the reverend had already cut some timbers and set them to dry as he knew that the windows could not be made with green wood or they would warp. Governor Phillip promised the building was on a list to be constructed.

Mary Johnson and Annie soon sorted the children into two age groups. The other girls with broken limbs or injuries looked after the very small ones, and Annie and Mary began educating the older ones.

Annie was delighted to discover that Reverend Johnson had brought boxes of Bibles, slates, and chalk with him.

Jamie was thrilled that his lessons were to continue. Soon, the older free children and three young convicts under the age of fourteen were sitting and doing lessons with slates and chalk.

The three convict children, Elizabeth Hayward, John Hudson, and George Youngson, were starting to read from scratch.

Jamie Campbell explained to them that this place was a new beginning for them all, and he told them why they needed to learn new things. Here, class status was irrelevant; if they worked hard, they could become what they wished. Nothing was beyond them, but they had to learn to read and write.

Annie smiled at his words, but she realised he was correct. She had been taken to meet the new surgeon again, as Doctor Bowes-Smith would soon leave with the *Lady Penrhyn* when it departed for China.

The resident surgeon, Doctor John White, checked her arm. It needed realignment.

Leaning against Doctor Bowes-Smith's chest, Doctor White reset it. He also moved the splint slightly and re-bandaged it.

Somehow, Annie bore the pain and did not pass out. Leaning against this man's chest reminded her of the last time Oliver had taken her in his arms. The ache of her arm eased, and the pain was now tolerable. However, the pain in her heart remained.

At least now, Annie found that she could move her fingers again without them tingling. The regular movement and the perilous descent from the ship down a rope ladder one-handed had moved the bones slightly. With the limb reset, she could finally sleep peacefully and pain-free.

The area's odour wafted through the wide valley, and the summer heat intensified the stench. The small settlement needed sanitation. Although two privies had been dug, toileting facilities were inadequate, and the bushes around the camp were soon covered with excrement. When the rains came in torrents, this flooded into their only freshwater, causing the creek to become fouled quickly. Dysentery soon set into the colony. More public facilities were desperately needed.

With the stores unpacked, it was found that half the volume remained from what they expected to arrive with. Food was rationed to seven pounds of salted beef or four pounds of salt pork, three pints of dried peas, seven pounds of bread flour, six ounces of butter, and one pound of flour or rice per week. Female convicts and the marines' wives received two-thirds of the male convict ration weekly. It was so scant an amount that the convicts' anger caused more than ire. Thefts were followed by floggings and banishment.

With rations unable to be resupplied, Annie knew there couldn't be any waste. If a person couldn't cook, they didn't eat. There was no facility for a communal kitchen, but groups gathered and combined their rations to bulk up the meal. Thefts from stores brought dire consequences. These were brought home to the settlement when three convicts were caught stealing. Each man received a sentence of one hundred and fifty lashes.

Most of the convicts were forced to watch the flaying. The audience was splattered with the blood from the pulverised flesh from their backs by the vicious scourging of the cat-of-nine-tails. From past experience, the onlookers were aware that if the convict passed out, they would be nursed back to enough health until they were well enough to receive the remainder of their penalty. It was unlikely that they would live long enough to receive the full punishment.

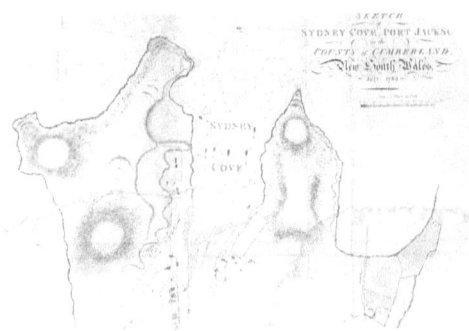

Chapter 14   Farming Failure
February 1788

$\mathcal{T}$he temperature in this new land was life-sappingly hot. At 105°F and nearly 100% humidity, some crew decided a dip in the clear water was in order.

It was the afternoon after the Norfolk Island contingent departed, and a shout of astonishment was heard from the foreshore. Many ran to see what caused the call and found two incidents occurring simultaneously.

Two lads from the *Prince of Wales* had been teasing their cook by shaking the hawker rope connected to the shore. They fell off, and the three ended up in the water. Sadly, the African cook could not swim and sank beneath the surface.

While they were searching for him, another shout was heard. One of the men on the foreshore saw an eight-foot crocodile sliding into the water. A larger fourteen-foot one had been seen in the shrubbery near the camp earlier in the month, but today, this one seemed to be interested in the missing cook as it swam towards the splashing.

Screams abounded, and they drew a crowd.

Annie and Mary Johnson tried to keep the children away, but Jamie and the older ones ran to the shoreline to observe what was happening.

What more evil creatures would this land produce? So far, they had seen sharks, snakes, shiny black spiders and now these alligator-like creatures. Earlier that week, a large black spider had been found slowly walking across the floor of the women's tent. Snakes had invaded other dwellings, and ticks were also a problem, as were the numerous flies, mosquitoes, and midges. The undulating song of the raucous cicadas was like a heartbeat of the bush. The ebb and flow of their cry was like the breathing of an unseen giant. The constant vibrations grated on their ears, and some evenings, the insects sang well into the night, making sleep difficult. Mornings started with the raucous calls of the myriad of unusual birds that abounded in this land.

With fear now etched into the watchers' eyes, the cook's body was eventually fished out of the sea. Thankfully, the crocodilian creature had not attacked him.

More settlers were falling victim to dysentery every day. No one was immune to the ravages of this illness. Even some of the ship's captains and crew fell ill.

Thankfully, no one had smallpox or any of the other lethal diseases that spread through the villages at home.

Doctor Bowes-Smith had mentioned that Surgeon John White had brought some smallpox scabs with him for variolation or inoculation of the newborn children and people of the colony. Both doctors had described to Richard Johnson how these dried scabs were placed up the nostrils of the children and inoculated against smallpox. This system had been used for over fifty years and seemed to work well. Lady Mary Wortley Montagu discovered this treatment in Constantinople in 1717 and brought the information back to England with her. Four years later, the Princess of Wales advocated further testing, and they discovered that it worked. Since then, it had been used as a widespread treatment for the killer disease. Doctor White planned to ensure that all those born in the colony would be protected from the disease.

The hospital, such as it was, was treating convicts; the free settlers were usually treated in their tents unless they were desperately ill, and the crew remained on their ships and treated by the sawbones on board. Three convicts had died in just one day; more were ill and likely to follow them; to top it off, the water situation was becoming serious as they needed fresh, clean drinking water, and the Tank Stream was now fouled by effluent washing into the creek.

The hospital was just a canvas awning, admittedly a large one, but still, it was just a tent and entirely ill-equipped for such a major dilemma. Doctor John White was in charge, and he was the doctor Annie had met earlier. He was the official surgeon for the settlement and had some medics working under his authority.

It was quite evident that the situation he was now facing meant that many of the leading citizens of the new colony could face the same dire circumstances as the convicts. Initially unaware of the cause of the illness, it was spreading indiscriminately. Eventually, anyone who drank the water became ill, and there was not enough wine or spirits to go around. Even boiling the water was not viable, as there were not enough pots to supply the entire colony of over two thousand souls. Most were crew or soldiers.

With sickness and hunger now sweeping through the small settlement, the date of the first month in the bay passed with no acknowledgement or celebration.

The tension in the infant settlement was tangible, and when four convicts, Barrett, Lovell, Hall and one other, were caught stealing a live pig and bread, they received the full force of the new laws.

The governor had already warned everyone about the instant

consequences of theft of supplies. All were sentenced to death. Barrett had already been part of a planned mutiny and was a well-known troublemaker; however, he had been warned, and now the consequence was he was to lose his life.

The following day, a large native fig tree with small leaves was chosen for the hangings. It was slightly to the south and out of direct sight of the settlement. Barrett, the instigator of the crime, was hung from the new gallows tree and buried nearby. Rather than follow him immediately, Lovett and Hall were given a twenty-four-hour reprieve.

Soon after dawn the following morning, the two condemned men, plus two more who had been caught stealing the evening before, were marched to the tree to await their execution.

As they mounted the ladder to the gallows, the governor, being lenient, issued the four of them a reprieve. However, one was chosen to be the settlement's hangman instead of banishment. Death may have been preferable to the other three as they were banished from the colony. They may have made for the French ships but were never seen again.

The French reported that they had refused them passage.

The sanitation situation was now critical.

Everyone was still defecating where they wished, and with the heavy rains, the vile sludge flowed into the drinking water. With over one hundred patients ill, many were now housed in the tent hospital; something needed to be done urgently. The doctor called in for assistance in the hospital, and Annie was surprised to find that even Doctor Bowes-Smith and the other ship's doctors were hard at work in the overheated tent.

She had gone in to get her arm seen again. Even though the aching had eased, she was unwilling to trust it for strength. Having already had it reset once, and that had hurt terribly, she did not wish to have that occur again. Twisting it was strictly forbidden.

Only days after her visit to the hospital, Annie took over all the classes. Mary Johnson was now tending to her husband, who had fallen ill with the debilitating illness.

Annie liked Reverend Richard, as he reminded her so much of her beloved father. To hear he was now prostrated with this sickness was sad. Mary kept vigil by her husband's side while Annie kept up the lessons as best she could. Instructing such a range of children was taxing at best.

~

Hours blended into days and days into weeks.

Each person was fighting to survive. Annie made friends with one of the native girls, who showed her what was safe to eat.

The plans for the settlement's gardens were finally showing some progress, but they still needed to be planted with a full crop. When they were sown, the heat had initially been a setback. Many of the seedlings succumbed, but those that survived seemed to have now settled into their new surroundings. At best, this crop would only be used for seed for another one. Far more fertile land was required to grow enough food to feed the settlement.

Privies were finally built and now set well back from the water source, and hopefully, the illnesses would ease. Water was vital to life's progress in the colony, and the Tank Stream was their only clean water source. Once the water source contamination had been identified as the problem, three wells were being dug near the hospital tent.

Richard Johnson's health made some progress, and he was soon moved from the hospital to their tent. Mary and Annie continued to nurse him. Soon, he was back on his feet but remained on light duties for a while. He had some marriages to perform, but otherwise, his duties were somewhat curtailed.

Annie also took to watering their precious young fruit trees. In his spare time, Reverend Johnson had found a decent plot of soil and planted the small citrus trees they had purchased in Cape Town. They kept these in their cabin and tended them carefully.

In the middle of this illness outbreak, the governor assembled a group of intrepid explorers, including Captain John Hunter, Captain Arthur Sever, and Lieutenant William Bradley, accompanied by Seaman Thomas Webb and one other crew member from the *Sirius*. The group set off in a small cutter to investigate other bays to the north. Captain Hunter had already surveyed the local bays in Port Jackson and made a detailed map. The stunningly beautiful bay was vast, but Broken Bay, which was to the north, needed investigation.

On many of these ventures, they encountered friendly natives and often sought to communicate with them. They carried trinkets of beads and straw hats for trade. On this exploration trip to the north, the governor elected to join them. Captain Cook's maps indicated other bays that may have better water supplies than Port Jackson.

The day after the cutter passed through the heads, a fourteen-foot creature that looked like another lizard-like beast was seen circling one of the ships in the harbour. One of the sailors declared that it looked like an alligator, but its snout was a different shape. It was more bobbled than the long, wide mouth of the American alligator. The creature sank beneath the surface and vanished. This animal was a third larger than the previous sighting the week before, so it was not the same creature. It also was not one of the huge land goannas they saw shinnying up the trees. This beast had been sighted soon after landing.

Annie heard all about it from Jamie, who arrived full of exciting news when he came for classes. Being free, he was one of the few who could wander where he wished. He was often seen haunting the foreshore near the ships or with his cousin. He was excited that there were sharks in the bay and crocodilians, too. She ruffled his hair and laughed, as only a young boy would be excited over such lethal creatures.

The changes on the foreshore occurred quickly in the short time the fleet had been in the bay. Gone were all the trees, and a tent city had sprung up on the western side of the Tank Stream. Tents were designated for the governor's residence, his senior officers, and more for the barracks and convict abodes. A prefabricated house was in the process of being erected for the governor. The first of the female tents were up close to the reverend, and the men were near the marines. Various marines who had brought families also had their own tents in between the two areas. More tents would be erected as soon as they had people spare.

When the time elapsed for the governor's party to return, the remaining leaders were afraid of the group's demise as the day came and went with no sign of them. It was no use sending out a search party as no one knew exactly where the group had gone. So they worked hard and set up the new town, praying they would return.

The Johnsons had their tent near the hospital and close to the sloping ground designated as the assembly area. Thankfully, both were nowhere near the men's quarters; therefore, Annie did not need to be near the male convicts for any reason.

In the next bay eastwards from the settlement, the clearing for a second larger farm was now occurring. The cut saplings were again stored for later use, and hundreds of men worked the designated garden. The red-coated marines stood guard in the sweltering heat as the convicts cut the trees, split some for fencing, dug the root balls out, and tilled the virgin soil. Although this bay could have been better dirt, it was all they currently had to work with.

In England, the soil had been tilled for thousands of years, and the workers had never struck dirt that had never been cultivated before. At home, farms had been fertilised, improved, tilled, and worked for generations. Here, the work was backbreaking and soul-crushing. Even getting a pick in the compacted earth was difficult. The heat often overcame the workers. However, the changes were occurring quickly with so many hands working together. When they did manage to break the soil, they had to be careful of the shiny black spiders that they had been told were lethal.

In the short time since the farm was started, nearly five acres had been cleared in the second garden area. Kangaroos were seen grazing in the bay, and the realisation that fencing would also be needed added to the time required for the garden preparation.

While the men were doing this, women were sent off collecting local 'greens' and samphire to eat. This last plant they called the asparagus of the sea. The succulent leaves grew along the waterways and were a known edible food source at home; although a slightly different species than in England, it tasted similar. The greens they knew they could eat because of the interaction with the native women. They had been observed collecting them, and through means of hand language, they knew them to be edible. However, what was an adequate source of food for the thirty or so Aboriginal people in a tribe was woefully inadequate for a group of fifteen hundred hungry people. They needed to get the gardens growing and fast.

Trading food was a regular occurrence. The Aboriginals would swap freshly netted fish for various other foodstuffs, like speared wallabies. Soon after the first landing, some of the children were befriended by the indigenous children who had come to collect the pink or white berries on the surrounding trees. These fruits were found to be delicious, crunchy like an apple, but with a taste of crisp pear. The native children spat out the pips from the centre, and the settlers' children were soon invited to join the harvest. Sadly, the trees were quickly stripped of their bounteous crop, and the fruit was rationed out with the other supplies. Richard Johnson decided to collect and plant some of the seeds.

While the other girls' injuries healed, Annie was still not cleared to work in the gardens. Her break had been far more severe; with both bones in her arm broken, it was mobile in the wrong place. With the minister now well on the road to recovery, she taught alongside Mary Johnson. The older children now had to do their share of the work. This entailed collecting wood for the many fires required to cook their meals and, where possible, collecting shellfish along the water's edge. Again, with fifteen hundred to feed, the oysters and other shellfish in the nearby bays soon were exhausted. With the morning chores done, the day's heat hit with a vengeance; the children settled down under the shady trees to be educated.

Once the children were released after classes, and this may be due to rain rather than the time of day, Mary and Annie were often seen walking along the foreshore, often arm in arm.

Annie's left arm was still useless, but that did not stop her from paying a call to the horses. They were now in a stable yard behind the governor's tent. This was an easy walk from the Johnson's place. The bay stallion would neigh and whinny at her approach.

Mary laughed at his antics and was amazed at the bond her charge had formed with the magnificent beast. He would often run back and forth along the fence as she drew near. Her offerings to him were usually only a handful of local grasses plucked as she walked, but he accepted them willingly. The mares and colts were amazingly healthy; one had dropped her foal. The new filly would become one to build up the herd.

Once the governor returned, Annie wondered if she could continue these visits as they were his private animals. However, there was no sign of this illustrious man. The cutter was now well overdue. He had left on March 2nd and was due back a week later, and having only taken supplies for a short time, the colony was worried.

It was not until the ninth day that the small cutter was finally seen returning, with the explorers none the worse for their adventure. The two Sirius crew members were excitedly bubbling over the expansive bay they had mapped. Thomas Webb, one of the sailors from the *Sirius*, was waxing lyrical to Jamie over the flats there that may one day make the most wonderful shipbuilding ground. The Webbs were a nautical family that was into boat building in England. His brother Robert was also a crewman on the *Sirius* but had gone to Norfolk Island with Olive, and another brother, James, though still in England, was a skilled shipbuilder. All the men in the family had sailing in their blood.

It did not take much to get Thomas talking to Jamie about the bays' possibilities. Jamie then related the trip to the Johnsons and Annie before class the following morning.

The bay to the north, marked on Cook's maps as Broken Bay, was of great interest for further development; however, the decision to remain in Port Jackson had been made. There were wider bays here that were easier to build on.

While the governor had been away, two of the convicts had been speared and killed by some natives; two others were missing. They had been collecting rushes on the water's edge and had not realised they had trespassed on some sacred area. Or mayhap it was because the colony had eaten so much of their food. For whatever reason, tensions were now high, and soldiers were on alert.

~

Jamie arrived at class one morning in early March. "Miss Annie, my cousin James said them Frenchies is gone."

Annie smiled. "Those Frenchmen are gone, Jamie. Correct English, please." His words had brought relief to her, though.

Jamie sighed resignedly. "Those Frenchmen, miss. Well, they have sailed away. No one knows if they went north or south, but they have gone. Cousin James said all that is left is a sign that marks the grave of something called a Curé."

Annie explained, "That's a French word for a minister of religion, Jamie. Like a vicar or Reverend Johnson. It is sad that the man died in a foreign land, and I doubt that he will even be remembered." The discussion about the French killing the tribe on the southern bay had disturbed the Johnsons and Annie greatly.

~

With all the livestock unloaded the fortnight after they arrived, they took their time unloading the dry stores. They used a hastily constructed jetty in Sydney Cove near the entry to the Tank Stream. The food and other provisions were placed in the newly constructed stone-based storerooms. This building was the most precious of any in their settlement; it was guarded twenty-four hours a day.

It was six weeks since the first ship had arrived in Port Jackson. The food storeroom was one of the first solid structures completed, as the food was the one thing the young colony could not be without. It was made from cut saplings and then daubed with mud, which dried to a firm render in the summer sun's heat. The barrels and grain bags were stored here, and armed sentries were placed outside to protect the meagre supplies from theft. The sandstone base had been quarried from the headland near the new gardens.

Rats from the ships had also become a problem as they ate through anything, and there were also local bush rats. Even the wattle and daub buildings were not impermeable from these. They also had to be stopped from attacking the stores, but how? Only a solid stone building would achieve that.

The ships also contained a prefabricated building that was to be erected as soon as possible. The site was currently being prepared. This would become the centre of government for the time being. With the ships now emptied of their precious cargoes, the *Charlotte*, *Lady Penrhyn,* and the *Scarborough* were discharged from naval duty; however, they did not leave port immediately as illness had struck some of their crew. Doctor Bowes-Smith was now attending patients on board the *Lady Penrhyn*. Unwilling to travel with an ailing crew, the vessels stayed close to the settlement.

There were now over two hundred ill with dysentery, and theft of stores was increasing. The guard was doubled on the storehouse, and punishments were now carried out in sight of the convicts to deter them.

It didn't work. Food production efforts began in earnest, with more area cleared and prepared for gardens. Extending food supplies was the main goal of the convict labour force from morning to evening. A few, like Thomas Eccles, had little experience with gardening. Betty Bird and Mary Love worked with him when possible, teaching him about the health of the soil.

Of the hundreds of animals purchased in Cape Town, few remained alive. Even the governor's sheep had died from eating an unknown toxic plant. The loss of each beast was a great tragedy, as they were supposed to be the colony's breeding stock.

Annie's care of the horses proved to be their saving grace. None had perished, and they had all arrived uninjured, if somewhat undernourished. Along with the horses and twelve of the pigs, although most of the sows were due to deliver their litters very soon, a mere twenty-nine sheep survived both the trip and the first storm that hit the day the women were landed, and one pig had also been struck by lightning. Many of the poultry had died en route from various causes; however, about a dozen turkeys, some geese and ducks remained. Only two hundred of the chickens were alive, and these were to be bred as quickly as possible. These beasts and birds now had to be the foundation stock for the colony. None were to be consumed. When one or two were stolen or died, the entire flock or herd was in jeopardy and, thus, the colony.

Tragically, only seven cattle, six cows and one bull survived the voyage, and that again was because Annie had insisted on the life-saving slings during the storms. They were the most valued beasts as they were to provide both milk and meat. Annie's care of the stock had meant they, too, survived the journey. They were kept close to camp but were permitted to graze as there was not enough dry fodder for them.

Hunting parties were sent out, but they often returned empty-handed.

When possible, food was traded with the natives. The settlers had large seine nets that caught large schools of mullet. The native men would then trade speared kangaroos for a quantity of fish. This worked well for both groups. Initially, the natives stole some fish until they realised they would willingly be traded for other food. A brisk trade became regular whenever a school was netted.

Captain Hunter spent much time exploring the bays and inlets surrounding their new settlement. He often sought out Richard Johnson for a chat when he was in the colony and came to know Annie quite well.

Annie liked him as he never made any move on her. He was more like a grandfather. He would greet her by name and bow a welcome when he arrived. He was happy to have her nearby while discussing his faith with the Johnsons. She discovered he had done divinity at university before turning to the sea for his career. If he came in the evenings, which he often did, he would escort her back to the women's tent for her safety. She remained safe as she was under the protection of such a high-ranking officer and the Johnsons.

Life in the struggling colony settled into a routine.

Annie's arm was still giving her trouble, and it remained in a splint and was unusable. Doctor White checked it regularly, but the sling was hot and uncomfortable. On her last visit, he encouraged her to use her fingers but try not to twist her arm. The first time they met, he had reset it. Now, his new bandaging meant only one strip of cloth sat between her thumb and fingers; the rest of the strapping was down her arm to her elbow. She no longer had to keep it in the sling. Captain Hunter had one of his crew whittle a shaped splint for her arm, which meant it was far more comfortable. With all her fingers now freed, she began to find life a little easier. Brushing her hair or even doing up her new apron for work proved impossible as she still could not twist her arm, but others were always around to assist. If by any chance she was too slow, and the other women had gone, then Mary Johnson could always be relied upon to help.

The bond between the two women had grown. By the time *Lady Penrhyn*, *Charlotte*, and *Scarborough* were ready to leave in May, the settlement looked like it had some structure; the prefabricated building was complete, as was a cottage for the Johnsons, and other wattle-and-dab buildings were under construction. Mary was not looking forward to the day Annie had to go to work in the gardens, but hopefully, that was some time away. Having a kindred spirit to work beside had been a blessing for them both.

~

On the day the *Lady Penrhyn* sailed, Doctor Bowes-Smith did the rounds of the various people he needed to say farewell to. Annie was one of them. He came to see her after his farewells to Richard Johnson.

School had been let out for the afternoon when she saw him leaning against a tree trunk with his arms folded. "Hello, Annie Gentle; I've come to say my farewells to you and the Johnsons."

Annie smiled. She had hoped he would do that.

His next words to her made her suck in her breath. "Annie, I have left you to nearly the last goodbye so that I can say something to you. The night you spoke to Elizabeth Colley after she lost her child was something I never expected to hear from the mouth of a convict, but then I came to know you better. Your words that night were good and true and spoken from the heart. Annie, strive always to believe them."

Annie bobbed a small curtsy. "Thank you, sir. I do and will."

He smiled in acknowledgement. "I don't know who you really are, but you have no need to be subservient to me."

Annie smiled shyly, knowing he was correct.

He nodded in acknowledgment of her thanks and continued, "I feel that even your arm being broken in the care of the horses was a God send, for otherwise you would have been landed with the other women. I could no more have kept you safe than I could have helped the others. Because of that injury, you are here teaching and have been placed in the loving care of the Johnsons."

Annie smiled again at his words, for she knew them to be true. She appreciated his care. She was teary as it was, as being May 5th, it was the first anniversary of the birth and death of her daughter. It was significant as it was also the day the *Lady Penrhyn* was to leave.

Over the year, she tried to imagine their daughter's appearance as she grew. Oliver's face and her hair, or vice versa? Her glassy eyes spoke volumes to the doctor. She said, "Thank you, doctor. I was glad you were on board, as compared to the other ships, they did not fare so well. Doctor Altree was, well…" she hesitated before adding, "…um, adequate at best, but you seemed to care too. That compassion made a world of difference to us."

The doctor had not moved or touched Annie.

Mary watched the two interact as she packed up the slates. She saw Annie's head drop, and then the man placed a caring hand on her shoulder, but that was all. However, the words he spoke so softly carried across the grass. "Annie, I also know that today would have been your child's first birthday; I want you to know that I remembered. I will keep you in my prayers and hope you will do the same for me. Do you have any messages for home?"

Annie nodded. His compassion and care had once more brought a lump to her throat. It took some moments before she could say, "Thank you, sir, and I will strive to do as you say. As to messages, I have but one. I dare not let my parents know my situation, so I still will not tell you my real name."

Over the journey, Annie's story unfolded to the doctor, and he knew her parents to be a rectory family, but not who or where they were or from where. Some details she had left out, she now filled in.

She lifted her head, saw Mary close, and slightly dropped her voice. "You know I am not using my real name, but will you tell the Marquess of Bowbelle that I am safe and well? He called me his 'gentle Annie,' and he was the father of my child. That was why I chose the name sir. If he could let the midwife know that I am both safe and well, that would be good." The date also meant that it was nearly a year since she had last seen Oliver. "Sir, can you tell him we are hungry? He may be able to assist."

The doctor nodded. "I shall, Annie, and let me say it's been my honour getting to know you. Stay strong and upright, my dear, and trust that God has things in control. We cannot always see His hand at work, but He does not make any errors. Keep your faith strong, dear girl." He gave her a bow, then took his leave.

Annie stood watching him stroll down the hill from the school area. She didn't hear Mary approach but felt the loving hand on her shoulder.

Mary's compassion was stirred. "Annie, dear, did I hear correctly? You lost a child?"

Annie was grief-stricken at the memories the doctor's conversation had stirred. She merely nodded, knowing the confirmation of such a comment would ostracise her.

Mary said, "I'm guessing that it was not consensual?"

Annie shook her head. Finally, she was able to clear the lump from her throat. "No, he was my employer, and he was drunk. I was in the wrong place at the wrong time. It was a year ago today that I lost her." She didn't wish to explain more, but the tears flowed unnoticed down her cheeks.

Mary slipped her arm around Annie's waist. "It happens, dear. I knew there was something that you weren't telling me. I felt you would reveal all when you were ready."

Annie stood gazing at the now retreating figure of the doctor as he headed to the jetty.

As he stepped into the longboat that was waiting for him, she turned to Mary and replied, "What Oliver did to me was not consensual, but even as he ravished me, I was in love with him. I was planning to leave his house soon, as his wife had just had a son, and I was employed as her paid companion for the duration of her confinement. She had delivered a boy that week. I couldn't risk staying that close to him, feeling as I did," She sniffed in an unladylike manner, then finished her comment, "and then it was too late to leave."

Mary was gutted for her young friend.

Annie watched as the doctor's boat reached the *Lady Penrhyn* before continuing. "The week Oliver's heir was born, he had his way with me, and soon after, I found I was with child, so I stayed for six months until I could no longer hide my condition. The worst had already occurred and did not reoccur. I stayed because I could no longer return home and had nowhere else to go. I told my parents I had moved to Scotland with another employer. When our daughter was stillborn, I dressed as a highwayman, held up their coach as they returned from church, and handed him our dead daughter. As I rode away, I heard his distraught cry as he realised she was not breathing. I never even named her. I collapsed soon afterwards, still dressed in my highwayman outfit.

I was told later that it was because of his wife's accusation that I was arrested as a horse thief. However, I was sent here for highway robbery as the horse escaped."

That was an abbreviated outline of what happened, and Annie now expected to be rejected as a fallen woman. She thought that now she would need to walk away from the loving placement and seek work in the gardens.

Instead, Mary enfolded a very teary Annie in her loving arms.

The ropes tying the *Lady Penrhyn* to the shore were hauled aboard, and Annie saw the doctor come to the railing and wave to them.

They responded and watched in silence as the ship rounded the point. The *Lady Penrhyn* was gone.

Suddenly, it was all too much for Annie. Mary's compassion was the final straw. It was as though a dam burst. The doctor was her last tie with home.

Annie's sobs broke Mary's heart. Mary said, "Annie dearest, you must trust God that He will see you safe. There will be some unseen reason for you being here. We are like the knots on the back of a tapestry, but He can see the entire beautiful picture on the front." Mary paused and thought before adding, "Mayhap even asking your friend for food could well be the reason you are here. I heard you ask the doctor to pass on that message."

Mary's care bolstered Annie's resolve to stay strong.

With the ships now gone, Annie felt even more alone.

Behind her, Captain John Hunter and Richard were discussing building a church somewhere. The odd word from their conversation floated to them. When the breeze dropped, they could not help but overhear her story. The knowing glance they gave to each other meant they would both watch over her closely.

Aware that she still had six years to serve, Annie knuckled down to build a new life in this raw place. She must try hard to put the memories of Oliver behind her.

That, however, was much easier said than done. She did not wish to enter into any relationship with any man other than Oliver, and he was not available.

Chapter 15   Food, Glorious Food
Late 1789 - Early 1790

Even though Annie's arm was healed well enough to do manual labour, she kept it bandaged for protection. The need for food was extreme, and all hands were needed to help. The two-year supply of food for six hundred that was sent out with the first fleet did not account for the spoilage and the needs of the ships' crews.

The other eight hundred or so men who had been in the settlement on the day of Governor Phillip's speech were crew from the eleven ships. Once three vessels had left, nearly double the number of people on board the ships for the quantity of food that was sent. Fifteen hundred hungry mouths had eaten their way through about half of the food.

~

Annie was still working with Mary Johnson when a long boat crossed the bay and took one of the indigenous men captive. The man refused to give his name, and he arrived with a rope around his neck and protested loudly.

Richard was furious and insisted that they release him.

Governor Phillip would not; he wished to try to communicate with him.

Annie saw the compassionate look the tall, dark-skinned man gave her and gasped with surprise. He was the one confined, but she was the one with her arm bandaged.

Richard discovered that his name was Arabanoo and not Manly, as the governor had been calling him.

It took time, but his incarceration was eased when he showed no sign of escape. Annie realised from her friendship with some of the local children that he could have slipped away easily. However, he was curious and chose to remain to learn what he could.

Eventually, he was taken back to visit his people often; however, he always chose to return to the town. Bennelong later joined him, and he was more adept at communication. He had learnt some English words that had eluded Arabanoo.

Governor Phillip supplied them with clothing and taught them to use cutlery and eat at a table. Neither liked doing this.

~

With virtually no new wheat grain to sow, decisions needed to be made before the existing supplies were exhausted. The need for new farmland and readily accessible food was the main priority for the governor, but it seemed that no matter what they tried, they could not farm the rugged virgin soils in Sydney Cove. Food would not grow at Farm Cove. Few, if any, of the new settlers were farmers and those who had been sent to Norfolk Island. Thomas Eccles, Betty Bird, and Mary Love were some of the exceptions.

However, they did not realise that farming a new land would be so fraught with difficulties. To add to the colony's desperation, the five cows and two bulls escaped only five months after landing.

Captain Hunter was charged to keep his eyes open for them on his expeditions. They evaded all efforts to find them, but cow pats were found, so they were alive somewhere. He did, however, find a possible area to farm further up the western end of the extensive bay.

~

By October 1788, nine months after arriving, Governor Phillip was in a situation where he knew that running out of food before more ships came to rescue them was a forgone conclusion. Starvation was now inevitable. Most of the unneeded ships had been sent on their way, and they were left with the *Supply* and the *Sirius*. The supply ships promised by the navy had not appeared. The decision was made to send the *HMS Sirius* to Cape Town for food. He was fully aware that the trip would take some six months to return if he was lucky, but a decision needed to be made. That left the two settlements with the smaller *HMS Supply* between them.

Watching the one-hundred-foot ship leave Sydney Heads was a sad sight for everyone. The *Sirius* planned to head eastward at a very low route and be pushed by the prevailing wind. No known vessel had followed this route, but sailing against the mammoth seas was not an option for an unpowered square sailing ship.

Seven months after the settlement was started, rations were cut. All male convicts received the same as the women, but now they were cut again.

With more convicts sent to Norfolk Island, only six hundred people remained in the colony. However, babies were being born with far too great a frequency. Doctor White duly vaccinated them with his primitive inoculations, and it seemed to work as well as he had been told. With the remaining ships gone, the number of people living in Sydney Cove had lowered, but they still needed to eat. Even six hundred persons were too many for the meagre supplies they had on hand. Much of what they had was sent for the new settlement on Norfolk Island. This infant town was also demanding food.

Things were dire.

Hopefully, the farms on the island would soon start producing useful crops, but it didn't look good. England said they would send more ships, but none had arrived.

Before Captain Hunter departed on his life-saving trip, he had recommended that land at the end of the vast bay looked like a better prospect to farm. After various expeditions, a new government farm was established near Rose Hill, some fifteen miles west of the main settlement. The first wheat crop in Sydney Cove had already failed; not a single grain germinated in the colony's hard soil and summer heat. That had necessitated further exploration up the bay. In November 1788, just after Captain Hunter had sailed away on the *Sirius* to seek food, Henry Dodd was given permission to start farming further inland. It was soon growing crops well. Here, the soil was much better.

As they found out later, Captain Hunter had sailed the *Sirius* around Cape Horn at the bottom of South America, where he stayed in the roaring forty winds and was taken to Cape Town. He restocked as fast as he could with not only food and seeds but medical supplies and livestock, then headed eastward again.

Leaving Table Bay on the anniversary of the landing in Port Jackson, she headed back to the infant colony again. The perilous voyage across the mountainous seas saw Captain Hunter arrive in Sydney Cove on May 8th 1789. The ship had sailed right around the world in eight months. The cargo was life-saving after stopping to restock in Africa, but a single shipload was only a stop-gap for the ailing colony. Its arrival coincided with a smallpox outbreak.

Within a year, the first land out west had not only been cleared but had produced the colonists' first real food grown in the country. Vegetables were grown, and then some meagre quantities of wheat, barley, and a small quantity of flax, corn, and oats were harvested; the crop was considered excellent but not enough to ward off starvation.

Annie and many of the women were each given a plot of land to till and grow what they could. Richard and Mary had come to hold a church service, and he wished to see how the garden was going. They brought Captain Hunter with them so he could see first-hand what the soil was like. He watched as Richard bent down and took a handful of soil, spat on it and mixed it into a lump with some spit. When he opened his fist, the soil didn't stick together. "Oh, Annie, this is much better than it was before. I see you have dug in lots of vegetable matter. It no longer balls like the clay soil."

Annie grinned at his praise. "Thank you, sir. I did what you said and have a manure pile. The soldiers used to throw out the stable sweepings, but I have asked them to pile it up for us. We are all using it." She pointed to the heap of steaming mess that had just been delivered.

Captain Hunter had not visited the farms for some time. Annie had met him often at the Johnson's house, and she was not shy of him. Although unmarried, he had never made a move on any of the girls; therefore, he was always greeted with a smile. He greeted her by name. "Annie, did the men dig over the virgin soil, or did you do it yourself?"

Annie chuckled. "Sir, I tried but didn't have the strength, as my broken arm made the heavy work impossible. So Governor Phillip sent out a team of men to dig it over first. We didn't even have the tools or strength to make a hole in the hard soil."

The group walked over to the rest of the new gardens and checked each plot. Only Annie's was fully fenced with a brush fence. This stopped the small wallabies from eating what she was growing, but it didn't stop the birds. However, she had strung twine crisscrossed over the entire plot. Again, none of the other girls had done this.

Most of the seeds were needed to plant for the next year's larger crop. The farm was extended, and more of the virgin ground was put under cultivation. It was hard work tilling the virgin soils. What native food they could source, they ate quite willingly, but as with the greens and samphire that was adequate for a small tribe of thirty, it was barely a nibble for over six hundred. Native sarsaparilla vines still twined along shaded gullies; currant bushes that bore fruit on the ridges in autumn and New Zealand spinach were all consumed.

Annie heard that even the governor tried eating raw beach beans and was violently ill before discovering they must be cooked before consumption.

Thankfully, the fish were plentiful, but she was getting very sick of eating fish no matter how many different ways it was cooked. Netting schools of mullet, they traded with the natives for speared kangaroo and other foods. This worked well until the natives tried to take some of the tools. They did not understand they were unable to be replaced; they were chased, and the items were retrieved. Sadly, the misunderstandings became the start of various skirmishes.

For some time, things jogged along well; then disaster hit with a vengeance. Arabanoo took the Judge-Advocate, David Collins, to meet his family. In the area where they should have been, there was silence. There was no noise, no footprints in the sand and no sign of anyone there. As he walked through where the tribe's encampment had been, it was empty. But there were bodies everywhere. Smallpox had ravaged the clan, and those who had not died had fled.

Arabanoo stood alone. He stood in the clearing and said, "All dead, all dead!"

It was not long after this visit that the news filtered through of a great calamity. Smallpox had ravaged many of the local tribes around Sydney Cove, and they had all gone. Most were dead; the rest had gone bush. Arabanoo found and nursed two of the young girls from his tribe, but sadly, he contracted the disease and died a month later.

Annie was sad the nice man had died in such agony. However, the children, Boorong and Nanbaree, survived, and one remained with the Johnsons. Boorong took the name of Abaroo and decided to stay with the Johnsons. Whether that was in honour of her kinsman or for some other reason, Annie never found out. She met this girl often at the Johnson's house and had learnt some words in her language. She had also met one of the young boys who brought the Johnsons native berries to swap for fish. Nanbaree stayed with Doctor White.

Drought followed the disease, and still, no ships arrived with food. Following smallpox, syphilis, tuberculosis, and influenza, measles ravaged the remains of the tribes in the area. Fewer than half the tribes remained, and many of them showed signs of one or other of the diseases. The arrival of more convict ships would bring more illness and not enough food.

Governor Phillip donated his personal allocation of one hundred fifty pounds of flour to the dwindling supplies, but that tiny amount only deferred starvation. Each officer gave what they had, but many complained bitterly about sharing with the convicts.

Gone were the laden tables to celebrate King George's birthday on June 4th as they had done the first year. Gone was the luxury of butchered stock of any kind. That first banquet had included mutton, pork, ducks, fowls, fish, kangaroo, salads, pies, and preserved fruits that had been planned for future celebrations. This year, the date was all but ignored.

Supplies of alcohol were limited, with no allocation at all for convicts. They drank water or lemon myrtle tea, which was slightly safer as it was boiled.

Rations throughout the infant settlement were reduced again and again.

~

The following year, no food had arrived from Norfolk Island. As they had no ship stationed there, so none was expected. Therefore, ten months after Captain Hunter had returned to the colony from Cape Town, both the *Sirius* and the *Supply* set sail to take supplies and more convicts to Norfolk Island to ease the burden on the main colony. Hopefully, they would bring back whatever produce the island farmers had ready. The trip would only take a week either way, and they should return by Easter.

However, when they arrived on March 13th, 1790, bad weather looked to be setting in. Before the weather changed, the two ships managed to unload their passengers. There were one hundred and sixteen convict males, sixty-seven convict females, twenty-seven children and sixty-five more marines.

Unfortunately, there was no produce to bring back.

The farms there had failed.

The *Supply*, a smaller armed tender at best, waited a day or so and finally managed to get their stores ashore. When empty, it signalled that they were leaving their anchorage; the *Sirius* could move in to unload. However, the *Sirius* was a larger twenty-gun, one-hundred-foot-long naval ship, and the bay was unprotected from the winds.

The anchorage was not secure, so the larger *Sirius* moved to a different bay to remain safe after unloading most of her stores. She planned to take the convicts they had just unloaded back to Sydney.

Sadly, this decision was ultimately a bad one.

On March 19th, just before noon, she was blown onto the rocks. Captain Hunter had desperately tried to save the ship, but even with her sails furled, the wind caught her, and she hit a submerged reef.

Thanks to the crew's efforts, most of the remaining stores were saved, but the personal possessions of those on board were lost, and thankfully, no lives were lost.

The disaster was that the *HMS Sirius*, the settlement's flagship, had sunk. Captain Hunter remained on Norfolk Island to assist where he could. Guilt wracked him, but he knew he could have done nothing to save his vessel.

Those on shore had watched in horror as the colony's main ship was rigged with a line to shore to haul off the remaining supplies as best they could.

Then, everyone watched as the wind still swirled frequently, and each wave that crashed worsened the condition of the afflicted vessel.

After all of the crew were off the stricken ship, including the majority of the accessible stores, Captain Hunter abandoned his stricken but beloved leaky vessel. This was his second shipwreck, but it was the first with him at the helm. He stood on the headland watching the sea claim his beloved lady. He knew a court marshal would follow.

With everyone safe but the island unable to feed everyone, the *Supply* loaded up what people it could and reluctantly returned to Sydney Cove to report the devastating loss of the larger vessel.

As the island's crops failed, the colonists were marooned with barely enough food for everyone's daily rations. The smaller ship could not fit all of the convicts on board, and it needed to leave to source more food, or they, too, would die.

Lieutenant Phillip Gidley King had no choice but to cut the rations in half again, as now he had to feed the hungry settlers and a mass of new people.

John Hunter remained on the island and knew he would need to return to London for an investigation into his handling of the ship. For the moment, he had little to do. He now had time to think and pray. He walked along the foreshore and spent time fishing to bolster the meagre rations of the settlement.

For months, he was marooned until Governor Phillip chartered a Dutch ship, the *Waaksamheid*. Norfolk Island was its first destination, and the vessel brought both food and a passage off the island.

Both the island and the settlement on the mainland now had no choice but to wait until supplies arrived… if they arrived.

~

Annie was now working alongside the other women in Rose Hill on the government farm. It took some days after the *Supply* arrived for the news to filter through. Annie was thrilled that at least the nice Captain Hunter had not been hurt, but she was sad he had not returned. They tried as hard as possible to make things grow for the government. She had been there since she was given the all-clear for manual labour. The only means of watering the thirsty grain crop was with a bucket. However, sourcing fresh water was a constant problem. The river near Rose Hill was tidal, so the only freshwater they had access to was from a small creek. There was now a small dam constructed that contained the flow. From this dam, the girls had to walk constantly to get buckets of water. It was hot, back-breaking work. Most could carry two at a time, but Annie could only carry one. Their overseer eventually had one of the convict carpenters make a yoke that sat on her shoulders, and she could hang a bucket off each end. This worked well.

On Saturdays, Annie knew she was supposed to be working her own plot. However, knowing that Mary and Richard were coming for the Sunday service, she had watered her plants in her tiny plot early. She was now free to spend time with her friend. Mary's occasional visits were the only bright spots in her routine. If she watered her broad beans and turnips early, she had time to spend chatting. She had made three trips to the creek before mid-morning and had time now to chat.

~

With the loss of the larger ship, the only thing that could save them now was praying for more boats to come with food.

Sadly, when the ships did come in 1790, their arrival brought near disaster to the settlement.

The *Lady Juliana*, the *Neptune* and the *Justinian* sailed into a cheery welcome, expecting their arrival to be the end to rationing.

Not so!

What they brought nearly crippled the colony. The one thousand and six convicts who had left London in reasonable health were now emaciated. They collected more in Cape Town from the wreck of the store ship the *Guardian,* which had left a little earlier. The Second Fleet discovered that the main supply ship had never made it to New South Wales.

With more mouths to feed on the vessels, the ships' captains decided to cut rations on board, and on the overcrowded lower decks, the convicts were not permitted any time on deck. With no access to sunlight, decent food, or medical assistance, the emaciated, skeletal humans that arrived made the colonists gasp in horror.

Those that had not died on the voyage were riddled with disease, starved, lice-ridden living human skeletons. Nearly a quarter, over two hundred and seventy-three convicts, had died on the voyage, and it had not taken long for word of the deaths to trickle through to Rose Hill. Nearly five hundred of the new convicts were put straight into the hospital, and more died over the following months.

When the news arrived at the farm, Annie fell to her knees and thanked God for sending her with Captain Sever and Doctor Bowes-Smith to care for them. He had insisted that provisions were adequate if not downright good.

He had also permitted access to the fresh air and sunlight of even the worst offenders. On the trip out, they had consumed just one bad meal that made them ill. They were clean, the ship was new, and most of the convicts were allowed time above deck when weather permitted. Admittedly, for the majority, that was not as often as they had hoped. Annie knew that some of the more rebellious women had been manacled, and Captain Campbell even had a need to resort to thumbscrews for a few.

~

Some months later, Mary Johnson came for another visit.

They sat chatting, and she had told Annie that by eight months after the arrival of the Second Fleet, over forty per cent of the convicts had died.

Mary had not been able to voice her disgust to anyone but Annie. She now poured out her aching heart. "Richard has had long conversations with the governor. Annie, something needs to be done from London. If John Hunter had been here, he would have agreed with Richard. Arthur Phillip is often too ill to deal with this situation."

Mary, who was normally very passive, was pacing the area as she spoke.

"These poor dears came with private contractors instead of the navy, and these wretches thought to sell the food on arrival and make a profit. That failed. They caught the sharp edge of the governor's tongue."

Annie had never seen her calm friend in such an anxious state.

Mary raged for a while and then abruptly said, "Annie, they get paid for how many embark, not how many arrive safely and in good health. The poor creatures were kept in chains and locked below decks the entire trip. Not seeing the light of day until they landed here. It's inhuman!" She rose and paced the small allotment.

Annie had never seen Mary so irritated, even angry. She had no words of comfort, but she could give her a hug and proceeded to do so.

Eventually, they sat down, and Mary continued to describe the changes in town.

Annie's concentration was fixed on a thought she had just had. She was staring at an inanimate object as she thought about the one person who *could* do something. She wished there was some way that Oliver knew about what was going on. She wondered if the doctor had managed to visit him. She sighed, wondering if the changes she had glimpsed in him had remained or if he had fallen back into his spoilt little rich boy behaviour. She doubted she would ever know.

In the year she lived with them, Mary had inveigled the entire story out of Annie, including shameful details of her wanton behaviour later on. Annie still flushed with deep embarrassment over her behaviour with Oliver that night. Yet his rejection of her hurt even more. She was already carrying his child; not much more could have occurred. They had kissed only once after that.

After Mary's diatribe over the state of the convicts, she realised Annie had fallen silent. She saw the far-away gaze now in Annie's face and reached to touch her friend's shoulder. "I gather you still miss him?"

Annie nodded a little tearfully. "More than I should, Mary," she sighed. "If I could write to him and…" Annie froze; she couldn't do that. She gave a small shake of her head, "Oliver is in a position to do something about this mess, but I can't do it, Mary; I can't open myself to the hurt and rejection that could bring to me."

Mary patted her hand.

Annie gasped, barely able to speak. She said with vivid clarity at the self-revelation, "I'm as selfish as he is, Mary, but I'm so over being hurt and then rejected, not that he's free anyway."

Mary enfolded Annie in one of her wonderful hugs. "Everyone is entitled to self-preservation, dear girl. He hurt you badly, and even though you love him, he is still married to someone else." Mary brushed back a dark blonde curl from Annie's eye. "If he were free, I bet he would come if he knew you were here. But Annie, dearest, neither is he free nor here. You have to move on."

Annie sank into Mary's caring arms. "I know, Mary, I know it all, but that doesn't make the wanting any less. I love him so much it hurts here." She punched her heart with a clenched fist.

"I know, sweet girl, but it will fade in time. Find a man here and settle down." Mary encouraged her friend to do this often; Annie shook her head each time.

As expected, Annie pulled from her arms, shaking her head, and said, "No, Mary, I shall never marry anyone but him." Annie jumped up and stood gazing at nothing.

Mary watched, and then she, too, rose. The two women walked arm-in-arm in silence for a while. "Show me the other gardens, dear."

Colin, the overseer, and the other convict women were all hard at work. The overseer had given Annie permission to have Mrs Johnson visit today, so she was greeted warmly by all the other workers.

They wandered around the plots and then returned to Annie's garden.

After they were out of earshot of the others, Mary wanted to change the subject; she said, "I must tell you of an incident Richard had. He was visiting a sick and dying convict from Yorkshire, and unsure of how to start about the serious side of his visit, Richard mentioned the atrocious weather. The young Yorkshireman then proceeded to astound Richard by saying. 'Vicar, you are not here to talk about the weather; you're here to talk about my soul, so get on with it, laddie.' With that, Richard did, of course, but I thought the abruptness of his words somewhat peculiar. Many know when their time is approaching. Death, I mean. This man did, for when Richard returned the following day, he had died. Richard had said the final prayers with him. The poor wretch had made peace with God and was content to commit to the Lord's care. The poor man was but a walking skeleton."

Annie knew all about starvation. The scant rations they had needed to last as long as possible. "Mary, I saw hunger on our ship as it took so long to arrive. Supplies were low for the last months. But now, so little grows here; it's disheartening."

They returned to Annie's garden after a casual stroll around the rest of the plots.

Mary had been waiting until they started talking about gardening. "Annie, I brought something special for you." She dug into her reticule and pulled out a small parcel. "Richard's garden is doing surprisingly well. So far this year, we have picked oranges, strawberries, cucumbers, peas, and grapes. There were some delicious guavas, even though the tree was only small. Last year, I picked not less than a thousand cucumbers from our vines. Any that were damaged, I pickled them up for use later."

As Annie opened the small gift, half a dozen of the juiciest strawberries sat in her hand. "Oh, Mary, these look delicious." Annie threw herself into her friends' arms for a hug of thanks.

Mary was delighted that her gift was appreciated. "Careful, you don't squash them. These are better than the ones Richard took to the governor. Richard told me to stay and make sure you ate them yourself, so eat up now, dear."

They seated themselves again on a small patch of grass in the shade of a big tree off to the edge of the gardens.

Annie had learnt that being allocated a garden in this area had been fraught with difficulty. The tree roots sucked what little moisture there was from the ground.

Months later, she requested a different plot and was rewarded with some lush black flood soil. Here, her plants grew well.

Mary watched the joy on Annie's face as she bit into the luscious berries. The fruit was so large that Annie could only nibble at them. When she had finished, Mary drew another gift from her oversized reticule. "Richard said you are to have these runners. Plant them where there is good moisture and support the fruit with dry grasses, like straw. They are called strawberries for a reason. You must pick them as soon as colour shows, or the ants, slugs, and birds will get at them. They will ripen after picking." The second parcel contained a dozen strawberry runners. These were like gold in a starving colony. Annie burst into tears and again threw herself into her friends' arms. Hugging Mary was like hugging her mother.

Within the hour, the precious gift had been planted in the damp, fertile soil she had tilled so lovingly. Thanks to Richard's advice, Annie's plot was surrounded by a lightweight fence of sorts. She had used native vines to tie the thin, straight branches together, and then she used this to grow various sorts of vine fruit and vegetables on it. The fence kept out the kangaroos and gave her plants a better chance of survival. It was lightweight and could only support beans and broad beans, not pumpkins and cucumbers. She had chuckled as she had never really liked broad beans, so the quartermaster was delighted when she handed all her crop of broad beans into government stores. She was thankful he had no idea how many of the lovely crunchy green runner beans she ate as she picked them. Not many had made it to stores.

Annie remembered cutting the strawberry runners from her parents' plants and throwing them away. The thought that such a gift should bring so much joy made her giggle.

As Mary watched her toil, then laugh, she enquired the reason for her mirth.

Annie's face was alive with delight. Thoughts of home typically made her sad, but not today. "Mary, I used to cut these off and throw them away at home. Mama used to say the best fruit only grows on the first plant of the runner, but now I can test that for myself."

Mary smiled. "Dearie, Richard would like to bring Captain Hunter out to see the farms. He hoped you would not mind a visit from him."

Annie smiled. She liked the captain, and Richard was always welcome. She nodded assent with a grin. "I didn't know he was back from Norfolk."

The men visited shortly before John departed for England in March 1791. He had wanted to say farewell. "Annie, I wished to say a word of encouragement. When your doctor left, he asked me to keep an eye on you. However, I have travelled often, so I have not been here much. The reverend and his good lady will continue their care of you. Keep the faith, dear girl, and trust our good Lord that He has your life in hand."

Annie nodded. She was in awe that the esteemed captain had singled her out, a convict. She gave the lovely gentleman a deep curtsy and said thank you.

~

The appalling state of the Second Fleet's arrival was followed by more ships. Over the next two years, more vessels arrived, bringing more convicts. Food was not the only problem. There were no buildings to house the new convicts. Men could be placed in makeshift tents, but the women needed to be somewhere safer.

Timber buildings were hastily constructed, and the growing colony was a hive of activity. Thankfully, many of the convict ships brought food in excess of what was needed on board. The pressure was easing with the Rose Hill farm now producing well, but the colony was not yet out of trouble. One bad season could still spell disaster, but supplies had finally arrived. The decision was made that while convicts arrived unannounced, rationing would continue.

The Third Fleet, consisting of eleven more ships, arrived from July to October 1791. They brought nearly two thousand more convicts and, of course, their accompanying military and crews. Thankfully, they also brought excess food.

Annie loved Mary's visits with Richard, who did services for those in this area. When the Johnsons arrived, they were filled with news. Three more ships arrived individually rather than as a fleet. The *Pitt* came first carrying over four hundred more oppressed convicts. Disease had struck on the voyage out. The crew were decimated, and some of the convicts ended up manning the vessel to bring her safely to the cove. However, the *Pitt's* arrival brought mixed blessings. For yes, she brought more mouths to feed, but she also carried a partially assembled vessel named the *Francis*. This small craft was to remain in Sydney Cove for use in the colony. She was not huge, but the forty-one-ton schooner would again give the settlement some means of communicating with Norfolk Island regularly. One convict was a girl named Annie White. She was temporarily placed at Rose Hill before being sent to a farm. The two Annies eyed each other warily but soon became friends. Sadly, she only remained a few weeks before leaving to work further west on a new farm overseen by the Tremains, a Cornish couple.

~

The next ship to arrive was the *Royal Admiral* in October 1792. She had another two hundred and fifty male convicts on board, and there were many conversations about where to place the hoards of felons now arriving in the cove. Many were set to work on road gangs, a few were sent to farms as workers, and the unlucky ones were set to work in the quarries. They spent their endless days breaking rocks and hewing stones. Colin told Annie that these men were already dejected as they arrived in the middle of an early heatwave. He'd fallen into conversation with one of the new men. Sam Garney had been sent to one of the newer farms just west of the town. He was one of the lucky ones. However, with no wagons, the only way for them to get to their farm was to walk in the heat.

The *Kitty* was the last ship to arrive that year, and it brought the blessed relief they had been praying for. She was filled with stores. One of the convicts on board was Susanna Nairn, who had given birth while in Rio de Janeiro to a little boy whom she named John.

Mary met this girl and offered to have her assist in the school.

Mary and Richard visited shortly after word had come of the *Kitty's* arrival. All they knew was that she only had forty convicts on board and was filled to the brim with food.

Mary said, "Annie dear, I heard that the *Kitty* brought wonderful things, but listen to the list of stores. There are 282,567 pounds of flour, 165,360 pounds of pork, and 126,000 pounds of beef. They have not unloaded it yet, but Richard wanted me to tell you as soon as we knew."

The joy of hearing this news made Annie sink to the ground and weep with relief. Finally, they had enough food.

Chapter 16   Gentle Annie

*T*he Reverend Godfrey and Anne-Marie were worried that they had lost contact with their only child.

Annabella Soames had supposedly been in Scotland for nearly six years, or so her parents thought. They were very concerned that they had not heard from her and wondered why, but they had no one to ask. She had left no forwarding address or even the name of the person she was working with. The marquess had not mentioned anything about her when they saw him at church. Then, after some years, Reverend and Mrs Soames heard from their friend, the midwife, that he, too, had left the area.

The big house had been shut up. All they knew was that his wife and son had left him, and then they had both died. The marquess had vanished with no information of where he had gone.

Meanwhile, in New South Wales, Annie was living her life as Annie Gentle. Many times, she had been tempted to write to her parents and confess everything, but there was no way to send a letter anyway, not that she had any paper. After so long, she had almost forgotten the pampered life of Annabella Soames in favour of the convict, Annie Gentle, who had calloused hands and tanned skin. Her gardening work in the new colony had toughened her.

Day in and day out, she tended her garden plot and worked on the government farm. No matter her desires, she had chosen her name to remain incognito from her family to shield them from her disgrace, first from having an illegitimate child and then as a convict. Her name was chosen as a nod to Oliver, for it was all his fault. Her feelings for him had not diminished over the years, but she knew she would never see him again. She had never let any man grow close to her. She had shunned all of them, and, with the shortage of women, many had tried to draw near.

As days blurred into one another. The tedium of gardening never waned, but it gave her a reason to rise in the dawn light. She thought back to the frustrating days caring for her aunt or the months working for Verity. She shuddered when she remembered how cruel that woman was. Her empathy for Oliver grew. He had no way out of the marriage. Verity may have had a beautiful face, but she was emotionally ugly. Working in the newly tilled soil gave her a measure of contentment. She would plant a seed or runner, and it would grow if she tended it well. The hot summers were a trial as the plants wished to curl up their leaves and die. Annie tried everything she could to help them survive. The lattice of twine over the plot was covered with tree fern fronds, and these eased the sun and, therefore, the heat on the valuable plants. Although the production of food gave her pleasure, it also meant that she had far too much time to think. Every day, her mind turned to either Oliver or their daughter, often with tears. It had taken a few years for the men to stop bothering her with offers of everything from becoming a housekeeper to marriage. All were refused with a firmness that left them in no doubt of her intent. None ever neared first base with Annie Gentle. For some reason, the men respected her refusal of even a dalliance and finally left her in peace. Annie was still hurt at the knowledge that she would never know the comforting arms of her beloved Oliver again. She savoured the memory of the times she had been enfolded in his strong embrace.

Over the intervening years, Mary Johnson had even stopped suggesting the idea of marriage. She was surprised Mary had not come for a visit again after the *Kitty* arrived some weeks ago. She was usually full of news. The last time she came, she told her that the governor was leaving in December.

Then, in late 1792, Annie saw a sight that stirred memories. Loving the spring sunsets, she lifted her head from her toil to see how close the sun was to setting. As she did, she caught sight of something that sent shivers up her spine. Initially wondering if it was a mirage, she heard a horse whinny and knew the vision to be real. Looking into the setting sun, a figure was silhouetted in the orange light. However, it was an amazingly familiar sight, and it brought a smile to her lips. The spectre was of a horseman dressed in the same sort of cape and a tricorn hat that she had worn to haunt Oliver. There were few horses in the colony, and she wondered if it were the governor's stallion, but if it was, who was riding it, surely not the governor? He would not even know about her ruse. Maybe he was just out for an evening ride. It couldn't be Oliver as he was in England with his wife.

In the intervening years since her arrival, she had stopped thinking of Oliver as the marquess or even Marquess Oliver. Now, in her mind, he was just Oliver. She had called him that a few times to his face, but normally in anger and also in her letter. He was Oliver in her private daydreams. Her Oliver! Those were the dreams where their daughter had lived, and she was a happy little girl living with two happy parents who were deeply in love. Dreams of freedom and a place in society. Dreams of clean hands, a full stomach, nice clothes and dreams of living happily ever after. Dreams of her parents enjoying their granddaughter. But, her dreams invariably ended at dawn and the start of a new day or with a crack of a whip and a catty remark to make her keep working.

The rider reappeared each evening for over five months, never drawing closer and always silhouetted against the setting sun and then vanishing as she arrived back at the women's residence. Through the hot summer, Annie began to look forward to the sight at the end of each day. Then, one day, the horseman wasn't there. She stayed in the garden working late, just in case he was held back by something. Finally, she went indoors when it was too dark to work anymore.

The horizon was devoid of the spectre for a week, and then when it reappeared, she stood gazing at it. Her heart started racing as she realised that the rider had drawn a little closer today. Annie found her heart was singing; she held her hands clasped to her chest, and she had almost forgotten to breathe. Only one person would know the meaning of the caped rider. Only one person saw what she did, other than Bob, and she knew he would not be there. He couldn't be there, could he? Oliver was here somewhere. He was nearby and reappeared daily to watch her and ensure she got home safely. She realised he knew where she was, but why had he come?

The rider appeared each evening for the remainder of the week; however, each day, he came a little closer and appeared a little earlier. As the days grew cooler, the horseman was no longer just a silhouette in the setting sun but was still too far away to speak to her.

Then, on the morning of May 5th 1793, on what would have been her daughter's sixth birthday, and after more than six months of regular appearances, the rider came close enough for Annie to confirm it was definitely Oliver. However, this time, it was mid-morning when he made his appearance. He rode up to the edge of the garden at Rose Hill and sat on his steed, watching her work. She was on her hands and knees, head down, weeding and weeping, overwhelmed by memories of her loss. Her tears helped water the plants.

The horse whinnied, making Annie look up.

Oliver sat on the governor's bay stallion, wearing the familiar tricorn hat and cape. He watched her, unsure of her reaction to his presence; he stayed seated but grinning.

She was hesitant about what to do, so she pulled herself up and brushed off the loose dirt from her hands and skirt. Unaware of her actions, she found herself being drawn towards him.Frozen to the saddle, he could still not judge her reaction until she asked quite bluntly, "Oliver, why are you here?"

No bowing or using his title of marquess, no My Lord, no kowtowing to him, just his name, uttered with a passive affection. His excitement nearly overwhelmed him. She was not angry. He had been so uncertain as to her reaction that he had been fearful of approaching her, or he would have come earlier. Mary had told him to trust her, but he hadn't. He knew he had to take the next steps gently. Annie had never been afraid to stand up to him and made him rethink his actions in life more than anyone else ever had. She was someone very dear to him, his gentle Annie. Someone whom he had defiled and whom he had missed like crazy when she had gone. He put his hand out to her, then dropped it again. "I came because you are here, my gentle Annie. I came because Verity is dead. I came because I want you, Annie. I want you so much it hurts."

A flash of hurt and anger swept across her face, "I told you, I am nobody's mistress, Oliver. I am my own woman or will be when I serve my final year." Annie stood her ground. "I'm no whore; I never was, and I never will be. Here, life has taught me many things, but a man's power over a woman's body is something I have no wish to have forced upon me again."

Oliver was now off his steed, abandoning it to go where it wished, and he slipped through the timber fence. He had not yet touched her, but he so wished to draw her to him and kiss her silly. The stallion recognised Annie's voice and stayed close to the fence. As Oliver spoke, he hooked a finger and brushed off some spots of dirt from her sun-browned cheek. "No, my gentle Annie, not as a mistress, but as mistress of my home and heart. Annie Soames, I wish to marry you if you will have me, although I am not worthy of you."

Annie was determined to clear the air before she answered. "Why Oliver? Because you shamed me? Because your shrew of a wife had me arrested? Because of what you did to me? Because of your guilt?"

Oliver understood her anger and hurt and knew he needed to answer her truthfully. "All of those things, and yet none of them! Yes, I shamed you, and I can never say I'm sorry enough. I buried our daughter in the family crypt under the name of Anna Marie Soames-Quilpie. I told Verity everything after you brought me our child. It is why she hated you and had you arrested. I never received the magistrates' letter until it was too late, as I was busy with our child. I was burying our daughter when it arrived. Then, for the week following, I was in no state to know anything about it. Henry handed the letter to me a week later, but you were gone from the cells."

Her gaze remained on his face. He had the courtesy of looking embarrassed. He admitted he had got very, very drunk and remained so for some time. He continued, "Verity was livid, Annie, and she had no right to be as she had forced me to accept her son as my heir. So I locked myself in the office with the bottle; more than one, if the truth be told." Oliver watched for a reaction, but Annie gave none but a flicker of an eyelid.

She brushed away a fly but remained silent.

He said, "You know we had an arranged marriage, and up until Marcus was born, we jogged along all right. I got drunk for the very first time that night, and I hurt you because she flung at me that Marcus, my heir, was not my child, hence my questioning of you. I had wondered on our wedding night if she was as virginal as I had been told. She confirmed that night that she was expecting a child when we wed. My heir was not of my blood. But, my gentle

Annie, I was drawn to you well before then, soon after you arrived. I first glimpsed you at Sir Basil's place at his wife's funeral, and I wished then to know who you were. After you came to live with us, I watched your every move but dared not touch you." He expected a reaction from her, but there was none. She waited for him to finish his story.

He did. "In the intervening years, I have had much time to think about you and us. And that night when you were in my office, and I was fortified by far too much brandy, I dared to follow my lusts and desires and forced myself upon you. Even worse, I was so inebriated I remember nothing about it but your heavenly perfume. When you confronted me the following morning, I laughed because I had no idea how to react, but I was so very sorry. Guilt ate at me for weeks, but I wanted and needed you close to me. Then that damned spectre started appearing. Oh, my gentle Annie, I felt I was being punished for ravishing you. I thought I was going crazy, as my mother had done when I was young. The visions I saw were exactly as I had dreamed as a child. I had no idea it was you until the day you handed me our beautiful daughter." He swallowed nervously. "My darling Annie, I wanted you again so much; you have no idea how hard it was to turn down your oh-so-very tempting offer. That day, I needed you to leave my office, and quickly, I dared not relent. I was ready to leave Verity for you as I don't give a damn about society. I was ready to turn my back on all I knew and all my responsibilities to be with you. That day I last saw you, I wished to get out of the carriage and follow you, but I knew I needed to care for your gift to me. I did not realise she was not breathing until you had gone."

Annie smiled in understanding but stayed silent.

"Months earlier, when you told me you were carrying our child, I was beside myself in frustration. I wanted you with me, yet I knew you would have to leave. I purchased you a cottage in the next-door village, and then I was too fearful to inform you about it lest you leave me permanently. I knew that if Verity found out, she would attempt to hurt you in some way."

Annie nodded and said, "She did anyway." Her face still showed no emotion.

Oliver agreed. "I knew she would. She has had her comeuppance, though. She left me for some French fellow nearly two years ago, and they drowned while crossing the channel. Marcus was with them, so I gather the child was his."

Annie nodded. "That would be Francois Dubois; he visited often while you were away. I did wonder when I saw the child." She touched her chin.

Oliver looked surprised that she knew what had been occurring. He nodded, then drew a long, deep breath before saying, "Annie, I wronged you; I took what I had no right even to touch. I defiled you and betrayed your trust." He paused and then said the words he should have said so long ago. "I am sorry, so very, very sorry. I had made my marriage vows in good faith and intended to keep them. But those months of having you in my house and being unable to touch you…" His Adam's apple bobbled as he swallowed nervously, "After we had been together, and then the appearances of the spectre… well, they all made me rethink my entire life. I forgot that I had told you of my dreams. So, yes, I thought my mother's affliction had fallen on me, but you challenged me to reassess everything in my life of privilege. I failed you, and I turned to the bottle for a while. You stood up for what you believed in and told me to my face I was a shallow, self-centred, egotistical, poor-little-rich-boy who had never been crossed."

Annie grinned. "You forgot conceited, stubborn, and cheese-paring. I know that one hurt in particular."

Oliver chuckled. "No, I didn't forget them, but your words hit home far more than you knew. I remember every word you have ever spoken to me. Sweet Annie, I began to look into my life and realised everything you said was true. I did not like who I had become. Then my granny's words came back like an avalanche, 'Be the man you would want your daughter to marry.' I was not. If our Anna had brought home a man like me, he would have been met by the barrel of a gun."

She saw him swallow again, but she smirked at the image he portrayed.

"My dearest Annie, every word you said was true, and I wanted to change who I was. Verity didn't like me before the hold-up, but now she positively hated me. Before you handed me our child, I had removed the last of her privileges, including having visitors or going visiting. Her anger and hatred suited me fine. I wished for nothing to do with the cuckolding vixen… but I was still tied to her legally by my marriage vows."

Annie nodded. She understood but let him finish.

Oliver had not shifted his gaze from her beautiful mud-smeared and now freckled face. "After Marcus was born, I never returned to her bed." He plucked up the courage to lift his hand to her face and caress her downy cheek with his thumb, then brushed another tendril of fair hair away and tucked it behind her ear.

His touch was feather-light, but Annie tipped her head slightly, increasing the pressure from his fingers. She wished to throw herself into his arms, but she knew he needed to give voice to his words. Oliver continued talking, his eyes boring into her own honey-gold ones. "All I wanted was you, Annie, as I've never wanted anyone before. I still do, and I always will, but far more importantly, I need you and love you."

Annie smiled; those last three words were the words she had dreamed of hearing, as now he was free. Relief washed over her, and she chuckled. "The highwayman thing, I did it initially to make you pay for all sorts of things. I had no intention of keeping it going for so long, but then I found I was carrying your child. Our child, Oliver! She would have turned six today." She looked at him apologetically. "I knew about your mother's illness, but I have since heard what she suffered, which many women experience after birth. Many, if not most, recover, but some don't. They have a name for it, but I don't remember what it is. Oliver, it is not something that will ever affect you. It is brought on by childbirth; your nightmares as a traumatised child were just that and not madness."

He thumbed her cheek. "So I have since heard, my dear. Bob's mother said something along those lines. I sought her out shortly after I discovered where you were. On the day of your hold-up, Bob finally told me his part in the story. I had no idea you had been with his mother." His hand had crept around to the base of her neck. "Annie, dearest gentle Annie, I wish to kiss you. I wish to hold you tight and never let you go. Annie, I love you, but I will not touch you more without your permission."

Annie's reply was to take a step towards him and place her filthy hands on his snowy white linen shirt possessively. "You are the only man I have ever been with, Oliver, and the only one I ever wish to love." Her arms slid around his neck, neither of them caring about the smudges her dirty hands had left on his crisp white shirt.

He enfolded her in his arms and lowered his lips to hers. The world around them faded away. Neither cared that they were now being watched open-mouthed by all the other garden workers and the overseer. They were totally absorbed in their embrace, knowing it was something that both had desired for many years. A long, deep, and loving kiss that was freely given and willingly taken guilt-free. One so full of promise of a life together. He was now free to be hers and had come halfway around the world to claim her. Oliver broke away first, but with his lips still so close to hers, he murmured, "I love you so much it hurts." Giving her no chance to reply, he occupied her lips again for some time. When he drew back this time, he said, "My darling girl, I have heard of the horrible reports of the landing from your Doctor Bowes-Smith. He said you were kept safe, but, my dearest Annie, I feared the worst for you. However, you say it was not so?"

Annie relished the embrace and stayed comfortably in his arms. "No, Oliver! No man has touched me; none but you! The seas were so bad in the south that I was thrown against a bulkhead and badly broke my arm whilst caring for your steed." She glanced at the stallion, who was standing with his head over the fence, waiting for her attention. She still wondered why Oliver was riding the governor's horse. Flashes of that horrible scene invaded her mind. "I was not landed when the other women were. I was with other injured girls and the girls who were heading for Norfolk Island. Oliver, it was horrible to watch and be unable to do anything to help those on shore." She buried her head in his shoulder, thinking about that first landing. Then, her shoulders began to shake as she wept at those horrible memories. She had wept often over the years, but this was a release on a much deeper level. This time, she had Oliver. This time, she was also weeping with relief. She would no longer be alone.

She had bottled her emotions for so long, and they flooded out like a champagne cork popping. It was five years since she had wept in such a way.

He felt her tears soak into his shirt. He held her tightly while gently rubbing her back, bringing security and comfort.

As her tears slowly subsided, Oliver could barely hear her words. Annie's voice wavered as she spoke of that horrific morning. "Oliver, I saw things no daughter from a rectory should ever dream about. Things I can't un-see. Our friends were brutally violated in front of us. What little clothing they wore on landing was torn from their bodies until they lay bleeding, naked, and unresponsive on the foreshore. A few of the convict women adored the attention and encouraged the men on, but most were unwillingly violated. Age was no barrier to the carnal pigs on shore. From the young girls to the older women, all were attacked, and the men slaked their lusts on the prostrated, almost unresponsive bodies of my friends. Most were fighting as hard as they could, but their abusers egged on the next, the next, and the next. When one abuser was done, another jumped on to ride them until they had taken their fill; sometimes, even two men worked on the poor woman at once. Oliver, the scene was far more than merely degrading; it was evil. Doctor Arthur Bowes-Smith stood near me, watching in horror. He was screaming and yelling for them to stop. He called until he was hoarse, as he was aghast and disgusted. With no longboats at hand, he had as little chance of stopping the situation. He was tempted to jump in, but being unable to swim would have been no use. Had we still been roped to shore, I'm sure he would have climbed down the rope, but we were anchored further out in the bay. The scene on the foreshore was a violent orgy. No, it was more than that; it was mass violation and carnage. The doctor said he would report this to the highest authority and ensure it would never happen again. I do hope he did."

Annie lifted her face to his; her tear-stained eyes tore at his heart. "I wished you were here with me so I could have turned to you for comfort."

He could see she was still grieved at the memory.

After a shudder, she continued, "Many children were begotten that day, and there was no way of knowing who the fathers were." With her arms now wrapped around him, she sought refuge in his shoulder again. He was so strong and safe, and she needed him. She breathed in his clean, masculine scent, then relaxed.

Oliver was gutted, but he didn't know what to say to ease her pain; however, he softly replied, "Your Doctor Arthur Bowes-Smith did report the abuse in London, my love. He filed his surgeon's log, making sure that the details were recorded; I know, for I was with him as he did so. He did everything possible to ensure it never happened again. Not that I saw anything myself, but lending support with my title helped him be believed. When we go home, we shall work together to see that a lot of those being transported are better treated. Many officials over there thought he was exaggerating things. The doctor also added other things that needed to be addressed before more ships were sent. He mentioned that the civilian doctor assigned to the convicts on your ship was incapable of his work, and he presented the document transferring the convicts to him only weeks into the journey. That, too, needed to be addressed. He requested that only naval doctors be sent. While Verity was under virtual lock and key at home, I spent much time with him after his return to England. He sent a message and told you to keep praying." Her head nodded against his chest.

Oliver knew it was best to tell her the sad news now while she was in the security of his arms. "My darling Annie, I must tell you that he passed away six months after he arrived in London. I had gone home for some time to ensure Verity had not strayed while I was away. I discovered that her filthy Frenchman had been meeting her in secret. Bob had let me know. I had the cuckolding swine banished from our shores as an enemy of the realm. On my return to London after Christmas, I had planned to meet with Arthur again; I sought him out only to find he had died in my absence. He was only thirty-nine, and there was so much I wished to discover. He was a man I planned to get to know better and work with, but sadly, I never received that chance. My love, I wish to return and continue his impassioned work for the convicts. He passed his baton to me, and I have willingly accepted that role. I will tell you that I was given his diary from the voyage out here. Having read through it while waiting for a ship, I had an insight into what you went through. I handed his personal journal over to the admiralty as I felt it was a document that needed to be kept for posterity."

Annie drew back in his arms, aghast. "Oh, Oliver, Doctor Arthur is really dead? He was so nice. My time on board would have been far more difficult without him."

He nodded sadly. Oliver laid his cheek upon her head. "He told me of a certain conversation he overheard. It was the day when you told a woman of the joys awaiting us in Heaven."

Annie nodded against his chest again. "I did, as I believe we will see our daughter in her full perfection once we're in Heaven."

Choked with emotion, it took a little while for him to answer. "I will look forward to that day, my love." After a time, he spoke again. "Annie, our Anna was so perfect. When you placed the basket in my arms, I had so hoped to hear a cry. When you rode away, I pulled back the blankets and saw her exquisite little face, but her downy cheeks were bluish and stiff. Her pale hair was just the same colour as your own. I wished she would open her eyes, but she was cold, and I knew she would never gaze on my face and call me Papa. I freely admit that I wept then as I had never cried before. That day, my old life fell away forever, and I was washed with shame at what I had done to you. I felt all that was good in me died that day. But Annie, after that terrible week, I did not turn to the bottle again." He lifted Annie's chin and pecked her lips with a quick kiss. "Verity was disgusted with me, but I no longer cared about her. I cradled our daughter until it was time to lay her in the crypt the following morning. I would not relinquish her to anyone. Knowing it was the only time I would get to hold her, I sat cuddling her in my arms all night. At dawn on the morning of May 7th, with Bob's help, I placed her in my mother's casket next to my tiny sister's body so she would never be alone."

Annie's lip quivered as he spoke. Her daughter now had a name and was safe for eternity. She wept quietly again as she listened to his tale. A tear fell onto her head, then another. Oliver was weeping, too. The grieving parents were sharing their loss for the first time.

When Oliver fell silent, Annie sniffed and said, "I did the same, Oliver. She never breathed. She was so perfect, but Ermie did all she could, but nothing worked. She was all I had of you, and if she had lived, I would have loved and cared for her. I also would have stayed and let you know everything she achieved and encouraged you to see her."

The sorrow of the loss of their child was finally aired.

Annie again wept for their daughter. So much had happened so fast that she had never had time to release her. Now, she could name their daughter Anna, their perfect little Anna. Only Oliver could understand exactly what she was feeling and bring her the comfort she needed. Now, she released the pain of her loss to the father of her child.

He had bottled up his feelings as he had no one to speak to but Bob. It was not the sort of thing you could discuss with your head groom. Oliver felt as though he had been kicked in the stomach. He had not given Annie any support until it was too late. His selfishness consumed him over what he wanted, and he did not think about her. He had not even known where to make enquiries. He had no idea she loved him so deeply, even after what he had done to her. He should have thought about asking the midwife, but it never occurred to him. He had not even realised that the woman was Bob's mother. Alcohol had so befuddled his brain that he had not been able to think straight. He had been grieving the loss of their child in his own way. He was already married, so he knew he could offer Annie no more than financial support or ask her to become his mistress. He felt that Annie would not accept that aid or his immoral suggestion. He had long ago let a needy family have the cottage he had bought for her.

Annie felt him kissing her hair, and then she heard him say over and over again, "I'm so sorry, so very sorry." His voice broke, and the emotion poured from him. He had said the words years before, but this time, he meant them.

Once her sobs eased again, she lifted her teary face to his. His question needed answering. "I love you so much, Oliver, but I am a convict. I'm not even permitted to marry without approval. How can I return to England and be your wife with my background?"

Oliver's small chuckle was comforting. "Annie, it took me over two years to find you. Yes, I knew you had been imprisoned. Verity enjoyed rubbing that in my face when I roused from my drunken stupor, but I had no idea you had been transported. All she said was that you were no longer in the area. I searched but drew a blank at every turn. It was not until your doctor friend told me in 1790 that he sought me out and gave me your messages. When I looked for you everywhere, there was no Annie Soames on any manifest or in any gaol. After the doctor's return, I knew where to look and saw a name I knew so well: Annie Gentle, my very own gentle Annie. I knew then I would follow you wherever you went when the time was right."

Annie had pulled back in his arms to watch his face as he spoke.

"Then, a few years ago, after Verity and Marcus drowned, I was free to follow you; I found I could not mourn for them, so I fled to London. My only problem was that no ships were coming here, but I could prepare for the voyage. I rented a warehouse on the docks and started buying things Arthur said were needed. Eventually, I came on the supply ship, *Kitty*. Your doctor mentioned a severe lack of food, so I brought everything I could." He paused before admitting his nervousness. "Sweetheart, I have been here for six months, waiting for the required permissions and arranging somewhere for us to live. I knew you would recognise me, but I stayed away until I sorted things. I was so very fearful that you would not want me near you, let alone marry me. Having said that, Mary told me otherwise, so, my sweet, I have made arrangements and transferred your final year to me as your future husband."

Her head jerked up at those words, and she said, "The governor needs to give approval for a marriage, Oliver, and he's gone."

He quickly kissed her lips, then grinned. "I know, and I have it in writing right here. Arthur Phillip gave it to me before he left," he tapped his coat pocket.

Annie still needed persuading, "But I'm a convict; how can I be a marchioness? You will be ostracised by society. Cut off from all you know."

Oliver slid his hand lovingly over her tanned cheek, "You mean the same society I have already rejected? The one that thrust a cuckolding shrew upon me because she was from the same class? I will willingly forgo all that to have you in my life, Annie. I know nothing of your background except that you were some poor relation of Sir Basil's. I tried to contact him, but he is still in Italy. My darling girl, I care little for society. I do, however, care for you and am prepared to cast all aside for you."

Annie pulled from his embrace with a smile. "Dearest Oliver, my father is your rector in Bowbelle Village church. Mother is, or was, Anne-Marie Armstrong, sister to Sir Basil. Uncle Basil wrote my reference. I was Aunt Violet's companion-cum-personal maid after her accident."

Oliver was overwhelmed. "But Anne-Marie Armstrong looked after me when Mother died." Memories of the lovely girl washed over him. "Then you are gentry too?"

Annie nodded. "I thought you knew that. When you named our daughter Anna Marie, I thought you must have known it was my mother's name. I am Annabella-Marie."

With a shout of joy, Oliver crushed her to him again and murmured, "I had no idea, my beloved, none whatsoever. No, my love, she was named for you, and my mother's name was Marie. I knew the ministers' name was the same, but they never asked after you."

Annie smiled. "When I found I was carrying your child, I wrote to them and told them I had a new job in Scotland and would not have time to say farewell. I also told them where I was going was isolated, with little contact with the mainland. They think I left your employ many years ago."

Oliver was astounded that she had even protected him from her parents' ire. "You amaze me, my darling, that even then, you protected me when I did not deserve it. I find that God has been laughing at me for some time. I'm learning to listen to Him, but old habits are hard to shake. Will you help me, gentle Annie? Will you be my wife? I'm so glad I asked you before I knew your background."

Annie realised all her dreams had come true. "Yes, Oliver, I would be delighted to. However, I shall continue your reform." She chuckled and stepped close to him once more.

He said, "Willingly!" Oliver lowered his head and took possession of her lips. Tomorrow, she would be his forever.

The overseer, Colin Newstead, finally came over to enquire who this man was and why the caped man was manhandling one of the women. Surprisingly, Annie did not seem to object either. He watched with some jealousy as she returned his passionate kisses and embraces with great contentment. He arrived beside them.

Releasing her a little but without relinquishing his hold of Annie, Oliver introduced himself by his full title.

The overseer stood with his eyes and mouth wide open; then his jaw slammed shut. Gawking at nobility was just not done. The man before him was a real live marquess, and he was holding Annie Gentle as though she belonged to him. More than once, Annie had given Colin the edge of her tongue for making advances to her. He thought she was a cold fish who would give no man the time of day, let alone a casual tumble in the hay. Women were in short supply in the colony, and for her to hold out against them frustrated him no end. Now Colin found she was up close and personal with a real-life marquess. His jaw dropped open again. Speechless and confused, the man stood and gaped at the embracing couple before him.

Oliver realised his confusion and added to it by asking in an authoritative voice, "Well man, what say you? Did you particularly wish to ask something?" He felt Annie chuckle against his shoulder, but her face remained well hidden.

Colin remembered his duty as overseer was to protect the convict women. He mumbled something about manhandling the convict women, and the visitor was not permitted on the property without permission.

This was the opening Oliver wished for; "Oh, you mean this?" He dug into his pocket, withdrew a folded document, and handed it to the overseer.

At that, Annie moved from within the circle of his arm to stand beside him.

Colin opened the envelope and saw words written on it; however, he was unable to read and was holding the envelope upside down; he looked at the paper blankly.

Oliver reached out and carefully took it from his grasp, realising the man's inability to decipher its meaning. "It says that Annie Gentle has been transferred into my keeping. I have other documentation that I will produce in good time to the appropriate persons, but Annie Gentle has just agreed to be my wife. So please, sir, mind your manners near my fiancée." He felt Annie stiffen slightly under his arm.

However, Annie gazed lovingly at her beloved and said with a chuckle, "Oliver, please behave." She laughed again at her chastisement, knowing Colin had made moves on her.

Annie's adamant refusal to his advances had left him in no doubt about her lack of interest in men. Therefore, he was surprised at her words. She was apparently on first-name terms with the marquess.

She looked up at Oliver adoringly and explained. "Oliver, Colin is a good man and is just doing his job. He has kept us safe and well protected from the unwanted attentions of other men." She saw the confusion on her betrothed's face and a smile flutter across the overseer's lips. "Colin is a convict too, and he is our guardian, but he's a trusted one, and I class him as a friend, but that is all." She met Colin's astounded gaze.

He was confounded. Did she consider him her friend?

Annie smiled and explained to the overseer who Oliver was. "Colin, I've known Oliver for some time. Long before I arrived here, he is the reason I would let no other man near me." Annie felt Oliver relax a little.

At hearing the words she said to Colin, Oliver said somewhat contritely, "Sorry, my love, I told you I would need your continued rebukes. I find I am quite possessive over you and jealous of another man's slightest attention towards you," He smiled at the overseer, "…even if he has his job to do." He dropped another quick kiss on her lips. After a few moments, Oliver turned to Colin. "The upshot is, sir, that I shall be removing her from the government farm today, as we are to be married tomorrow by Reverend Johnson. I would invite you, but I feel we should keep our ceremony private." He looked down at Annie and said, "Mary Johnson said something about her standing as a witness for you. She admitted she knew of me, so they have already read the banns."

Annie was delighted. "Really? That's wonderful! She knows all, Oliver. They both do."

Oliver looked at the other convict workers watching them. "I dare say it's impossible to keep it quiet, but tell them Annie is marrying Oliver Quilpie, and please don't mention the title. I will make it worth your while." Oliver dug into his pocket and drew out a five-pound note.

Annie grinned and nodded.

Colin's head bounced in agreement, and he reached out for the money greedily and nodded again. "Of course, sir, I mean, Your Lordship, I mean My Lord Marquess." His mouth again dropped open and stayed that way for longer than it should have. He felt so rich and had not even had to steal the money this time. His eyes flicked to Annie's. "Miss Annie, dare I offer my congratulations?" He spoke as he stowed more than three years' London wages in his pocket, not that he was paid as a convict.

Annie smiled as she turned to crawl through the fence to the horse. "You may, Colin, and thank you. You may also have my garden plot; I don't think I'll need it again. I may come back for some cuttings, but otherwise, it's yours."

Colin doffed his hat to them and watched them leave.

As they left the gardens to retrieve her possessions from the female servants' accommodations, Annie stroked the stallion's muzzle, and he lipped her hand as he had done many times before. "Hello, boy; I hope you don't mind carrying us both?"

The horse threw his head up a few times.

Oliver was not surprised to see the rapport between her and the somewhat cantankerous stallion.

Annie stroked the velvety muzzle again. "I won't ask how you are riding the governor's horse, but I know this beautiful boy well."

Oliver joined her at the stallion's side. "I ride him because he is now all but mine. When Arthur Phillip returned to England last December, he knew all about you and your care of this beast *en route*. He could imagine no other person to look after him as he needed to. So, my darling, he's ours until the esteemed gentleman returns, if he does. Well, if the truth be known, Arthur gave him into your care. So I hope you don't mind, but I'm really riding your horse." He gave her a wicked grin and chuckled, saying, "Well, you rode my horse without permission." He gave her a quick kiss, then laughed.

Annie was stunned. "He's ours? Really and truly? What's his name?"

Oliver watched her hug the stallion's neck, "I believe the governor named him Pegasus."

Annie chuckled, "Ahh, the winged horse that sprang from Medusa's blood. Apt! Except that he is not white, and you are not Bellerophon."

Oliver flicked the reins over his steed's neck and gave Annie a hand up. It was six years since she had been on a horse, and she had forgotten the thrill of the experience. He said, "Trust you to know the history of the name."

Annie shrugged. "I studied Ancient Greek, amongst other languages, with Papa."

Oliver looked at his fiancée, stunned. "You are like an onion; you have so many layers, and each one is completely different from the next."

Annie chuckled. "I hope I don't smell so bad."

Oliver almost blushed at the memory that the comments conjured up. "No, but I will be buying you more of that delicious violet scent that nearly drove me crazy."

Annie snuggled into him as they slowly rode across the seventy-acre farm.

By noon, Annie and Oliver had returned to the female quarters. They had taken the long route to have some privacy and a long, passionate kiss. Annie packed her few things and joined him outside. Her possessions were now wrapped in Oliver's old cloak that she had kept all through the years, and it was now tied to the saddle. Oliver had brought her a new royal blue velvet hooded cape, and she was now warmly wrapped in his lovely gift. She sat sideways in front of Oliver on the stallion's back. As they left the accommodation block, Annie was sitting cradled in his arms with hers wrapped around him. It occurred to Annie that she had no idea where they were to stay that night. "Oliver, there is no accommodation in town; where are we to stay?" She had automatically assumed that they would sleep together that night.

Oliver planted a kiss on her upturned lips. "There are some benefits to being nobility, my darling gentle Annie, as I'm sure you will soon find. It seems that even here, I have friends in high places. Arthur arranged everything before he left." More he would not say, but this room was Arthur Phillip's old abode was more than sufficient. Tonight, he would relinquish it for her, but they would share it tomorrow. With Major Francis Grose in charge of the colony, Oliver had been somewhat on tenterhooks to see if what he had arranged with the previous governor would be honoured. It was, and it was those arrangements that had held up his appearance. He had managed to build a small cottage for them in Sydney, and it was now finished. Recently, he had needed to go to Sydney to confirm plans for their wedding. He furnished the completed cottage whilst there.

Annie had barely left the government farm for the five years she had been in the Parramatta area. Having spent the first year with Mary and Richard Johnson, she was transferred to the government garden at Rose Hill after receiving the all-clear from the doctor. Consequently, she did not know her way around the new community. She sat on the front of his saddle, leaning back comfortably against his chest, with his arms holding her securely. She was gazing around her but unable to wipe the smile from her face. Many of the original tents that had been there when she arrived had been pulled down in favour of shanty wattle and daub cottages. They were primitive, to say the least, in comparison to Oliver's grand house in England. Since her arrival, she had heard that a military compound had been built but had not seen it.

As they drew closer to the military redoubt on the low hillside in Parramatta, Oliver told her that when Governor Phillip had left Sydney Cove, he had relinquished his personal residence to Oliver for his use. As they rode along leisurely, Oliver explained that the governor had personally undertaken to do their paperwork due to the issue of names. It had taken weeks to prove his own identity and sort everything out. Initially, Oliver had been thankful that no one here knew him, but that also meant no one could vouch for him. It was only when he mentioned the death of Doctor Bowes-Smith, only six months after his return to London, that the penny dropped with the governor. Bowes-Smith had made reports in London about the well-being of the convicts; he had apparently made recommendations that were supported by a member of the nobility. Those despatch reports had been brought with the Second Fleet, and Oliver had been mentioned on them.

Oliver had admitted that it was indeed him and that it was because of Annie that the doctor had made contact with him. He smiled when he thought back to the moment Arthur Phillip realised that Oliver was on his side and not there to feather his own nest. In their few weeks together, Arthur and Oliver had talked and rehashed much about the first journey. Since then, more convicts had arrived but little food. Oliver had tried to come with the Second Fleet, but they had no room for him on board when they discovered what he wanted to bring. As private owners, the captains would not even take the food Oliver had in store. The captains intended to make their journeys profitable, so they carried their produce. When he eventually arrived in Sydney Cove, what he heard about that Second Fleet trip horrified him. Had he been on board, he wondered if he could have done anything for the poor wretches. Of the one thousand or so convicts who had embarked on those wretched ships, a quarter had died *en route,* and another quarter had died soon after landing. Five hundred of the walking skeletons were unloaded directly into the hospital, and it was thanks to the skills of Doctor John White that half of them lived.

Oliver had come on a ship that brought life-saving supplies. He had stocked up with chests of clothes for Annie, realising from what the doctor had said that there was nothing available in the colony for her to wear. He now knew that any garments excess to her requirements would be left with Mary Johnson. She could give away what she did not require herself. Annie was one of the first convicts to receive permission to return home, and that had taken some fast talking from Oliver.

It was only when he poured out the full story of his abuse of Annie and his wife's jealousy and the trumped-up charge of highwayman that Arthur Phillip signed the documents. Unbeknownst to him, Mary Johnson and John Hunter had validated Annie's story. By the time Oliver had been in the colony for some weeks, the Johnsons had become close friends. Being the governor meant that socialising with the convicts was out of the question, and to keep the New South Wales Corps in check, he needed to stay distant. To have a like-minded friend was a delight, even if only for a few weeks until he departed in December on the *Atlantic* with Bennelong. Arthur Phillip was not well. He was racked with pain and knew he needed specialist treatment that he could receive only in London.

Chapter 17   Till Death Us Do Part

*T*hankfully, the *Kitty* on which Oliver and his goods had arrived carried more food than convicts.

On arrival, Oliver donated his immense food consignment for government use. When the governor heard about this, he expressed his thanks profusely.

According to Doctor Bowes-Smith, the colony was starving, so Oliver subsidised the purchase of as many stores as the ship's hold could carry.

Every nook and cranny was stuffed with produce, seeds, and implements. For this reason, his extra 'luggage' would not fit into the holds of the ships of the Second Fleet.

The food he had brought, plentiful as it was, eased the conditions but did not cure them. Only adequate local productivity would do that, or the cessation of transportation.

Rationing was eased but not removed, as they still had no idea how many convicts would arrive without warning.

Oliver's only request to Arthur Phillip was that his title or name not be recorded anywhere.

The governor agreed.

When Oliver requested permission to marry Annie, Governor Phillip said they could not marry until she had only one year left to serve, which would be the day she was captured.

Oliver arranged the service for that date. They were to be married in a private ceremony on May 6th 1793, and Richard Johnson performed the marriage of Oliver Christopher Quilpie and Annabella-Marie Soames.

With Arthur Phillip gone, only Doctor John White, in whom Oliver had confided, and Mary and Richard Johnson knew their real identities.

John White and Mary Johnson would act as witnesses at their nuptials. Thinking back to the ridiculous palaver of his first huge wedding, Oliver smiled, knowing that this was what he wanted, just Annie, nothing more, nothing less. She was his world.

The Marquess of Bowbelle smiled as he looked at the beautiful girl in his arms. Tomorrow, they would marry, and Annie Gentle would vanish from all records. Arthur Phillip had made arrangements for that before he left.

Oliver knew that Annabella Soames would be listed as arriving on a foreign ship and that Annie Gentle would leave on it later. Should anyone ever enquire after her, she would die soon after sailing.

As reluctant as he was to leave her side, he knew they must part for the night. He was surprised when she said, "You are not staying with me?"

He shook his head. "No, my love, we shall start as we mean to go on. From today, we are to conform to society's rules."

Her crestfallen face eased when he said, "You need a long bath, my darling," he said politely. "I could not find perfume, but there is a cake of soap for you."

She chuckled and agreed. She was filthy, and she stank. Yes, she needed a bath.

~

When Annie awoke the following morning in the big feather bed, she wondered where she was. She even pinched herself to make sure she was awake.

The past twenty hours came flooding back to her, and she relaxed. Today, her dreams would come true. By tonight, Oliver would share the bed, and they would be man and wife.

Knowing that he was waiting for her somewhere in the area, she stretched languidly again and slowly slid her feet out under the warm blankets.

The chill of the air hit her like a bucket of cold water thrown over her. She chuckled. For the previous six years, her accommodation had gone from a hard convict ship berth to a leaky tent, then to a wattle and daub shack with no windows and various creepy crawlies as bunkmates.

Although she didn't like spiders, the ones that were bigger than her hand and ran fast only seemed to eat the annoying mosquitos. Some of those spiders were brown, and others were dark with striped legs, but they seemed harmless enough. She didn't like the slow-moving, black, shiny ones.

The girls sharing her shack had learnt quickly not to leave their clothing or shoes on the ground, as they would attract spiders.

One of the children had found one of these evil death creatures in their blankets the week they landed. Later, Abaroo told them these creatures could kill a person easily. Snakes were often seen in and around the campsite, especially in the first weeks while they were still clearing the settlement.

Annie had heard that one of the convicts had been bitten, but as another sickness was beginning to spread, she had no idea if the man had died from the snake, spider or illness.

Now sitting on the edge of the double bed, she saw that there were still embers in the fireplace. She decided to add a log or two and kindle the fire, and soon, the room was warming.

Last night, she unashamedly confessed that she was disappointed he would not be staying the night.

He wished he was but said, "If I do not leave now, your reputation will be ruined even before we have a chance to start on the right foot."

After he showed her the trunk of clothing, they returned to the dining room and away from the temptation of the big bed.

She had slept in a fine linen nightgown with lace trimmings that Oliver had brought for her. She had not had night attire for a long time. She smiled when she thought about him choosing such an intimate item of apparel.

Oliver visited Ermie soon after the doctor returned with news of where she was. He retrieved her clothing and then purchased more. He had brought it all with him.

The enormous travelling cases of her possessions now sat next to his trunks on the floor of her room.

Last night, he had packed enough for his needs for one night away. He said he would collect her in the morning when they would go to Sydney to be married.

When she had arrived in Rose Hill five years ago, the track was a narrow pathway freshly cut through the rough scrub. The original military redoubt buildings had been hastily erected tents with one or two that were wattle and daub. A few had been whitewashed with clay and lime.

When they arrived yesterday, she noticed a cluster of timber houses, one of which was somewhat larger than the others.

Oliver had ridden straight up to this larger building. She wondered what the road would be like now. He had it all arranged, and she had no need to worry about anything.

When they arrived, he had lifted her down, and while hiding behind Pegasus, they enjoyed a long and passionate embrace.

With the fire sparking to life, she wondered if she should ring a bell or even if there was one to ring.

She had no idea what the procedure for the morning activities was, so she was about to walk to the door and peep out when it opened.

The young maid received a surprise. "Oh miss, you're up! And you have the fire going already. I'm so sorry I'm late, but I never expected you up so early. Us gels is normally up before anyone. I was going to creep in and get your fire going for you so you could wake up in a toasty room."

Annie chuckled. Oliver had warned her not to mention being a convict, and Annie Gentle was now dead. She replied, "I'm an early riser, so I did it myself. I was hoping for some water to wash in, though."

The girl bobbed a curtsy. "Oh yes, miss, I'll go get some."

The maid ducked out of the room and was back in a jiffy with a jug of hot water.

The layout of this building could be taken in at a glance.

The house had only a few rooms, and the kitchen was at the back. To reach it, one had to step across the corridor.

Annie thought back to the day she had that lovely violet-scented bath at Oliver's house. In a way, it had been that bath that had brought her here. The wash she managed to have in the hip bath last night had been adequate, and although she now felt clean, she longed for a long, hot soak in a big tub. She knew that there was a well here, so the military compound had water on demand.

By the time the girl had flung open the curtains and made the bed, Annie was dressed in one of the gowns Oliver had brought from home. She had no idea how he would explain her arrival in the colony, as they had not discussed that. She was sure that Oliver had that worked out, too. Either that, or she would have to stay out of sight for a while.

Her wash in the basin removed the sleep from her eyes and freshened her considerably. She was about to wander outside when there were more noises.

Another maid came in carrying a loaded tray. A footman of sorts, probably a convict, followed with a small table. He placed it down, took a white tablecloth from under his arm, spread it out, and left.

The feast that was set before her was bacon and eggs, cooked just the way she liked them, golden-brown toast, lemon marmalade, and curls of butter, things she had not seen for years.

Annie nearly wept with the delicious food. How did they get butter when there were no cows? Had Oliver brought some of those, too? She presumed that he had, or there would be no butter.

The maid who had first come in said, "Mr Quilpie said that you liked your eggs hard and your bacon well-cooked, miss; I hope that is right?"

Annie's eyes were wide with astonishment that Oliver had indeed noticed such small things. She had eaten with the family only a few times, and that included a few breakfasts. She said, "They are absolutely perfect. Yes, that is the way I like them; I call them both crispy."

The maid said, "Miss, he brought us some butter, too. I don't know where he got it unless he brought some cows on his ship. It's ever so long since I've had that treat." Without waiting for an answer, she curtsied and left. The other maid was tidying the room and setting a chair for her.

Annie chuckled. Trust Oliver to have discovered the cows had wandered away. Doctor Arthur must have told him about that. She gazed at the delicious food in front of her.

Having not used a knife and fork for six years, sitting at a table and using proper cutlery was strange. She found that, being a convict, certain restrictions were placed upon them. Owning a knife was one thing that was frowned upon. She had only been issued with a spoon; that was all she had to eat with for the last six years. However, as there was only usually stew, gruel, or porridge to eat, so it was all she needed. The so-called bread on the ship out was what they called hard tack or ship biscuits, and they had arrived in huge barrels.

They were sent with two years' worth of food and were supposed to arrive with over eighteen months' supply, but with so many storms on the way out, much had spoiled. The two years' worth of hardtack had been about the only thing they had access to during the frequent rough weather, so it was all but gone by the time they arrived.

She waited until the maids left and was alone before the first tear fell. He really did love her.

It occurred to her that Oliver had meant it when he said he had been watching her, even how she liked her eggs. Thinking about why she liked them this way made her chuckle. With hard eggs and crispy bacon, she wrapped them in a table napkin and stuffed them in her pockets when she rode on Midas or Aladdin. The cook at the rectory always made extra for breakfast for her, and she thought no one had noticed when she was at Oliver's house.

With no one left in the room to watch, she placed the bacon on the toast, dumped the egg on top, then walked to the window and munched it in a very unladylike way. She would have to spend the rest of her life sitting at the big table in Oliver's dining room, using cutlery and living the la-de-dah life of a marchioness.

Today was the last day she was Annie Gentle. She giggled with delight. However, that thought brought her up short; she said to herself between mouthfuls, "Gentle Annie Soames, soon to be Quilpie. As of today, your life will change. Your dreams will come true with the man you love, but then what? Are you now going to sit back and play Lady Muck, too? Or are you going to do something useful with your life?" She thought back to something Oliver had said yesterday when talking about Doctor Bowes-Smith and his work. She wondered how they would do that. Working at the point of arrest was a starting point. Separating the men from the women and having female guards is needed. When she was incarcerated, she had only seen male guards. It took little imagination to know what they got up to. The women also needed privacy and better facilities. A bucket and no privacy to relieve themselves was disgusting. That needed to be sorted, too. She also had ideas about keeping the women occupied. Once she and Olive started teaching them, they behaved much better.

Eating her breakfast quickly, she wanted to talk over her questions with Oliver.

After her delicious meal, she had just finished cleaning her teeth with the cloth and powdered charcoal she had made for herself when she was informed that Oliver arrived.

The maid said that he was awaiting her in the other room.

Knowing that there was only one main bedroom in this building, plus some tiny staff rooms, Annie realised he would be in the sitting room-cum-office.

Annie had many questions for her fiancé. Yesterday, she had been so overwhelmed that he had actually come for her that she didn't ask him anything.

When she entered the room, Oliver had his back to the door. The swishing of her gown made him turn and hold out his arms to her.

She needed no second invitation and was soon swept into a passionate embrace.

They fell apart some minutes later when the maid entered.

She said, "Sir, I have found the gown you wished to have packed. I have placed it with your clothing in the small chest and the other items you requested for Miss Soames. Also, the carriage will be brought around shortly, sir."

Without waiting for an answer, she bobbed a curtsy and left.

Annie spun around to him. "A gown? What gown, Oliver?"

Oliver bent and gave her another quick kiss before answering. "I brought you the most beautiful gown to wear for our wedding, my sweet. It's made by London's top designer, and I must say it's lovely. Having previously been married to a woman who demanded the finest of everything, you deserve no less. However, I would never permit her to use the services of Madam Dominique. Verity was livid with me. However, this gown is one of Madam's exotic creations. It has a matching bonnet, and if we were having a fancy do after the service or a ball, you would be the belle of it. You will be when we eventually get home." He saw her stiffen.

Annie frowned. "I just realised that I can't, as I was never presented, Oliver; how can I go to a society ball?"

Oliver chuckled. "Ahh, but my darling, you will be married, so you will need to be presented again anyway. Mind you, I will probably keep you locked up in an ivory tower and bearing many of my children before I let you out to be exposed to the evil world."

With a laugh, she gave him a love punch on the shoulder. He chuckled. "Ooh, that hurt. You are stronger than you look."

She chuckled again and said, "And flexible, too. Wait until later, and you will find out much more about me."

Oliver said, "My darling girl, nothing about you surprises me now." She cocked an eyebrow at his comment. "Okay, well, almost nothing," he chuckled.

She was about to leave the room quite sedately when she stopped, turned and said, "Have I told you how much I love you?" Their departure was a little delayed as she intended to show him how much he meant to her.

~

The carriage ride to Sydney was a two-hour journey over a now well-worn track. As it had been a cold morning, Oliver packed a selection of warm blankets and added a couple of feather pillows for comfort.

In the years since Annie journeyed westwards, the original two-wheel track had been widened and improved. Still, the fifteen-mile trip seemed to take forever, not that they minded. They utilised the time for many kisses and not much conversation as they knew the driver could overhear them.

When their carriage came to the outskirts of the town, Annie hardly recognised the place. Gone were most of the tents, as now a higgledy-de-piggledy assortment of wattle and daub buildings were scattered throughout the small valley. It was no longer recognisable as the shanty town of tents she had watched being built was gone. However, it was not the 'New Albion' that Governor Phillip and the Johnsons spoke about either. Although there were many new buildings, it stank. "Oh, Oliver, it's changed so much."

There were so many gardens and farm plots and even a windmill. It had changed beyond recognition.

Her head swivelled from one side of the carriage to the other. "Do you know Governor Phillip wished to call the settlement New Albion? However, Doctor White told me that someone suggested it be named after the Home Secretary, Viscount Sydney."

Oliver chuckled but remained quiet. He knew Viscount Sydney, Thomas Townshend, as was his given name. Thomas was thrilled the new town had been named after him. Oliver watched her mounting excitement. Oh, how he adored her.

She continued, "I can't believe they have got all this done in such a short time. Oh, Oliver, you should have seen it when we arrived. It was all bush, and the men had to clear an area before we could even erect the tents." She vividly described the first view of the bays when they first saw it.

Annie set about trying to describe the landscape before the trees were removed. "One look at the rough scrub-lined bay was enough to send my friend Olive Gaskin into fits of tears. She went to Norfolk Island to live. Reverend Richard brings back messages for me, but she married Nathaniel Lucas, and they have three children. They have two-year-old twin girls and a new baby boy named William."

She had been snuggling against Oliver for most of the trip, but as they entered the town, she sat up and now sat demurely on her seat, looking like the gently bred lady she was in reality.

Oliver sat gazing lustfully at her, knowing that they would be married soon.

Annie was overwhelmingly happy. "I'm so looking forward to seeing Mary Johnson as it was just after the *Kitty* arrived that I last had any time with her. She had come to tell me that she was with child again. They lost their first baby boy, and then about two years ago, they had a daughter, whom they gave an aboriginal name, Milbah Maria, but it sounds like Melba when she says it. I have not seen their little boy yet. Richard said, they named him Henry Martin, but I'm sure he's as cute as Milbah."

Oliver gazed at her while she spoke. He loved the way her lips moved; they were so kissable. That was something he did before answering her. He smiled and said, "He is."

She kept chatting about the Johnsons and their love of gardening, about the oranges, vegetables, and meat they supplied for the colony. "Oliver, Arabanoo told me that the local name for this area is *Warrane*, and the people who lived here were the *Gadigal* people. He was from a different tribal group as he was from the other side of the harbour."

After a while, she realised Oliver was not replying to her excited babbling. "My beloved, am I talking too much?"

"Never, my sweet." Oliver watched her mobile mouth as she spoke. He had done this often at home as she read to Verity. Not that she had been permitted to converse much when Verity was around, but the way Annie's lips moved was almost provocative. He also loved listening to her musical voice when she was reading. She could have read the book of Numbers from the Bible, and he would have found it interesting.

She said something else, and he realised he had not heard her.

She had no idea how absolutely lovely she was. "Pardon, love. I am enjoying just watching you talk. Do you know how beautiful you are when you are speaking? Your mouth is like a cupid's bow, and all I can think of is kissing you again and again." He proceeded to do this again.

Annie chuckled and pushed him away. "We'll be seen, Oliver; behave yourself." Instead, she took his hand and interwove her fingers with his. She stroked the back of his hand and rested against his chest.

He said, "I wish today were over already." His arm pulled her close, and she rubbed her hand up and down his leg. Her actions did things to his body that he found hard to hide.

She giggled.

Oliver groaned. "I wish I had made arrangements to stay in town after the wedding, but I simply was not going to have our wedding night in a squalid little hut. I will use Arthur's quarters at Parramatta until we can leave; it's where you stayed last night, but I have a surprise for you, too. The relieving major stays in the military quarters as I did on arrival. They are comfortable enough, I suppose, but not for a honeymoon. I'm not sure if Francis Grose is happy about the arrangement, but he had quarters out there already, and he's not the governor, only acting governor. His wife remains in town here."

Annie lowered her voice and said, "You could have stayed last night."

He shook his head. After another long kiss, he said, "Arthur said you can return home any time as long as your term has expired before you set foot in England. So that means we leave here about Christmas time."

"I can leave early?" She gave a little jig of excitement. "I don't really care as long as I can be with you."

At that moment, the carriage drew to a halt outside the Johnson's abode.

Oliver leant over and kissed her quickly, saying, "That, my darling love, is a given."

Richard and Mary greeted them as they pulled up.

Within moments, the two women were in each other's arms, hugging and chatting.

Oliver watched as Mary took her friend indoors. He felt somewhat bereft with her gone from his side and stood watching her depart.

Richard suggested that they leave the women to do what women did. They had to prepare for the wedding, which would occur as soon as the doctor arrived. He noticed Oliver's eyes followed Annie until she was out of sight.

Richard tapped him on the shoulder. "Come on, Oliver, we have things to do."

Oliver reluctantly followed Richard. The quicker they prepared, the quicker he would have her as his wife. The first thing he needed to do was to unpack her gown and deliver it. He sighed and set to work.

~

Milbah carried a basket of tiny pink wax flowers, as they were the only thing blooming near the wattle and daub house. She walked in front of Annie and Doctor White, who escorted her down the grassy aisle.

Milbah grabbed and threw large handfuls of petals in Annie's path.

The doctor had been let into Annie's secret as he and Oliver had become friends.

Unbeknownst to Oliver, Arthur Bowes-Smith had written to John soon after his return to England. The Second Fleet had brought his letter and revealed Oliver's assistance. It was he who had told the governor about the peer's assistance to the doctor.

Thanks to Mary, Annie knew that the doctor had befriended one of the convict women, Rachel Turner, and they had a child in September of the year before.

John said, "Melba dear, just throw a few at a time rather than big handfuls."

Milbah turned and frowned at him because he had not said her name properly, then continued to do as she wished.

Annie chuckled.

Mary waited for Annie, holding Henry.

Oliver was in front of Richard and turned as John dug him in the ribs.

Annie was wearing the gown Oliver had brought for her, and she looked just like a London bride would have.

The marriage ceremony started as soon as Annie stood beside Oliver. Again, she entwined her fingers with his and gazed up at him in adoration.

Only an hour after arriving in Sydney Cove, they stood under a tall gum tree on the banks of Port Jackson in front of the minister and his wife.

Before they even became aware of the passing of time, Richard pronounced them husband and wife and said, "You may now kiss the bride."

With Richard, Mary, and John watching, Oliver took his wife in his arms and kissed her. At first, his kisses were tender, but then he drew her close, and his kisses became deeper and more heated.

Annie, forgetting where she was, returned them with delight.

They broke apart when Milbah asked her mother, "Why is Uncle Oliver eating Aunt Annie?"

Oliver chuckled, realised where they were, and released Annie. "Later, my love," he whispered softly.

Richard gave them a blessing, and the newlyweds stood around chatting while he packed up the items he had used for the ceremony.

Twice, Richard dropped things, and with a moan, he muttered, "One day, we'll have a church that will fit as many who wish to come and a place to put everything."

Annie had been chatting with Mary. "What does he mean, Mary?"

Mary sighed and said, "Since Governor Phillip left in December, the man he left in charge has overturned many of Arthur's edicts. The first to go was that convicts no longer must attend services. This goes against the advice given by the king himself, as do the land grants he issued to his friends."

Richard had overheard and said, "Not now, Mary dear." He gave a nod to John's presence.

Mary nodded, realising the doctor was still there. Thankfully, he had been deep in conversation with Oliver. She mouthed, "Later," to Annie.

The doctor had to return to the hospital, but he asked to check Annie's arm before he left.

Annie still had twinges of pain and, on his occasional visits to Parramatta, saw him give her arm the once-over each time.

Oliver observed the inspection with interest. "Does she need further treatment, John?"

The doctor lifted his eyes to Oliver's. "No, but as she won't be working in the gardens now, it should help the pins and needles she's still getting. I'm sure it is more from carrying the heavy buckets of water than the broken arm, but we'll know soon enough, young Annie Gentle Soames, eh?"

"I used a shoulder yoke most of the time, sir. Anyway, I'm Annabella Quilpie now, doctor." Annie knew that Oliver had revealed his title to him, and he had been sworn to secrecy along with her friends. Richard and Mary, of course, knew everything as Annie had told them about Oliver long before his arrival.

Once Richard was packed up, the small group returned to the cottage. Mary was walking beside Annie with Henry still held in her arms, and Richard had Milbah on his back as they walked next to Oliver and Annie.

Richard said, "I told you God had a plan, Annie."

Annie smiled at Mary and then glanced at Oliver. "He does, and I told you both that I would not marry anyone but Oliver, and now I have." She skipped with joy. "And now we have a year-long honeymoon before us, and I'm looking forward to that with great glee."

The men kept walking as they had to stow away the items used for the wedding.

When they were far enough away, Mary said,"About that..." and she gave Annie a talk about marriage that her mother would normally have given her.

Annie's eyes were wide open as she listened with rapt attention. "You mean I can enjoy it?"

Mary put her finger to her lips but nodded vigorously. "Absolutely!" Her one word reinforced that action.

Mary prepared a luncheon, cooking a young injured cockerel that had been attacked by crows and serving it with a selection of vegetables they had grown. In the years since they had been in the colony, Richard and Mary's garden had flourished as few others did in the town.

When others had given up, Richard was allocated their land, then assigned more convicts to till the dirt, and he gave instructions on how to improve the soils with compost made from food waste and stable matter. His plants didn't just grow; they thrived. His gardens were often the talk of the town.

John White returned for luncheon as Oliver had invited him and was somewhat envious when the topic of gardening came up for discussion. John said, "With Governor Phillip now gone, Major Grose has begun allocating land for the production of more food. I have been given one hundred acres just out of the town. I have a team to clear it and till the soil, but I'm wondering what will grow best there. Do you have any ideas, sir?" the surgeon asked Richard.

The set look on Richard's face did not reflect contentment.

John wondered what he had said wrong.

Mary explained, "Doctor, I shall let the cat out of the proverbial bag. In his wisdom, the acting Governor has overturned both the king's and Governor Phillip's edicts of the convicts being at regular worship, amongst other things. He has refused permission to build a church with government assistance. Also, he has taken away the convicts who work in our gardens in case they are encouraged to assist with the building of a church. Considering the food needs for the colony, we now have the bare minimum needed to keep the water up to the plants. He has also refused Richard's use of the river barge to Parramatta."

The group looked at the young mother in astonishment.

John spoke first. "That's ridiculous, sir; you are by far the best gardener in the colony, and if I could emulate but half of what you have achieved, I'd be thrilled. As to the church, what are you going to do?"

Richard turned to the doctor and, with a surprising flash of anger, exclaimed, "Do? What shall I do? Well, I shall build it myself. That's what I shall do."

All were surprised that Richard unleashed his bottled-up wrath.

The minister folded his arms angrily. "Yes, Mary, that is what we shall do, and we shall start next month."

Oliver grinned. "Annie, dear wife, once we have had a honeymoon, it looks like we have a church to build. I was wondering how we were going to occupy ourselves until we left. It seems the good Lord has it all in hand."

The utter delight that was written on Annie's face was almost laughable. "Really? We can help them?"

Oliver turned her calloused hand over in his own. "These hands are very capable ones, my beloved wife. If they can tame an unbroken Arabian stallion or three and also grow food for others, then my sweet, I do not see why they cannot assist in building a church, but you will need to teach me."

Annie threw her arms around her husband's neck. "You are the very best of husbands."

Oliver chuckled at the joy of such a project. "I know, my beloved; just make sure you remember that." He silenced her further comments with his lips. Aware that everyone was watching them, it was only a peck on her lips.

The doctor looked at the very unusual couple, a marquess and a convict. Yet, knowing their story, he was sure this relationship would work. He shrugged and said, "So much for taking it a bit easy, Annie. That arm of yours has to last you a lifetime. If you wish to assist with the construction of the church, you may, but you will be holding, not cutting, do you understand?"

She gave him a grin and a nod.

Chapter 18   Adventure Honeymoon

*A*nnie and Oliver stayed only as long as was polite. Oliver was itching to return to the cottage in Parramatta and begin their honeymoon.

Over the remainder of the luncheon, they had put their heads together and planned a uniquely shaped church. It would be cross-shaped so the three groups, convict, free and military, would not have to sit next to each other.

As they were leaving, Mary had loaded Annie up with a selection of leftovers from the luncheon.

As Oliver was deep in conversation with Richard and John, the women stowed the basket in the luggage rack on the back with their clothes.

Annie had changed from her glorious gown and donned a new travelling dress before saying farewell to Mary and the girls in her household.

Abaroo came and gave her a big hug, said something that only Annie could hear, and then shrank back into the shadows.

By the time Oliver and Annie made their farewells minutes later, she had vanished from view.

Richard had an outline and now had to work out how to construct the building. It would need to be wattle and daub, but if he made the uprights as logs rather than saplings, then the construction would be much stronger. He set about drawing up proper plans and, by the end of the afternoon, had put in an order for the lumber he required.

Meanwhile, Oliver and Annie were well on their way back to the cottage in Parramatta.

Although they had already been together physically and had a child, Annie had now become somewhat shy about what was ahead of her.

Oliver knew something was concerning her as she had fallen silent. Wondering what could possibly be the matter, he thought the only way to find out was to ask. "Annie dearest, something is concerning you, but if you do not tell me, I shall be unable to assist."

Annie turned to him with reddened cheeks. "It hurt the first time, Oliver, but I want to be with you again that way. I want to have your children and be a good wife, but I'm scared. Mary chatted with me and said that it should be enjoyable and even fun, but I felt great pain."

Oliver heaved a sigh of relief. "Sweetheart, it hurt because you had never been with a man. Since then, you have been born a child, and well, to put it quite bluntly, you will have stretched. This time, there should be no pain at all, only pleasure, I promise."

She nodded, then snuggled up to him again. "I remember when I told you I was carrying your child and that when you kissed me, all I wished you to do was to take me again on the chaise lounge in your office. I had no idea I could be so wonton. The desires you stirred in me were, well, even now, they are almost frightening."

Oliver had his arm around her and had drawn her close to him. "The desires I had for you were so wrong, but in my drunken stupor, I did not restrain my lust. Now, what is ahead of us is good and proper. I must admit I am looking forward to tonight in a warm, soft bed."

Their conversation was silenced for some time as he pulled her onto his lap. They had travelled about six miles along the fifteen-mile road when the carriage bounced over a particularly bad hole.

An ominous crunch made the carriage lurch; then, it leaned heavily to one side.

Oliver knew in an instant that one of the wheels had broken. If a horse had thrown a shoe, they could have walked the remaining distance, but they were now stranded in the middle of the bush with the coach now sitting at an odd angle.

The coachman carefully opened the door to enquire about their well-being. "I'm mighty sorry, sir, but oi thinks you are stuck here until I can get a spare wheel. It's bust beyond fixin', sir."

Oliver opened his mouth to speak when Annie butted in. "Can you ride to Parramatta and bring back a spare one tomorrow morning?"

The coachman knew the man to be a gentleman and that he was not used to roughing it. In his short acquaintance with Mrs Quilpie, he was pretty sure the lady would be able to cope with most things. "Oi can missus, but will you'se be all right here for the night? There ain't be no wild animals to hurt you, but you might be mighty cold."

Oliver was horrified. "But, Annie…"

Annie smiled and said, "Trust me, Oliver, this will be a honeymoon we will never forget." She turned to the coachman and said, "If you unharness the leader and hobble the other horse, then you should easily make it to town before dark. Be assured that we will be fine here. The dingos will stay away from the fire. Oliver will assist you with the horse."

By this time, Oliver and Annie had alighted from the stricken vehicle. He gaped at her suggestions but went to assist the driver. One glance at the spokes on the wheel showed three were shattered, the metal rim buckled, and the felloe on one side was broken in half.

Less than ten minutes after the carriage stopped, the coachman rode off, leaving the honeymooners standing in the middle of nowhere.

They had managed to move the broken carriage off to the side of the road before they unharnessed the beasts.

The area they had broken down in had a wide grassy clearing nearby. The second horse was hobbled and left to graze along the road edges.

The coachman set off to Parramatta on the leader, and the newlyweds quite literally watched him ride off into the sunset.

Once the horse and rider had vanished from sight, Annie turned to her new husband and said, "Well, husband mine, your education is about to start. Tonight, we are having a wedding night in New South Wales, convict style. First, we collect wood and then set up a campfire. We've had enough food to eat from that huge luncheon that if we get hungry, then we hunt for something to eat like I had to when we arrived. Maybe a goanna or a possum. There's a creek, so we have water…"

She saw Oliver's look of horror. She doubled over laughing. "…or we open the hamper of leftovers Mary gave us."

Oliver's face was filled with relief. "I am not eating any of those grubs you told me about. Nope! No matter how hungry I am, I will draw the line at those wiggling things."

Annie chuckled. "Well, hamper or not, we will still need a fire. So we need to collect wood as it will be cold tonight."

With daylight fading quickly, they collected as much wood as they could. A tree had fallen some time ago, and many of the older branches had smashed as it fell. "Before you pick up the wood, check for snakes, Oliver. It should be cold enough that they are not out, but be careful anyway."

He was intrigued when she walked around hunting for some firesticks, as she called them. She chose a thin, straight, freshly dead gum twig about the thickness of her finger and an old, well-dead chunk of soft and spongy bark. She also pulled a few strands of her hair out and twisted them around her fingers to make a loop. She pulled off her shoes to hold the bottom chunk of bark with her toes.

He watched, intrigued. "Annie, what are you doing, sweetie?"

While still concentrating on her work, she said, "Well, we have firewood. Do you have any flint or a tinderbox?"

Oliver shook his head and then squatted down beside her to watch. "No, but how do you make fire with sticks?"

Annie was busy powdering some of the dry bark and looking for harder patches to start the friction. "The top stick is a freshly dead gum stick. The bottom one is an old dead branch, or you can use a bit of soft bark. But preferably something that will cause some heat. The hair is to catch the spark. I've done this a few times before, but it's not guaranteed." With her tongue poking out the side of her mouth, she set to work. Her hands twisted and rubbed down the length of the stick. She soon saw a wisp of smoke, added the hair and powdered bark to the bottom, and then kept twisting.

Moments later, Oliver watched as the smoke turned into fire. "Oh my Annie, that's another layer of your onion!"

She nodded and said, "Hmm, but not something I will use much in society in England, methinks."

Within an hour, Annie had Oliver organised for his first night camping. With the fire going and the blankets and pillows placed near the fire. Mary's hamper was placed on a couple of small branches to stop the ants from raiding it.

He watched as she cleared the ground before laying the thin coachman's oilskin wrap on the ground. He felt so useless. He could only watch her prepare for the evening.

She added the pillows and warm blankets, turned to her husband, and said, "Husband mine, behold the begetting bed." Her hands were on her hips, and she threw back her head and laughed at his shocked expression.

As it was nearing twilight and the fire had not yet burnt down, they raided the hamper.

Amongst the wood that Annie had collected was a green gum branch with a forked end. When the fire had burned for a while, she poked this into the side of some of the bread and carefully toasted the thick, buttered slices.

Oliver watched in awe.

She looked up and caught his gaze. "When I arrived, we were all like you. None of us knew how to live in this country. Through Mary and Richard and their interaction with some of the native children, I learned much about local foods. Abaroo, the smallpox-scarred Eora girl at their house, often visited the Johnsons. A year later, about half of her tribe died of the disease. We had no idea anyone carried the illness, but it was the only way the Aboriginals could have become sick. Arabanoo was another of the Aborigines, and he nursed her, and one of the other child, Nanberry, then caught it and died. Abaroo was known as Bagaroo when she came but changed to Abaroo when she became ill. I often wondered if it was in homage to Arabanoo, who nursed her. Araboo is free to come and go as she wishes; she speaks some English and taught me some words of her language."

Annie knew her well from the year she lived with them. Abaroo occasionally called in at Parramatta and taught Annie what foods to eat and how to prepare them. Annie, in turn, helped her new friend learn her language.

Annie had used this knowledge to supplement her rations in the years of near starvation in the colony. She decided not to tell him too much, as sleeping on the ground would be enough of a shock for Oliver for one night. The rest of the information would follow in the following months. However, her eyes scanned the surrounding bush to see if they were being watched.

As the sun finally sank behind the scrubby bush, the two of them packed away Mary's feast.

Rather than leave it on the ground for the ants to find, Oliver placed the hamper back into the carriage for safety.

While he was busy doing that, Annie found a bush and relieved herself. Oliver had needed to do the same and did so while Annie was tending the fire.

As the evening darkened, Annie and Oliver watched the flames lick the new branches they added.

Oliver had never experienced outdoor life or sat around a wood fire before. The coal at home didn't have the same ambience. For him, this was all new. He felt vulnerable and unsure of what to do next.

As the darkness fell, Annie pointed out some of the stars she had learned about. Venus was the first to appear, and by the time it was dark, the Southern Cross and pointers were visible.

The May sky was filled with a myriad of twinkling stars, and the crackling of the burning twigs made them pull the blankets back a little from the fire.

Once the bed was prepared, Annie reclined on the blankets invitingly.

Oliver did not need words to know her intention.

The light from the fire illuminated her face. Her kisses warmed him, and soon, the emotion of the evening saw her unbuttoning his shirt.

As they undressed, Oliver pushed a blanket near the fire to warm.

Item by item, their raiment was soon divested and placed carefully on a log out of the ants' and spiders' reach.

The stars, cicadas, and possible audience were nearly forgotten.

Oliver was still unsure if what they were doing was wise.

Her kisses diverted him adequately.

Annie had just taken off her new chemise when he drew up the warmed blanket to cover them.

Annie chuckled and said, "No one will see us, Oliver. We are here like Adam and Eve were, starting our marriage under the stars. They would have done much as we have, but without the blankets and feather pillows. The fire is enough light to see me, and you once said you wished to see all of me; well, I'm here, and I'm all yours."

Looking was not exactly what Oliver had in mind, but it was a good start; his gentle caress shot bolts of delight through Annie.

Their previous coupling had been so fast and so unexpected that this time, Annie wished to explore him and his anatomy. He did not even remember being with her.

The firelight showed her he was ready for her. She drew him down on top of her and waited for the pain, but there was none, just pleasure.

Oliver's desire for his new wife made the blood pound to his nether regions. He wanted her, but he promised to pleasure her, and that's what he planned to do. They had their lives before them, but tonight must be for her. She was right; this was a honeymoon they would remember forever. He promised he would not hurt her. He intended to take the evening slowly.

That's apparently not what Annie wanted. She pulled him on top of her and wrapped her legs around him.

The warm blankets did indeed become their begetting bed. Knowing that she had conceived after their first coupling, she wondered what they would do if she had a child in the colony.

Temporarily sated, Oliver rolled off her and drew her to him as they lay looking up at the stars. "Did I hurt you, sweetie?"

Annie curled up to his muscular body. "No, it was as you said. Having a child has changed my body. But laying a large melon will do that."

Oliver chuckled.

With the evening cooling, Oliver drew the other blankets over them, and they dozed while enfolded in each other's arms. Just before they slept, Oliver said quietly, "I love you so much, Annie Quilpie. I just want to make sure you know that."

Annie's answer was to lift her head for a long kiss. "Ditto, Oliver; I love you too." She was so drowsy that he hardly heard her words. She was asleep in moments, and he lay looking up at the sky above, deep in thought, with her curled up to his side.

Some time in the middle of the night, Annie woke, and realising the fire had burned down, she scrambled from the blankets and pulled another big log onto the coals.

Oliver stirred and watched her nubile naked body silhouetted as the flames licked the log. She had always been slim, but now her frame was gaunt. The years of near starvation and hard outdoor work had made her shed every ounce of condition she had carried. She still had bumps natural to a woman, but gone was her voluptuous, curvaceous figure after playing 'go fetch' for Verity.

As Annie crawled back into their bed, Oliver was now fully awake. "Hello, wife, I do hope you are not tired, for I seem to have my second wind."

The light lit up their bodies as the tongues of fire began to consume the new log.

Oliver was determined that Annie would learn what the joys of marriage were all about. This time, Oliver ensured she was properly fulfilled.

Her shouts of delight and whimpers of pleasure made Oliver grin. When he took his fill of her, she squealed with delight, and they completed the act in unison.

"Oh, Oliver, what was that?" She asked in awe at what had just occurred to her.

As she snuggled in his arms under the blankets, he said, "That, my darling love, is what marriage really is. It's what I should have let you experience last time, but I could not wait. Hopefully, this will happen most of the time we are together."

Annie rubbed her hand over his prickly cheek. "I'm going to love being married to you, Oliver Christopher Quilpie. I'm going to love having your babies and for you to use your title to help people. I presume that is what you meant by picking up Doctor Bowes-Smith's baton."

Oliver tilted up her chin and kissed her. "It is, my sweet, but I will not discuss another man on my wedding night, even if it's a dead man. I think I will be quite a possessive husband, my darling."

Once again warmed by the fire, they settled to sleep.

Oliver lay watching the stars above while Annie slept in his arms. He realised he was happy. He had never known such absolute contentment. He was lying on a rug, stark naked, in the middle of the bush with nothing more than his lady love. His wife! Annie was worth giving up everything else in his luxurious life. Should she refuse to return home, he would be content to stay here with her.

~

They were awoken in the pre-dawn light, with Oliver being poked through the blanket. They were surrounded by about a dozen tall, near-naked Aboriginal men; they all had spears.

Annie was not awake and had thrown her arms above her head, thus showing she was unclad. She heard giggles and woke.

Oliver realised her state of undress and pulled the blanket up to cover her. He sat up in their makeshift bed and realised his clothing was out of reach.

Annie, now wide awake, clutched the blanket to cover her breasts and said, "Me *dyinmang,*" she said, pointing to herself, "Oliver's *duba.*" She showed them her ring. In the dawn light, she saw a row of grinning white teeth surrounding them. She pointed to Oliver and said, "*Mullamang,*" then to herself again, "*Duba.*"

The chuckles surrounding them made Oliver wonder what she had said.

She translated for him. "Abaroo told me the word for an aboriginal wife is *dyinmang,* and woman means *duba. Mullamang* is the word for husband. She only told me yesterday when we were saying goodbye. So, I might have said it wrong. She said they have their spears visible, so we should be safe. When you don't see them, you should worry, Oliver. They slide them in the grass and can pick them up with their toes in an instant."

One of the younger men leaned over and said not so quietly, "You speak real good, Miss Annie. You learn to make good fire, too. We come tell you get dressed quick; your people coming."

While he spoke, he waved the others away, and they melted back into the bush as he spoke.

"I, Bidgee Bidgee, Abaroo's blood brother, she say you good to her. You be plenty quick; they come soon." Then he was gone. He melted into the dim light as soon as he finished speaking.

Once alone in the opening, Oliver grabbed their clothing while muttering under his breath.

Both hastily dressed under the blanket just in case the men were still watching.

Annie was giggling so much that she found it hard to pull on her stockings.

Oliver had been all but caught *in flagrante delicto* with his wife. He couldn't see the funny side of things.

On the other hand, Annie was nearly beside herself in fits of laughter. "Oliver, if I had told you that they may appear at any time, would you have... well, done what we did?"

Oliver was horrified. "Absolutely not!"

She threw her arms around his neck and kissed him. "Exactly, husband mine. They are sometimes called the ghosts of the bush for good reason. Bennelong, whom Governor Phillip took back to England with him, is part of the same tribe. Nanberry, who lives with John White and Rachel, Bidgee Bidgee, Ballooderry and Maugoran are all related to Abaroo. They have the most amazing ability to appear and disappear in an instant. Abaroo told me Bidgee Bidgee is a brilliant mimic of people and animals. However, I had no idea that Abaroo had taught any of them English. For all I know, they could have been watching all night."

The look of horror Oliver gave her set her off again in a peal of laughter.

"Oh, Oliver, they have children too, but they don't have blankets; they use animal skins. Abaroo tells me they always sleep near the fire as it keeps the dingos away. Like us, they are good people, and all the ones I have met are lovely and helpful. They are willing to trade food; if we get a chance, we must try how they cook duck. The bird is drowned and encased in mud. Then the ball is sat in the coals. It's delicious. However, there are rogues in any group of humans. We have invaded their land, but more often than not, we trade with them, and they are kind and honest. I have had far more trouble with the soldiers than them. Abaroo liked my strawberries, but they wouldn't take them unless they left me something in return. I often found containers of native berries, a speared possum, or sometimes a fish in place of my missing fruit."

Once clad, they set about folding up their 'bed' and packing the carriage with the now almost emptied hamper.

No sooner had the sun risen above the tree line than a vehicle was heard coming down the road.

Annie was sitting in a lady-like manner on the log as though she had only been waiting for ten minutes.

Oliver was flicking his eyes on the bush where the boy had vanished. He could not believe they had disappeared so fast. He had seen that one of the lad's front teeth was missing and had been amazed that he had a six-inch spike through his nose.

He said, "Annie, I had no idea the natives were so… well, clever, I suppose, and they are so dark. I understand why they are called the ghosts of the bush. I've never seen someone vanish so fast."

Annie knew what he was feeling. "Yes, they are, both black and skilled at many things. I, too, was fearful when I met my first one, but through Abaroo, I learned a lot. She taught me the secret of fire-making. They have a different skill from us, but they do not need to drink tea from cups with a little finger held aloft or how to bow or curtsy to a king; they do know how to make fire and dig for roots and witchetty grubs. They live on the land without harming it. They take what they need without leaving a trace that they were here. If it were not for their assistance, we would all have died. I, for one, will be thankful to every one of them."

As she spoke, the carriage arrived.

It took an hour to replace the wheel as they had to somehow make a lever to lift the carriage.

The luggage and hamper needed to be unloaded, and Oliver and the coach driver used a long, freshly fallen branch as a lever. The blacksmith, who had come to ensure the wheel was correctly installed, fitted the wheel on and inserted the pin to hold it in place.

The wheel was loaded on the blacksmith's cart, and the two vehicles set off for the final miles to Parramatta.

Oliver took Annie in his arms as soon as the carriage door shut. "I so wish I had met you so much earlier in my life. I would have been a very different person."

Annie shook her head. "No, Oliver, we are who we are today because of what we have both endured. There must be no more '*ifs*' or '*buts*'. I know what Verity was like; I know about that part of your story, Oliver, and now you must experience a bit of what my life has been like here, for you will need to know that to understand me fully. I have changed a bit over the years."

Oliver nodded, unable to answer. If last night was an example of what she could do, he wondered what else he would learn about her. He knew she was unique. He had seen her wild rides on his horses that any sane man avoided. He knew that life would never be boring with Annie in his world. He had also learnt just how important God was in her life. He was front and centre of all her decisions, and his time with Richard and Mary over the past months had shown him a new way to live. For once, he began to like the man he was becoming.

He said, "I can tell you one thing, Annie Quilpie; when I return to England, I will be treating my staff very differently. I can't believe what an egotistical upstart I am."

Annie smiled. "Was, Oliver! By the time we have finished building the church, you will find that you have muscles you didn't know about and that we are all humans made in God's image. You will be working next to hardened criminals, and you will hear their stories. There is no difference between convict and free, peer or pauper. I have learnt much about people in the years since my arrest. My friend Olive was arrested for theft, but her real name was Olivia Gascoyne. She is gentry, too, and we bonded quickly. Oliver, I learned to love all of the women; they are from all walks of life. When in chains, class is irrelevant."

Chapter 19   Building the Future

$\mathcal{B}$y the time they had been married for a month, Annie had already had her monthly flow once. Although saddened that she had not conceived soon after they married, they had plenty of fun practising.

Mary's words after their wedding told her that the act of marriage was supposed to be fun as well as productive. Her words included something that surprised the newly married couple. "God made that side enjoyable for both of you, so enjoy it. Remember these three words: recreation, relaxation and reproduction."

Annie had discovered the truth of two of those words but was still waiting for the last one to occur.

They had already discussed names for future children. Maxwell and Olivia were two names they both liked. All that needed to happen now was for her to conceive; however, she was still woefully thin.

The rickety building they shared beside the military redoubt in Parramatta was small, but the bed was soft and oh-so-comfortable. However, there was little, if any, hanging space, as the governor really only had his uniforms.

Oliver had mountains of clothing, as he had also brought not only Annie's old clothing but a massive travelling case of new apparel for her as well as some three large cases of his own attire.

Annie had great fun trying on all her new items while they were cloistered in their bedroom.

Oliver had approved what looked best on her. Two gowns he refused to allow her to wear unless modified. The *décolletage* was far too low for the colony full of lustful men. Unless she sewed in a false neckline, he would not permit her to wear those two gowns in a sleazy, female-starved convict town. She already turned heads wherever she went. Her clean, fair, curly hair was unusual in this squalid place. On the farm, her hair looked brown, caked with oils and filth. Her fair curls had been invisible. Now, she was nearly back to her beautiful, vibrant self. She did not need to attract unwanted attention from lustful eyes.

Oliver now freely admitted he was already jealous, but his decision about the dresses was more to protect her.

On arrival in Sydney Cove for their wedding, Oliver admitted that he had paid for a small dwelling to be built for them. He waited until this was complete before he came to collect Annie.

It was a whitewashed wattle and daub cottage near the Johnsons house, and thankfully, Annie was delighted with their first home. Compared to the immense palace-like building in England, the entire cottage was the size of Oliver's bedroom.

She admitted with a giggle that she knew the size of his bedroom as she had ventured into his room to steal his clothing.

He feigned a shocked look.

They still had no idea how long the church would take to build, but the construction materials had been piled up and ready for use by the time their honeymoon was over.

Their return to Sydney was welcomed by their neighbours, Richard and Mary.

In the weeks since they were married, the cottage that Oliver had commissioned was now fully furnished. It was only one large room with a movable divider to screen off the bedroom. This area was off to the left side, and the eat-in kitchen had a fireplace to the right, with a kitchen bench near the open fire. A table filled the middle of the room.

The cottage had an overhanging gable roofline with a verandah on one side. Here, another rustic bench seat was constructed.

Annie noticed the luxurious-looking bed. The frame was not the typical French polished four-post bed found in England, but the base had been made from stripped saplings and cobbled with mortise and tenon joints. Their new mosquito net could easily be hung over it. Where Oliver sourced a feather mattress from, Annie didn't ask, but it would be used with great enjoyment. The whitewash, really just white clay with some crushed shell grit in it, had dried to a smooth but somewhat gritty surface.

They moved the one case of clothing they had sorted to wear in the colony and set it beside their bed. The room had some unusual hangers along one wall near the window, but they were actually branch offcuts protruding from a backboard. On the other side of the window was some shelving.

Again, the cabin had very little storage space, but it still had more than at the official residence in Parramatta. The bedroom area was the size of Oliver's closet at home, and he knew it would take some getting used to. Hopefully, they would be outside working most of the day.

The remainder of their full travelling cases were placed around the table as extra seating.

After a month-long honeymoon, the newlyweds became used to a new person with whom to share their lives.

Oliver's first marriage had been disjointed from the start.

Annie had been without luxuries for so long that such things were a delight. She had shared a pallet bed on the ship out, but snuggling up next to a fully clad convict woman who stank was not the same as sleeping next to a virile, naked husband. She had to relearn to have nice things and to be served instead of serving.

Oliver had to learn to do without many of the luxuries he had been born with. Through it all, they laughed a lot.

While in Parramatta, Annie showed Oliver her garden. They picked everything they could before heading to Sydney. She carefully dug up her strawberries, leaving one or two runners for Colin, who now owned the plot. They would need food in Sydney, and that meant starting a vegetable garden at their cottage. These plants would be a good start.

As thanks, Colin had swapped produce from other plots, and they left with a quantity of fresh vegetables.

Bidgee Bidgee had come to say farewell and brought them a wallaby tail to make stew. In return, Oliver gave him one of his tricorn hats. Wearing it with pride, Bidgee Bidgee minced away from them in the exact manner that Major Francis Grose walked.

The pair watching his departure failed to hold back their mirth.

Their friend turned to wave, gave them a grin, and then vanished into the bush.

~

Three days into the church build, Oliver realised he was doing something useful and enjoying himself. He worked side by side with his wife, assorted convicts, an aboriginal girl, and a clergyman. Boxing at the clubs in London or riding in Hyde Park or Rotten Row used very few of his muscles compared with the work he was now doing. His hands were blistered, and he had many splinters, but he didn't care a hoot.

Annie was working by his side, lifting the smaller logs and weaving the vines through the standing saplings.

Both returned home to their tiny cottage each evening, covered in daub and sawdust, but they were happier than ever.

Oliver had sourced a large hip bath from somewhere, and although they could not stretch out, they could wash before falling into bed exhausted.

Mary and Richard's convict maid and Abaroo, if she were around, would cook up a storm and feed all the workers before they headed home, so all any of them had to do was wash and then head to bed.

The Johnsons also complained about the aches and pains of manual labour.

The Quilpies grinned and nodded, knowing that they still had more activities planned for when they were alone.

Occasionally, one or the other of them was asleep before their spouse joined them, but most nights, they released the physical union.

Each night, the newlyweds slept entwined.

They were content.

Oliver had never been without staff to cater to his every whim until he boarded the ship to come here.

At home, luxuries and whatever food he desired were provided without fuss. His valet kept his clothing in order and dressed him; here, he missed none of those things. Having Annie with him was enough.

She delighted in teaching him the basic joys of living.

By the time they were three weeks into the construction, the walls of the unusual church were nearly up, and the first of the roof beams were in place. When the walls were completed, they would add the trusses for the roof on those.

Oliver discovered that they even had to build the ladders on which they climbed. He found the manual labour of building something not just useful but exhilarating. His instructor was a convict whom Oliver learned to respect. Max Slater could turn his hand to build anything.

Richard and he mulled over how to attack each stage of the construction. He watched in awe as the skilled craftsmen adzed each main roof beam. The skill needed to turn a round log into a square beam was not easy.

Oliver tried it, and Max, the carpenter, laughed at his effort. The craftsmen explained that the bloodwood in the middle gave the timber immense strength rather than splitting a log and getting two lengths from each one. Adzing off the sides and squaring them gave the entire building a more solid foundation. By splitting the logs, the strength was halved.

Each log had been felled and had been drying for over two years. It was now stripped of bark and dressed for use.

Oliver considered himself well-educated until he realised that his studies in the classics and languages were useless for living on a land like this. He was a novice and willingly took instruction from a skilled carpenter, who, he discovered, was a master pick-pocket.

Another convict taught him how to fish with a hand line made from twine and a local vine. They used oysters as bait on hooks of bent nails and caught a large bream. This was far more rewarding than fly fishing for salmon in his streams at home. Hunger honed his need to succeed.

When specific skills were needed for the next stage, and they were not needed on the building site, Annie and he would wander down to Farm Cove and try to catch some fresh fish for dinner. They were often successful, returning with enough for both households.

That evening in bed, Oliver lay waiting for Annie to join him. His bare chest was exposed above the blankets; his arms were above his head.

Annie luxuriated in the hip bath in front of the fire, and he enjoyed the view. Both were now used to the physical exertions.

Oliver discovered that due to the manual labour, his muscles were taxing the seams of his shirts to the point that Annie needed to make repairs on one of them.

One shirt had been torn, and Annie used it to cut up and add gussets to the other shirts.

He chuckled at her ingenuity. At home, he would have thrown out the item; here, he had no way to replace them. Annie used every linen scrap and even made some handkerchiefs with the remaining fabric. His physique filled out, and his skin shone with health and vigour as it had never done before. He had tan lines on his arms and loved the warm winter sun.

Tonight, they were chatting as she bathed.

Oliver said, "Annie, did you know that Max is a thief and he is serving seven years? We were making the scarf cuts for the trusses today, and somehow, we got onto the subject of why he came out. I had no idea that so many workers in England were underpaid. You tried to tell me, but I was willing to trust my agents and leave the nitty-gritty of salaries for them to sort out. I had no idea until you told me everyone was trying to subsist on a mere pittance."

Annie smiled, remembering the accusations she had thrust at him. She said, "Where money is concerned, I have discovered that greed comes to the fore. Few people will ever have enough of the glittery substance, and the temptation of money makes many otherwise trustworthy people fall victim to the lust for obtaining more. Colin was here for the same reason. Food for you was a luxury. You only had to say what you wished for dinner, and the cook made it for you. But the villagers and poor of London ate what they could find. Sometimes, that meant catching river rats and eating them as they had to do on the hulks. Poaching was a necessity, not a luxury. Many here received seven years for trying to survive. The only thing the rich and greedy like more than money is grog. Here, they don't care what kind it is as long as it makes them drunk. Some of the home-brew moonshine or hooch they brew here is all but lethal."

Oliver frowned. She didn't exactly say his agents were crooks but realised he would thoroughly check his books when he went home.

Annie stood in the bath, letting the excess water drain off her body and unashamedly standing in full view of Oliver. He had found a lady in the colony who had made perfume from some native violets, and he had purchased a tiny flask of the delicious scent. Annie had added a couple of drops to her bath water tonight. The heady smell filled the tiny room with an aroma of luxury.

Memories washed over Oliver, and flashes he had thought forgotten flooded over him. She leaned over and picked up a cloth to dry herself off, and Oliver groaned with desire. He remembered sniffing the settee to try to catch her scent. He never needed to do that again as now his eyes feasted on her every move. He knew that very shortly, she would be beside him in bed, naked as the day she was born. He watched his wife dry herself and was already lusting over her alabaster body.

Trying to focus on the mundane to quench his ardour, he said, "Max is teaching me things I had no idea about. I'm learning about cantilevers, cambers, chamfers, slopes, scarf cuts, and overhangs. I had never considered how a roof was made before or why it stayed up. I knew about flying buttresses on the cathedrals at home, but I had no idea how to brace a joint or smooth timber. He had me using a spokeshave to chamfer the edges off the beams. I wondered why he worried about the necessity of doing these until I had to hold one of the beams while he fixed them to the other side. The chamfered edges meant they didn't give me splinters."

Annie was now dry, and she extinguished the lamp as she came to bed.

Their small cabin was warm and toasty.

Outside, the frost had settled on the ground, and they knew the morning would be cold. Tonight, their bed would be warm as they once again took their fill of each other.

Oliver no longer cared about the giant spiders running over the whitewashed walls. Each night, the new cheesecloth netting over their bed was dropped, and they could sleep in peace without the creatures, geckos falling, or mosquitos buzzing them.

One of the huge hairy creatures had fallen on their bed in Parramatta, and he discovered just how fast they could run. The honeymooners had moved like lightning as the large spider ran up the bedclothes. To avoid further occurrences of that, he had purchased a bolt of loose-weave cheesecloth, and Annie had made a tent-like canopy over the bed. He had added a screw and hook to the ceiling and hung the net tent from that. They had made a second net for the cottage.

Cocooned in their own little love nest, they needed no one else.

Tonight, Oliver reached out for her as she slipped beneath the covers. He would drop the sides of the netting after their lovemaking. He was not concerned that she had not fallen with his child as they enjoyed exploring the intimacy of their marriage. Both knew that she could conceive, and they had time on their side.

Before their marriage, Oliver had never slept a full night with a woman in his arms. He had visited Verity's rooms when she permitted, but that had not been often. She did not like him remaining after they had been together and usually banished him within moments of completing the act. With Verity, there was no afterglow after their mating. The physical act with her was making love to an inanimate doll. With her arms above her head, she didn't respond to him, so he didn't try to pleasure her. He used to take his fill, then leave her.

With Annie, she would snuggle up to his side and lay an arm possessively across his chest. He would feel her soft breath on the hairs of his neck as she slept. He had never known such contentment; wrapping his arms around her, he, too, slept. He realised he was happy, deeply, and satisfyingly happy.

~

By the time all the trusses were completed and tea tree shrubbery collected for the thatching, the possibility of a new Quilpie was manifesting itself to Annie. They had been married three months, and she had finally missed a flow. Knowing that once she started to eat good food again when her garden produced well, her monthly flow would become regular again. That had indeed happened.

The tea tree thatching would take a long time to complete as it was much more difficult to use than the sedge or Norfolk reed at home. There was just enough of the native rushes to place a single row before covering it with tea tree branches. From inside the building, it looked properly thatched, but from outside, the native shrub made the roof look unusual. The native rushes meant the water should run down the stems if water did seep through.

The strange cross-shaped church now had thatch rafters awaiting their covering, and an enormous pile of dried rushes awaited installation.

Richard knew of an area of wetland some miles down the harbour that was host to a vast area of these rushes. Not enough for the entire roof, but certainly enough to install a single layer. The seating would be arranged with the longer nave to fit the convicts, and the side transepts would seat the free settlers in one wing and the military in the other. This way, the three groups were kept separate.

On the day the thatching was completed, Annie and Oliver stood watching the last sheet of lead capping be applied to the roof's central peak.

Oliver noticed that Annie had been holding her stomach during the past week. He had seen her do this before when she carried their first child, but he wondered but did not ask.

As Annie had carried a child before, she knew what was ahead of her, but she had no idea if marital relations could continue while she was expecting. After a long conversation with Mary that morning, Annie ascertained that they could continue enjoying the benefits of marriage. She now just had to work out how to tell Oliver he was to be a father again. And this child may well be his heir. "Oliver, you know this church has three branches of the building; it works, doesn't it? It makes a cross."

Oliver watched intently as the last sheet of flashing was passed onto the roof. "Yes, sweetheart, I think it will work well. It will mean that the congregation can attend worship in peace and in all weathers."

This morning, Oliver helped the final bunch of vegetation get tied together with copper wire that held it all together. Now, only the final section of lead flashing on the top needed to be added. He knew that the entire building had cost under £70. It was a lifetime of funds for a convict but only the value of one evening coat for him. He had assisted in the costs with a donation to Richard. When Oliver explained the value was less than one outfit from his tailor, his friend accepted gracefully.

Annie tugged at his hand to get him to turn to her. "It's not the only thing in threes, Oliver."

His attention was now focused on her. "Huh, like what, my gentle Annie?"

Her face shone with love as she gazed at him. "What is one plus one, Oliver?"

A puzzled frown sat on his brow. "Two, why?"

Annie was bubbling with happiness, "Wrong, it's three." She took his hand and placed it on her stomach.

The realisation of her action confirmed his suspicion. He was over the moon. "Are you serious? You're with child again?"

Annie giggled. "Yes, but shhh, we're only just married; we're not supposed to have a history, remember."

In his elation with her news, he grasped her around the waist and swung her around.

She didn't need to hear words to know of his happiness.

Mary watched on as her friend announced the joyous news to her husband.

Richard stood beside her and looked puzzled. "Is there something I should know?" He remembered how Mary had told him of her exciting condition. Sadly, their first son had died, but they had two healthy children.

Mary nodded.

Richard's face was flooded with relief. "Is that why she's not been helping with the build this week? I thought they must have had a fight."

Again, Mary nodded while chuckling. "No fighting for those two love birds. No, I kept her busy with other things so she would not be lifting anything. She's only a bit late, but we're not taking chances. With her history, she's concerned a little."

While the two couples were still occupied with discussing babies, the church building was completed unnoticed.

Oliver slid his arm around Annie's shoulder, and they walked to their friends to share their good news.

Mary dug Richard in the side. "Act surprised."

"I will," he said, grinning knowingly.

Oliver and Annie arrived at their friends' side as Mary and Richard were grinning from ear to ear. "You know, don't you?"

Richard gave a slow nod. Mary elbowed him somewhat angrily. He said, "Ouch! What was that for?"

"I told you to act surprised," Mary chuckled.

Richard was laughing. "Why? It's not like they haven't had enough practice. I'm delighted, of course; we both are."

Oliver flushed scarlet at the comment but said he was happy. He also had much to discuss with Annie. He knew that staying in the colony was not an option, and he wished to get home as fast as possible.

With the church's completion, the seating construction was already underway. As proper church pews were far too expensive to make, Richard settled on stumps and slabs of timber for the simple seats. They would eventually be replaced as pews were made, but it would be a quick way of getting the church open for services, and he wished to do that as soon as possible.

The finishing touches could be done after the services started. The inside needed whitewashing, and the seats were to be set in place as each was made.

Richard also wanted shelving and a cupboard built into the vestry. The books they had brought would soon be able to be unpacked. He planned that the church would be a multi-purpose building, and shelving along the walls of the nave meant their library could be used by others. Eventually, a public meeting house would be constructed, and the library would move in there, but for now, this would do.

Few knew that he had more than four thousand two hundred books in storage, not to mention numerous Bibles and hymn books. He still had to get the glass out of Government Stores and have windows made, but that would come later.

Oliver left Richard to oversee the tidying up of the lead ridge capping to spend time with his wife.

Without even saying farewell to their friends, they walked down the hill to their cabin and sat on the grassy embankment outside their front door to discuss their forthcoming child.

The arrival of this baby would be vastly different to the loss of their firstborn. Oliver had been unable to be part of her life through that, and the joyous news of the impending birth had brought back a flood of memories that both were finding it hard not to voice.

They needed to be alone to cope with the emotions washing over them both. He was overwhelmed with guilt about how he had treated her the last time.

Annie realised that he needed to voice his concerns. However, she was so excited that all she wanted to do was hold him close, which she had been unable to do before.

Oliver had his arm around Annie's shoulder as they talked, but he now turned her to face him. "Annie, my darling love, although I am delighted with this news, I am also concerned. My gentle Annie, I wish the child to be born in England. Not about birthright or anything, but because medical services there are better. Here, everything is… um, primitive, to say the least. This means that we should enquire about a passage home immediately. With the church finished, it is time we left Mary and Richard to get on with what they are here to do."

Annie was not yet feeling ill, so she knew her condition was very early. "Oliver, I would like that above all things. If my reckoning is correct, the baby should arrive in about April, but my term expires in May."

She was not voicing what was on her mind, but she realised that the child would be born while she was still a convict.

Oliver had already worked that out. "I don't care, sweetheart; we're going on the next ship home. I have Arthur Phillip's letter; a few weeks here or there should not make a huge difference. We'll have to keep our heads down for a bit. Annie Gentle is dead; he arranged all that too. She left on the foreign ship that brought you."

Annie gasped and chuckled. She knew Oliver would have sorted that out.

~

Within a week, Oliver had found that two ships were due to depart. The *Boddingtons* and the *Sugar Cane* had both arrived loaded with very troublesome Irish convicts.

The two vessels discharged very healthy convicts and sold the excess supplies to the colony. Both vessels planned to make a quick turnaround and set sail for home as soon as possible. The paperwork for both ships was currently being processed.

As Oliver sought to work out the passage home, Richard and Mary were preparing for the first service in the new building. Although the governor's edict for the convicts' church attendance was unpopular, many were content to attend Divine Worship when possible, for it meant a short cessation of their convict duties.

Major Grose overturned that rule and demanded that the services be held at six in the morning rather than seven, which meant that fewer attended the service.

Mary and Annie sat together, talking babies, while Oliver and Richard discussed possible church names.

They came up with an eminently suitable name. In homage to Governor Arthur Phillip, they both liked the name Saint Phillip's, Sydney. Richard realised he would need to bless the building as there was no bishop present. However, as the building was unconsecrated, it was to remain officially unnamed. The name would be used unofficially until the dedication could occur.

The date for the first service was also set. August 25th, 1793, would be the auspicious day. Unfortunately, the day was windy, and the windows were merely openings in the walls. The boxes of glass panes that Richard had brought with him remained locked in Government Stores, and Major Grose refused to release them to him. Glass, being in short supply, needed to be requisitioned. Richard had done that already, with no response from the acting governor. He had stored the church glass under government care for safekeeping. Major Grose would not release it.

The day finally arrived. Mrs Grose and some other persons of quality in town attended, with Oliver and Annie sitting next to Mary and the children.

Many convicts filled the nave, and surprisingly, many of the military seats were occupied. Overall, Richard was content. However, Mrs Grose complained about the chill inside the church.

After the service, she mentioned that the wind whistled so severely through the unglazed windows that it made the service uncomfortable.

Richard bit his lip, trying hard not to smile, but gave the major a dirty look. He had placed them next to the opening intentionally. He already knew how cold the church was, as he'd been in the building frequently. He had allocated her pew to be in front of one such opening. He reapplied to the Commissary for the panes of glass set aside for the church, and even though his wife had complained about the chill, Major Grose refused the request.

Richard knew the precious material was sitting awaiting his use, and he had even had the sash window frames made ready for installation. They were sitting awaiting glass. He was angry, livid at the expense he had gone to for the congregation's comfort, only to be thwarted by the acting governor; however, his hands were tied. Arthur Phillip had gone and left this man in charge. As the only person in the five-hundred-seat church who complained was Major Grose's wife, she may have a better chance of overturning the acting governor's mind than he would himself.

Oliver knew he was already on the man's bad books as he occupied the best premises in Parramatta. He stayed well out of the argument.

After the church was finished being built, they spent some time during the week out at Parramatta in the more comfortable abode. Knowing they were now to leave, Oliver did not wish to contribute to any bad feelings.

At the end of August, they returned to town for a visit to celebrate the first service.

Oliver realised their woodpile had vanished. He set to chop some firewood while Annie visited Mary. Oliver cut his leg with an axe while working. He thought it was nothing serious as it didn't hurt much, but not wishing to worry Annie, he wandered down to the hospital so John White could look at it. His arrival at the building was met with him being shown a seat in a large waiting room. He felt a little light-headed and leaned against the wall to wait his turn.

What seemed only moments later, a convict girl shook his shoulder. Oliver wasn't sure if he had fallen asleep or passed out. He tried to see who was in front of him, but his eyes wouldn't focus.

John White was kneeling on the ground, covered in an apron smeared with blood. "Well, aren't you a bad patient? You passed out, Oliver. So while you were out cold, I sutured your wound with roo tendon, so it should heal quite well now."

Oliver was still battling to focus. "Roo, what? Did I pass out?"

The doctor smiled at his friend, nodding. "Kangaroo tendon, Oliver. I have few supplies here, so I use what I can. Many substances can be used to sew up an injury. Gold thread, silver, copper, kangaroo tendon, black horsehair, linen, wire, animal intestines, cotton, silk, and even whalebone can be used. My supplies are so scant that I have had to make my own. I reboil the needles and keep the tendon threads in alcohol. When you came in, you should have said you were bleeding. Those cases are always seen first." John looked up at Oliver to see that he was still very pale and woozy. "Head between the legs, my friend, or you will pass out again. I didn't rouse you until I had finished treating you."

After a few minutes, with his head held down over a pool of blood, Oliver was feeling much clearer. "Thanks, John. I didn't think it was that bad a cut. I saw some blood, but it wasn't hurting that much."

The doctor smiled. "It was a six-stitcher, Oliver. Next time, leave the axe work to your man."

As the hospital tent was only a short distance from the cottage, John made sure there were no emergencies and took a five-minute break, hoisted Oliver up, and escorted him home.

As Oliver had not yet told John about the news of their child, he took the opportunity to do so and said, "John, we're going home as soon as I can get passage. The only problem is that Annie's term will not have expired before the child is born."

By the time Oliver was helped outside, the cool, fresh September air had roused him enough for him to be able to walk by himself.

John released his friend but continued to escort him to his house. "Oliver, you told me the governor had the paperwork sorted. What did it say? Was it an Absolute Pardon or just permission to leave the colony?"

Oliver's frown met John's gaze. "A what? I didn't open it. He handed it to me with the transfer of Annie's papers. Come in, and we'll have a look."

As they reached the cottage, Oliver knocked and heard Annie call for him to come in. He poked his head around the door to check that Annie was clad as she had surprised him a few times by greeting him in the-altogether. Thankfully, she was making butter, so she was fully clothed. "Hello, love, I have brought a visitor."

Annie looked down and saw the cut and bloodied trousers. "Oliver, what have you done to yourself?"

Oliver bent and kissed her. "A bit of a nick, love; John sewed me up with kangaroo tendon, so I might be able to jump better next time."

John followed Oliver inside and was greeted by Annie. He filled her in on the wound and told her what she needed to do to keep it clean. While they talked, Oliver retrieved the paperwork. As he returned, John noticed a massive grin on his friend's face.

"You're right, John. Why didn't I notice this before? He dated it from the day he wrote the letter."

Annie had no idea what he was talking about. "Wrote what, Oliver?" Rather than tell her, Oliver handed her the previously unread document. Annie dropped her eyes to read the official script. She gasped and said, "I'm free already? He gave me an Absolute remission of the sentence?"

John took the document from her hands. He, too, perused the writing. "This is an Absolute Pardon, all right. You are free, Annie and have been since the governor wrote this. So you were free when we married. I can't work out why you didn't read this before, my friend. This is like gold out here." John's eyes dropped to the document he held. He had not seen one before, but it was spelled out in full. He read the paragraph aloud. "Annie, Oliver, listen to this:

As of December 12th 1792, I, Arthur Phillip, His Majesty's Governor of the said Territory of New South Wales and the Islands thereunto adjacent, taking into consideration the unremitting good conduct and meritorious behaviour of Annie Gentle and deeming her, the said Annie Gentle, a proper object of the Royal Mercy do hereby absolutely remit the remainder of the time or term which is yet unexpired of the original sentence or order of transportation passed on the said Annie Gentle in the year of our Lord, one thousand seven hundred and ninety-two. Signed, Arthur Phillip."

John smiled before adding, "Therefore, she was free to leave the colony from that date, but of course, she won't be leaving under that name anyway."

The sheaf of documents that Oliver put on the table sat ignored by the happy couple.

Oliver had even forgotten John was there watching. "Annie, my darling gentle Annie, I'm so sorry. I should have read the paperwork. Some of Arthur's comments now make sense."

He went to take her in his arms when John coughed. The doctor said, "If you three are going to get all lovey-dovey, I'll head back to work. Annie, come and see me sometime, and we'll talk about babies." He turned to leave, "Oh, and bring Oliver; as if the child comes on board, he will need to know what to do, so ensure you come along with her."

Two months ago, the *Boddingtons* arrived with a full load of Irish convicts, so she was now clear to sail. The filth and stench below had taken time to clear. She was to leave in mid-October with her sister ship, the *Sugar Cane*. That only gave Oliver and Annie weeks to sort out their possessions and sign their cottage over to Richard to use as he wished. Richard was also given Pegasus. Oliver doubted the governor would return, so the minister could use him to breed with his mare.

The colony's development now hinged on a regular supply of food. Richard needed the horse for transport, and they had discovered that the stallion would also pull a small cart. Oliver had done what he could, and now it was time to care for his growing family. He promised to send more food, just in case.

With Annie now expecting their second child, time was of the essence. Even leaving in October was cutting the time close. There was a strong possibility that the baby could well be born on the ship. Oliver also decided that he would change his lifestyle once he was home. Gone would be the drinking. He had hardly missed the nightly brandy since he had been in the colony. His preconceptions had been challenged over many things. These men had become friends. They did not know his title or status in England. Oliver was one of the reverend's friends here in Sydney, and that had been enough. No one ever asked about his background, but he had volunteered that he was a free settler. Working alongside convicts, both long and short-term crooks, he realised how he had treated his staff had been abysmal.

Chapter 20   Going Home

Over the last week of their stay, they disposed of their few possessions amongst their friends. Annie realised that the clothes Oliver had brought for her would be well out of fashion by the time she returned home. As Mary had few gowns, Annie gave her most of the excess apparel. She knew that with her growing condition, only the very full, high-waisted dresses would fit her in the coming months. Unable to purchase any suitable baby fabrics, Annie kept a few muslin gowns that she would chop up and make outfits for the child while on board. She also found some lengths of flannel lining the bottom of the cases. She kept these for the baby's napkins. She also discovered a length of woven cream wool she had intended to make into a cape. This would be good as an outer napkin, so it was packed for repurposing.

Although Oliver knew saying farewell to Mary would be hard for Annie, they hoped to see them in England one day. Annie's farewell to Pegasus was far more difficult. The stallion had come across the small paddock with his tail held high in the air and high-stepping his way towards her. The beauty of the creature was enough to stir the soul. Each day, she had gone to hug him and give him a handful of special feed. Soon, she would be gone, and he would receive no more treats. She knew Richard would care for him well.

The time for their departure arrived. Oliver had booked two adjoining cabins for them and a third one for their luggage.

As a farewell gift, Doctor John arrived with a large box. "I had no idea what to get you, but I thought something from the Antipodes would suffice. Knowing Annie's penchant for taming wild horses, this was an obvious choice. This is a child's rocking horse of sorts. It's to be suspended by ropes from a hook on the roof or, better still, a verandah. It works as a swing. I once saw one on a patient's visit and commissioned one for you so you would have a tangible memory of your time here."

Oliver accepted his gift and gingerly looked into the flat box, wondering how a rocking horse would fit into a three-inch thick package. There were two flat pieces, two round bits that looked like branches, and a long bolt with a nut. Tipping out the contents, the two men quickly constructed the swing. There was also a bundle of rope that obviously fitted through the various holes. The entire swing was held together by just the one long bolt that hinged the horse like it was being ridden. The two round branches were for the hands and feet and fitted into holes in the headpiece. The simplicity of the design was ingenious, and Oliver knew that Annie would be delighted for their child to be riding this. On return home, he would have it mounted in the nursery. He thanked John profusely and said a final farewell with a manly hug.

Only one month earlier, the large box of medical supplies that Oliver had brought with him on the *Kitty* had finally turned up. It had been mixed up with the food stores and was not discovered until shortly before their departure. John was delighted when he finally received this gift. Before leaving London, Oliver had sourced everything medical that would fit into the large lockable box. Arthur Bowes-Smith had mentioned how little there was. Oliver had forgotten about the purchase until he cut his leg, so he went hunting for it. Its contents were packaged as tightly as possible. It contained every new gadget he could buy, from long lengths of suture fibre to bottles of ether and pure alcohol. A wooden monaural stethoscope and bloodletting equipment, a pair of delivery forceps, a glass cupping set, a pair of new amputation saws, and a large range of surgical implements, including fifty scalpels of various shapes and sizes, two catheters, one for men and one for women, and many more items.

John was delighted and embraced Oliver with another big man-hug. However, one or two things that John had hoped to find were not in the box. Oliver noticed and asked John what to send on the next ship. John wrote an extensive list of his needs, including wormwood, which he had run out of.

Oliver now had the list of items in his pocket that he had promised to send when he arrived home. Subconsciously, he added more suture thread, although his leg had healed without issue. The twice-daily dousing of potent alcohol had stopped any infection.

The final day of farewells brought tears from Mary, but they came with a promise to visit when they eventually returned home. Once the promise was extracted, the two couples parted. Oliver and Annie walked out on the small, now rickety jetty she had watched being constructed when she arrived. The memory of Doctor Arthur Bowes-Smith returned afresh. "Oliver, we have much to do for this place when we get home. I know John will have given you a list of things, but Richard asked me to see if we can hunt out an assistant for him. Although Richard is amazing, to me, it is John who is the unacknowledged hero of this place. Most of us would have died, but for him. I will admit that Parramatta is growing to such an extent that it will need its own minister, but it will also need a doctor. Richard is burning his candle at both ends, trying to minister alone. Mary is worried about his health, but John can't be in two places at once either, and they need more than the tiny clinic that is out at Parramatta."

The *Boddingtons* weighed anchor mid-morning on October 13th 1793. It caught the outgoing tide, and a soft westerly breeze carried the small ship eastward out of the bay. Over six years of Annie's life had been spent in this harbour, and she was a vastly different person from the girl who had arrived. Oliver stood at her side and watched the expressions pass across her face. The sadness sat on her brow for a while, then the corners of her mouth turned up when she heard Pegasus whinny. It was like a final farewell. Mary and Richard stayed on the jetty until the ship had rounded the headland. Milbah had nearly fallen into the water, and Richard hoisted her onto his neck to keep her safe.

As the ship left the jetty, Annie and Oliver caught sight of John standing at the entrance to the hospital. What the doctor had achieved in the time he had been in the colony was truly amazing. If he ran out of things, he had learnt to improvise. He often used the indigenous medicines he had learned about, including squashed witchetty grubs from under the tea tree shrubs for burns, and he traded fresh fish for puff fungi for infections.

Bidgee Bidgee came with a regular supply of other local medicines. Whoever would have thought of using kangaroo tendon fibres to replace sutures? Oliver was pleased he had not known what was occurring that day, or he might have objected. As it was, no infection occurred, and it had fully healed, albeit with a scar to be proud of.

The departing couple stood watching the receding shoreline until the towering headlands at the harbour entrance had faded into the misty distance. Only then did they go below to their cabin. They had stayed on board the previous night to settle in whilst in the calm waters. Now, the westerly wind carried them on the gently rolling seas. As they travelled further from shore, the reminiscences of the journey out washed over them both. Annie related the many huge storms they had suffered. Oliver told her of his fears about the ship's foundering and that she would never know of his love for her. Every morning on waking, he told her of his adoration of her. Annie would wrap her arms around his neck and snuggle into him. They never tired of touching each other. Annie was still somewhat overwhelmed that she could touch him as she wished. Morning sickness was now pronounced, and Oliver discovered the benefit of getting her a mug of black tea as soon as he could.

~

As the months passed, the couple were frequently seen on deck with his arms around her, often holding fast to the railing and watching the rolling waves pass them by. Every mile they traversed was one closer to home and a new life together. The ship's captain, Master Robert Chalmers, kept their special place on the poop deck for them. The other passengers were mostly emancipists who had also been given Full Pardons. He had been let into the knowledge of Oliver's title as he had needed to be shown Annie's paperwork so she could leave the colony. Nothing, however, was entered in the captain's journal about her conviction. Annie Gentle was dead, and Annie Soames no longer existed either. Oliver and Annabella Quilpie were newlyweds on an extended honeymoon, travelling around the world.

By the time the small vessel reached Cape Horn, Annie's condition was showing. Her bump was larger than it had been before, and she presumed this was because it was her second time expecting a child. She wasn't showing at all just over four months along last time. She now had a well-pronounced curve on her sylphlike figure and could feel movement. They had a month before the first stop.

After being becalmed for nearly a week once they turned the cape, their arrival at Rio de Janeiro was a welcome port of call. They had experienced storms, but nothing like on the way out six years earlier. The stop meant replenishment of food supplies, but the way north would mean that unless the wind changed, they would need to tack and wear all the way across the Atlantic Ocean. While in the town, they delighted in a carriage tour and saw the impressive arches of the *Lapa Arcs*. The incredible water aqueduct had recently been reopened after refurbishment. It had originally been built nearly forty years earlier to bring water to the gold mines; now, it supplied water for the town.In the heat of the December weather, Annie had become very faint. At Oliver's insistence, she was taken to see a Portuguese-speaking doctor in town. Both Annie and Oliver spoke a little Spanish and thought they could make themselves understood. Her shape at five months along was now much bigger than she had previously been. She was continually hungry and decidedly uncomfortable. At five months last confinement, she had hardly been showing. She was only a little over that time.

Oliver had gone with her to the hospital in town and waited outside the doctor's room until a grinning doctor called him inside. The dark-haired, moustachioed man beckoned him into the office. "*Sente-se por favor, senhor.*" Oliver realised that he was to sit next to Annie; he did as he was bid. Annie was sheet white and silent. Oliver looked concerned. "Annie, what is wrong?" She was unable to answer. So he turned to the doctor and repeated his enquiry, "*O que está errado?*"

Thankfully, the doctor did not give a long spiel in reply but said, with a huge and silly grin plastered on this swarthy face, "*Nada, senhor.*"

Annie found her voice. "Oliver, he said we are having twins."

The doctor's dark head nodded profusely. "*Sim! Dois bebés,*" he said while holding up two fingers.

Aghast, Oliver repeated, "Two babies? Twins?" He didn't know whom to look at. His eyes turned from Annie to the doctor again.

The Portuguese doctor said, "*Sim, Sim, dois!* Yes, two, *senhor.*"

Annie's nervous giggle brought Oliver back to earth with a bang. She turned to her husband. "Oliver, the doctor said that twins often come early. This means that the babies may arrive before we get home, and, sweetheart, there is no doctor on the ship, so you may have to deliver them."

If he was shocked by the news of this information, his stomach now fell through the floor of the office. He felt as light-headed as when he had put the axe through his leg. Both John and Mary had given him some brief instructions on what to do if he needed to deliver their baby, but he had not taken notes. Now, he had to settle with a Spanish/Portuguese translation via a doctor who seemed to laugh a lot. He purchased scissors, twine, and towels, and he remembered that John had said he would need all of those things. Now he duplicated everything and put them in a bag they called the 'go' bag.

Annie forestalled him from buying one dozen scissors. "Darling one, we will only need one pair of scissors, even if it's twins. We will need many more napkins and warm wraps as we arrive in winter. They can share the crib."

He nodded, and they stocked up on everything possible, including new maternity gowns and night rails for Annie, as the doctor had said she would get much larger than last time. Oliver wondered if they would manage. They had to; they would have no choice. They would be parents to an instant family, so much for arriving home before they were due. Oliver had asked the doctor if it would be better to stay in Rio de Janeiro until the twins arrived.

The doctor replied, "*Vá velejar.*" Then he made the sailing sign and shooed them out of his office. Oliver presumed that meant 'go sailing'. He nodded his understanding. All he could do was talk to Captain Chalmers and see what he recommended.

Their conversation made the captain re-think his plans for an extended stay in port. Knowing that the normal summer winds in the area were north-easterlies, he hoped that one of the rare southerly busters would blow up. His barometer dropped slightly, so he set sail on the next tide. Hopefully, the coming change would carry them quickly to the equator. Once there, the winds often changed to a south-westerly as they headed into the winter. He would hoist every sail and set off as soon as possible. They may only have eight weeks to make the trip before the babies came, which allowed them to come a month early. Time being of the essence, news quickly spread around the crew that a bonus would be promised to each sailor if they pushed the ship to its top sailing speed. Shore leave was willingly cancelled, and within twenty-four hours, the ship had hoisted its sails, weighed anchor, and was underway. With the prospect of a bonus of £5 per crewman from Oliver, every effort was made to catch every breeze.

~

Christmas was celebrated at sea with a stiff westerly breeze pushing them northward. The equator was soon behind them, and the winds changed to the southwest. With no tacking, the vessel tackled the waves with gusto. The white sails billowed to their full measure. Sails were tripled, and every square inch of breeze was captured and propelled the *Boddingtons* homeward. The eight square sails caught every breath of wind, and the eight triangular sails filled every possible position on the masts.

Every day, Annie grew bigger, as did her appetite. Doctor John White had told her to walk if possible, and on a moving ship when one's centre of gravity was off-centre, that was a hard ask. When calm enough, Oliver would wrap his arm around her and do a circuit on the main deck, as it was the largest area available. The rains put paid to the outside exercise, but Oliver made her walk up and down the length of the ship on the gun deck. She didn't like doing this as the stench of the convicts from the previous voyage still oozed from the ship's timbers. It brought back too many memories of her own voyage south. However, Oliver insisted.

With so few passengers on board, they ate with the crew in the mess room. The captain made them sit at his table, but the crew filled the spare places as the only other passengers were two emancipists. The passengers and crew had merged into a friendly, happy bunch in the months at sea.

Thankfully, violent storms and dead calm days were few and far between. On the 10th of March, 1794, land was finally sighted. However, it took five days to reach port. They landed on Annie's twenty-seventh birthday. Oliver had requested they be taken to Portsmouth rather than London. As Annie was almost rotund, this was a stop that the captain was very willing to make as it shaved a week off their trip. Oliver knew that the fifty-mile journey home would be, by necessity, a very slow one. As the Navy used the route daily, he knew roads from Portsmouth to Horsham were good. Hopefully, Annie would cope with the jostling of the carriage.

In March, those on shore were surprised by the ship's arrival at the naval dock. The captain had carefully navigated his way through the myriad of ships and hulks moored in the harbour and then through anchored naval vessels to the main dock. He knew there was a long, gently sloping gangplank from this wharf that Annie could negotiate with a little more ease than a rope ladder. Oliver willingly paid the crew their bonus.

Once the harbour master realised the imminency of a twin delivery, he queue-jumped the *Boddingtons* and permitted the Quilpies to disembark. Annie had back pain but no real contractions yet. She knew the time was close but feared to tell Oliver. At least they were on shore, and the naval hospital was within sight. However, she wasn't sure if the naval hospital was the place to give birth, but there should be a midwife somewhere in Portsmouth. She wanted Ermie to tend to her, so she remained silent.

Annie was seated in the harbourmaster's office as there was nowhere else Oliver could leave her while he arranged the transport. She had quietly mentioned that he was not to forget to bring the 'go' bag with him, just in case it was required. In less than an hour, a coach and four were loading up the minimal luggage they had with them. Annie knew that with a five or six-hour trip ahead of them, she should still have time to make it home, even if she went into labour now. The coach set off at a cracking pace and slew around the corner so quickly that Annie was thrown against Oliver. He rapped on the communication door, and the coachman slid the small door open. "Yes, gov!"

Oliver was livid. "I said to drive with haste, not with danger. We want to arrive in one piece, not smashed up on the way. Ease up on the corners, drive safely, and do not force past other vehicles."

"Right o'! I'm sorry, gov." The driver slammed shut the communication door and slowed his pace slightly.

They were soon leaving the buildings of Portsmouth behind them. Oliver sat cradling Annie against him to ease the jolting of the carriage. She was clutching his hand. As he breathed in the violet scent of her hair, he said, "This reminds me of our wedding night; we were sitting in the same stance when the wheel broke. I learned just how capable you were that night. I would have had no possibility of starting a fire in any form. You knew exactly how to do everything. Even to making a toasting fork."

Annie smiled through the first of her contractions. It was too soon to let him know that the babies were coming. Soon, she knew she could not hold back the cries. She said, "Necessity is the mother of invention, Oliver. When you need fire and have no flint, you quickly learn what you need to live. Abaroo taught me a lot. Governor Phillip had promised Richard a stone or even a brick building for the church. As that didn't occur, we cobbled together a wonderful wattle and daub building for, how much did he say, £67?"

"Yes, £60 of which he paid in Spanish dollars, some I had donated to the cause, and the rest he sold his fine produce to the government and made the money that way. Grose is going to find that taking away Richard's convicts will not be a benefit to the colony. He had so few now that he may even have to give up one or two of his farms. I gave Richard the cows I brought on the *Kitty*. I believe the *Britannia* left shortly before us to purchase more cattle in Cape Town." Oliver thought back to Francis Grose's bias toward the work of the church. He had no idea if his objection was from a lack of faith or purely because he didn't want convicts forced to worship, but he felt it was much more profound. Richard had also been told to cut the length of services down to only forty-five minutes, and by the time they left, he was only permitted to hold them at six o'clock on Sunday mornings instead of daily services. Before Oliver left to travel to Sydney two years ago, he may well have agreed with the major; however, since his many conversations with Richard and Mary, he had learned the vast difference between religion and the true Christian faith.

While he had been in Sydney making the arrangements for their cottage to be built, Richard and he had sat on the grassy embankment discussing this exact topic. Oliver had never had anyone to teach him about what the Bible was and how to live Jesus's teachings. He had never thought about why he went to church, and he had tried to avoid going whenever he could. He had followed his father's example of attending once a month, and normally, it was for a service of Morning Prayer. He liked the sung Psalms but hated the long and drawn-out boring sermons. In London, he had been known to even doze off during them. Oliver was lost in reminiscing about that conversation with Richard. He hardly noticed that Annie had fallen asleep on his chest. Richard had loaned him one of the Bibles from church, and he remembered going back to the half-built cottage and looking up the wordy passage about where

Jesus condemned the Pharisees in the first few verses of Matthew, chapter 23.

"But he that is greatest among you shall be your servant. And whosoever shall exalt himself shall be abased, and he that shall humble himself shall be exalted. But woe unto you, scribes and Pharisees, hypocrites! For ye shut up the kingdom of heaven against men: for ye neither go in yourselves, neither suffer ye them that are entering to go in. Woe unto you, scribes and Pharisees, hypocrites! For ye devour widows' houses, and for a pretence make long prayer: therefore ye shall receive the greater damnation. Woe unto you, scribes and Pharisees, hypocrites! For ye compass sea and land to make one proselyte, and when he is made, ye make him twofold more the child of hell than yourselves."

Oliver realised he was equal to the Pharisees in rank. He had to stand strong in his faith and not be a puppet leader. He had to be faithful to Christ and what he now believed. He had to be a leader and not part of the problem. He cringed when he thought of his old selfish life. He was determined to change. With Annie beside him, he knew he could. Others now relied on him.

The revelation that Jesus also hated the religious fervour that annoyed him so much was a delight for Oliver. He hated those who gave outward lip service to the church but cared little for their fellow man. He could see his old self in his own criticism. He smiled. He had changed because of Annie. His life was better because of her, and he was a better man for her being in his life. He felt he could say to his grandmother that he would be content if his daughter courted a man as he was now. After they moved into the cottage, Richard slowly and patiently explained what Annie had already told him. God wanted us to love him. It is plain and simple with no strings attached. God was just like a parent caring for their child; sometimes, He disciplined his children, but it was always because He loved them and never hurt them. He always guided them to follow Him. Jesus was the pathway that God provided to us so we could return to Him, but it is our free will to follow Him or not. Those words had been a puzzle to him until their wedding night.

While lying on the grass when broken down on the night they married, Oliver decided to follow the Lord wherever He led. He and Annie had not long consummated their marriage, and they lay on the blankets watching the stars above them. She had fallen asleep in his arms and curled up to his side. The sounds and smells of the bush around him were strange, and he held his new wife protectively. Oliver had never seen a sight so lovely. That night, he had lain awake, watching the glory above him. Earlier, Annie pointed out the Southern Cross and the pointer stars. They watched as an occasional shooting star zipped across the sky. He realised that he and Annie were like the insignificant tiny stars above their heads. One particularly long shooting star shot across the entire night sky, and the words of another Bible verse from Psalm 119 came to him. Verse 105 said, *"Thy Word Is a lamp unto My feet and light unto My path."* The shooting star was like God, showing the way for him to travel. He had travelled around the world to find Annie but realised he had also found God. Not in the sermons, not in church, nor in the words of mankind; he found God in the heavenly realms above. That night, his entire life changed. He had had so little time to have any real conversations with Annie before they married that he had no idea her faith was so much a part of who she was. He had been stunned to find she was brought up in the rectory of his own parish church. She had made a comment earlier about being a rectory girl, but he had presumed she had been a maid in one. In the time they had been on the ship, Annie told him of the family connections and how she knew so much detail of his childhood nightmares. Oliver remembered an older girl looking after him while his mother had been ill and after she died. He had never associated that girl with Annie's mother.

Annie's faith, purity, and compassion were some of the things that first drew her to his attention. She never bit at Verity's catty remarks; she never lost her temper. Now, in the months they had been married, he realised that her faith made her so different. He could not wait to get back and get to know her parents better. However, he was aware he needed to deal with their wrath, but he deserved whatever they dished out to him. With Annie resting on his chest, his heart had never been so full. Her deep, even breathing allowed him to gaze down at her as she slept. He'd never known such love before and knew how precious she was to him. Her face had dropped, and he could no longer see it. He turned and sat watching out the window as they traversed the miles. His mind went back to Sydney. Major Grose had also cut Richard's access to the river ferry to Parramatta, but with Pegasus now at his disposal, that trip could be accomplished much faster than by the slow boat. Another person who had become a bit of a thorn in Richard's side was John Macarthur in Parramatta. On the grant Major Grose had given to his friend, Macarthur and his wife had started to build a house not far from the redoubt. Oliver had met them quite a few times, and although he liked the Scottish wife, he could not say the same for the suave husband. He had met such characters in London and avoided them like the plague. Their meetings were not always congenial, as John Macarthur knew Oliver to be friends with Richard.

Oliver wondered what they would have thought if they had known of his title. He imagined that his welcome would have been vastly different. He smiled, knowing that he would have flouted that tidbit of information in years past. He had managed to live for nearly a year in the colony with very few discovering his status. Those had become trusted friends, and they had not spread the word. Even Colin had stayed quiet about his discovery. They had met again before departure, and Oliver thanked him again for taking care of Annie. He received another £5 as a thank you. Hopefully, they could keep the knowledge of their trip quiet. If word spread about her conviction, he decided he would publicly defame Verity for her cattiness and cuckolding. He had already struck Marcus's name from the family tree.

As he sat mulling over these thoughts, he noticed that Annie was awake and now was occasionally squeezing his hand quite tightly, and her breathing became deeper. She had done this about half an hour ago, but his fingers were almost numb this time. "Annie, are you all right?" He had not looked down at her until now and saw her face pale and that she was in pain. The look she gave him tore at his heart. "Are the babies coming?"

She nodded, then burst into tears. With little that he could do to help her other than cuddle her, he did just that. The pains were still thirty minutes apart; hopefully, they could travel the final two hours before the babies arrived.

After a few more contractions, he realised they were getting closer. He started timing them.

Within an hour, they were down to fifteen minutes apart. He knew that once they turned off the main road closer to home, the road deteriorated into a country lane. He did something he would never have done a year ago. He dropped his cheek to Annie's head and prayed. He said, "Dear God, pave the way before us and let us get home in time."

The carriage wheels rumbled over the miles. The pains were ten minutes apart by the time they were nearing Horsham, then down to five only a few miles later.

Oliver was trying to remember what Mary had said, and the word breathing kept coming to mind. "Annie, Mary said something about keeping your mouth open when breathing and yelling if you wished."

Annie nodded. She had been doing deep breathing, but the pain was getting bad. They hit a large pothole in the road, and a gush of fluid came from between her legs. "Oliver, my waters have broken. This will make things happen fast. How far away are we now?"

Oliver was panicking but didn't wish to show Annie. He said, "Five minutes, sweetheart. Can you hold on?"

Annie had no choice but to grab Oliver. "Oh, Oliver, if only I could, but it doesn't work that way. They will come when they are ready. I didn't want the birth to be like this. I don't want to lose them like I lost Anna. I can't risk them, Oliver."

As they spoke, they turned into the long driveway at the house. "We're nearly there, sweet Annie, just a couple of minutes longer."

Annie was travailing in great pain. "The last time I was in labour, I had been able to walk around; sitting still is nearly killing me. I can feel a head. I have to take off my drawers. The first baby is coming."

The carriage pulled up at Bowbelle Hall's front door as she finished speaking. As always, the usual staff was on duty and ready for any eventuality. Today, however, they would all be tested on how well they were trained.

Chapter 21   Homecoming

*H*enry Greening stood with his mouth open at the scream emanating from the coach. Annie felt that contraction violently. The moment it passed, Oliver burst from the carriage door, "Henry, gather everyone; Annie is about to give birth to twins. Bring Mrs Durham and mobilise the staff."

Henry stood immobile.

Oliver noticed his butler had not budged. "Henry, move it… now! And get the small bag on the carriage floor. We'll need it; the babies are coming." Oliver leaned into the carriage and scooped Annie into his strong arms.

As they entered the door, Annie said, "Oliver, I have to be sick." They were passing the foyer stand, and she grabbed one of his hats and filled it, then handed the smelly item to the startled butler. She said, "Oliver, your office chaise lounge now. I won't make it upstairs. They are coming right now!" She groaned in agony.

Hearing her words, James, the footman, flung open the den door and ripped off the dust covers. He grinned; Annie was back.

Oliver carried his precious bundle to the couch where he had first abused her. They had come full circle. That couch was now to be repurposed as a birthing bed. Oliver gently laid her on the chaise lounge and packed her back with velvet cushions. He had just settled her when his housekeeper arrived.

Seeing Oliver intended to leave, Annie reached for him. "Don't you dare leave me this time, Oliver! You got me into this; we'll see this through together." She clutched his hand again and prepared to deliver their children.

He nodded nervously. "I won't leave you, my darling Annie." His heart was in his mouth. He had promised never to leave her. He looked up at a noise near the door. He noticed the multitude of staff now at the door. "Lady Annie does not need spectators," he said angrily.

Knowing they were about to expose his wife's private area, he shot orders at them. "If you want to do something useful, go and clean the nursery;

there are twins coming, so duplicate everything. And remove the dust coverings from everything. We are home to stay." He glanced down at Annie when he heard her say, "Get Mama now!" He nodded, "James, send someone to the rector and Mrs Soames and bring the midwife to my wife."

He looked at his footman again. "Better still, James, go collect the midwife yourself and take our carriage at the door; tell her it's urgent. Henry, I want you to go and collect her parents in another carriage personally. Scoot!" Henry passed him the 'go' bag.

Oliver flicked his hand as he was wont to do, and all the excess staff vanished.

Henry grinned. Finally, his master realised who Annie was.

Oliver released a smirk. He wondered exactly how many of his staff knew who Annie was. He presumed that most of them were aware of his search and stayed silent to protect her.

As the door slowly shut, Oliver heard one of the maids ask, "Did the marquess say that was Lady Annie? Did they get married?" Oliver smiled as they vanished. Then, he heard an excited cheer from outside the room. He chuckled, knowing exactly what that meant for his household. With a silly grin on his face, the murmur of voices faded away as his concentration returned to Annie. His fear had gone, and he was looking forward to their new life in the impressive house with his beloved wife and children.

No, it was no longer just a house; it would be their home, for Annie would make it one. A place of warmth, love, and fun. The love he felt for Annie was nearly overwhelming. Yes, he had married the love of his life, and he would stay with her forever. She had brought the vibrancy of living into his being. "I'll never leave you, my gentle Annie. I'll stay by your side forever. I promised you that, and I will not break it."

Mrs Durham arrived to help with the delivery. The first thing she did was ease off Annie's wet drawers.

James had gone to fetch Ermie, and Henry had just driven off to fetch her parents in another carriage.

Oliver quickly shooed out the footmen who brought the hot water and other paraphernalia, and then they prepared Annie to deliver the first of their babies. Towels and a pitcher of hot water had been placed beside Mrs Durham, and Oliver discovered that the best place to be was by Annie's head. He had initially wished to stay well away, but Annie ended up half-sitting and half-leaning on his lap. He was glad he was not standing; otherwise, he may have passed out. He discovered he was not good with the sight of blood.

She turned and said, "Ready, Oliver?"

He leant down and kissed her wet brow. "No, sweetheart, but that's not an option anyway, is it? I love you so much, and today we become a family, my darling Annie."

Annie groaned and said, "Juditty, the first one is coming." Her words were uttered in a strangled voice.

Her crushing grasp had almost pulverised Oliver's hand. He had not realised she was so strong. The scream that echoed around the vast room made him weep with fear for her well-being. His lusts had now caused her so much pain, and last time, she had all but done it alone and delivered a dead child.

As she relaxed against him before the next push, she gazed up at him with such love in her eyes. "Have I told you lately how much I love you?"

With her affirming words, his face shed the years of stress and anxiety; the loneliness of his youth was now a thing of the past. He didn't just have Annie and the children; he now had an entire house full of a new family to get to know and love as Annie did. "You have, my darling, gentle Annie, but we will tell each other daily and time and time again over the years."

Annie nodded, knowing he was happy. Once again, she took a deep breath and pushed their child into the world.

Soon, the soft squall of a child's cry broke the quietness of the office.

Oliver watched in awe at the moving infant Mrs Durham now held aloft. The baby was a boy; that much was obvious. The babe took a deep breath that turned him from a greyish blue to a healthy pink and then released a loud bellow. His howl showed that he was fit and had good lungs. He may well have been six weeks early, but he was strong.Outside the room, a cheer erupted. Oliver bit his lip and chuckled.

Mrs Durham beamed at the marquess. "Sir, you have a son, and he's a healthy young chappie at that."

Oliver knew she was aware that Marcus had not been his child and said, "Yes, Mrs Durham, this time, we all have a son and heir. This time, a true one, a new Earl of Martindel."

His housekeeper grinned knowingly and met her employer's eye with a glint of happiness.

Oliver kissed Annie's brow as she snuggled into his warm embrace.

The housekeeper smiled at the loving couple before her. She knew that Verity had admitted to the marquess that the child she had born was not his but her lover's. She had guessed that the moment she saw the babe. She and most of the other staff were pleased when Madam Muck ran away and took her son. Even more so when they heard that they had drowned along with everyone on the ship, she felt sad for the other passengers, but it freed the master. Lord Oliver had been able to go and find his Annie. All the staff had been horrified when they discovered what her ladyship had done to Annie. Bob told her about it when they met Doctor Arthur. When Lord Oliver announced that he was going to find her and bring her back, relief flooded over all the staff. They had put the household to sleep in his absence. The furniture was covered, and the staff were given fully paid holidays on a rotating roster. A few were still away.

When Annie's nice doctor arrived from New South Wales and remained cloistered in the office with Oliver for some hours, the final piece of the jigsaw fell into place. Juditty knew of the love child and of its death, but even Bob and Ermie had no idea what had happened to Annie. She had just vanished. The doctor had told Lord Oliver that Lady Verity had been responsible for Annie's conviction.

Juditty knew that life at Bowbelle Hall would no longer be the quiet, oppressed house it once had been. It would become a warm, loving home filled with the joy that Annie would bring into their midst.

Digging into the bag the marquess had brought, Mrs Durham tied and cut the now empty cord, wrapped the child and handed the baby boy to his father.

Annie rested against him, gazing at the perfect babe in her arms. "What will you name him, Oliver?" They had long ago agreed that he would name the boys, and she would choose the girls.

Oliver grinned. "We discussed this, and I agree, Maxwell. Our friend Max told me it means a *great stream*. Considering we have just circumnavigated the entire world, I think that's appropriate. I liked the name before I met Max. It is eminently suitable. That one great big stream we have traversed to be together. However, it will also remind me daily of our friend Max, the convict, and his needs, but sweetheart, I would like to add a few more names: Arthur John for our Sydney doctor friends and Oliver after me. However, we should wait and see if the next one is a boy too; he can be Richard Godfrey."

As they sat in the afterglow of the birth, both gazing contentedly at the small child, noises were heard in the foyer.

Annie's mother burst through the door, and her father was beside the butler. Hard on her mother's tail was Ermie.

James hovered near the door but was banished by Oliver, as was Henry. Oliver waved his hand to make both men leave, and the door closed behind them.

Annie realised she needed to be with her mother. "Oliver, take Max to Papa while I talk to Mama for a moment."

Still cradling his son, Oliver carefully negotiated the buckets, discarded bloodied towels and other paraphernalia that sat on the floor of his normally pristine office. He went to meet his father-in-law to introduce his son to his grandfather. Further confessions would need to wait.

As the door quietly closed behind him, Annie took her mother in her arms. "Mama, I can't tell you everything right now, but the marquess is your son-in-law, and he's just gone to introduce your grandson to Papa. Will you stay while I prepare to deliver his sibling?"

Anne-Marie was stunned at the news but nodded. "Twins?" Annie nodded. Anne-Marie presumed that her daughter had just returned from Scotland, but there was obviously much more to their story.

Ermie had quietly taken over from her friend, Juditty.

Juditty Durham had willingly relinquished her position in great relief. She didn't mind catching a baby, but the afterbirth was messy, and Ermie was used to this. For there to be two babies at once was enough for her to expel a long sigh of relief when the midwife arrived. She hovered in case she was needed.

Ermie interrupted the mother-daughter reunion. "Sorry, Mrs Soames, but Annie, sweetie, you need to get up and walk to turn the babe." Ermie hoisted Annie's gown up further and felt her stomach.

Annie nodded. "Mama, can you get Oliver for me, please?"

Her mother was somewhat flustered with her daughter calling the marquess by his Christian name. "Yes, of course, darling, but…"

Annie cut her off. "Mama, I will explain everything later, but I need Oliver now, please."

Her mother went to relieve Oliver of his precious burden and send him back to his wife. Anne-Marie was reeling from the unfolding situation. Henry had explained little except that Annie needed them urgently. He had not mentioned that a birth was imminent, let alone in progress. It was seven years since they had heard from her. She passed Oliver with a nod and took the baby. She had not seen him for nearly two years.

Oliver returned to Annie's side and listened to Ermie's instructions. He helped Annie get on her feet and then walked her around the room.

For half an hour, the two walked, and Annie was told to stretch and bend a little to help the child move position and turn. After a while, Ermie felt her stomach again and said that the babe had turned. "Annie, you delivered last time on the birthing chair. Do you want to try on your back or…" she looked at Mrs Durham with a frown "…or squatting."

Annie saw her quandary. "She knows Ermie; I had to let her know a long time ago."

Oliver gasped.

Juditty Durham met Oliver's eyes and saw him flush with embarrassment. She smiled, realising his remorse; however, she also knew of his continuing love for Annie.

Annie could feel a contraction coming. "Squatting, I think, Ermie, but how long will this take?"

Ermie shrugged. "It could be minutes, dearie, or it could be another half-an-hour. I've known them to wait a full day before they decide to come."

It turned out to be only minutes; the pains returned with a vengeance. Annie's mother came at the first cry of pain.

Ermie was intrigued that Annie had persuaded the marquess to stay for the births. Men usually refused to be part of a birth. Annie saw her puzzled glance at her husband. "He's staying, Ermie, and he knows that."

After twenty minutes of heavy contractions, Annie was still on her feet and leaning into Oliver for support. She asked Ermie to check her progress. She felt she was close.

Ermie said, "You're crowning, Annie, positions, everyone." Ermie looked at Oliver and said, "Sir, if you are staying, you will need to be seated on the chaise lounge and support Miss Annie." She showed him how to sit and then positioned Annie between his legs so she could squat and be supported.

Oliver smiled at the midwife. "She's Lady Annie now and about time too."

Ermie guffawed and said, "I agree, sir. Mrs Soames, can you hold the bowl for her?"

Olivia Mary Violet Annabella was placed in her mother's arms fifteen minutes later. The perfect little girl looked just like her older sister had. She had a golden fuzz and a rounded face; only this little girl opened her eyes to the world and let out a cry that was music to her parents' ears. Annie turned to Oliver and wept. "She's perfect, Oliver, and she's breathing. She will be Olivia, and then Mary after Mary Johnson, Violet as it is eight years to the day from Aunt Violet's death and Annabella after me. They are named after our convict friends to remind us we are all equal in god's eyes." She felt the wetness of his tears on her neck as he kissed her. She felt him nod and murmur, "Perfect."

This time, there were no apologies. His words of love were for Annie's ears only. "She's Anna's little sister, sweetheart. One day, we'll tell them all about their big sister. One day!"

Her mother heard the couple's soft utterances and finally understood what had puzzled her for a long time. Annie had carried another child of his, and it had died, one born out of wedlock. Her heart wept for her daughter, but for now, that was irrelevant. They were married and had two healthy children. Twin grandchildren, what a joyous blessing.

The delivery of the two afterbirths made the pain of the births a breeze. Having been through this before, Annie warned Oliver she would scream and make the windows of the mansion shudder. She wasn't wrong. The agony of the final part of the delivery was now complete. Ermie cleaned Annie up and told Oliver that he could carry her to bed as soon as she finished feeding the babies.

Ermie promised to call on her the following morning, but she had another child to deliver. "I will see you settled first, dear. The other lass is not in labour; I need to break her waters as she's overdue."

While still on the chaise lounge, Annie quickly adjusted her dress, Oliver undoing the back of her gown. She fed both babies while her mother and Oliver watched as she juggled feeding two at once. They had placed a velvet cushion under each wiggling, mewling bundle as Ermie showed her how to place them. Within fifteen minutes, both were fed and asleep, just two hours after their arrival.

The four adults still needed to have a long discussion, which was best done in the privacy of the master bedroom.

Oliver scooped up Annie and carried her to their suite. She wrapped her arms around his neck, and their whispered conversation was inaudible to others.

The reverend was cradling his grandson, and he followed his wife and granddaughter up the stairs. Both tiny babies remained asleep.

Oliver and Annie knew her parents' retribution must now be faced.

When Verity left, Oliver had completely stripped the soft furnishings in the Lady Chamber and burnt it all. For more than a year, the room remained empty. Nothing of Verity's remained. The room sat unfurnished until shortly before he left for Sydney. He had ordered the redecoration of the entire suite, converting Verity's bedroom into a closet and her immense closet into a new bedroom. She had taken most of her clothing with her, but the remaining gowns were given to the staff. He had not seen the conversion complete. The burnt furnishings were replaced with the most exquisite furniture from other suites; the drapes were now heavy velvet. He had ordered that the room be aired daily, and over the intervening years, the cloying perfume had evaporated. Before he left, he had told Juditty to make the room smell of violets, and it did. He grinned when he entered the room. It was perfect.

The lovely room was decorated with new cream curtains with gold and violet highlights and tie-backs. The new magnificently carved bed had a huge pelmet overhanging the head and was draped with similar colours, only in creamy silk brocades and violet highlights. The room was decorated especially for Annie. As he placed her on the side of the bed, he realised she was still in her gown, which was covered in blood. He needed to remove the soiled garment and clean her up. Issuing instructions on which cases to bring in, her night rail appeared in a matter of minutes, as did a large ewer and jug of hot water. His staff had already unloaded the luggage carriage, which had arrived soon after the first baby had been delivered.

The maids had already started unpacking her cases into her new dressing room.

After Oliver placed Annie in the completely refurbished elegant bed, he let her get comfortable. He waited attentively, arranging pillows and making her feel at home. Then Oliver shooed away the helping hands and soon had her stripped, washed and helped her into the bed. He had done it all himself.

When she was ready, he gave her a quick kiss. "Now, to face your parents, my sweet. I am as nervous as a small child being disciplined. And I deserve everything they will yell at me."

Annie reached out for him and cupped his beloved face. "Oliver, trust them. Be truthful and accept their judgement."

Oliver nodded and, after another kiss, opened the door to his parents-in-law and children. Ermie and Mrs Durham carefully removed the babies from their arms, and Oliver ushered in the older couple.

The two ladies took the babies upstairs to their new room.

The door closed quietly behind the clergy couple as Oliver prepared himself for the wrath he so richly deserved.

The expected chastisement was not forthcoming, but the utter disappointment he saw on their faces was more punishment than a tongue-lashing would have been.

Annie intended to tell them somewhat delicately what had occurred when Oliver blurted out to her parents. "I violated her, sir; I stole her innocence, and I was married and could do nothing to repair what I had destroyed." His comments were met with silence, so he continued. "I got drunk and had my way with her. I will not explain much more than saying that Verity had just admitted that the child she had birthed was not mine, and I took it out on Annie. It's all my fault, and I will bear full responsibility and accept your wrath and whatever chastisement you wish."

Annie's father lifted his head and looked long and hard at his son-in-law. Eventually, he quietly asked, "Are you sorry, son?"

Oliver felt like he was a five-year-old. His eyes swam with the unshed tears of his remorse. He nodded, then said, while gazing adoringly at his wife. "More than you can ever know, sir; I have loved your Annie for so long, then I lost her. I was crushed until I found out where she was and that Verity was responsible for her incarceration and transportation."

Oliver's look of adoration was enough for her father to forgive him for what he had done. He and Annie obviously adored each other. "I will say nothing more other than ask, have you confessed your actions to the Lord? Only then will you be able to forgive yourself, for I am not your judge."

His loving words could have knocked Oliver over. Again, Oliver nodded. A tear of repentance escaped from his eye. He nodded. "Often, sir!" Oliver moved to Annie's side.

Over the next half hour, the entire story unfolds, from Annie's highwayman spectre to spite him to Verity's spite and her vengeance.

They told her parents of Annie's conviction and transportation.

She briefly described the colony and the trip out there. More of her life would follow at a later time and day. Annie told them about Oliver's arrival, her interaction with Reverend Richard and Mary Johnson, and that she had first been assigned to them.

Through it all, the older couple sat listening in virtual silence. Occasionally, they would ask a question, but mostly they listened. They were obviously hurting but also greatly relieved she was back.

Oliver had never seen such love in action, but the embrace they both received from her parents melted him. He wept unashamedly. These two put the love of the good Lord into action. They showed Christ's forgiveness in such a way that he was overwhelmed. He had never seen such compassion, tolerance, and forgiveness, so he gazed at his rector in pure awe. Annie had told him to trust them. She knew them so well, and she was of the same mould. Oliver's confession was made honestly, and the absolution was given with love. The new family would have many more discussions later, but he knew he was forgiven and accepted.

~

Two weeks after the birth of the twins, Annie was permitted downstairs. Knowing how very ill and weak she had been after Anna's birth, she had complied and stayed in bed. She lapped up the luxury of what being a marchioness meant. Even though they could not be together as husband and wife, Annie insisted that Oliver share her bed each night.

Rather than hire new maids for the nursery, a plethora of young ones wished to rotate through night duty and care for the infants. Annie insisted on feeding them herself. She fully intended to be a hands-on mother.

Her return brought a joyous freshness to the house. She noticed that rather than just one maid, many of them took turns coming into her room to do a small service for her. Each thanked her and welcomed her home.

Eventually, the two village girls, Alice and Milly, who had bathed after her that fateful week so long ago, were promoted to nursery maids and would care for the children. Both girls were from large families, and Annie knew they were experienced at looking after babies. The two girls moved into the nursery upstairs with the babies and took over their daily care.

As Annie insisted, the twins were brought to her room to feed. As soon as she was permitted out of bed, she made a trip to visit her babies. She found Oliver there already. He was gazing at his sleeping children, but he had something by his side. A large flat package sat on the floor. As he turned, she saw what it was. He had put his new carpentry skills to good use and made a second rocking horse swing for the second twin; only this now was made of a pale oak, not red gum. He had duplicated John White's gift. Although it would be many months before they could use them, he had made a twin to the rocking horse that would also be suspended from the ornate roof of the nursery. She understood his pleasure in his work as she realised he had made this himself. Bob probably assisted a little, but it was the first time Oliver had ever done something like this. He took great pride in the fact that his ability to do such a simple thing worked well.

Annie walked to him and slipped her arm around his waist, greeting him with a long and loving kiss.

After a while, they stood looking into the cribs. She said, "Max and Livvy are two perfect little miracles. We are so very blessed, Oliver. We have so much, my love, that we will have to implement our plan as soon as I am well. Without Doctor Arthur Bowes-Smith, we may never have had this opportunity. I may not have even survived the trip, but for him. We owe it to his memory to ensure that the occupants are treated more humanely on future convict ships."

Oliver turned to his wife and drew her into his arms. He bent down and drew a deep breath of her violet-scented hair. He said, "That smell of violets haunted my dreams, and I had no idea what it was. For some reason, everywhere I went in the house, I could smell it."

Annie smiled as she remembered both maids had also reeked of the perfume. Everywhere they went that week, the three of them left the lingering scent of violets. As they also cleaned his room, the scent would have lingered there as well. However, it was that week she had also stolen into his room and taken some of his old clothing. She had intentionally dropped a handkerchief in his wardrobe that was covered in the scent. Her confession of this made him chuckle. She still had his cape and would never get rid of it.

Alice and Milly left them with their children and quietly left the room.

Oliver lovingly kissed her and then softly said. "All I remember about that night was the violets. The scent remained on my clothing and hung in my room for days." He dropped his voice so the maids would not hear should they still be within earshot. "It was quite strong, especially on the office couch! After you had gone, I would sit on the floor and breathe in your perfume. It was as though the aroma had burnt a brand in my heart. Having said that, I can never apologise enough. If only..."

Annie lifted her hand and placed her fingers on his lips. "No, 'if only's' Oliver; our future is before us. The past is forgiven, and tomorrow, we move forward to help others in the future. We have a family, and the bonds of love will bind us tight. These two will lead us on a merry dance, much as I did for my parents. They are named after two convicts, so I would expect no less. I was a hoyden, and you turned me into Gentle Annie. I learned much in those years apart, and we will put that to good use, for I know how to help them." She chuckled, adding, "However, I would prefer not to have to start the fires each morning with sticks. Oliver, unlike us, these two already have a head start. They have not only each other but us too. We were both alone, but no more. You are my soul mate, and I never wish to be apart from you again."

Choked up with the emotion he had been too afraid to show until he met this girl, Oliver took some time before he replied. He occupied her red cupid-shaped lips with his own, then said, "You never will be alone again, my darling, gentle Annie Soames Quilpie, for wherever you go, I will follow. You see, I love you."

Much work was ahead of them, and they would ensure the plight of the oppressed would be eased where possible, but that was for another day. The soft whimpering sounds of waking babies finally broke them apart.

Mrs Elizabeth (Betty) Fry

In later years, from 1814,
Mrs Elizabeth Fry and her twenty-thousand helpers, many of whom were
peers, did much to aid the condition of the female convicts.
Each female convict was given a gift pack with fabric, wool,
knitting needles and numerous other items to occupy themselves on the
journey to a new life. They were able to sell the items they made
and make some money for themselves.

(See *A Lady in Irons.*)

Elizabeth and her brother, Joseph Gurney,
inspected the goals throughout England and Scotland,
suggesting ideas for the improvement of the prisoner's conditions.
Glasgow Prison was one of the few that passed inspection.

(See *Scotch at The Rocks*)

More books are coming set in this era.

When Upon Life's Billows is Captain John Hunter's story and
will continue the story of the colony.
John Hunter's story is the first book in the
Hunter to Macquarie Collection. (1795-1822)

Reviews *of my books help bring them to the attention of other readers who are more likely to read something from a new-to-them author if it has more reviews (even if they are star ratings).*

The voyage

The First Fleet Journey 1787-1788

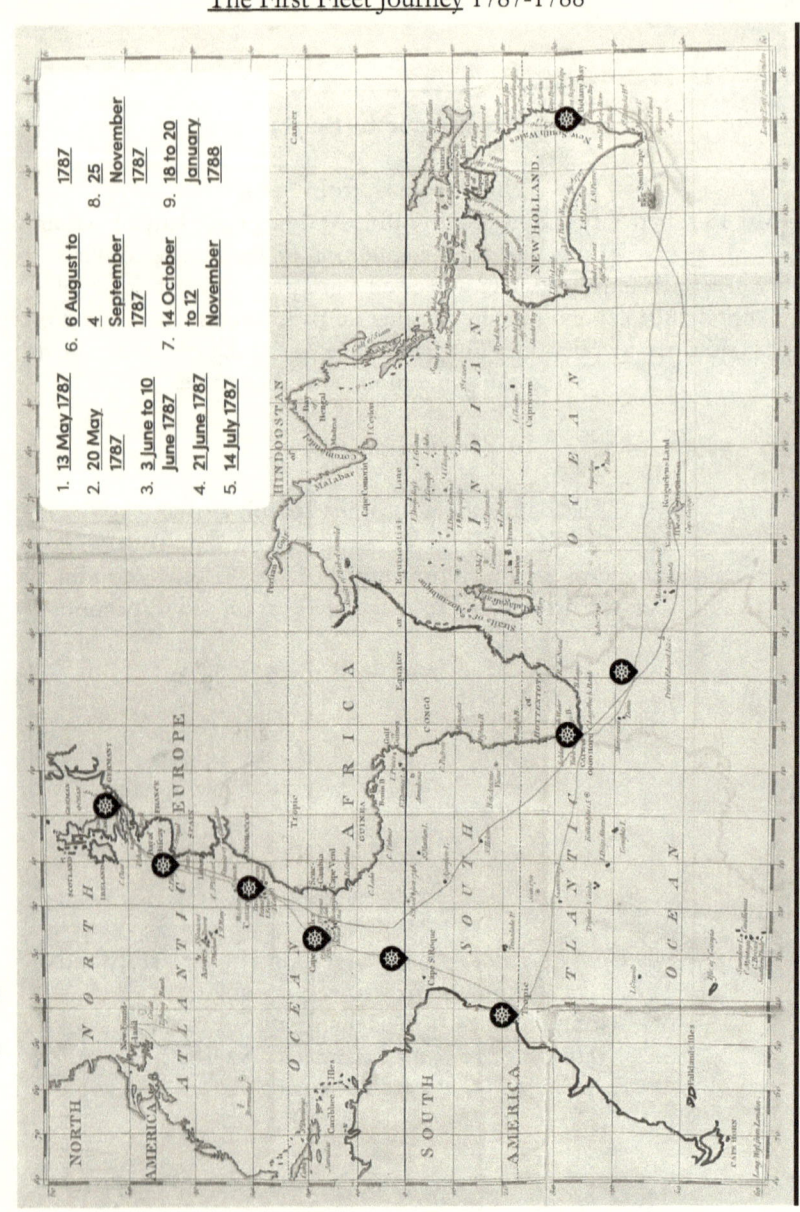

1. 13 May 1787
2. 20 May 1787
3. 3 June to 10 June 1787
4. 21 June 1787
5. 14 July 1787
6. 6 August to 4 September 1787
7. 14 October to 12 November 1787
8. 25 November 1787
9. 18 to 20 January 1788

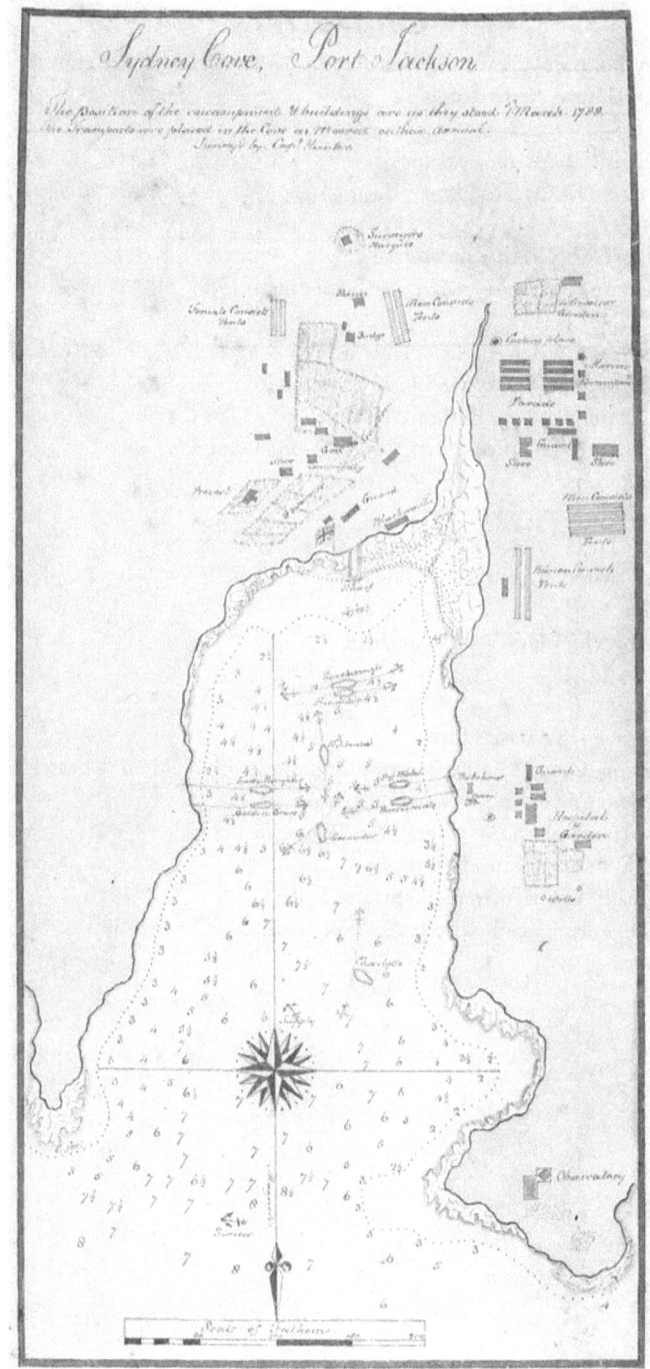

Sydney Cove settlement in 1788

Female convicts top left. The minister and judge were in between male and female convicts.

Characters

Rev **Godfrey Soames**, curate and later Rector of Bowbelle Village church.
m 1765 **Anne-Marie Armstrong**
Children 1
#1 Annabella Marie (**Annie**) Soames b 17/3/1767 (Annie Gentle, aka Gentle Annie - Oliver's pet name for her) (3 horses, Basil's *Midas,* Oliver's *Aladdin,* Phillip's *Pegasus)*

Sir **Basil Armstrong**, Annie's maternal Uncle - Armstrong Keep
Violet Armstrong, paralysed wife, died 15th March 1786

Oliver Quilpie, Marquess of Bowbelle -b 1760 *Bowbelle Hall,* horse *King's Majesty.*
m1 1785 Marchioness **Verity** died 1792 drowned
#1 Marcus Neville Quilpie, Earl of Martindel, b 9/1786 d 1792
m2 Annabella Marie (**Annie**) Soames b aka Annie Gentle, *see above*
   Children, 2+
   1 **Anna**-Marie Soames Quilpie
   b & d 5/May/1787
   2 Maxwell (**Max**) Arthur John Oliver Quilpie, twin
   b 15 March 1794
   3 Olivia (**Livvie**) Mary Violet Annabella Quilpie, twin
   b 15 March 1794

Nigel Hawthorne - Sir Basil's butler
Henry Greening, Oliver's butler, married/widowed with children & grandchildren
Juditty Durham Oliver's housekeeper
Erminetrude (**Ermie**) Wilde - Midwife at Bowbelle Village
Bob Brown, her son and head groom.
Colin Newstead - Convict overseer in Rose Hill
Alice & Milly - village maids who had a violet bath. Nursery maids
Maxwell Slater
Jenny m Max

Real people - *I have tried to portray all of them as accurately as history permits.*

Governor Arthur Phillip

Captain John Hunter

Major Francis Grose

Captain Campbell and nephew **Jamie**

Doctor John White

Rev Richard & Mary Johnson- the first chaplain

http://www.fellowshipfirstfleeters.org.au/revrichardjohnson.htm

Doctor Arthur Bowes-Smyth - his journal is online for free.

http://acms.sl.nsw.gov.au/_transcript/2015/D02131/a138.html

Margaret Frownes (Maggie), aged 45 - died Oct 1788 in Sydney

Olive Gaskin/Olivia Gascoigne, a real person, is herself: See bibliography.

She married **Nathaniel Lucas** Nate, and Olive married and had children.

(the Lucas's twins died at age 2 when a tree fell on their house).

Mary Love (arrested with Betty Bird - Betty Eccles)

Betty Bird married Thomas Eccles and later became the housekeeper at Government House and the colony's dairy maid, dying at age 105.

Thomas Eccles married Betty Bird, and they eventually had 13 children

Convict women on board Lady Penrhyn (+ Olive/Olivia)

Elizabeth Colley (who lost a baby boy to stillbirth) went on to marry and have more children. (partner to Thomas Jamison on Norfolk Island, and they had five children)

Elizabeth Lees, Elizabeth Hipley, Ann Inett, Susannah Gough, Nathaniel, and Olive Gaskin/Olivia Gascoyne all went to Norfolk Island.

All the convicts mentioned, other than Annie, and their crimes are real.

The ship captains and other historical characters are mentioned in history.

About Annie's friends - *their stories are as true as I could find.*

Olivia Gascoigne aka Olive Gaskin - Olivia Lucas (1761–1830)

Olivia Gascoigne was found guilty on 5 March 1785 at Worchester, England, of stealing 13 pieces of gold coin of the value of £13/13/-, and one piece of foreign silver coin from a dwelling house. Her death sentence was commuted to seven years transportation on 28 December 1785. She arrived in Sydney in January 1788 aboard the Lady Penrhyn as part of the First Fleet.

Gaskin/Gascoigne was sent to Norfolk Island aboard the Supply shortly after her arrival in New South Wales. Also on board was **Nathaniel Lucas**. The couple were married shortly after their arrival on Norfolk Island in a civil ceremony. The marriage was solemnised in 1791; they had 13 children, 11 of whom survived infancy. The couple returned to Port Jackson in 1805. Following her husband's death, Olivia Lucas moved to Van Diemen's Land (Tasmania) in 1818 with six of her surviving children. She died at Launceston on 10 June 1830; her age was given as 69.

https://peopleaustralia.anu.edu.au/biography/lucas-olivia-25601

Olivia had eleven children while living on Norfolk Island. Her first child, Ann, born on 2 March 1789, was one of the first children to be born there. The very first child born at the new settlement was called Norfolk and was the offspring of Lieutenant Philip Gidley King and convict Ann Inett. A year later, twins Mary and Sarah were born to Olivia; however, they died at 18 months of age when a tree, being felled by Nathaniel, descended upon them. Olivia's arm was broken in the same incident. The other children were William (1792), Nathaniel (1793), Olivia (1795), John (1796), James (1798), George (1800), Charles (1801), Sarah (1803), Mary Ann (1805) and finally, Thomas (1807). In typical fashion of the era, the names of children who died were recycled and given to children who were born later. Mary and Sarah were the names of Nathaniel and Olivia's mothers, and John was the names of both their fathers. The family left Norfolk Island in 1805 when a decision was made to abandon the settlement. Olivia's final two children, Mary Ann and Thomas, were born in Sydney. The Lucas family moved to Sydney, where the marriage broke up in 1816, and Olivia, with six of her children, moved to Port Dalrymple in Van Diemen's Land (Tasmania). Nathaniel died in 1818, aged 54, and, during the previous few years, several of his sons commuted from Van Diemen's Land to Liverpool, where they worked with him.

https://www.dianakupke.com.au/page6d.php

Elizabeth Eccles—*aka Betty Bird*—*Winifred Elizabeth Bird was arrested with Mary and John Love. Soon after their arrival, Betty Bird and Thomas Eccles moved to Norfolk Island*, where they married. They had many children and later moved back to Sydney. Thomas died, and Betty became housekeeper at Government House Parramatta and later took over the dairy. She lived next door to the dairy and died aged 105. Her story is told in "Convict Shadows of the Past" By Sara Powter.

Elizabeth Colley After losing her baby on the Lady Penrhyn, she became a partner of Thomas Jamison (from the Sirius) and later a surgeon on Norfolk Island. Five children were born into this union. Thomas later took her home to England despite having a wife and children there.
https://peopleaustralia.anu.edu.au/biography/colley-elizabeth-eliza-30584/text37911

Doctor Arthur Bowes-Smyth

Was the senior surgeon on the *Lady Penrhyn* but was employed to oversee the wellbeing of the soldiers and crew. Doctor Altree, the convict's doctor, fell ill shortly before sailing and by their first stop, he was relieved of duty. Doctor Arthur wrote a detailed journal of the voyage, which is available online for anyone to read. After leaving Sydney it took him eighteen months to return to London. He reported the horrific contusion to London, but by then the Second Fleet had already sailed. The *Kitty* was sent out to relieve the hunger, but his pleas were supported by a member of the aristocracy. He reported the orgy after the women landed as the ship he was on was in full view of the vile sight. It was his book that inspired my story.

Bibliography

Voyage details - Lady Penrhyn
https://dictionaryofsydney.org/entry/lady_penrhyn
Lady Penrhyn history
https://firstfleetfellowship.org.au/ships/hms-lady-penrhyn/
https://dictionaryofsydney.org/entry/lady_penrhyn#ref-uuid=3d9dabe5-2805-a1ea-2186-4b09f3397593
First Fleet trip
https://pursuit.unimelb.edu.au/articles/the-first-fleet-and-australia-s-unforgiving-weather
https://sydneylivingmuseums.com.au/stories/first-fleet-ships/20-may-1787
https://firstfleetfellowship.org.au/library/seamen/
Dr Arthur Bowes-Smith - journal
Arthur Bowes-Smith, illustrated journal, 1787-1789. Titled `A Journal of a Voyage from Portsmouth to New South Wales and China in the Lady Penrhyn, Merchantman William Cropton Sever, Commander by Arthur Bowes-Smith, Surgeon - 1787-1788-1789'; being a fair 22 March 1787 - 12 August 1789; compiled ca 1790
http://www.gp.org.au/first_fleet_surgeon.html
 & File :- 6mxwWq4okVPdg
https://collection.sl.nsw.gov.au/digital/6mxwWq4okVPdg?_gl=1*dky93i*_ga*OTQxNzc4NTYyLjE2NjA0Mjk3MTk.*_ga_CYHFMM592Q*MTY2MTEzMjU0OS42LjAuMTY2MTEzMjU1NC41NS4wLjA.
(*Transcript*) http://acms.sl.nsw.gov.au/_transcript/2015/D02131/a138.html
Nautical shipping terms
https://www.hnsa.org/manuals-documents/age-of-sail/textbook-of-seamanship/the-ship-definitions/
Olive Gaskins/Olivia Gascoigne history
http://www.fellowshipfirstfleeters.org.au/lucas_gascoigne.htm
Smallpox
https://www.nma.gov.au/defining-moments/resources/smallpox-epidemic
William Bradley's Diary
https://acms.sl.nsw.gov.au/_transcript/2015/D02131/a138.html
Thomas & Robert Webb
https://hmssirius.com.au/thomas-webb-seaman-hms-sirius-1786-and-hm-supply-1788/
https://peopleaustralia.anu.edu.au/biography/webb-robert-29848
The sinking of the HMS Sirius
https://firstfleetfellowship.org.au/marines/the-wreck-of-sirius-at-norfolk-island/
https://environment.gov.au/shipwreck/public/wreck/wreck.do?key=7956
Convict Transportation
https://www.records.nsw.gov.au/archives/collections-and-research/guides-and-indexes/convict-transportation-nsw
Colonial /Native food plants.
https://media.australian.museum/media/dd/Uploads/Documents/38627/ams370_vXXII_07_LowRes.eaab05e.pdf
https://www.sl.nsw.gov.au/learning/food-colony/food-they-tried-grow
Early Parramatta
https://www.parrapark.com.au/assets/Things-to-do/Google-Arts-Culture-Tour/PP_WalkingTour_ColonialRoseHill_A4DL_web.pdf
Rev Richard Johnson
https://adb.anu.edu.au/biography/johnson-richard-2275
1st St Phillips Church
https://dictionaryofsydney.org/entry/christian_church_architecture
Kangaroo tendon sutures
https://www.nursing.virginia.edu/news/flashback-stitches/
Further Reading
Journals of the First Fleet
https://en.wikipedia.org/wiki/Journals_of_the_First_Fleet
Elizabeth Colley
https://peopleaustralia.anu.edu.au/biography/colley-elizabeth-eliza-30584/text37911
Dharug/Dharawal Language resources
https://dharug.dalang.com.au/language/dictionary

Glossary

Aboriginal words - Dharug/Dharawal dialect

Dharug/Dharawal Language resources
https://dharug.dalang.com.au/language/dictionary

Dharug Tribe -the Aboriginal people from Western Sydney to the central Blue Mountains area. Known as Freshwater People. **Eora** Tribe are the Saltwater people)

Dharug Language resource:-
   https://dharug.dalang.com.au/language/dictionary? query=thank+you&type=English&numeric=Exact&dialect=All#
Eora language resource *(William Dawes journal) https://www.williamdawes.org/ indexes.html*

Gurung = child/baby
Duba/s = Aboriginal woman/women
dhulay or *mula.* = Aboriginal man
Binya = pregnant
Baragat = frightened
Fella = pigeon English for person
Chook= a chicken
Gunnya = aboriginal tent
Garmit = black cockatoo (large black parrot)
Garraway= white cockatoo (large white parrot with yellow crest)
didgeridoos= hollow branch used for instrument
gunya/humpy - Aboriginal dwelling
Badu= water
biyanga = father
Wilbung - currawong
Garraway - wind
Birrong - stars
dyinmang, is wife
Mullamang is husband.

If you loved this book, these are similar. (*All are stand-alone stories*)

First Fleet Convict Era Trilogy 1788-1800

Gentle Annie Soames

Her dreams lead to unexpected outcomes. An Australian First Fleet story.
A First Fleet story with the descriptions taken directly from the Journal of
Doctor Arthur Bowes Smith was the doctor on board the Lady Penrhyn.

Annie Soames is a girl beloved by the community but not afraid to voice her desires. That leads to trouble, illicit love, and a world turned upside down.
Oliver Quilpie, the newly married Marquess, finds his arranged marriage unsatisfactory; he is irresistibly drawn to his wife's companion. Unfortunately, he can't keep his hands off her. In retaliation, Annie copies his every move while riding, dressed as a highwayman. However, she has now fallen in love with him. This ultimately leads to her arrest and banishment to a distant land.
After some years, Oliver's wife dies, and his thoughts turn to Annie. He seeks to find her, but she has vanished. He is horrified to discover she was transported to New South Wales as a convict on the *Lady Penrhyn*. Will Annie want to see him?

ISBN 9780645441574   ISBN ebook 9781923097063   LP ISBN 978-1923097346
https://mybook.to/GentleAnnieSoames

Long-listed in the Historical Fiction Company Competition 2024

The Emancipated Potter

Sydney Cove 1788 to Parramatta 1795
Not all felons are convicts, and not all convicts are felons.

Colin Osborne's serene life as a talented potter is disrupted by a self-important peer. A single punch sends Colin across to the other side of the globe.
Aggie Gibbs is a young convict girl being hunted by a wayward soldier. The two find themselves in a town of criminals and lecherous men.
Captain John Hunter is Colin's mentor, and he paves the way for a new life for his young friends. Then disaster strikes, and he must leave.
Can Colin keep Aggie safe? Will they fulfil Captain Hunter's wishes to build a decent life for the convicts destined to live out their lives in the penal town? Will John ever return to New South Wales?

Paperback ISBN 9781923097476   ISBN ebook 9781923097483

Paternity Unknown

Sydney 1788 - 1800 The Aftermath of the First Fleet landing.
Can forgiveness be that easy?

Connie Waterson is traumatised after she became one of the victims of the attack when the convict women were landed on February 6th, 1788. She finds herself expecting an unwanted child. Along with her friends, she must learn to cope with the challenges of their new environment while protecting the life growing within her.
Nigel Bray is a young convict who almost instantly regrets his carnal actions on the day the prisoners from the *Lady Penrhyn* landed. Knowing that Connie is the unwilling recipient of his base desires, Nigel does what he can to ease her path. He is racked with questions: is the child his? Will she ever forgive him? What must Nigel do to win Connie's trust?

ISBN 9781923097438   ISBN ebook 9781923097445   LP ISBN 978-1923097452

The Hunter to Macquarie Collection 1795-1822

When Upon Life's Billows

Sydney 1795-1821 - Governor John Hunter
Keep Your Friends Close, and your enemies Closer.

John Hunter loved his life at sea. The wind blows where no man knows, and John is caught in a storm. His ship, the *HMS Sirius,* was wrecked in 1790. Five years later, he became the second governor of the rough and filthy penal settlement of New South Wales. From a place he once loved, he now seems to be in the wrong place at the wrong time, trusting the wrong people.
Helena Rosedale is not your typical female convict. She fiercely battles to prevent the men from abusing her, earning her the nickname "*Helena the Hellcat.*"
Crispin Milroy, alone in the world, serves on the new governor's security detail. Can he win the fair lady's heart? Life in 1795 in Sydney Cove is harsh at best. Food is scarce, and disease often ravages the settlement. Life throws everything at these three, yet somehow, they manage to survive. Why does John trust this young couple when others betray him? What trials must Helena and Crispin endure to make their new lives in this unforgiving town bearable? How can John ease their path?

ISBN: 9780645783339   ebook ISBN: 9780645783346
May 2025

The Saddler's Song
London 1790s to Parramatta 1840s

George Ellis is the son of a tanner living on the outskirts of London. When disease strikes his family, he is left alone and hurting, seeking a new life for himself. After hearing from a friend about the chance to start a business in New South Wales, he sells everything he knows and departs. His cherished violin is his most treasured possession, and his gift for creating beautiful music is kept hidden from all but a select few.

Ben Parker is a saddler, like George; he is also alone in the world. Ben also sells up to move to the new colony. The two young men meet and combine their skills to start afresh in a new world. During the journey out, George's skill as a violinist is revealed. On arrival, they find accommodation with a family with many lovely daughters. Two of these girls steal their hearts, but how will the business survive in an animal-starved land with limited access to leather? What is the saddler's song?   ISBN : 9780645783353   eISBN: 9780645783360

Coming 2025

Tuppence to Pass
London 1800s to Parramatta 1820s

Josh Callan is a London lad making the most of the life dealt to him. Stealing from the man who killed his father gives the family a new direction. Josh gets arrested for theft, but the judge belittles him, saying he's not worth tuppence. As Governor Macquarie's term begins, he is transported to the penal colony of Sydney as a convict. He proves his worth and lands on his feet, becoming the governor's groom and confidante.

Life in the Colonial town opens opportunities they could never have dreamed about in England, but can Josh find his niche? Where will this strange friendship take him?
      ISBN : 9781923097070   eISBN: 9781923097087

Coming 2025

His Majesty's Pageboy
London to Emu Plains, Australia, in the 1800s

Jack Turner was born into a life of pomp and privilege that was not rightfully his. He was brought to the royal court for his protection. By age ten, he served as King George the Third's pageboy and was known as Lord John. For years, he struggled against society's immorality and people's shallowness; then, he met an unspoiled young girl whose purity stood out amidst the mire of humanity. He is unable to pursue her before his life hits a wall.

Martha Alexander is the daughter of a wealthy shipping merchant. She has been presented to London's second tier of society, where she meets the young man of her dreams. She is expected to marry well, and Lord John sets her heart fluttering. However, her father's drinking shatters her future. He was made to sign all his possessions away while drunk, unknowingly including his daughter. Refusing a forced marriage changes her life. How did these two young people end up as convicts in Australia?   Paperback ISBN 9781923097308   eISBN 978192309792

Coming 2026

A Fist Full of Holey Dollars
Sydney Cove 1810+

Captain **Rudi Greenwood** is a solitary man trapped in a job without a purpose in a land where alcohol is the currency and rules are frequently ignored in the pursuit of wealth.

Bethany Edwards is a grieving widow expecting her late husband's child. Rudi's attraction to the lovely widow compels him to reassess his views and contemplate someone new. She seeks Rudi's help and support, but is that all she truly feels?

When **Governor Lachlan Macquarie** asks Rudi for help improving the roads, a casual remark alters Rudi's life and affects the entire colony. To tackle the alcohol issue, he proposes creating a new currency. With Bethany by his side, will he rise to the governor's challenges? What actions lead to him being despised by the exclusives and free settlers in the colony?
      Paperback ISBN 9781923097407   eISBN 9781923097414

Coming 2026

Far From the Whispering Sheoaks
Set in Australia in 1817+

Fanny Little was in the wrong place doing something she thought was legal. Her actions led to her arrest, trial, and banishment. She was assigned from the female prison to ex-soldier Gordon McKenzie and soon found herself in the despicable and humiliating situation of being sold in the public marketplace.

Phil Bentley is a man running from his jealous uncle. He is seeking safety on a secluded farm half a world away. With the community backing them, can Phil save Fanny from Gordon's vile abuse? Why is their relationship destined to spark controversy? And who is Jas? Why does Gordon wish to harm the child? Will they ever escape the shadows pursuing them?
      Paperback ISBN 9781923097315   eISBN9781923097322

Coming 2026

Bound Down in Iron Chains
An Australian Historical Tale, set in the Boys' Orphanage in Sydney in 1818+
Smuggling, Rum and Ructions

Howard Marlow is a studious and honest London bookkeeper. When asked to help a friend's brother with his bookkeeping, he unknowingly helps a crime gang. He is arrested, convicted, and transported. On arrival, Howard is assigned to the boy's orphanage, where a possibly crooked soldier is in charge. He is asked to use his skills to decipher bookkeeping entries that make no sense. He discovers his love for the affection-starved boys at the orphanage.

Naomi Buckingham, a convict girl, is thrust into the harsh reality of the orphanage alongside Howard. She is assigned to the orphanage, but it is far from the refuge she had hoped for. The supervisor is a man who does not respect women. With no one to rely on but the new accountant, she grapples with the question of trust.

Naomi is the key to breaking the bookkeeping code and cracking the case wide open. Can Howard use his brains to save them both? How do they become involved with some of the worst criminals in the New South Wales penal colony?

Paperback ISBN 9781923097353   eISBN9781923097360
Coming 2026

Unlikely Convict Ladies Trilogy 1792-1840s
Dancing to Her Own Tune
Co-authored by Sheila Hunter and Sara Powter
Sydney 1790s to England 1830s

Annie White is released after serving seven years as a convict in Sydney. She has a visitor who helps her start a baking business. Annie is then asked to assist another ailing man, **Sam Corbett**. She nurses him back to health, and a relationship blossoms between them. They settle into a life together, barely making ends meet, when she realises she's expecting a child. Sam's past is laid bare, and he must come to terms with the revelations. They both must confront their accusers and discover that the answers to their questions are not what they anticipated. Their life experiences seem to cling to them, and unable to shake them off, they end up back in England. They must face their ghosts and recognise they are not who they think they are. How can they transform their anger and spite into love and forgiveness? The Dance of Life goes on.
ISBN 9780645110715   ISBN9780645110722

Long-listed for the Historical Fiction Company Competition 2022
Amelia's Tears
Parramatta 1828 – England 1840s
From Tears of Sadness to Tears of Joy.

Amelia Westaweller awaits her assignment in the Parramatta Female Prison. Forced to leave the relative safety of gaol, she is assigned and now faces her worst nightmare. A foul man claims her and makes her life a living hell. Then, her world goes black. A glimmer of hope arises when she hears from her brother, Jim, who has enlisted a friend to help her. She writes to Jim, pouring out her heart and telling him of the horrors of her new life. He encourages her to stay firm in her faith. All she can do is pray. When Major **Ned** Grace, her brother's friend, enters her life in Parramatta, he starts to ease her path. Things have changed, as now she has a child in tow. How can Amelia forge a new life for herself? What man could want her with her background and a child at her side? Who is the gentleman who turns her tears of sadness into tears of great joy?
ISBN: 9780645110739   eISBN: 9780645110746 Hard Cover ISBN 9798420617953

A Lady in Irons
England 1800s - Parramatta 1808+

Katy Harrington is mourning the death of her husband after he died in a shooting accident. Barely coping, she awaits the birth of their child. If it's a girl, she must hand the family home to her husband's brother. The day after giving birth to a daughter, she and her daughter are left on the side of a road. She collapses and is found by someone she thought had died in a fire ten years before. **Perry White,** badly scarred himself, nurses her back to health. They marry and move in with her widowed friend, Mary.

After some years, she discovers her husband and friend in each other's arms. Now living in a love triangle, she flees. Grasping the only straw available, she intentionally gets arrested and is sent to a colony far away. By doing this, her marriage can be annulled.

What happens in the Colony is different from what she expects. Governor Macquarie comes to her rescue, but what of Perry and her children?
ISBN: 9780645110784   eISBN:9780645441505

NO MORE, MY *Love*

Hunter Valley, NSW, 1820s

Jess Elkin is distraught when tragedy ravages her family. Now widowed, she becomes the victim of a carriage accident and is nursed back to health by the driver.

Marcus Ryan, a hard-headed woollen mill owner, was not expecting to fall in love. Yet, when Jess's fortunes suddenly turn for the worse, Marcus must decide how far he will go to pursue her. Years after following her to Newcastle, Australia, Marcus vanishes. Jess is left wondering if he will keep his promise to return to her... Will she ever see him again?

ISBN: 9780645441536   eISBN 9780645441581

Long-listed in the Historical Fiction Company Competition 2023

The Vine Weaver

Hawkesbury River area 1820s+
New Beginnings and Old Threats

In the 1820s, in Australia, **Joel and Hetty Walker** lived on a secluded farm on the Hawkesbury River, which became a healing haven for the protection of young convict women. A series of events brings **Fran Rea** to Hetty's attention, and she is taken to the farm. Fran and Hetty develop a cottage industry under the compassionate eye of farmhand **Hector Macdougal;** Hector's loving words change lives. It is to him that Fran turns when threatened.

The vines now must draw them close to survive the future revelations, and of those, there are many.

ISBN: 9780645441512   eISBN: 9780645441529

Long-listed in the Historical Fiction Company Competition 2023

https://amazon.com/dp/0645441511   https://amazon.com/dp/B0C6Z552Y2

The story continues in "Scotch at The Rocks"...

Scotch at The Rocks

Glasgow, Scotland, early 1800s to The Rocks, Sydney 1830s

Orphaned children Brodie Stewart and Heather Anderson live on Glasgow's streets. Although hungry, somehow they survive and keep out of trouble. Heather finds a job and looks to be settled; things go pear-shaped for them both. Eventually, they marry by declaration, yet even that gets messed up, and they are both arrested soon after they make their vow. In 1838, they were transported to Sydney as convicts. Heather arrives within weeks of Brodie, and they are assigned close to each other. They are now living on the docklands in Sydney, called The Rocks. They now have to forge a new life halfway across the world from their homeland.

Adventures abound, and Brodie gets press-ganged. While he's away, Heather's life changes and soon, she's officially selling Scotch Whisky at a shop in The Rocks.

You can take a Scot out of Scotland, but where did the Scotch come from?

ISBN 9780645441550 ebook 9781923097001 Large Print 9781923097254

https://mybook.to/ScotchatTheRocks

Waiting at the Sliprails

The Bathurst Road 1830s
A Convict's Tale

Bea Dawes's term of conviction nears an end, and she has few options other than marriage to a stranger or going on the street.

Jack Barnes, the hired drover, wants a wife. Bea accepts his offer; then, she discovers that he could be gone for months, leaving her alone with **Billy and Netty,** part of the tribe of an Aboriginal tribe who live on his secluded farm. Bea learns to love her husband and also this wonderful aboriginal couple. Drought ravages the farm, and Jack must hit the long paddock with the flock. In his absence, a visitor arrives, threatening to destroy everything she has worked so hard for. Can Bea touch his heart? Can she cope? Will the drought ever end? And when will Jack return?

ISBN: 9780645441543   eISBN: 9781923097032

https://mybook.to/WaitingattheSliprails

August 2023

PenCraft Award Winner for Literary Excellence, Christian Historical Fiction 2024

Convict Shadows of the Past
Two Jennifers, two hundred years apart

When she discovers her convict family history, eight-year-old Jenny Kellow learns that she was named after a convict from nearly two hundred years ago. Inspired by her grandfather's stories, she delves into her ancestors' convict past. From him, she hears tales of bushrangers, convicts, and life in the early colony of Parramatta. She embarks on a journey to retrace the footsteps of her convict great-great-great-grandmother to honour her. Jenny's quest begins with microfiche in the '60s, where she finds out about a small tin mining town in Cornwall and the production of a cheese that set London alight. She uncovers that her ancestor, **Jennifer Kellow,** brought her cheese-making skills to Parramatta, where she taught others the craft. Echoes of the past can still be heard if you know where to listen. Who was the first Jennifer, and what does she have to do with cheese? Why is she so elusive? Did Jenny's ancestor, Jennifer, ever see those two small crosses carved into the bricks of the Female Factory? Would Jenny ever uncover her ancestor's story?

ISBN: 9780645783315   ISBN ebook 9780645783322
A NaNoWriMo 2022 book winner

In Defence of Her Honour
London 1800s to Parramatta 1819
Will the real man of quality please stand up?

Bill Miller was raised and educated with the sons of the family. The youngest, Bert Edison-Browne, had been his best friend. However, jealousy intervenes when Bill's excellent schoolwork curtails their friendship. He wins a scholarship and enters Oxford University. When Bill's father dies unexpectedly, Bert insists that Bill take over as butler, but it's more to oppress him. Bert's jealousy grows and festers. He is now looking for a way to rid themselves of their new butler. A ruckus ensues, and Bill is arrested for assaulting Bert.

Molly Ross, the housekeeper's daughter, will vouch for him. It's too late; Bill has been arrested and is soon sentenced to be transported. With Bill gone, Molly now fights to defend herself from Bert. After hitting him with a pan, she, too, is arrested and sent to Sydney. Bill and Molly arrive with letters of introduction and compensation from Bert's father. Soon, they will be running the best inn in Parramatta with an endorsement from the governor.

ISBN 9780645441567   ISBN ebook 9781923097049
Long-listed in the Historical Fiction Company Competition 2024

I Can't Stop Tomorrow
Irish Famine 1840s to Avoca Beach, Australia

Escaping bigotry and prejudice in Ireland, the O'Shane family lives on a secluded farm on the west coast of Ireland. The potato blight soon decimates their farm. It's always darkest before dawn, and the two remaining girls cling to the hope of a new life. With the kindness of strangers, the eldest girls, **Clare** and **Kerry O'Shane**, head to their cousin, Sal Lockley, in Parramatta, Australia.   A new, wonderful life awaits them both. **Shéamus Connor** is the annoying teenage boy who reluctantly draws Clare's affection. However, living in a convict town means ruffians abound.

John Moore is a bad-tempered and troubled Irishman who is content to live alone on another secluded farm until he discovers Clare and two other lads need rescuing.
Can John protect her from the pain inflicted by an evil world?
Can Shéamus find his lost love who has fled?

ISBN: 9780645441598   ISBN ebook 9781923097056

Madeline's Boy
England 1830s to New South Wales 1840
The race to protect an Orphaned Boy
All is not straightforward when money and titles are involved.

Orphaned, afraid and on the run, Chip must flee.
Madeline was his mother's best friend. Maddie now needs to keep her charge safe and alive. She must give up her life to protect the boy she has loved since birth.
Months after Chip's parents' demise, Maddie sets out to deliver Chip to his Uncle Humphrey, who lives in Sydney. Through him, she meets Chip's friend Tim, who falls for Maddie— but will they find happiness?
The menacing presence soon finds Chip, and Maddie needs to hide him again. They are moved from hidden farms to secret valleys, ending up in an aboriginal encampment.
Can Tim find a way to be with Maddie? And if so... Will Chip ever be safe?

ISBN: 9780645783308   ISBN ebook 9781923097094
Long-listed in the Historical Fiction Company Competition 2024

https://mybook.to/MadelinesBoy

Jam or Marmalade for Tea
England 1820s to New South Wales 1825 (Governor Brisbane Era)

Martha Hamilton is the eldest of four orphans struggling to survive on their own. She is caught stealing, tried, convicted, and transported to New South Wales. With her family gone, she becomes despondent. Life holds no meaning for her, and the ocean waves look inviting.

Captain Guy Manning is a frustrated and injured redcoat soldier returning to Sydney for a new assignment. He notices Martha trying to jump overboard and rescues her. How do two cats bring them together?

A convict ship is no place for romance, and she's far too young anyway, isn't she?

Can Guy save her and forge a life together for them? What connections does he have to try to save her siblings? Why is marmalade important for their future?

Paperback ISBN 9781923097933 eISBN9781923097285

A NaNoWriMo 2023 book winner

https://mybook.to/JamorMarmaladeforTea

A prequel to 'The Lockleys Parramatta' series
(Free novella with newsletter signup)

Unshackled Lives
Set in England &Australia in the 1800s
Australian historical fiction of early colonial days

Ned Lockley is the second of four sons of the Duke and Duchess of Gracemere. As his mother's favourite, his childhood years were blissful, but he needs to grow up, and quickly.

A whirlwind romance is followed by a loved one's betrayal. The following emotional turmoil is hard for Ned to cope with, especially amid a collapsing, immoral society.

Ned can't stay as even his family is falling apart. His mother's words to remain true to himself and his faith make him leave everything he knows. How did Ned end up in New South Wales in charge of placing female convicts? Will he ever find happiness or discover who Charles is?

ISBN 9781923097377 eISBN 9781923097384 LP ISBN: 9781923097391

A 100-year, six-part Australian Colonial series
The Lockleys of Parramatta 1800-1900

Hands upon the Anvil
A blacksmith's life and love are more than work
Parramatta 1830s

Eddie Lockley's parents were transported for their crimes. Can a steadfast lad rise above his origins and guide others to succeed in a land of opportunity?

Ten-year-old Eddie longs to help his mum and dad. Living in a convict town with his family, the keen youngster has been working with the local blacksmith since his sixth birthday. But when a lieutenant doesn't stop abusing his older brother, the young boy yearns for the day when he can stand up and end the torment. Though he's thrilled when his mentor offers to send him off to learn his letters, Eddie fears he won't be around to watch his sibling's back. But as he takes on the biggest adventure of his life, the brave believer soon discovers that God is looking out for everyone he loves. Does this young man in the making have what it takes to change everything for the better?

ISBN 9780994578235 Ebook ISBN 978-0-9945782-5-9 Hardcover 9798496177368

https://mybook.to/HandsUponTheAnvil

Out Where The Brolgas Dance
Gold is found, and so is love
Parramatta 1840s
How can a question change so many people?

It's the 1840s, and discoveries across the Blue Mountains continue. Major Mitchell's new road is complete, and towns are planned and being built. Abundant land is available for those who want it. Eighteen-year-old **William "Wills" Lockley** has laid a solid foundation for a respectable career as a blacksmith, but the Lockley lust for adventure flows deeply within his veins. He dreads the monotony of work at the blacksmith's forge and yearns for adventure in a new frontier. Wills meets six Englishmen (*Coping with what is now known as PTSD*) who have the means to make his dreams come true. What they discover changes the Colony and their lives forever. Gold fever ensues. While in the West, Wills must deal with an uncertain romance. Does Cathy even want him?

ISBN 9780994578242 Ebook ISBN 978-0-9945782-6-6 Hardcover ISBN 9798755445504
LP ISBN 9781923097155

https://mybook.to/OutWhereTheBrolgas

Diamonds in the Dirt
Diamonds, love and money… but there is much more to life.
Parramatta 1850s

The youngest Lockley son, **Luke Lockley**, has completed university, and his life has no direction. No job, no money, and no love. Desperately alone, he prays for guidance. How can Luke trust that God has a plan for him if he can't even find a job? He does the only thing he can … he prays. Within a week, life has changed … oh, how it has changed as his brother Wills turns up with a suggestion. Would Luke be interested in joining the expedition with John Evans? **Reverend William Clarke** needs assistance with a government mineral survey. The challenges, adventures and finds are life-changing for many. However, it gives Luke meaning, purpose and direction. The condition of his heart problems also takes a turn. Can he walk away? Will she wait for him?

ISBN:9780994578273 Ebook ISBN: 978-0-9945782-8-0 Hard cover ISBN 979-8788011141

https://mybook.to/DiamondsintheDirt

The Earl's Shadow
Who or what is the 'shadow'? How does it affect so many?
Parramatta 1860s

Charles Lockley is the Earl of Coxheath. He spent his youth as a convict in Parramatta and had no idea he was an Earl. He had minimal education and few social skills; his eldest son, **Charlie**, is no different.

Now faced with mortality, Charles has to work out how to live the remainder of his life after a near-death experience. He is called to step way out of his comfort zone in London. His action will change the world for many. The echoes from the past still haunt Charlie. London is calling the family, and they can't postpone the trip. How does the Cobb and Co. coach driver **Jim Leslie** fit in? And precisely what is *'The Earl's Shadow'* that he speaks about? What happens if the 'Shadow' is gone?

ISBN: 9780645110708 Ebook ISBN 978-0-9945782-9-7
Released June 2022
https://mybook.to/TheEarlsShadow

Once a Jolly Swagman
An old black Billy Can contain the secrets of an incredible life
An Australian Historical Novel Inspired by songs of The Seekers
Set in 1870s Parramatta and Kent, UK

Rick Lockley, battling his family's expectations, runs away to find himself. **Jack**, a jolly swagman, takes him under his care. Even after years together, Rick knows little about the old man.

On his death, Jack leaves Rick his precious billy can; the contents reveal Jack's identity. Stunned, Rick must travel to England to finalise Jack's wishes. There, he uncovers Jack's life of love, betrayal and a link to his own family. Rick also discovers there is much more to learn about this enigmatic man.

ISBN 9780645110753   Ebook ISBN 978-0-6451107-6-0
Released Sept 2022
https://mybook.to/OnceaJollySwagman

Jonty's Journey
Gems, Love, Artists and a Golden Lion
Australia and South Africa 1880-1902

Sydney Jeweller Jonty Evans' passion for gems takes him to Africa at a volatile time. There, he finds the diamonds he wants and is given a lion cub. However, Jonty is all but kidnapped. His experiences in the Transvaal plunge him into questioning everything he knows about life. Soon, nightmares haunt him. (This is now known as PTSD.)

Upon returning home, he nearly ruins his chance with **Lottie** before it even begins, and he finds adjusting hard. Lottie's father, **Luke** Lockley from Parramatta, takes him under his wing and directs him to someone who can assist.

Jonty is then called back to Africa as a liaison and reunites with his lion, Chimbu, after saving the life of his security detail. His life journey introduces him to remarkable artists, politicians, poets, rebels, and the scapegoat soldier Harry Breaker Morant. Can Jonty lay the past to rest and find his lost peace?

ISBN 9780645110777 HC ISBN 9781923097124   Ebook ISBN: 978-0-6451107-9-1
Released Feb 2023
https://mybook.to/JontysJourney

Co-Winner of 1999 NSW Senior Citizen of the Year, In the Year of the Senior Citizen

$\mathcal{M}$attie

The Story of an Australian Convict Child
An Australian Historical Story inspired by real Life.

An orphaned child, Mattie is convicted of petty theft, sentenced to seven years, and sent to Australia. She meets another convict woman who, at her death, gives Mattie a chance for a new life. She makes the most of everything that comes her way, earning her freedom, falling in love, marrying, and becoming a mother. But life is not kind to her.

She meets bushrangers, moves to the gold fields in Bathurst, and starts a store. Yet, she is the kind of woman who made Australia what it is today. Can she survive alone in a man's world? She is a remarkable woman who breaks down all her barriers.
(Mattie's story continues in The Lockleys of Parramatta - bk 4 & 6)

ISBN 9781503252370 & ebook AISN BOOTTEDBTO
(The story continues in The Earl's Shadow & Once a Jolly Swagman)
https://mybook.to/Mattie_sh

$\mathcal{R}$icky

A boy in Colonial Australia

Ricky English and his mother immigrated from England to join his father in the new Colony of Sydney. Upon arrival, there was no sign of his father. Ricky's mum uses the tiny amount of money they brought to get lodgings in a run-down building. Things go from bad to worse when his mother dies; he is thrown out of the rooms, and the caretakers confiscate all their possessions.

Ricky lives on the streets of Sydney Town as a street waif. Ricky finds safe places to sleep and befriends freed convicts who can help him survive. One day, he encounters a lost child and helps reunite her with her family. These people try to help him, but he insists on doing things his way because of his stubbornness. However, he has found a mentor and confidante. The story follows him through his life. He survives and turns his life around, helping others along the way. ***(Will's story continues in Jonty's Journey)***

Paperback ISBN 9780994578211   Kindle ASIN: B00MLYN6IG
https://mybook.to/Ricky_sh

$\mathcal{T}$he $\mathcal{H}$eather to $\mathcal{T}$he $\mathcal{H}$awkesbury

Four Scottish families brave a new life in a strange land.

Mary Macdonald and husband **Murd** and family; her brother **Fergus** MacKenzie; sister-in-law **Caro** MacLeod; cousin **Alex** Fraser and all their families who have had to emigrate from the Isle of Skye during the "Clearances."

The story follows the four families from Scotland on the ship out to the NSW colony in the 1850s. Mary does not cope with the changes and losses that occur in the first months in the colony. The other women in the family rely on her, and she nearly crumbles. The families struggle together through accidents, losses, trials, floods, and hard work and forge a strong bond with their new country. Trials, tribulations and triumphs see the four families make a firm mark in their new homeland. The immigrants from Scotland helped make Australia what it is today.

ISBN 978994578228   ebook AISN B01A21JYWQ   Large Print ISBN1533473641
Available on Amazon/Kindle & Large Print
https://mybook.to/TheHeathertTHawkesbury

Sara's Author Bio

Sheila Hunter and Sara Powter were a passionate mother-and-daughter team of amateur genealogists. While working together on their family tree, they made many captivating discoveries. The greatest was finding four convicts who held very different perspectives on life in the colony from the military. These four felons were sent to Australia from 1792 to 1814, during the height of convict transportation. Before passing in 2002, Sheila adapted some of these histories into enchanting stories, her Australian Colonial Trilogy. Sara later had these published. Sheila left a fourth unfinished story, inspiring Sara to complete it. However, before she did, **The Lockleys of Parramatta** were created to see if she could do justice to her mother's work. The first two in the series were completed before attempting to finish **Dancing to Her Own Tune** for her mother. (*Sheila wrote the first 30k words*)

Vividly living through the Colonial Era, these books delve further into the theme of overcoming adversity in Colonial Australia and how it developed, the demise of the Convict system and the discovery of mineral wealth.

Sara skilfully intertwines precise archival data with a captivating narrative to craft a collection of stories about faith, love, loss, and redemption.

Two hundred years after her family arrived in Australia, Sara continues the Australian Colonial stories that start with **Gentle Annie Soames**, a saga about the First Fleet. Her **First Fleet Trilogy** is now complete. Following this chronologically are **The Hunter to Macquarie Collection,** the **Unlikely Convict Ladies Trilog**y, and The **Lockleys of Parramatta. The Convict Birthstain Collection**, set in the mid-1800s, follows. All the stories are stand-alone novels.

See Sara's web page to keep up to date with more stories.
With an online store available for a signed copy of Sara's books.
https://www.sarapowter.com.au/   (*Australian Postage only*)

Feel free to email me at
saragpowter@gmail.com

BOOK BUB
 https://partners.bookbub.com/authors/6273615/edit

FACEBOOK https://www.facebook.com/profile.php?id=100063887262514

Do you want the book *UNSHACKLED LIVES for FREE?*
Download from Book Funnel after you sign up.

Amazon Aus QR

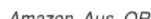

FREE Newsletter signup
From my web page.

www.ingramcontent.com/pod-product-compliance
Lightning Source LLC
Chambersburg PA
CBHW031949240626
47153CB00003B/913